THE FACE OF HEKATE

TAPESTRY OF FATE

BOOK 6

MATTHEW LARKIN

INCANDESCENT PHOENIX BOOKS

The Face of Hekate
Tapestry of Fate Book 6
MATT LARKIN
Editors: Sarah Chorn, Regina Dowling
Cover: Felix Ortiz, Shawn T. King
Map: Francesca Baerald

Incandescent Phoenix Books
mattlarkinbooks.com

TITAN ERA
OKEANUS
THULE
HYPERBOREA
ILLYRIS
SALON
KELTIA
RASSENIA
MNEMOSYNIA
OLMECATL
THRINAKIA
TARTESSOS
KARKHEDON
KARTH
KEMET
TIWANAKU
MEMPHIS
TIWANAKU
NUMIDEN
OSIRION
THE GREAT VELDT
KUSH
HY-BRASIL
KONGO JUNGLE
KGALAGADI DESERT
AZANIA

KER-YS
XIRONG
ISSEDONIA
NYXLANDS
ARIMASPIA
HYLEAN WOODS
KIMMERIA
PHLEGRA
THEMISKYRA
KOLCHIS
KOLCHIS
AXEINOS SEA
PHRYGIA
IOLKOS
ILIUM
ARAD MOUNTAINS
BYBLOS
PHOENIKIA
TYROS
OLYMPIAN MOUNTAINS
ELLADOS
PHAEAKIA
DELPHI
THEBES
ITHAKA
ARGOS
KORINTH
KROKYLEA
KRONION
MERITUN
LESVOS
SKYROS
NAXOS
RHIOS
PHOEBA
LYDIA
HELION
AEOLIA
ATLANTIS
KNOSOS
ATLANTIS
OGYGIA
THALASSA
UGART
NESHIA
BADIAN STEPPES
NINEVEH
ASUR
BABILIM
BABILIM
KISSATU
EMPTY DESERT
DURANKI MOUNTAINS
SUMERU MOUNTAINS
NYSA
TAKHKHASILA
BARBARIKON
PATALIPUTRA
HINDUSH
DHANYAKATAKA
KUMARI KANDAM
FLAMING MOUNTAINS
JADE MOUNTAINS
YAN
JINYANG
YINDAI
XIANYANG
YING
GEBI DESERT
XIAO
XIANG
BO
WANGGEOM
WAKOKU
YAMATO
DANGUN
KUNLUN MOUNTAINS
YUESHANG
VYADHAPURA
NUSANTARA ISLES
HAWAIKI
NUSANTARA
MUGEDANG
DREAMING DESERT
DREAMING LANDS
BULU
RAPAI
MU
SHALMALI
HURSAG MOUNTAINS

THE WHISPER

It starts with a whisper, a haunting intimation of a World askew. That we are, in the end, caught in a death spiral, time nearly played out, whilst entropy tugs ever harder upon the Wheel of Fate.

Looking now into the dying embers, we at last apprehend Truth, and in it the revelation that the vaunted tales of old were not what we thought ... And neither, in fact, were we.

For if we have lived before, might not all we've dreamt be but our souls' memories of Worlds become dust ...

A QUICK NOTE

For full colour, higher-res maps, character lists, location overviews, and glossaries, check out the bonus resources here:
https://tinyurl.com/hw52dzss

And if you liked this book, be sure to check out my offer for a free novella at the end.

PROLOGUE

Gloaming Era, Golden Age

Fate was, by definition, Fate, and thus immutable. As the avatar of history, Amirani knew this better than anyone; despite his gambit, despite his desperate need to avert the end he had foreseen. That Vorsanos and the rest of their so-called Gnostic Cabal could offer some means of skirting destiny presented a hope so enticing—however unlikely—he found himself pacing about the cathedral in Vulgeth, pretending to examine the statues gracing the alcoves.

Was what Vorsanos claimed even possible? Could they change the course of the future? Didn't that fly in the face of the existence of Oracular sight?

He was in the midst of his wanderings and musings when Narada —Veles now, he reminded himself—entered from a door in the east wing. Though Amirani could tell he was not alone, Veles's companion clung to the shadows. Or they clung to him. Either way, Erlik remained draped in the darkness.

"I have already beheld the form you now wear," Amirani admitted, peering into the tenebrous depths of the cathedral. "I know what has befallen you."

With a groan that might well have been a growl, Erlik lurched into the candlelight of the nearest column, though half his form still lurked in shadow. Still, it was enough to offer a haunting glimpse of the vampire.

His skin had grown pale, almost translucent, and seemed stretched too taut over abnormal bone structures. A sharply arched brow. A nose turned upward, and ears warped into leaves, like he had become a cross between man and bat. The tableau was completed by the leathery wings folded behind his back. The vampire bore no shirt, though he had draped a cloak over his arm, perhaps so he could conceal himself as a Man if desired.

A petty urge to point out that he had warned Erlik about the price of sorcery rose in Amirani's breast, but he suppressed it. Such recriminations served naught and no one, least of all considering he had allowed Erlik to follow this course out of necessity. Desperate need—Ananke—as governed so many of his actions. Maybe all actions ... The illusion of choice stripped away by the single, all-consuming mission to forestall the dissolution of the World.

Instead, he fought his repulsion and laid a hand upon the vampire's forearm in some semblance of the kinship they had once shared. Oh, but Erlik was a kind of ghost now, and worse, he had transmitted his cursed state to others. The taint of it consumed him, even as his spawn spread over this new world.

The prices they all paid.

"Now that we are gathered," Vorsanos said, hand upon Amirani's shoulder, "I can take you to the Bastion."

"These streets remain perilous," Amirani stated.

Erlik snorted. "As if I cannot control my own kindred?"

Amirani inclined his head in acknowledgment of the point. While he couldn't imagine the vampire bloodlines would dare assault their high progenitor, still, Erlik's words implied a great deal more control than he suspected the fallen Watcher actually possessed over his creations.

"Nevertheless," Veles said, "there are catacomb tunnels we can take to the Bastion. Secured tunnels that run beneath Vulgeth."

"And cross through the ruins of Falias," Amirani said.

No one answered that. Erlik disappeared back through the same archway he had come from, then Veles beckoned Amirani and the others to follow him. The passage led into a corridor, from which Erlik unlocked a side door and slipped down a staircase, vanishing into the darkness below.

Vorsanos paused by the door to light an oil lamp. "The Cabal will only be complete when you join us, old friend. After all, who matters more than the one who opened our eyes to the Lie?"

The Lie. That was what they called the Archon deceit that had bound the Watchers?

Were he to join their ranks, to share more of what he knew— more than they could conceive—maybe he could find allies. But Amirani had pledged himself to the Fates now, and he was bound to *Fate* itself. They sought to break the Wheel of Fate, not grasping he was, in some sense, partly responsible for its existence. Oh, yes, he too wanted to destroy its hold upon the souls of Man, but doing so required a more delicate touch than his erstwhile brethren could manage. He had sworn not to trust them again, and he must abide by that oath, for he had given all he was to his final gambit.

If there was to be hope for Man, it would come from the Destroyer.

Vorsanos led him down labyrinthine passages, ever deeper into the old city, revealing excavations that ought never have been made. The Gnostic Cabal had rejected the Archons and yet still tried to harness power from one of them. Of course, so had Amirani in stealing Agni's Flame, so he supposed any charge of hypocrisy he might level against them would ring with bitter hollowness.

The shadow-drenched passages were lined with crypts and oft displayed skulls embedded in the walls. He heard dripping water and imagined they passed nigh to the city's sewers, even caught a whiff of reeking dampness. They came round, at last, to the heavy iron door that Erlik had left ajar.

Amirani had expected it would lead them back into Vulgeth, but rather, the door opened into another staircase descending further underground. He cast a wary glance at Remiel. Was it possible they had lied about rejecting the Archons in order to entrap him? Could they have fallen under Naamah's sway?

She nodded encouragement, and he followed—with growing reluctance—as Vorsanos guided him into a subterranean fortress set apart by iron grates. The Cabal Bastion. Supernal wards were carved into the stone before those gates, perhaps intended to hold back spirits and demons, though Erlik himself had passed within and stood at the entrance to a facade not unlike the cathedrals above. More double doors three times the height of Men. More spiked arches, though these joined up with the cavernous ceiling.

Vorsanos's lamp did little to illuminate the vault above them, but upon buttresses Amirani could make out hints of carved gargoyles that would peer at any who crossed here.

He followed the others through the gate and inside the Bastion proper. Erlik drifted off into shadows, and Remiel and Veles headed for a lounge.

"Join us when you are ready," Remiel said. "After you've seen."

Vorsanos waved a hand for Amirani to follow, so he did. The man unlocked a back chamber, then shut the door behind them when Amirani had entered, and set about lighting a massive brazier at the room's heart. A series of quicksilver mirrors ran along the perimeter of the circular room, each set into its own alcove.

"They are not perfect," Vorsanos admitted, coming over with the lamp once he had the brazier blazing.

"Scrying mirrors," Amirani said. "You claimed the scrying mirrors of the Sluagh."

"Yes and no. I have modified these to show more than other places in this world."

A chill had the hair on Amirani's arms standing on end. "To show *what*?"

"We don't know where your Oracular visions came from. But they showed you things about the future ... allowed you to realise the Ontos long before the rest of us. If we want a chance at true Gnosis, we too must have access to Oracular insight."

Amirani peered into the depths of quicksilver. And deep it was, seeming to tug upon his very soul. To pull him from the now into some murky sojourn out of time. "Oracle Mirrors. You created these to see the future."

"I have seen ... visions that crush the very heart of me. I have beheld a future which steals away all I thought I knew."

Amirani closed his eyes a moment. "Prescience is the most complex of burdens." And did this mimicry of prescience bring the Cabal closer to being his allies or simply make them more dangerous enemies?

"Join us."

Amirani opened his eyes to stare at the other man. "You said you had proof that Fate could be altered."

Vorsanos nodded. "I had been refining this design already when I came across something that changed ... everything. Something that allowed me to breach the bounds of time and begin perfecting these devices. Even ..."

"Even what?"

Vorsanos shook his head. "Better you see the proof, first." The fallen Watcher led him beyond the mirror room, down into what Amirani could only think of as a dungeon.

An orichalcum gate bounded a single cell at the end of the hall. The flickers of his lamp adumbrated a form within, a woman huddled in the corner, wrists resting upon her knees as if in meditation. She lurched to her feet at their approach.

"Kronos!" she snarled.

"A timewalker," Vorsanos said to Amirani. "She came here through time, and I have used her device—which thus far seems specific to her—to both improve upon the mirrors and begin constructing a means for *us* to move through time."

He heard the man, but Amirani could not tear his gaze from the golden-eyed, dark-haired woman in the cell. Even less so when she drew nigh, gaping at him, her expression one of utter shock. And beyond those eyes, he saw ... Aditi's reborn soul.

PART I

Let us take it as a given that every statement must be either true or false. Let us take it as a second given that events are predicated on causes. Thus, if we imagine the future, we may consider that an event will or will not occur, based on causes. If we say that the event will happen, this is either true or false. If it is true, then the event could not have not occurred. Whatever cannot not happen, must necessarily happen. The future was determined by necessity, that is, by Ananke. Everything is thus governed by Ananke.

— Urania, Analects of the Muses

1

PANDORA

Gloaming Era, Golden Age

*T*ime had, by turns, flown and crept, muddling into an endless whorl. Pandora could not have said how many years had passed whilst she languished in dungeons beneath Vulgeth. Perhaps two, perhaps five, perhaps longer still, for in the perpetual gloom of the lamplight hold, she had lost all ability to judge.

She had passed the years thinking, meditating, or working through the training the Amazons had imparted to her, trying to keep her edge. But time dragged on and it grew harder to bear. She played games in her mind, solving mathematical puzzles, writing poetry, or pursuing any other complex activity to stave off the madness.

Sometimes, one member or another of the Cabal would come to speak to her and demand answers about the Box and its workings. Pandora offered them precious little information, but nor did she dare outright refuse them. If she did not speak to them at all, they might stop coming down here. And theirs were the only faces she saw, hateful though they proved.

And then Prometheus had come, alongside Kronos, and looked at her, not quite as though he knew her, but as though he knew *of* her. Perhaps, though he had not before encountered her, prescient insight had warned him of her coming? She could see no other explanation for how intently he had stared into the depths of her eyes as though peering into her soul. The sensation had left her jittery and unnerved.

Prometheus had departed with Kronos—Vorsanos, here—before Pandora had gotten a chance to speak with her beloved, and she was left with no choice save to return to her contemplations.

She had been wrong about so many things. She ought not to have come to Vulgeth, yet she had been so certain she could find the answers she needed. Hekate had warned her she would lose the Box here—a thought the interminable years had given Pandora ample time to stew over—and still Pandora had dared to believe she could cheat the future.

What was the start of this? Pandora chuckled to keep from screaming.

Maybe it was when a misguided timewalker stumbled into the midst of the Gnostic Cabal and showed them time could be breached.

It did not surprise her when Prometheus returned, alone, what she judged to be, perhaps, two days later. Pandora rose and moved to the bars to her cell, gripping them to stare into her beloved's sapphire eyes. Her orichalcum fetters clanked against her cage. With her gaze, she implored him to help her. "Prometheus ..."

"I do not know that name."

Pandora was trembling, terrified beyond sense she might lose this one chance at her freedom. A mischosen word could send him away. After so long down here, she had begun to imagine spending the rest of her life rotting in the dark. Then he had come to her, a beacon of light taunting her with a single way home. And she ached for fear of losing sight of it. "Not yet, I suppose."

"Then it is all true, isn't it? Who are you?"

He had known her, when first he had encountered her on Helion, during the Ambrosial War. Already, he had known her name. Because she was always meant to tell him now. "I am Pandora." How much was she to tell him now? Could the future be made better—or worse—by her speaking too freely? Or by her reticence? She had mulled over those questions in the time since she had first seen him here and come up with only a half-formed answer: she would tell him as much as she needed to in order to secure his aid, and no more.

Pandora had come here to gain knowledge of the past, not to impart knowledge of the future. Despite all that had befallen her with the Cabal, perhaps she might yet escape this place with some of that knowledge.

"Well, Pandora, here I am called Amirani and I have seen the device which brought you here."

The Box! "I need it." It came out harsher than she'd intended, bursting from her mouth before she could stop herself from speaking.

Amirani shook his head. "The Cabal guards it too closely. Though they cannot use it—and are uncertain why—they have spent years adapting it to build devices which they can operate."

Indeed, Vorsanos and the others had come to her many times, asking why the device would not work for them. Prometheus, in creating the Box, must have somehow limited it. Pandora could use it, and her granddaughter Kirke had used it. Perhaps only those of her bloodline could manage it. Though she had succeeded in bringing Herakles along, so she was not certain of the details. He called Athene—another of Pandora's granddaughters—his adoptive mother. But if he was also of the line of Athenian kings, perhaps he too shared Pandora's blood.

"The others believe your presence here, a woman from outside this time, may serve as proof that Fate is not immutable."

Oh, how fervently Pandora would have liked to believe that. With such desperation she clung to that hope, rekindling its flame each time the ravages of Fate extinguished it.

And Amirani read the thought writ plain upon her face. "Neither of us remains quite so sanguine."

She clutched the bars even tighter. "Time is an ouroboros." Amirani closed his hands over top hers, his grip gentle. "If you do not know me," she asked, heart hammering at his tantalising closeness, "why then do you look at me that way?"

"I did not know your name. I never said I did not know *you*. The intangible stuff of you that is but motes of Light contained within a temporary shell, that part, I have known from the first days."

His words, the sound of his voice, caressed. And yet the potential import of his meaning—that she had either lived before or he had seen her in his visions eons before her birth—slammed into her and left her gasping for breath. It took her shamefully long to remember how to work her tongue, much less make use of it. "You have to set me free. I cannot remain here. No matter how hopeless Fate seems, I have to *try* to make right all the inequities of time." She stopped herself short of revealing their daughter and the terrible future she would unleash.

Amirani nodded once, not seeming the least surprised, and from his black coat withdrew a ring of keys. After selecting one, he unlocked the bars to her cell, then motioned her forward to remove her orichalcum fetters as well. As those chains fell away, a rush of Pneuma flooded back into her and Pandora shuddered from the sudden return of her power.

The Phoenix wakened to life and flames burst from her hands, leapt along her arms, and singed her tattered tunic. The spirit inside her had lain quiescent so long its ire now threatened to explode. Before the flames could burn away her clothes, Pandora closed her palms together and willed them back inside.

"You hold the Flame," Amirani said when she opened her eyes and saw him watching her, mouth hanging open.

Pandora chuckled. So many things she wished she could tell him. "It's the Phoenix."

"The what?"

"You'll understand in time."

He took that in stride and grabbed her hand, pulling her along behind himself.

"Where are you taking me?"

Amirani led her down a series of tunnels, catacombs in various states of decay. Pandora could not shake the sense of some foulness permeating the air of this sepulchral place. Sputtering torches in wall sconces cast sporadic wells of light amid the gloom. "I cannot get the Box for you, but the Cabal built something." He did not slow as he spoke, taking twists and turns in the darkness without hesitation. "Larger devices—or perhaps one device in four segments—spread across the continents, beneath the cities of Dark Faerie, connecting the four ruins. They call them the Time Chambers. Soon, they intend to activate one, and this they think to use to thwart Fate. They consulted me in the fine-tuning of the device here. I believe I can use it to send you home before they begin their own sojourns in time."

Time Chambers. That was how Kronos had fled from her Era, after escaping Tartarus, to reach that distant future Era where Hekate had blanketed the world in snow and mist. "I don't think the Time Chamber here still exists in my time."

He glanced at her but did not ask what became of it. "The working theory holds that, to move one through time, the chambers must also cast one through space. That's why they needed multiple destinations."

"You mean, in addition to sending me to the future, it will send me to the ruins of another of these cities of Dark Faerie."

"Mmm." Amirani led her round another bend. "We must hurry. There is chaos in the city above. Strife within the vampire bloodlines bodes ill for Mankind."

Whilst tempted to inquire about the details, the burdens and sorrows of past Eras would only serve as a distraction from Pandora's real mission. Still, the idea of leaving behind the Box sounded foreign almost beyond comprehension. The device had become, despite her ambivalence toward it, like a part of herself. She believed Amirani when he claimed they could never reach it, and yet—

Around the corner, a nightmarish creature surged forward, all distended limbs and an unhinged jaw exposing hideous fangs. Instinct took over and Pandora's hand shot toward the closest of the torches. Flames leapt to her hand, casting all save herself in darkness. The creature—it looked like what she'd faced in the Vulgeth ruins of her day, save for its feral aspect—had already flung itself forward. With her flaming hand, Pandora seized the abomination by the throat. Having her Pneuma drained through her blood once was enough. With a shriek, she slammed it against the wall.

Her smouldering fingers punched through hardened flesh, and she felt muscle char and crunch beneath her grip. Its throat turned to ash, then the whole monster went up in flames. Smoke and cinders and gristle spilt from her hand.

Pandora winced and snapped her wrist to fling the gore away. "What is it?"

The shock that had washed over his features vanished. "One of the breeds of vampire. A side effect of the creation of the Veil. Keep moving."

He led her into a circular chamber, intent to drag her across. But something set onto a podium in the middle of it brought her to a stumbling stop. Because she had seen it before, when she had confronted Kronos before the Titanomachy. "That's the Tablet of Destiny."

Amirani stiffened but allowed her to draw him to a stop whilst she plodded over to examine the stone slab. It was plain stone, though engraved with strange glyphs not unlike those she had beheld in Hekate's grimoire. There were eight lines carved upon the tablet. Names? Dates?

"We have no time to ogle over treasures the Cabal only half-understand."

She whirled on him. "Do you understand it? You always know so much more than you reveal, lover." Letting slip the nature of their relationship in the future had been a deliberate choice, a move designed to throw him off his guard.

Amirani did not miss a beat, though. "Whatever I withheld, I must have done for good reason."

"I—"

A whirring buzzed through the stones beneath their feet and set the catacombs to trembling. Pandora's ears popped.

As she recovered, one set of the glyphs upon the Tablet began to emanate faint blue light, and both she and Amirani swivelled to gape. "What the …?" Gingerly, she brushed her fingers over the carvings in the Tablet. The radiance emitted no heat, only a pale gleam.

Her companion, though, had turned from the pedestal and began casting about, seeking for something. Or someone. A man eased around the corner, cautious, his hand upon the hilt of sword longer than any she had before seen. His clothes were strange, even for this Era, a long black coat over an embroidered white shirt.

"Amirani," the man said, his command of the local language tinged with a foreign accent.

"You came through the Time Chamber," Amirani said, even his mind apparently reeling at the implication. "They intended to first activate it this very day."

"You sent me," the man confirmed.

"I …" Amirani sucked in a sharp breath, for once speechless.

The stranger looked to Pandora, watching her with a wary glare. The Tablet was definitely reacting to this man's presence. His gaze swept over it, briefly, but he did not seem to make the connection nor much care about the stone's purpose. "Is she human?"

Amirani stole a glance at Pandora as well, coming out of his shock. "Yes."

The man abruptly lost interest in her. "Where is Erlik?"

"At this moment, I think he is preparing for the activation of the Chamber." Oh, but that had clearly already happened. The moment the device became ready, someone came through from the future. As far as Pandora could gauge, that implied the furthest back anyone could travel was to the moment of the Chamber's creation. It made sense, she supposed, given that the devices were designed to send one between them and could not send one to a point in which no two of the Chambers existed.

The stranger took Amirani's words as confirmation of his mission, whatever it was, and hurried from the chamber without so much as another word.

Regardless, Pandora was left parsing the revelation of his presence. As Amirani had implied, the future existed. It had always accounted for the existence of these devices. The ouroboros encompassed all that was or ever would be.

Perhaps her lover read the creeping despair that seized her upon her face. "History is merciless."

"Still," she said. "We must strive against the chains of Fate."

Amirani offered a nod of confirmation, respecting her determination. Or perhaps humouring her desperation. He led her into the room beyond the Tablet, a massive spherical chamber with a purpose she could not doubt. The bottom half of the orb was filled with water, rimmed by a walkway which joined to the device at the heart of it all: a massive orrery conjoined to an adjustable astrolabe. The mess of interconnecting gears made plain the chamber's relationship to her Box. The builders had studied every mechanism of one device and recreated it on a massive scale

As Pandora ogled the wonder of the machine, Amirani set to fiddling with the innumerable dials and levers and adjustable panels. She watched him, taking in all he did and all she saw of that device. But something seemed ... off.

"I don't think that's correct."

He looked at her, curiosity plain in his sapphire eyes. She had used the Box so many times, she had gained an intuitive grasp of its workings. This thing was not so different. Simpler, perhaps, because it had only three possible destinations in space and, from this point, could only go forward in time. Together, they worked at setting the device until she was fair certain, as much as she could ever be, that it would allow her to return to her own Era.

Without the Box, she would not find it easy to correct a mistake, she reminded herself. As with that device, this one might not allow her perfect control. At some point, the only choice lay in the testing of it or not.

On impulse, she laid a hand upon his cheek, and he turned from what he was doing to look hard at her. "One day, you must reveal to me all the whirring gears of your mind." He looked like he might say something but instead shut his mouth and held her hand with his own. "You have to go," she said when it became plain he had no words for this situation. "I must throw the final lever alone, lest you become swept up in the shift."

They both knew the timeline could not endure such a thing.

Amirani squeezed her hand once more, then released it. As he departed, he cast a final, mournful look her way. What truths did he know that she still had not realised? But she felt herself growing ever closer to the answers.

When Amirani had sealed the door, leaving her alone once more, Pandora activated the Time Chamber. Lightning coruscated along the orrery arms. The device whirred, its many limbs and walkways spinning in faster and faster orbits. The room trembled and whined from the strain. The water rose about the room's side, creating a hollow sphere of liquid. Lightning leapt from the blurring arms of the orrery to the encircling waters, turning them luminous.

The World bent back upon itself, light collapsing into a bubble. Everything blinked out.

2

HEKATE

46 Bronze Age

*B*acchic wine flowed through Thebian aqueducts, filling every fountain with the sacred brew. Women flocked to God's side, hearing his call from far and wide. They came from the brothels and the markets, from the manses and the alleyways. They flowed in from the landed estates outside the polis, having slain husbands and sons who tried to control them. Any man who refused them—who dared deny the Maenads as emissaries of the divine—tore him to pieces. They scattered limbs and feasted upon phalluses until, in the end, only those who joined the revels and sipped God's wine remained in Thebes.

Then, more came. Dishevelled or unclad, they flowed in through the gates from farmlands, from villages, from little cabins in the woods. Some Hekate recognised as witches, even one other sorceress. Some were Nymphs, thriving when at last free from the oppressive weight of male Titans.

They began to flow in from Korinth or came upon ships out of

Kronion. She knew that, in time, the wine would reach every polis in Elládos. Soon, no woman would remain bound by her societal chains. The edifices of man were already crumbling.

Thus drunk and smiling, she wandered the halls, no longer bothering with clothes. Modesty, like vanity, was but an affectation foisted upon humanity by its own pomposity. Now freed, she lay with any man or woman who caught her eye, she ate where she wished, slept where she wished, and never allowed the taste of the precious brew to leave her lips.

Stumbling along the garden path, admiring the moonlight, Hekate did not see the cloaked stranger until she collided with his chest. Chill hands seized her arms. Through the haze, she looked up into eyes glinting red beneath the shadowy recesses of that hood.

"Keuthos ..." she breathed. Could a revenant drink the wine? No, and the God would not approve of his unnatural presence, would he? No, she needed to summon the others and have him torn limb from limb. In honour of her old friend, she would feast on his flesh herself.

She drew in a breath to scream, but an icy hand slapped over her mouth, cutting off her air. Some powder—that tasted like oneiroi dust!—in the other hand tickled her nose and ... she ...

Everything blurred. Darkness took her.

Hekate awoke gagging on the honey-sweet taste of Ambrosia. A parade of horses pranced through her skull. The clatter of their hooves ushered in the most stupendous hangover in the history of time. She dared peek at the world and winced as a beam of moonlight hammered through her eyes, blinding.

A groan escaped her.

She turned to her side, realised someone had wrapt a himation around her, and pulled it tighter.

"She's free of it now," she heard a woman say.

"Can he claim her again?" another voice said. Keuthos?

A hesitation. "I can weaken him with a spell, though the process is long and will cost me." Another pause. "He will not stop hunting for her, though. Zagreus's rage pierces even through the aspect of the Elder God. He will come for her." That voice … Enodia?

"How can we escape him?"

A hand alighted on her shoulder, almost gentle, in a way she had never known Enodia to be. "She needs the power to confront him. Tell her to finish that grimoire."

Keuthos scoffed, the sound hollow. "There are no masters left from which she might yet learn. I wonder how much *you* might have to offer, sorceress."

"A great deal, had I the time. But I must attend to Dionysus if you are to escape his sight even for a moment." The hand withdrew. "There is truth in your words, Keuthos. Few remain who could teach Hekate at this stage. But there were others, in ages past, their wisdom forgotten in the buried halls of ancient wonders."

"Dark Faerie?" Keuthos groaned. "We have been to Gorias."

"The ruins of Falias lie in the Nyxlands. Guide her there, keep her alive, and she will find what she needs."

Though she struggled to focus on their conversation, the blissful oblivion of dreams rose to claim her.

❧

WHEN THEY EMERGED *from the depths of Olympus, Kronos led Hekate not toward the crumbling steps that would descend the mountain but rather onto a side path that wrapt around the peak.*

"What are we about now?" she demanded, unable to infuse her words with the bite of bitterness she'd hoped for.

"Long ago, I discovered something, a relic of the first Era of the World. A record, if you will, of destiny itself."

Their path forced them to press against the cliff, gazing at a sheer drop plunging for hundreds of feet. The view sent Hekate's heart racing and sweat slicked the same palms with which she steadied herself against the rock wall.

At last they reached a wider shelf, then had to squeeze through a narrow crevasse separating the mountainside. From the look, a quake had opened this rent, albeit one long back, given how wind and rain had eroded the outer edges.

WILD TRIBES INHABITED the woodlands in the northernmost reaches of Phlegra. So far as Hekate knew, neither the Elládosi nor the local Phlegrans knew much about these men they called barbarians. Those who knew of their existence spoke of them in frightened whispers. Savages. Men gone mad, living upon the edge of the Nyxlands, tainted by the Goddess of Night.

Yet, upon learning she could speak their tongue, the wood-dwellers brought them into their wooden huts, fed them venison—though Keuthos only pretended to partake—and treated them as honoured guests. While they wore leathers and animal skins around their shoulders for warmth, in the end, they were much like all Men, Hekate decided. Save, perhaps, for the fact their most respected elder was a wrinkled woman.

The way she studied Hekate over the campfire, an intensity behind those rheumy eyes, could well mean a witch guided these people.

She and Keuthos had travelled more than two months since her friend had rescued her from Dionysus's thrall, pushing hard for fear her adversary may yet pursue her. Whether she had earned Zagreus's ire, she surely deserved Hades's wrath. Given the dark king's power, that he should manage to see Zagreus reborn, and as a son of Zeus ... perhaps she could believe that. But that Hades should manage to somehow pull an aspect of an Elder God into the newborn defied all reason. The very thought of it had chills wracking her, nightmares parading through her sleep. Puissance beyond all ken coursed through Dionysus now, and she could not see a means of combating the madness he engendered.

"You cannot go north," the old woman said after gnawing on a gristly hunk of meat.

Murmurs burbled amid those gathered close enough to overhear. More than once, Hekate thought she heard the tribesmen speak of a "gate to Hel."

"Why not?" Keuthos asked, drawing an appraising look from the woman. The revenant-wraith held back from the fire, but if the barbarians had noticed his aversion to flame, they gave no sign.

"Death bleeds in the north. A fell wind sweeps through twisted trees. Things wake that ought to sleep forever."

Words spoken with a ritual intonation, a caution handed from generation to generation. Legends claimed that, while the Time of Nyx ended in the Nyxlands, and that there, and there alone, Nyx still held sway. Did eternal night truly reign in the north, or mere superstition? According to tales, Kronos had fought alongside Ouranos to end the Time of Nyx, and perhaps the fallen Titan could have spoken to what lay ahead, had Zeus not bound him in Tartarus.

"What is Hel?" Hekate heard herself asking, almost as in a dream. The name simmered with unspoken dread, a primal fear that coursed through these people like an icy mountain stream.

The witch fixed Hekate with a discomfiting stare, as though she could see the abrasions of Hekate's faltering soul. "The hidden place. It is *death*. The end of all things, when frost spreads like a sweeping plague, when light dims and shadows reign."

The Underworld, perhaps? An evocative term for it, one that struck such consuming awe in the wood-folk they dared speak it only in whispers.

So ... if a gate to Hel truly existed in the Nyxlands, did that mean a breach to the Underworld—or the Otherworld—lay north? Was it possible an actual bridge to Nyx awaited them should they push on, seeking the ruins of Falias?

Pressing these people would avail her little, she thought, given the looming dread that already seized them. As it was, their hosts thought her and Keuthos mad for their inquiries. The last thing they needed was for these people to decide them threats they must destroy.

The barbarians passed around a skin of honeyed wine, and

Hekate's pulse quickened at the thought of a mild intoxicant. After months without the taste of the Bacchic wine, after so long ... Her fingers trembled, reaching for the skin. Just a taste, something to help keep the nightmares at bay for—

Keuthos's icy grip closed on her bicep, the revenant having come closer to the fire than she had thus far seen. "We must rest. We have far yet to travel." Her friend fair dragged Hekate to her feet. Gratitude warred with indignation within her. A petulant urge arose to yank her arm away and seize the precious draught that might obviate all the myriad torments whirring within her.

With a grating effort of will, she allowed Keuthos to guide her back into the small wooden hut the tribe had granted them. She had to duck to enter the doorway, and only at the centre of the dome could she stand upright without brushing her head against the ceiling.

Keuthos guided her toward the rear of the hut and forced her to sit beside the dim light of a fat-burning candle. The revenant's ruby gaze glinted with unspoken condemnation that had her wanting to shove him. Who was he to judge her? Keuthos may have suffered his own torments; it did not mean he understood the pains, the *terrors*, that cut through Hekate.

"We should not continue north. If we turn west, we could head through the wilderness. Perhaps make it over the Hnitbjorgs before the snows clog the passes."

He meant her to head for his original homeland of Hyperborea. While the thought of running from Dionysus held a certain appeal, it was not Hekate's nature, nor was it probable they could evade the gaze of an Elder God determined to find them for long. No, her only hope lay in whatever secrets Enodia believed lay in the ruins of Falias. Knowledge, the sorceress had said, might allow her to finish the grimoire and combat even such a foe as Dionysus.

"Can you not navigate the way to Hel?" Hekate asked.

"You place too much trust in the dead."

She scoffed at that. "If I cannot trust you, one of my oldest friends, whom am I to trust?"

Keuthos lifted his head enough for her to glimpse his wan, pale flesh. "I am yours, always." Despite his hollow voice and dire aspect, she knew he meant it. Keuthos and she were bound together, by choice or the threads of the Moirai, it mattered little. "I was speaking of the sorceress." What? Hekate cocked her head. Keuthos grunted, leaning back a little. "You didn't know. Enodia ... she is like me."

"No." That was impossible. Surely Hekate would have known. Would have sensed it, in all the time they had spent together. Wouldn't she?

"She is a revenant."

The words—the *doubts*—wormed through her heart, burrowing deeper. Had Enodia always been dead, or had she died since last Hekate had seen her? In Thebes, Enodia had departed before Hekate had recovered her senses. Keuthos had told her that he had sought some means of breaking Dionysus's hold over her and that he had found Enodia, agreed to work with her. What had passed between them, he spoke little of, but then, Keuthos had become far less garrulous in general since his death.

Swallowing, let alone finding words, proved a momentous challenge. If Hekate could have missed something so obvious, so glaring in import, how could she trust aught she thought she knew? "I ..."

"Given she withheld something so basic from you," Keuthos said, "what makes you think she has revealed all you need to know now?"

In truth, she could never know. But ... "She helped you save me from the most dire situation I ever found myself in. I could well have remained Dionysus's slave for eternity. He made me taste the flesh of Man. Brought out such primal lusts I could not even ..."

Keuthos growled. "All that proves is she did not wish you to remain a thrall to that abomination. Not that she is trustworthy."

No, no, no. Enodia had helped Hekate, time and again, along the long road of her life. She had first taught her sorcery, to say naught of the harnessing of the lesser arcana. How to control her necromancy and oneiromancy, how to use the psychic gifts hidden in her mind. "I have to believe that she sent me to finish the grimoire for my benefit. I have to know what lies within the Nyxlands, Keuthos." If she allowed herself to question *everything*, to hold naught as constant and given, indecision would paralyse her of necessity. Sometimes, trust had to be a choice, and she had to trust *someone*. "Without whatever secrets lurk in Falias, Dionysus will find me. He will reclaim his hold upon me. The creature won't be satisfied until he has brought me, and all Olympus, to utter ruination."

A long while, too long, Keuthos held her gaze in glowering silence. At last, he grunted. "Then we shall find the way to Hel."

ANOTHER MONTH, Hekate and Keuthos trekked north, at last breaking free of woodlands and passing around the nameless mountains that framed the barbarian domains. East would lay Arimaspia, land of Cyclopes and gryphons, where Man dared not tread and even Hekate had never thought to venture. Not after hearing the stories the Kimmerians had told of the wilderness, long years back.

But even fell Arimaspia held not a fraction of the dread evoked in Man by the name of the Nyxlands. The further north they pressed, the longer the nights seemed to drag on. For Keuthos's sake, they travelled only during those lengthening spans of darkness, making camp when the sun burnt the sky with its fleeting appearances.

They passed through endless fields of yellow, withering grasses, broken by copses of skeletal trees that seemed to watch her with palpable hunger. They trod over rolling hills carpeted with night-blooming flowers, then down into shadowed valleys clogged with bent oaks and nigh leafless beech trees. A chill wind from the north blew more oft than not, bearing a hint of decay and something more ... a reek she could almost *see*, one akin to the psychic disturbances when the Penumbra converged into the Mortal Realm.

Game was scarce, forcing her to ration what food they found. When they encountered animals, most had a feral, even malicious aspect to them. They bumbled into a wild boar as tall at the shoulder as the largest horse. It was a creature of tusks and bristles that would have gored her, had Keuthos not intervened, devouring the wretched thing's soul. The beast did, however, provide more meat than either of them could carry.

As the sun set, marking the start of another night of trekking, an ill presence upon the wind had Hekate casting about herself. They had camped within another wood of bent, leafless trees, taking what limited shelter they might claim from the first dustings of snow. She could make out little in the spreading twilight, so she embraced the Sight, peering into the Penumbra, and gasped. Etheric ripples thrummed along the ground like tremors, welling into trees. Even as she looked, a great oak *turned* its trunk, peering at her with hollow eyes. Dangling creepers edged toward their legs.

"Dammit!" Hekate broke into a run. More trees around them seeped into lethargic animation, their attempts to surround Hekate and Keuthos slow but implacable.

"Dryads have been watching us," Keuthos said, the revenant rushing to her side.

"Then why do they not strike?" Hekate demanded, forced to dodge around one crawling plant after another. While they could outdistance a creeping tree with ease, the spreading threat meant they had, mostlike, enjoyed their last rest for a long while.

"They await the appearance of their master," Keuthos answered. Even the revenant-wraith seemed lost as to how they might escape from the encroaching forest. "We must press forward. That they harry us so can only mean Dionysus draws nigh."

With sorcery Hekate might have compelled a dryad, bound it to her will, but not without time to prepare and cast. Such would prove impossible now, leaving her only one recourse.

Though already a bit short of breath from running, Hekate broke into a Kandamian spellsong. Her Supernal words evoked the tutelary spirit of this wood. Not the dryads who moved through it as though masters, but the land *itself*, blighted and warped as it was by the dark of the Nyxlands. Still, a remnant of some living entity lay quiescent beneath the surface.

Her words prodded and pleaded, her rhythm soothing even the moribund soul of this wretched land into wakefulness. With flattery and allusion to ancient glory, with evoked memory of what must have once been verdancy, she stirred the living wood.

Vines lurched at them, roots rose in attempts to snare ankles, forcing them to leap with Potency. Branches lashed at them, attempting to bar their way. Keuthos blundered shoulder-first into one, his revenant strength splintering dried wood into kindling an instant before it would have smacked into Hekate.

"For last, indelible glory," Hekate sang in Supernal, "for memory of what was lost, I call upon you to reject the hold of these dryads. For those who would revel in your bounty one final time, open the way."

A rumble built beneath the ground, followed by snapping roots as trees shifted, the land turned in a moil of heaving dirt and rocks and dust. In answer to her plea, to the power of her Pneuma poured into her desperate song, the forest *parted*. Trees edged to the sides, trunks bowing convex, offering a route through.

A denying, hissing shriek broke through the night, the dryads recoiling in wrath that any such being would defy them. That a spirit older even than themselves should assert its dominance, though it must have passed into oblivion in so doing.

In a mad dash, Hekate and Keuthos raced forward. They broke through the edge of the woods and found a vast field of crumbling stonework the likes of which she had never seen. Scattered trees even more decrepit than those they had left overgrew the outer city. The lingering bones of fallen glories hinted at once-soaring spires with sporadic enclaves throughout the ruin still standing.

"Was this Falias?" Hekate asked whilst passing beneath the broken frame of a buttress dripping with brown moss.

"I think ..." Keuthos rasped, turning about to take it in before casting another glance back at the dilapidated wood they had fled. "A legend in Hyperborea spoke of a city erected over a ruin of darkness.

Some claim the builders sought to contain the Dark, while other, direr tales claim they hoped to harness it."

If so, if the Hyperborean legend proved fact, another civilisation had built atop lost Falias, only to share its fate. A vast, dead city within the Nyxlands.

If answers lay here, they would have to find them with haste. The dryads might hesitate to close in on the ruins, but naught would stop Dionysus once he arrived.

TREKKING INTO THE CITY, the land began to slope inward. Cracked cobbles pitched toward the centre of a great circle, with the damage to structures growing more severe the further they pushed forward.

The whole of the ruin felt saturated with Khaos. It chafed her skin and grated her soul. It filled her nostrils with a reek not unlike the awful stench of her dreams of Aeshma. Was this the Hel the barbarians had so dreaded? Beneath the eaves of etiolated monuments, shadows grew so deep they seemed abysses into which she might plummet should she draw nigh. Tenebrous stretches welled and seethed on her periphery, still when she looked to them, then, from the corner of her eye, seeming to reach for her with grasping tendrils.

They came at last to a gaping crater, a caldera into which the shattered city had tumbled. Fragments of structures dangled upon the descending tiers, but at the centre lay an atramentous pit, a hole that seemed to bore right through Gaia and into a void of Khaos. The taste of the Otherworldly tickled her tongue. Bleak puissance scraped her nerves and brushed over her will, compelling, *daring* her to descend into those depths. A whisper of shadows promised visions of Ontos if she but braved the true Dark.

"Look." Keuthos pointed toward a structure. The half adjacent to the hole had fallen away, exposing the interior of yet another building that must have once stretched hundreds of feet in the air. The great spire had broken off, but Keuthos drew her attention not to the crumbling upper recesses but to an unprotected cellar. A dust-caked ruin, to be sure, but one with hundreds upon hundreds of bound tomes collapsed into random mounds within.

Tomes unlike most aught she had ever seen, other than the *Sefer Raziel* in her satchel and a handful of texts possessed by the Circle of Goetic Mysteries in ages past. "A library." Hekate could scarce believe her eyes. Such a wealth of knowledge, and in this place, it bespoke truths long forgotten by peoples modern Man had no memory of at all.

Even the Time of Nyx had held wonder, learning, secrets beyond dreaming. Would that she could question Kronos, demand to know why he and Ouranos and their allies had sought to bring down this antecedent age.

Or perhaps the squirming Dark at the heart of these ruins offered enough answer.

Careful of her footing—dust and pebbles skittered toward the pit in her passing—Hekate made her way to the ruined library. What they sought must be within. It had to be.

ONCE, this place must have housed a thousand tomes or more. Once, she could tell, shelves lined the walls, row stacked upon row. A handful of shelves on a single wall remained unbroken, though cracks splintered the stone of even these. Hekate traced a careful finger along the chinks, imagining the momentous quake that had devastated this city. It had ruined a civilisation. Had Ouranos caused the cataclysm or merely reacted to it?

It was one question that, mostlike, even these tomes couldn't answer.

The burnt-out ashes amid blackened leather covers told her something had set alight a fair portion of this library, though whether by accident or intent, she did not know.

Earlier, she had found lamps along the wall. Glass had once contained a flame inside, but the glass had shattered in the quake, and the means of lighting the lamps eluded her, forcing her to instead wedge a torch within the sconce.

Keuthos thumped a gap in the intact shelf. "One of the tomes is missing."

"How can you be certain?" She moved closer.

He pointed to regular markings along the spines. "These are numbers. The pattern is missing the third book, jumping to the next in sequence."

"You can *read* these?" Hekate's ability to speak the tongues of Men did not extend to reading unknown languages. But if Keuthos could understand writing from the time of Nyx ...

"No, the numbers are similar enough to old scripts I transcribed. The texts would take long indeed to translate, if I could manage at all."

Before Hekate could ask more, a growl rumbled into the library. *Several* growls, of something bestial and ravenous. Hekate and Keuthos spun, gazes drawn into the upper recesses whence came the sound. There, amid too-thick shadows, glinted several pairs of red eyes, looking down upon Hekate with a hunger of those who had not eaten in an age.

More revenants, and like Keuthos, they needed to consume flesh to survive. How long had these creatures haunted the ruins? Had they hibernated here since the fall of the Time of Nyx?

She had no time to seek such answers. More growls issued from outside. Without taking her eyes off the visible foes, Hekate backed toward the entrance, summoning Khione's ice to her fingertips.

The Dark gathers ... Mormo taunted.

Keuthos positioned himself in front of her. "When I say run, make a break for the city's edge."

Where Dionysus still hunted her? She needed answers, she needed power to combat the aspect of the Elder God, and she needed it *now*. More revenants crawled in from upper windows, scrambling along the ceiling like spiders.

All at once, those gleaming red lights surged forward, launched from the hidden recesses of the library like stones from a sling, all converging upon her.

"Run!" Keuthos bellowed, even as he leapt, colliding with another revenant in midair. His swiping skeletal claws tore through flesh and ripped out an eye as they landed. Continuing his momentum, he caught the creature and flung it at another of its kind.

That was all Hekate saw before a revenant was upon her. She thrust her hand forward, launching an icicle the size of an arrow. The missile exploded from her fingers, punching through the revenant's throat and sending it careening back. The ghost's daze lasted a bare instant, then it was surging forward again, claws stretching toward her face.

Hekate's Potency allowed her to catch its wrists, but the revenant's strength sent her staggering backward. She couldn't hold it long. The creature bared fangs, mouth dripping venomous saliva, a putrid stench of decay escaping its maw. Closer and closer those fangs leant until Hekate tumbled backward. The ghost sprawled atop her, its acidic spit dribbling over her cheeks, drawing a hiss of pain from her.

She shrieked, trying to force it away and drive it upward. It was like trying to lift a wriggling, gnawing mountain intent to devour. She couldn't—

The revenant was ripped off her, spun around to face Keuthos. The Hyperborean's fist collided with its jaw. A sound of crunching bone as that jaw dislocated. A second punch knocked the lower half of the revenant's face off completely.

"Fly from here!" Keuthos commanded, even as three more revenants bore him down. Blows fell like hammers, cracking the stone floor, sending tremors through the already unstable ground. The tangle of ghosts moved fast as any Titan, their battle a boggling blur.

She hesitated. Was there some way to help Keuthos? But he had bidden her flee, and she wasn't sure how else to aid her friend.

Grimacing, Hekate dashed over debris and fallen books, making for the broken wall they'd entered by. "Shit!" Abandoning Keuthos again felt like someone was slicing ribbons out her guts. What sort of friend would leave him to hungry ghosts? But they cared about Keuthos only because he forestalled them from feasting upon *her*.

A mad scramble brought her back onto the street. The oppressive dark of a moonless night meant she could make out so little ... save that, all around, gleamed more flickers of waking red. Tiny pinpricks of rubescent death closing in, cutting off any hope of egress from the city.

Hekate broke off in one direction, making it a dozen strides before the appearance of more revenant eyes forced her to skid to a stop. She spun, looked this way and that, until she spotted an alley. Alacrity was not a strong Pneumatikoi for her, but she poured all the Pneuma she could into it, sprinting down the almost pitch-black streets, desperately trying to avoid stumbling over the limitless piles of shattered rock scattered around these ruins.

A chasm rent the alley, a gulf three feet across. She spotted it only because it had swallowed a piece of the adjacent building, allowing starlight to spill into the alley. With a Potency-fuelled leap, she cleared the gap, coming up in a run. The alley opened out into what must have once been a main breezeway.

And all around, eyes in the dark turned upon her.

She had, in the end, crossed into the domain of Hel. The ghosts scrambled over rooftops, crawled on walls, raced down the street, closing in from all directions. All, save the abyss that had swallowed the heart of this ravaged city.

Surely, to descend into such a void would mean death. But what choice lay before her?

Many of the eyes down the main streets broke away, spreading to either side without warning. Even those ghosts she could see in the shadows, those that had raced toward her on foot, abruptly vanished into alleys as if great hands had swept them all aside.

No revenants closed in. All had paused, those who lingered watching with fell hunger in their eyes, yet they tarried, as if afraid to close with her. As if ...

The ground groaned, rocks splitting, shifting, as a torrent of roots ripped through the cobbles. Riding high upon a wave of fibrous destruction stood Dionysus, arms spread in announcement of his own peerless glory. Not even an army of hungry ghosts dared close with this vessel of an Elder God.

"Fuck!" No choice remained. With all she had in Alacrity, Hekate sprinted for the great caldera. Ill wind whipped against her, the very air thick with Otherworldly taint, a warning that ahead lay the darkest of powers.

Behind her, closing in, came a return to enslavement. Dionysus's perverse smirk had bespoken the myriad torments he would visit upon her, the things he would do and, stripping her of will, make her *grateful* for the abuses.

She could not spare the breath to scream in horror. Run, run, run!

Her skin tingled as Dionysus drew closer. An invisible hand caressed her limbs, begging her to return to the embrace of the god. The heaving ground burst apart as the stream of roots ripped through the city, pulverising, casting stones aside in a cacophony that swallowed all other sound.

The fickle ground sent Hekate stumbling, skidding, landing shoulder-first upon lurching cobbles. That impact sent bolts of lightning shooting down her arm. A groan escaped her, her heart trying to climb out of her throat. Dread swallowed her, and worse, an unbidden desire to surrender, her flesh and mind striving to betray her.

A Potency-enhanced shove sent her scrambling forward, a stumbling, lopsided run. Roots and vines sprouted all around her, reaching. Dodging to one side and the next, she fled until she reached the drop-off into the crater.

Below, almost invisible in the dark, she spied a steep slope that *might* have ended in a lower tier. The play of starlight could have been buildings caught in a precarious perch on the side. Or it could have been jutting rocks that could turn her to pulp.

"Hekate ..." The god purred, his hypnotic voice demanding she prostrate herself and beg his favour. To worship him until the end of time.

Hekate jumped into the void.

A FEELING OF FLIGHT. A timeless, flailing, careening through the swallowing dark. A fist slamming into the whole of her body at once, a deeper darkness consuming her.

When Hekate pushed herself up, she could not say if she had lost consciousness for an instant or longer. Her senses seeped back in. The rumbling that ripped through the city above meant Dionysus could not lurk far behind, which meant little time had passed.

She lay amid rubble. As awareness deepened, she stifled a cry. Shards of rock had punched through her thigh and torn open gouges all over her torso.

Slowly, her eyes adjusted to the faint hint of starlight reaching down this far. In threatening chiaroscuro, the space above loomed, dozens of feet out of her reach. Yet such a fall would not much impede the god when he came for her.

Groaning, Hekate dragged herself forward. What could she do now? She could try to use Mormo to bodily shift into the Penumbra, but even if she held out against the wraith's will in her current state, judging by the cloying shadows, this place already lay within an Echo convergence. The barriers between Realms were so tenuous here, the god would walk right through.

Lacking any plan, she kept crawling. Casting herself deeper into the pit would be better than allowing Dionysus to strip her of her mind once more. Unless, of course, the fall killed her and Aeshma reached out of Tartarus to snare her soul.

"Fuck." A rasping, weak, pathetic curse for the pathetic condition of her body and soul.

And yet, she kept crawling, hunting aught she could use. If Dionysus came, maybe she could catch him off his guard, wound him, maybe ... maybe ...

Amid the rubble, her fingers brushed over something cool and metallic. Though caked in dust, she could feel intricate grooves inset within. A blade? No, she realised, brushing away debris. A cube of some kind, but perhaps strong enough to bash in a skull?

In the wan starlight, she blew dust off the object until she could get a better look. What she beheld was ... impossible.

But the cube looked like the Box that Kirke had shown her so long ago, claiming it had allowed her to travel through time. What in Gaia was the thing doing here, buried in millennia of detritus?

Crunching stone and a shower of pebbles drew her gaze overhead. The growing shadow that loomed, blocking even the meagre starlight, announced the arrival of the god. His flow of roots had him descending toward her, taking his time, drawing out her rising dread.

She was lost either way.

She was damned either way.

Decision made, with frantic fingers, Hekate twisted the gears. She had no idea how to activate this device—or even if it would work for her—but she would seize any chance to escape enslavement. Any place, any time must be better than this.

"Hekate ..." Dionysus purred, voice slithering inside her mind like a serpent, wriggling and writhing, breaking barriers down, eroding the will that defined her.

"Work, damn you, work!" Hekate hissed, twisting and pushing.

"Come to me, my Maenad," Dionysus commanded.

The Voice massaged the depths of her until she found herself on her knees, only half aware her hands still worked in faltering desperation.

"Come to me ..."

She tried to stand, to reach her precious Lord, but her wounded leg gave out beneath her. Her finger pushed against the Box and the top popped open.

Her ears popped and everything vanished.

3

HERAKLES

728 Bronze Age

The tiny polis of Edoni lay in Phlegra, not far from the greater city of Iolkos. Travelling there, Herakles could not help but think of Jason and the voyage of the Argo. Such musings had him grimacing as he plodded the beaten path toward his destination. The Argonauts had wrought woe in Kolchis, and Theseus told him that Jason had done worse on his return to Iolkos.

Herakles was in no position to judge a man for dark deeds and violence. And yet ... still, Jason's motives sat almost as ill with Herakles as his actions.

Before drawing nigh to Edoni, Herakles broke from the road and kept to the brush. He doubted his prey lay within the city proper, but this Diomedes would no doubt have scouts in what remained of the ravaged polis.

Unshouldering his bow, Herakles slowed his pace and began scanning for spoor. A herd of rampaging centaurs could not well conceal their passage, even if they assumed no Man would dare follow them into the wild woods they had claimed. Herakles had given precious little thought to centaurs up to now, but Diomedes had changed all that.

According to Eurystheus, a herd of centaurs led by one calling himself by that name had charged into Edoni, slaughtered or abducted half the populace, and rent King Lykurgus limb from limb. "We cannot abide savages running about, murdering royals, now, can we?" Eurystheus mused on choosing the next of Herakles's labours and demanding he slay the centaur leader.

If Eurystheus perceived the irony in sending Herakles to murder a centaur king after such a statement, he gave no indication of it. Besides, as it happened, Herakles agreed with him. Not that kings deserved special consideration, but rather that Man must be protected from any creatures whose aggressions had progressed so very far. The shades of Herakles's sons watched his progress as evening set in, and he dared to tell himself he beheld hints of satisfaction in their eyes.

He had, whatever it had cost him, now completed nine labours and the end was in sight. On returning with the cattle of Helios, Eurystheus had directed Herakles toward the more meaningful task of slaying a skinless bull that rampaged around Argos. Herakles had no idea where the monster had come from—men speculated it had belonged to Minos, same as the Minotaur that Theseus had slain, but Herakles doubted it. Either way, he'd slaughtered the creature and ended its rampage, earning a solemn nod from his boys and the thanks of the Argosian peasants.

And he'd dared allow himself a smile.

Yes, he could see the day in which his labours would at last be complete and he would be free. He could see in the faces of Deikoon and Kreontiades and Therimachus the glimpse of his redemption. He had slain his kin, but he had fought and bled because of it. He had, for four years, taken no step that was not dedicated to appeasing the souls of those betrayed children. And they would forgive him. They *must* forgive him.

As expected, Herakles found little difficulty in discovering the earth churned and trampled by the passage of so many hooves. With an arrow nocked, he crept along the route the centaurs had followed, ever alert for sign of his prey. After the tragedy with the hind, he had debated no longer using the hydra's venom upon his arrows. He had only two such black-fletched arrows left ... and mayhap he ought to have destroyed them. They had wrought enough unintended evil already.

But the toxin proved shockingly effective, and he was heading alone against an army of centaurs. He needed to be certain he could slay their leader at a distance and get away before they swarmed him. Centaurs had strength beyond that of Men, and not even Herakles could fight so many of them at once.

No, range and stealth were his sole allies on this mission, and he needed to avail himself of both if he was to succeed here.

What had Lykurgus done to arouse the centaurs' ire? Such thoughts plagued him as he slunk through the wood. It hardly mattered, he supposed. It was not like any action on the king's part should have earned him so brutal a fate. So pained and terror-laced a death.

The centaurs had gathered in a glade, many dozens of them, cavorting and drinking from skins and stolen amphorae. Others wrestled, challenged one another to hurl javelins—with such force tree trunks ruptured from the impact—or raced circuits about the clearing. His gaze was drawn to a shoddily constructed wooden cage. Within huddled a mass of Men, bruised and dirty, clothes tattered, faces with the look of those left empty inside by dread prolonged beyond endurance.

Herakles ground his teeth. He could not well leave these men and women to be eaten, violated, or whatever else the centaurs intended for them. Which meant his intention to strike down the centaur king from the shadows would prove impossible. Now, he had no choice but to attempt to free the prisoners, though it might well cost him his life in so doing.

But neither could he hope to succeed by charging in and challenging the whole of the centaurs to battle at once. Instead, he crept around the fringe, observing. He watched the centaurs in their drunken revels, noting to whom the others paid deference. He became certain the large one with the matted beard was Diomedes. Though none of the centaurs wore clothes, that one bore a laurel wreath about his neck, and the others oft looked to him with the kind of fearful reverence Herakles had seen Men direct at Titans.

Maybe, if he waited until dusk, when the centaurs were woozy with drink and the light worked against them ...

But now they were dragging a squealing girl from the cage. Not more than nine winters behind her, and these brutes intended to feast upon her flesh. A pair of the centaurs tossed the shrieking child between them like a toy. One caught her and yanked her hair hard enough to rip a lock from her scalp.

This, he could not bear.

Herakles rose and strode into the clearing, waiting until the gazes of many centaurs fell upon him. The savages hefted spears and javelins or took menacing steps toward him flexing their bulging arms. They snorted and snickered and saw in him fresh meat.

"I am Herakles, son of Zeus!" he bellowed, neither drawing back his bow, nor removing the nocked arrow. If any of them thought to charge him, they would find a certain death for themselves. "I have come here to challenge King Diomedes to single combat. Should I win, I would have your word the prisoners go free."

The one he'd taken as king trotted closer until he could peer down at Herakles. Like a man on horseback, he towered over Herakles, even tall as the demigod was, forcing him to crane his neck to meet his gaze. "What would I gain from accepting such a challenge, demigod?"

Herakles frowned. Pride was ever the chief failing of Men and Titans. Why not centaurs, as well? "Kill me, and no one will stop you from feasting upon my flesh. Or spurn my challenge and live with the shame of knowing you refused to do battle with one born of a mortal woman."

Diomedes snickered and nodded his head at Herakles's weapon. "And you'll fight me armed with a bow? Is that how Men duel in this Age?"

Herakles withdrew his nocked arrow and slid it back into his quiver. Both quiver and bow he leant against an oak and spread his arms. "Choose then the weapons of our battle."

"Weapons?" Diomede bared blood-slicked teeth too sharp for Man or horse. Of a sudden, the centaur lunged. His swift blow caught Herakles in the temple and sent him stumbling.

Before he knew what was happening, Diomedes had seized his ankle. With a mad cackle, the centaur broke into a run. Herakles's back and shoulders slapped over the ground, ripped ragged for an instant before he managed to flood Pneuma into Steadfastness to harden his skin. His head smacked again and again upon roots and rocks as the forest rushed by.

Impacts sent spots of light whirring across his vision. Blackness threatened to creep in upon him. Herakles caught the edge of a protruding root as he passed, sending Pneuma into Potency, then yanked himself to a stop, sending Diomedes stumbling at the sudden resistance. The centaur crashed into a tree. The root creaked and ripped free of Gaia, rocks and dirt tangled in its fibres.

Before Herakles could orient himself, large hands had seized him in a grip with the strength of the earth. He was yanked off the ground and slammed against a tree trunk that groaned at the impact. Rough bark scraped over Herakles's hardened skin, draining his Pneuma.

Surging more of his life force to Potency, he gripped Diomedes's wrists. Even with his strength, it was a strain to pry them apart. The centaur's eyes widened in disbelief, and Herakles allowed himself the hint of a grim smile—all he could manage whilst exerting such effort.

He felt it as bones ground beneath his fingers. The centaur gasped in pain. Herakles released his grip, dropped to the ground, and slammed a fist into Diomedes's gut. The blow thudded as though he'd struck solid oak. Another and another, hardened flesh ringing but starting to crack like splitting bark.

Diomedes reared back to kick Herakles with his front hooves. Herakles caught one leg and yanked it sideways, snapping the carpal joint. Screaming, the centaur toppled to the ground.

Herakles hesitated. The centaur king was beaten. He could be compelled to concede and thus release the prisoners. In the wings, Diomedes's brood watched his action. Mayhap they would see mercy as weak, or perhaps they would be moved by compassion. But this creature was a Man-eater, a rapist, and a threat to all civilised lands. If Herakles spared him, he would return to haunt the World of Men once more, and all those he harmed would ask why Herakles had not ended it when he could have.

With a roar, Herakles slammed his fist into the centaur's throat. Diomedes's Steadfastness kept the blow from collapsing his windpipe. The first time. Screaming his rage, Herakles landed another and another blow, pummelling the cannibal king's face, neck, and torso. Until even Pneuma could no longer ward against his fury. Until flesh caved and bones crunched and his foe became naught save a macabre stain upon the forest floor.

Keening arose, a bellow of defiance, and Herakles turned to see one centaur held back by several others. The enraged beast sought to charge at Herakles, to avenge his king.

"Nessus!" a centaur holding him growled. "It was a duel fought fair." Wild eyed, this Nessus struggled against his captors, but to little avail. Just as well, for Herakles did not fancy having to crush another of these beings with his bare hands.

THE CENTAURS MADE move neither to hinder nor aid Herakles as he retrieved his weapons and set about tearing out the gate from the cage. A trickle of frightened Edonians poured from the prison, ones and twos at first, then more, until two dozen bedraggled men, women, and children followed in Herakles's wake as he left the glade.

He could not afford to take stock of those he had rescued, though. Not whilst an army of centaurs marked his every step with wrathful gazes, fingers flexing upon weapons which they made plain they longed to use on him. Though they might honour the terms of the duel and allow Herakles and the prisoners safe passage, he had made enemies here.

Part of him wanted to object. To shout at these creatures that they had been the ones to first attack Edoni. Did they think they could pillage without drawing response? Their longing for vengeance stank of foul hypocrisy. But maybe Men, too, were oft victim to such failings. Herakles had wrought death and carnage in every land he had ever walked, and oft with little enough provocation.

"You're really Herakles?" a young man asked him as they passed beyond the centaur's glade. They were, perhaps, free of immediate danger, but Herakles would not put it past this Nessus or others to come hunting for them soon. Before that happened, he needed to see these people to the closest polis. They needed shelter behind sturdy walls; preferably walls manned by archers.

"I am," Herakles said without looking at the Edonian.

"Unbelievable ... I just ... Ah, my father, he told me about you."

"Uh, huh."

"He, um, he said he trained you, as a boy. When you were a boy, that is, not he. He taught you the art of archery."

That drew Herakles up short, and now he turned to take in the speaker. "I was trained in archery by Eurytos of Oikhalia, grandson of Great Apollon."

The youth nodded with the kind of enthusiasm found only in teenagers. "Yes, that's my father. I am called Iphitos. I was visiting the court of Lykurgus in Father's name when Dionysus came and demanded Edoni's allegiance."

"Dionysus? You mean Diomedes?"

Now Iphitos shook his head and cast a wary glance about the wood, as if in warning that danger still clung to their heels and stalked their every step. Herakles took it as a sign to get everyone moving again, and quickly. "Dionysus, the wandering God of Wine, or so he names himself. He summoned the centaurs, including Diomedes. But that was not the true name of the one you slew. Rather it was a new identity Dionysus bestowed upon the forefather of the centaur race, Ixion. He might try to distance himself from his past, but he is one known well enough to us around Mount Pelion."

Herakles chewed upon that morsel of information a while in silence, at least until they reached the edge of the wood. "You're a prince. I suppose it best I see you home to Mount Pelion and your father, lest more trouble find you." The mountain was a lesser peak of the Olympian mountain range and lay not far afield of the route Herakles would need to walk to return to Mykenai, regardless. "First, I must escort the others back to Edoni."

"There's naught for them there unless much has changed in a short time. Dionysus has claimed it as his own. The God claims all of Phlegra, calling ... things ... to his aid. Centaurs, yes, and beasts of the wood, too. Even the Olympian Artemis was at his side, I saw, on the day they seized me."

Artemis? Oh, gods damn it all. Herakles was uncertain he wished to engage with this Dionysus. He surely did not want to challenge Artemis once more. She would not have forgotten nor forgiven what he'd done to her lover and might well slay him when next she laid eyes upon him. If he was to help the people of Phlegra against this threat, he'd need aid. He could call upon the former Argonauts, he supposed. Theseus and Telamon and the others. But mayhap even that would not prove enough.

Would Athene join them? She had said he ought to become a symbol of what Man could achieve even against a hostile world. But surely his adoptive mother did not intend him to fight Artemis and Dionysus alone?

"Then we all make for Oikhalia," Herakles said. "I trust you will see these people sheltered there."

"I am certain my father will pledge to see them cared for, given all they've already suffered."

THEY FOUND the royals of Oikhalia not in their polis but rather in a great camp along the Pineios River. Within this city of tents unfolded revels thrown by their neighbours, the Lapiths. Their king, Pirithous, whom Herakles knew mostly as Theseus's friend, was in the midst of wedding Hippodamia, Iphitos's cousin.

"Father and Pirithous spoke of alliance before," Iphitos said by way of explanation, though he too seemed taken aback. "Perhaps news of what had befallen the people of Edoni forced their hands into so swift a marriage."

Herakles grunted as the prince escorted him through the camp, looking for sign of his father. It was not old Eurytos whom they found, however, but a woman perhaps a few years older than Iphitos who, upon spying them, raced forward and threw her arms around Iphitos.

"We thought you dead!"

"Iole," the young man gasped, embracing the girl and swinging her in the air.

After a moment, Iphitos held her at arms' length. "Where's Father?"

"Hmm." Iole put her hands upon her hips. "Well, as I said, you were presumed dead, Brother. I am the heir now, and it seems fitting you bow in my presence."

Herakles expected Iphitos to bristle, to perhaps point out that, in no polis in Elládos could a woman inherit aught. Instead, the boy swept an elaborate bow. Upon rising, he pointedly and noisily scratched his stones before offering her the same hand to clasp. "An honour to make your acquaintance, your Highness."

"Ewew ... Father's in council with Prince Theseus of Athenai," she said, pointing at one of the larger tents.

"Theseus is here?" Herakles cut in. The Prince of Athenai had experience fighting creatures of the Otherworld and Men alike. Herakles would have need of his aid if he was to overcome the foes rising in Phlegra.

"Yes," the girl said. "But by council, I meant to say he's occupied.

With a king." Iole looked Herakles up and down with naked appraisal. "Who are you, anyway?"

"This is Herakles of Mykenai," her brother said. "He saved me and the others gathered over there from a herd of centaurs."

Iole bit her lip and cocked her head. "My gratitude, Herakles. Were it not for you, I might have become the Prince of Oikhalia."

"Uh ..."

She winked. "Oh, I didn't much want the title. Apparently the chief duty involves the scratching of balls, and I find myself little interested in such pursuits."

Her brother shrugged. "Mayhap you'd find it satisfying if presented with the right pair."

"Mayhap," she admitted. "Alas, I have no takers upon which I could test it."

Iphitos snickered. "Because you insist upon showing your claws before beginning the task, big sister." He cleared his throat, sobering quickly. "See that our guests receive the wine, if you would. I fear I must intrude upon Father's council."

Iole motioned for servants who quickly bore amphorae toward the Edonians. "Do so, yes, but after washing your hands. Gods forbid if Theseus should deign to shake those filthy things."

"You'd be surprised did you know what things Theseus's hands had touched upon," Iphitos teased.

"Be still. It could well be my future husband of which you speak."

The prince took that as a dismissal and retreated to the large tent where his father and Theseus were.

Herakles was left speechless by the siblings' exchange and could do little more than allow Iole to escort him to one of several logs laid out for revellers to recline upon. The girl shoved a goblet of wine into his hands, then settled across from him, bucking custom that should have prevented a princess from drinking with men. Her manner, brisk as a mountain stream, was refreshing in its way, and Herakles found himself smiling into his goblet.

Evening would not set in for a few hours. He'd have time enough to call upon his friend later, he supposed, and the present company proved, if somewhat disconcerting, not unpleasant. "You expect to wed Theseus?" he asked.

"Hmm?" She chortled. "Oh, I've no idea. Depends how fine an archer he is, I suppose. Father's a bit of a bore in that regard. He decided it was past time I was wed and has thus declared, with Pirithous's permission, that whoever can win an archery contest here shall have my hand. Because we all know skill with a bow is the best possible test of suitability for marriage. Ah, but Father's set on his contest and will not be gainsaid. Men." She shrugged, though not unhappily. In fact, a sly smile began to creep over her features. "Perhaps you ought to enter, yes, dear Herakles?"

"Me?" Dare he again give his heart to a woman, and with his labours as yet unfulfilled? Eurystheus would still bestow two more labours upon him once he reported that Diomedes—Ixion—was dead. But that did not mean Herakles could not arrange an engagement for once his travails were complete.

Could he go back to farming and peace and a family? Mother claimed his explosion of violence against his children was brought on by a curse. He need not believe it would happen again. Did he deserve a life when this was over?

Iole licked her lips. "You seem pale, champion. Does it intimidate so much? For all the beasts you've conquered, do you quiver at the thought of needing to take on a woman? Do you think the needful ..." She sucked in a husky breath. "*Labour* ... beyond your means?" She leant closer, though the space between their seats was great enough she could not have reached to touch him had she tried.

He wanted her, that he could not deny. Four years of penance, and he had not known love, and rarely a woman's touch, save a few animalistic romps in haystacks. Unable to stop himself, he cast furtive glances about for the shades of little boys in the hopes their judgement could guide his course. But they were nowhere. "Don't you know what happened to Megara?" he asked. As if he needed someone to snatch proffered happiness and pleasure from his grasp. As if he thought it meet he ought to suffer alone for the rest of his life. "What happened to the children we shared betwixt us?"

Now Iole leant back upon her roost. "Everyone knows." A pause. "You imply such could happen again."

No. Yes. He had no idea. In truth, he did not know how it had happened the first time.

"I would make you an oath to do right by you," he said, words coming up jumbled together.

The girl crossed one leg over the other, regarding him in sudden seriousness. "Since that day ... Since then, you have become a legend across Elládos and beyond. You fight monsters and evil. You fight to redeem your good name."

No, she didn't understand. Herakles had never once given a rat's arse about his name. He fought to bring peace to three little ghosts. It was their forgiveness he craved. If he helped others along the way, then even better, for he wanted no parent to suffer the losses he had suffered. But he did not perform these labours in search of praise. Not from the living.

"Shoot for my hand if you wish. I would not take it amiss should you win. I do not think I'd find a future with you an unpleasant one."

IN THE END, Herakles had resolved to join the contest. He had shot for Iole's hand, won the contest, and come face-to-face with his erstwhile mentor, her father Eurytos.

But the man who had himself taught him archery looked upon Herakles and sneered. "Not for *you*, Herakles." Even when Iole protested he had achieved victory, he shook his head. "No father would turn his daughter over to a man guilty of such crimes as this man has committed."

Each word struck like a slap. He had told himself he fought not for redemption in the eyes of the World, but for his children. It had not, until now, occurred to him he might *need* absolution before the rest of Mankind, should he ever wish to join them once more.

With dark musings, he sat on the edge of camp and pondered that happiness was never meant to be his lot again. His one chance at a life had died upon his own hearth flames, and their appeasement was now his only quest. His only mission to bring peace to his boys.

Stopping Dionysus was not part of that pledge ... but neither could he walk away from those suffering in Phlegra.

Still, no matter how much he focused upon his duty, it sat ill what Eurytos had said and done. The man had broken his oath to award his daughter to the contest's victor. He had violated the precepts of honour, and that, in the end, was a crime worse even than murder.

One day, Herakles resolved, Eurytos would pay for such wrongdoing. One day he would pay dearly.

4

ARTEMIS

728 Bronze Age

Sprawled across a divan like a discarded shawl, Ariadne tittered and chortled, perhaps too drunk to have grasped what Artemis had said. As God had commanded, Artemis had ventured to Naxos and brought the terrified Ariadne back to become his "bride," as he termed her. The God had forced her to imbibe so much of the Bacchic wine she'd been only half conscious when Dionysus had taken his pleasure from her in front of the gathered mass of his jealous Maenads.

Artemis had not wanted to do it.

Ariadne was Aura. Her cousin's reborn soul lay quiescent within Ariadne's breast, and so knowing, in moments of unguarded conversation, Artemis had *seen* glimmers of the woman she'd known and loved as a boon companion. Did she see Aura in Ariadne because of that knowledge, her perceptions tinted by belief, or did knowledge allow her deeper apprehensions of reality?

Either way, the wife of God spent so much of her time drunk

beyond reason, addled past coherent conversation. These moments of precious semi-lucidity offered Artemis the only chances she now had to reach the soul inside Ariadne. So, back against the hearth in the girl's room she sat, watching Ariadne, listening to her drunken prattle, and casting about for another glimpse of what was lost. She'd seen Aura in a subtle turn of phrase, a nervous tick, a smile. A laugh.

When she could, Artemis demurred to accept any more of the Bacchic wine. Sometimes God forced her to imbibe to drown her mind in his rubescent rivers and lose her tensions in his nightly orgies. When Dionysus exerted his will, Artemis had not the power to resist. His commands she would never again dare disobey.

For millennia, Artemis had resented her father's oppressive dominance of her will. She had hated how Helios had failed to acknowledge any fragment of her autonomy. Then Zeus came to power and she'd thought things might grow better. Maybe, for a time, they had. But paranoia festered upon Olympus, rotting that mountain from the inside out, and Artemis became a prisoner.

Now, she was a prisoner again and, this time, not permitted to indulge her will even within the dark spaces of her own mind. God suffered neither doubt nor disobedience in the acts, words, or very souls of his flock. Moments like these, when his attention must be elsewhere, offered her only reprieve.

"I thought I loved Theseus ..." Ariadne murmured, her words scything through Artemis's musing. It seemed the girl was not so drunk as to have forgotten the life she'd left behind. "But he left me there ... I thought I'd die on that island. I thought ..." Ariadne turned her lolling head to peer at Artemis with drooping eyes. "I considered ending my life. Climbing the cliffs and casting myself into the sea to escape a death by starvation."

Artemis heaved a weary sigh. Dionysus had told her he had reached into Theseus's mind and made plain his claim upon Ariadne. Part of her—and part of Ariadne, no doubt—wanted to loathe Theseus for what he'd done. She could have named him craven, to abandon the woman he'd promised himself to. In the middle of the night, whilst she slept, he'd slunk away, a guilty thief fleeing his crime. But then, who could have done better? What Man could set himself against the will of God?

"I saw the sails of your ship on the horizon." With a groan, Ariadne tried to roll onto her stomach. The movement caused her to slip off the divan, smack the floor, where she lay moaning. Before Artemis resolved to move to help, the girl pushed herself up on her elbow. "You know what I thought then, when first I beheld someone coming to Naxos?"

Artemis swallowed a painful lump in her throat. "You thought he had come back for you."

"But he was gone. Even my sister, gone. Did she run off with him? Did he leave me for her? Younger and more beautiful?"

"God is jealous," Artemis warned. "He may mislike if his wife openly pines for a mortal man."

Still on her stomach, Ariadne crawled to Artemis, wriggling snakelike. Bacchic wine had stolen her dancer's grace and left only this slithering, broken woman in her place. Artemis reached over to clutch her hand. An empty gesture of solidarity. It implied she could support Ariadne, but Artemis could not free even herself. All she could do was sit on the floor, clutching the hand of her reborn cousin whilst staring into her eyes. "He planted something in my womb."

She could not know that, Artemis wanted to protest. Not enough time had passed for that. But she had seen the obscene birth and chrysalis of Deianeira. Dionysus had powers beyond the ken of Man or Titan, and she could not begin to guess at the full extent of those abilities.

Unable to think of aught to say, she laid a hand upon Ariadne's cheek before drawing the other woman close. So close Ariadne's heavy breath ruffled Artemis's hair. Trembles wracked God's wife, and Artemis still could find no words of comfort to offer one denied the least agency in her own life. Such situation rubbed raw Artemis's nerves as it was; but Ariadne—God had used her body to carry forth his progeny. Ariadne had been offered no say in the matter, nor was she permitted to even resent Dionysus within the depths of her soul.

"Aura ..." Artemis whispered into the woman's hair.

But the wine had overcome Ariadne, and she'd slipped into slumber, her snores heavy on Artemis's shoulder.

Thoth, Artemis thought, only to realise she invoked one Elder God out of fear of another, for Pan had manifested within Dionysus, of that there was no doubt.

Long ago, Aura had hanged herself to escape this God. Back then, Artemis had wept and raged and trembled in fury that Aura would do such a thing and deny all who might love her and hope to help her. Now she understood.

Sometimes it felt there was no other way out.

Except, in Aura's case, even death had offered only temporary reprieve.

THE CENTAUR NESSUS tromped into Dionysus's throne room in Edoni. Choking vines had overgrown the hall, bursting with grapes ripe for the plucking. The fountains flowed with Bacchic wine, compelling all who passed nigh to indulge in the sweet freedom it promised. Too oft, Artemis found herself scooping a crimson handful up to her mouth.

Or maybe the loss of reason that followed was a blessing. It allowed her to forget, for a moment, the ruination of her life and her part in the recurrent damnation of Aura. In the silent hours when the revels would at last end and Hyperion had not yet set aflame the sky, Artemis had oft mused on how she might aid Ariadne. Ever, she came up empty-handed. The both of them remained powerless, and most times, Ariadne was mired so deep in the currents of God's might she had not the presence of mind to resent her circumstances.

Yes, that mindless devotion was a reprieve from the agony of churning thoughts. It served as welcome distraction from the knowledge of how little their wills amounted to in the shaping of her their lives. Be it God or Fate, their courses were plotted for them; the illusion of volition was but petty cruelty when it amounted to naught.

Thus, half drunk and atrabilious, she watched the centaur's huffing indignation as he raged about whatever had so offended.

Apathetic, she leant against a column to see how Dionysus would respond to the beast's frenzy.

Dionysus, ivy coiling about his wrists as he sat upon his throne, spread a palm upward to motion for Nessus to continue. The God, as ever, wore that antlered bone mask. Most of the time, it remained blessedly expressionless. When the mask smiled ... Artemis shivered at the memory.

"The son of Zeus burst into our camp and slew my father!"

That drew both Artemis from her reflections and Dionysus from his throne. "Which son?"

Indeed, it would not have surprised if Ares, who ostensibly owned Phlegra and seized on any excuse for battle, had come to murder centaurs in vengeance for what had befallen Lykurgus. She wondered, if God sent her to slay Ares, whether she could overcome the self-styled God of War in a fair fight.

"Herakles." Nessus spat a wad of phlegm upon the throne-room floor.

Artemis grimaced. *Him.* The one whose careless arrow had slain Orion and driven her, unwittingly, into Dionysus's arms in the first place. Oh, she knew it was an obscene abrogation of responsibility for her actions to blame another for her choices, but how very tempting it proved. She could trace the chain of tragedies back to him and hold him to account; what care had she if that same chain reached further and wrapt around his neck, as well?

Part of her even hoped God would send her to kill him, though he'd been one those who'd helped free Orion from his torment as host to the Boar God.

"The son of Zeus ..." Dionysus said, pacing closer to Nessus until he could stroke the centaur's mane in some profane mixture of petting and sensuality. God laughed, then, and it was glorious and terrible, filling the hall with depths that resounded in every soul present therein. "So they come," he said, when at last his fell cackles died away. "They come to challenge our authority, and thus we must show Olympus and its sycophants the path to the Truth. Call the centaurs, King Nessus. For we make ready for war. All Elládos will tremble at our passage."

Artemis pressed herself off the pillar. It was happening. It was really happening.

As if having heard her thoughts—no doubt he did—Dionysus looked to her and nodded. "When we have struck down demigods and his son, perhaps then Zeus will deign to descend his mountain and engage with us." Now that mask *did* grin, bones creaking as it moved. "Then, at last, my father will reap what he has sown in me."

5

——————

ATHENE

728 Bronze Age

After their father had hurled Ares from the steps of Olympus, Athene's brother had not returned. Though she could little blame him for his ire, she thought it did not bode well for the future of the Olympian Order. Father oft flew into vitriolic frenzies, fuming about his son being a traitor and how he was going to have the man's hands dangling from the walls as trophies.

In one such bout, Athene stood in the throne room, watching her father pace and stew, in turns mumbling or bellowing about her brother. Lost in her thoughts, she did not, at first, realise when he had whirled upon her.

"Is he with them? Is he now among the Unseen?"

"Uh ..." Athene shook herself. Eurystheus had sent Herakles after some skinless bull rampaging around the countryside, and, as yet, she had not been able to check on his progress. For all she knew, her son's spiteful cousin had already sent him off on some other fool endeavour. Athene ought to be by Herakles's side, watching over him.

Not standing here in this empty, echoing hall, listening to her father erupt once more about her sadistic brother. "Unseen?"

"Of course Unseen, you thick-headed cunt!" Lightning crackled in Father's eyes, but he scarce seemed aware of it. "They are everywhere! They are *nowhere*. How am I to contend with ghosts in the shadows? Why am I forever surrounded by imbeciles and traitors? And where the fuck is Apollon? Tell that useless Oracle he had best earn his keep upon this mountain."

That ought to prove a pleasant conversation. "I'll fetch him." It gave her an excuse to escape the throne room, at least.

"Wait!" Her father bellowed. "Just how many Oracles are there?"

Did he mean to count among them oneiromancers like Kirke? If not ... "Were I to harbour a guess, I'd say perhaps a dozen around the Thalassa world."

"Any stronger than Apollon?"

She did not like where this headed. "Prometheus ..."

Zeus growled and waved that away. "I ought to never have let that traitorous fuck out from the black of Tartarus." Let him out? Athene heard Nike had freed him, with aid from an unknown demigod she assumed was Herakles.

"Themis," she ventured.

Now her father groaned. "That cunt's in Themiskyra." Some silent debate waged inside him. "First try Apollon. If we have to, we'll sack the Amazonian city and bring them here in chains. But mayhap not worth the effort as yet."

The casual way he spoke of destroying a city left her shuddering, suddenly all too eager to hunt for Apollon.

Artemis's twin brother claimed the energies in Delphi enhanced his Sight, so he spent the majority of his time in his home there rather than in his palace upon Olympus. He was one of only a few Olympians Zeus tolerated to have outside his immediate view. Some weeks back, though, Athene's father had summoned the master of Delphi, and now he lingered upon the mountain.

After asking around within his palace, Athene found he had scaled the walls and was lounging on the roof, staring up at the crackling storm clouds that enshrouded Olympus. She had not Artemis's gift for the Pneumatikoi of Lightness, which meant it took Athene more effort to reach Apollon than she might have wished. By the time she stood over him, cold sweat ran between her shoulder blades and her hair hung over her face in a dishevelled mess. The Heliad wore naught save a linen sheet strategically draped over his hips, assuming his strategy was not one of modesty.

The golden-eyed, flaxen-haired Titan beamed at her as though it were perfectly normal for them to converse thus, and Athene decided showing herself the least flustered by his appearance would only encourage him. Thus, she ignored his state. "Father is asking for you."

Though Kirke's Nectar had given Father a semblance of the Sight, it had not answered the questions that haunted him. In truth, it seemed to deepen his misgivings and paranoia. Whatever apparitions he beheld in the shadows of the future, they obsessed him. Zeus had grown increasingly volatile in the days since, at times turning to lash out at anyone, servant or Titan, who happened to cross his path.

Whatever gaps in his vision, he demanded she and Apollon strive to fill them. Though the Heliad smiled at her now, she had seen him when he thought no one watched, grimacing as he looked upon her father. His sister had gone missing, and Apollon had not been the same. Cracks spread in the foundations of Olympus, and Athene could not see how to hold her faltering family together.

"He asks the same question, ever and again, as if the Sight were one of his slaves he could flog into obedience. It rankles his pride, I think, to imagine he cannot cow Ananke itself with sheer belligerence."

"I know you worry over Artemis, but I'd bid you watch your tongue," Athene warned. "This mountain has a great many ears."

"Hmm. But as it so happens, I lay up here watching the swirl of the ever-present storm. There are fascinating patterns, even in these clouds, called by Otherworldly might." Oh. Apollon was an aeromancer. He was up here using the sky as a medium to trigger his Sight. "As it turns out, I did see something pertinent to all of our questions. I cannot say what I am meant to make of it, as yet."

He meant, whatever he had seen, he did not know if it was wise to share with the king. Withholding information could earn him Zeus's ire, for certain, but presenting it in the wrong light could also bring that infamous wrath down upon his head.

Athene settled down beside the Heliad. "Tell me, then, and we can decide it together."

"Zeus knows the prophecy says his child will slay him. For this prophecy, he's turned upon Ares."

Athene nodded.

"But he has many sons, Athene. Many, spread across the breadth of Gaia, thanks to his countless liaisons with mortals." Rapes, Apollon meant. Another thought coalesced almost immediately after that one: Herakles. Let him not mention Herakles, please. She could not bear it if she were to lose her adopted son, and she could not think how she could keep him hidden from Zeus. "Do you recall the Nymph Harmonia?"

Athene thought for a moment. Harmonia was another of her many half-siblings, one whom Zeus had fathered upon the Pleiad Elektra. The Nymph had wed a mortal sometime during the Silver Age, and he had become a king of Thebes. "I know her. I've not seen her in this Age."

"She had a daughter, Semele, whom your father took a fancy in."

No. Athene's stomach churned at the thought of that. "But ..."

"Yes, his granddaughter." Apollon watched her trying to form words at that. When she failed, he continued. "He sired a child upon her, one Dionysus."

A chill took Athene then. Stories claimed that Dionysus had ravaged Thebes a generation or two following the Gigantomachy. Athene had been preoccupied in her travels with Prometheus, but she had later heard brutal tales of obscene debauchery and grotesque violence. Crimes perpetrated by another son of Zeus.

Her mother vanished around the same time, and Athene had, on occasion, wondered if the two events were connected.

"At the time, your father was still consolidating his rule in the wake of the war. He could not afford to antagonise Hera with another bastard, so he thought it easier to murder the pregnant girl than risk word getting out about his latest affair. Only, somehow, the child in the womb survived the destruction of its mother." Apollon paused, favouring her with a grim, bitter smile. "Small wonder then that your little brother should swear vengeance upon your father."

Athene's hand went to her mouth. Ares was innocent, at least of the crime for which Father had cast him out. And because of Father's actions, he now had a mad Titan on the loose, intent on bringing war to Olympus. "I ... All that was nigh seven hundred years back. Where has he been this past Age?"

"That I do not know. But he is powerful, Athene. And he is moving on Elládos even as we speak. He has drawn to himself an army of centaurs and makes plans to invade south of here, along the passes."

"We have to stop him!" Athene bolted to her feet.

"Do we?" Apollon, too, rose, holding the sheet over his nethers. "I suppose we must." Some hidden concern creased his face, an afterthought that chased away other worries. "I have some sons that live not so very far from there."

It sounded as though they might well stand upon the edge of another war between Titans. "All the sons and daughters of Elládos are in danger now. I must speak with my father before we depart."

He cast a wary look at her, nodded, then hopped off the roof.

"Of course Ares is not the fucking traitor," Zeus fair spat, still pacing around the throne room. "And that donkey's shrivelled cock Apollon ought to have told us that sooner. It's his fault, that feckless Oracle. I bet he planned this! And Ares ought to have known better. I have to do every fucking thing, don't I? I knew it all along, and you were all too damn blundering to see."

Athene didn't know how to respond to his tirade. Was he claiming he had never doubted Ares? Had he not, this very morn, cursed his son's name for a traitor?

"Well make yourself useful, girl, and get the arse-licker back here."

"But Dionysus may already be assaulting Phlegra and soon move upon Ellados itself. We must move to—"

"What am I, a moron?" Her father threw his hands into the air. "Would you have me face a perfidious son prophesied to slay me? Without the support of the God of War at my back? Fuck, Athene. Did I not know better, I'd think you in league with that ungrateful brat!" Did he mean Dionysus now? Ares? Athene trembled to see her father so unhinged. This could not be happening.

Surely, it was the strain of the culmination of Prometheus's dire prophecy. Were she to slay Dionysus, her father would rest easy, his mind would settle, and things would be as once they had been. It sat ill, thinking she must strike down her brother. Kinslaying was among the foulest of deeds, topped perhaps only by oathbreaking in the ranks of heinous crimes. But nor could she let the Titan murder their common father.

Besides, for the sake of the Mankind, she had to put the king's mind at ease. "I will attend to it, then, Father. You can rely on me."

&

SHE AND APOLLON took pegasi from Mount Olympus down to the villages around Mount Pelion. He insisted they first stop to call upon his son, Asklepoius, who worked there as a doctor, chirurgeon, and alchemist. Thus, Athene brought Nephos to alight beside the village and, beside the other Olympian, raced into town.

"My boy," Apollon said, clapping an arm around the demigod in a more open show of affection than she had expected. In her experience, few male Olympians cared a whit for their demigod offspring. Apollon seemed the exception here. Indeed, the other Olympian had long held it against Athene after Herakles had slain his son Linos, and only in the past year or so he began speaking with her civilly once more. "I had almost forgotten you said you intended to open shop in these regions."

"Injury and disease abound on the edge of the wilds," Asklepoius answered, guiding the pair of them to a hall set up as an infirmary. "Especially now."

"Now?" Athene strode forward, already fearing what they would see.

Line after line of beds, all filled with men and women. Some groaned in bouts of semi-lucidity whilst others had succumbed to blessed unconsciousness. She saw too many missing limbs to take stock of. Wounds were wrapt with bandages now soaked with blood, and a subtle odour of rot turned the air inside putrid.

"Centaurs did this," Asklepoius answered her. "They have run amok."

"Worse," Apollon warned. "They are no rudderless ship. Rather, the chaos they unleash is directed with purpose by one who would see Elládos conquered."

The healer scoffed. "That's impossible. Since the Time of Nyx, no foreign ruler has ever claimed so much as a foothold into our motherland. The Titans here are the strongest across the full breadth of Gaia."

"Complacence could cost us," Athene warned, then looked to Apollon. "We need to find Dionysus. Now."

6

THESEUS

728 Bronze Age

"Brave Theseus," King Eurytos said, "surely you cannot suggest we cede Phlegra to the centaur onslaught. Edoni lies uncomfortably close to Mount Pelion and the poleis along this very river."

Within the king's tent, Theseus stared at his goblet of wine, watching the way it sloshed as he eased it from one side to another. Some men, he knew, claimed he'd gone sullen in the days since returning from the Labyrinth. Men were ever wont to criticise how others lived their lives without having the least conception of the tribulations those others had faced. He'd found it hard to look his father in the eye knowing what he'd done to Ariadne.

Harder still to dodge Phaidra's incessant questions about what had become of her sister.

In whom might he confide that it was not the dark of those tunnels that broke him but a *dream*? To give voice to such cowardice would have made him seem a fool—and a craven besides. So, with rivers of wine, Theseus drowned the need to unburden. He let the gloomy musings take him. And he let the ignorant around him speculate about those things which they could not begin to fathom.

He would not have left Athenai for aught save the fervent invitation from Pirithous to attend his wedding. Pirithous had become his closest friend in the world, and one did not spurn an invite to a royal wedding from one's dearest friend.

"I'm not suggesting we abandon Edoni or Phlegra," Theseus said, imagining his words drawn out and drowned in the wine, along with his sorrows. "I'm suggesting we fortify the mountain passes between Elládos and Phlegra and cut off any invasion before it lands."

"You mean to funnel them through the coastal passage at Thermopylae."

Theseus nodded, not taking his gaze from the wine. "A few phalanxes of bristling spears would mean charging centaurs would impale themselves before breaking through. Archers in the passes would render the Olympian Mountains a death trap. If this Diomedes seeks to assault our lands, he'd have to swim the Aegean to do it. Unless you think the centaurs intent to build a navy."

"Not hardly," Eurytos admitted. "And if we hold out until the snows come, those mountains will become impassable, even for centaurs."

"Indeed." Theseus snatched up the goblet and threw it back, heedless of the wine that sloshed over his tunic and beard. What care he for decorum now? What Man ought to trouble himself over appearances after having looked straight into the wrathful visage of a God?

Everything meant so little now. Even the defence of his homeland was but a mental exercise, carrying no more weight than a game of draughts. He lived in shadows now. Maybe he had never truly left the Labyrinth.

He rose, offered Eurytos a nod of parting, and took to wandering among the gathered guests celebrating the wedding. Eurytos was hosting an archery contest with the prize the hand of his daughter, Iole, but Theseus found himself little inclined to seek his marriage at the moment. Even if Eurytos had not-so-subtly indicated he had hoped Theseus would shoot and win. Theseus had considered demanding to know why Eurytos then needed the pretence. Why, if he sought the Prince of Athenai for his daughter's husband, he could not simply propose it outright?

He had no patience left for the games of Men.

"Theseus!" someone called, and Theseus found himself strolling to where Orpheus sat beside the river. The bard had a large amphora of wine wedged into the silt and was skipping stones over the water's surface. Perhaps it was that both mindless pursuits appealed, but Theseus found himself plopping down beside his fellow former Argonaut.

Orpheus handed Theseus a bowl of wine and said naught while he drank.

"Two years, now, hmm," Theseus said, wiping his mouth with the back of his hand. "You, um ... you told me you planned to trek to the Underworld, of all places. Almost had me going."

The bard huffed before tossing another stone across the river. "Now, seeing me sitting here in the waning sunlight, you think I most-like made no such venture?"

"I find it hard to give much credence to ..." Almost hard. Almost, as if Theseus had not seen something equally outlandish unfold in his mind.

"Mayhap it is better that way. You would not like it overmuch should you hear what I had to say, and less so if you believed it." The bard snatched back his wine bowl and poured himself another draught.

"Tell me anyway," Theseus said. He doubted aught Orpheus could say would measure up to the untrammelled horror of the nightmare that had beset him upon leaving the Labyrinth. And either way, it behoved him to understand as much of the Realms beyond Gaia as he could. Once a man begins to suspect what lurks in the darkness, he can never again walk past shadows without peering into those depths in a mixture of dread and guilty desire. Like picking a scab, one could not turn from knowledge forbidden ...

Orpheus downed his wine. Something about the look on his face told Theseus that he, perhaps, *needed* to tell this tale. He had borne it inside his breast so long the rising pressure threatened to tear him apart. Maybe Orpheus saw in Theseus one who could, *would* heed what he had to say.

The bard drew a deep breath. "Well then ..."

ORPHEUS SPOKE of his encounter with Medea. Of how the witch—whom Theseus had reluctantly arranged to be sheltered by his grandfather at Troezen—provided him with drugs that helped him leave behind his mortal shell and venture into the shadows of the Underworld. Of how he'd sought, found, and *almost* managed to return with the soul of his beloved wife. And how he'd failed.

And, too, how he'd run from Dionysus, a monstrous presence from beyond the Mortal Realm. A being touched by something Primordial. The words left Theseus chilled. Night had fallen whilst Orpheus spoke, and speechless and dolorous, Theseus left the bard behind to relieve himself.

It was a simple thing, the most basic pleasure, that draining of pressure, and focusing upon it offered momentary reprieve from his roiling thoughts. The things Orpheus had spoken of offered no solace, serving rather to deepen the horror that beset Theseus.

Pirithous had brought a lake's worth of wine here, but it would not be enough to still Theseus's nerves, he knew. And yet, he had to try.

He found his friend in his tent, in consult with Herakles, of all people, and Theseus forced himself from his melancholy long enough to embrace the demigod and exchange warm greetings.

"I've something to discuss with you come the morn," Herakles said. From the way the demigod looked at Theseus, he could well see Theseus had enjoyed far too many cups for any sort of weighty talk at the moment. Of course, he had planned a few more before sleep seized hold of him.

"Might have to be closer to noon," Theseus said, slapping Herakles on the bicep.

Herakles folded his arms over his chest, glowering. "Perhaps consider a smidge of moderation."

Theseus shrugged. "It's a wedding." As if that had aught to do with his state on this or any other day. "And about the happiest I've yet seen Pirithous."

Though his closest friend was not looking pleased, Theseus had to admit. Herakles ducked from the tent without further comment, and Pirithous motioned for Theseus to sit.

Earlier in the day, they'd talked. Pirithous had introduced his bride, the niece of King Eurytos of Oikhalia. That time, his friend's smile had spread wide enough it might have cracked his face. His laughter had filled the tent, vast and booming. They had spoken of their adventures in Kalydon and upon the Argo, of their friendship. And though they left the nights they had spent in one another's arms unspoken, Theseus knew Pirithous was bidding farewell to such times.

Still, he would not have begrudged Hippodamia her claim on Pirithous. He wished them all the happiness in the world.

"Why the dour look?" Theseus said, slumping upon the ground beside the Lapith king. The man had a small brazier in his tent, but he'd let it dwindle down to smoulders, and with the tent flap closed, its ruby light cast sinister shadows over his friend's face. "Eurytos and I made a plan to confront the centaurs before they can push into Ellá-dos." A thought wormed its way through his intoxicated mind. "Are we too late for that?"

"My father is dead," Pirithous said, staring at the brazier rather than meeting Theseus's gaze.

"Fuck," Theseus moaned and crawled over to his friend to clasp his hand. "I mean, I'm so sorry. When did ..."

"It was the first chance I had to speak with Herakles, and he did not realise either, at first. I always concealed his identity for shame."

"Shame? You are a prince! What cause have you for shame about your lineage?"

"None, I suppose." Pirithous pulled free his hand to wrap his arms around his knees. "Leastwise not on my mother's side." A pause, and he levelled a heavy look at Theseus. "Do you know what happens when a centaur forces himself upon a mortal woman?"

Theseus preferred not to even consider such an event, and his expression must have made that plain, for Pirithous soon looked back to the simmering flames.

"Most oft, it's more centaurs that result, assuming the woman lives at all. Such birthings rarely end well. Sometimes, though, it's a Man child born."

Theseus was either too drunk or not drunk enough. "Are you … you're saying …" Pirithous had always remained reticent about his father. Never volunteered information about him, save to indicate some unease there.

"My father was a centaur by the name of Ixion," Pirithous said. "I share blood with others of his spawn, most notably Kheiron, his firstborn, who lives up on the mountain, and trained many a demigod. Kheiron resisted the savagery inherent in centaur blood, though he told me once it is a battle he fights each day anew. My other siblings are less fortunate. Nessus is among the greatest of them."

It was a lot to take in, and Theseus's wine-addled brain was struggling to keep up. "And Ixion died?"

"Herakles killed him as one of his labours, though only after meeting the son of Eurytos did he learn whom he'd killed. He'd thought he'd gone to slay the centaur warlord Diomedes. But Iphitos told Herakles that was a new name given to Ixion by the God, Dionysus."

The name struck a chord of primal terror in Theseus's soul. He felt a hand go to his mouth.

"So," Pirithous said, voice thick with the aftermath of tears, "Herakles sought to avenge Lykurgus's murder by slaying Diomedes, and he did so. But now Nessus seems primed to seek vengeance anew. I've no idea how far this will go, Theseus. I cannot say for certain how I'm meant to feel about it. Ixion was taken by savagery, but he showed me

—for the most part—measures of warmth. He was my father, and he's dead."

Theseus bit back his response that Diomedes—Ixion—had rent Lykurgus limb from limb. "So, the centaurs serve Dionysus?"

"It appears that way."

And a God intended them harm. Nessus's vengeance sounded worse than Theseus had expected.

"I still don't think we—"

Agonised screams cleft the camp's peace in twain. Roars and bellows, cries of anguish and terror. The wet sound of weapons impacting flesh.

Theseus leapt to his feet, stumbled over his own legs, and planted face-first upon the tent's floor. Pirithous scrambled over him, managed his feet first, and rushed from the tent into the night. Theseus followed with all the grace of a one-legged pig and burst forth to find a camp embroiled in utter chaos.

Centaurs—half revealed by moonlight and the smoky light coming off bonfires and blazing tents—charged about hurling torches and javelins with equal glee. They trampled men and women too slow to flee, sweeping up others into their grasp as prisoners. Four of the beasts seized up each of Orpheus's limbs then galloped off in opposite directions.

A single baleful cry escaped the bard before he was rent asunder, the pieces of him strewn across the charnel field.

Bile scorched Theseus's throat, choking down his scream of denial.

It happened so fast he could not believe what he'd just seen.

But Pirithous was already racing forward, spear in one hand and javelin in another. Theseus's friend leapt and hurled the missile, catching a charging centaur in the face. Drink had not weakened his aim.

Theseus drew his sword and wished fervently for a shield. This was not how he planned it. This was not how he intended any of this. They were meant to funnel the centaurs at Thermopylae. The thought ran again and again through his wine-addled mind, as if repeating it enough might force it to become the truth.

A centaur charged too close, chasing a screaming serving boy. With a single swipe, Theseus cut out one of the beast's legs. The centaur tumbled, end over end, and landed in a heap in the dirt.

"Brother!" someone roared.

Theseus turned to see Pirithous squared off with a centaur who held Hippodamia aloft by her throat.

"Let her go!" Pirithous shrieked. His spear trembled in his desperation. "She's naught to do with this!"

"You missed Father's funeral," the centaur—Nessus, Theseus had to assume—said. "Hardly the action of a dutiful son, boy."

"Release her," Pirithous said, edging closer. Now more pleading than demand.

"A shame I shan't get the chance to fuck her in front of you," Nessus said. "Ah, but then, war requires sacrifices from us all."

"No, no, no—" Pirithous broke into a run.

Too slow.

Nessus seized Hippodamia's head and twisted it around until it her face was turned completely behind her. The wail that escaped Pirithous was more bestial than even the cries coming from the centaurs. He lunged, his spear darting for Nessus's flesh.

"The blood of Zeus," another voice called, forcing Theseus to divert his attention from the battle betwixt Pirithous and Nessus.

And it was *here*.

The face in the wood.

A head of living bone and curling antlers upon a massive Titan form, naked, painted with spiralling tattoos.

The visage of Theseus's worst nightmare. Now he knew the name for it; his dread was one and the same as the baleful God claiming Phlegra and directing the centaurs.

"Dionysus ..." Theseus's voice was more sob than accusation. His sword drooped. There was no fighting such an entity. The being standing across from him was beyond Man or Titan. It was something timeless. Fathomless in its awful depths, the roots of it reaching far past this fragile world.

"A prince of Athenai," the booming voice continued, "and thus a descendant of Athene. The blood of *Zeus* must be drained away to the last blighted drop, the World cleansed of its stain in ichorous cataracts pouring from dying Titans."

Shapes moved in the shadows, Man-like in stature, but inhuman in their lurid motions. They converged upon this fell God, their terrible master. With every lurching shadow, Theseus beheld intimations of the end of civilisation. Dionysus was frenzy given form. Bestial and devoid of empathy or reason, he would tear down the edifices of Man and let savage nature consume the cosmos.

This creature had stolen Ariadne. Images flashed through Theseus's mind, his once betrothed assaulted by the God.

"I shall rip your soul from its tainted vessel," Dionysus promised.

Theseus tried to heft his xiphos, but terror seized his muscles and they refused to obey. What vengeance could Man hope to exact upon God? His lot was only to stand and suffer what abuses or fortunes the divine chose to cast his way. He could not even stand, for the colossal will of the being ahead of him crashed upon him like a towering wave and sent him to his knees.

He would be forever kneeling.

A scream of defiance ripped from Theseus's lungs. Slowly, as Dionysus drew nigh, the point of his sword lifted out of the mud.

Then he realised the scream came not only from his throat, but from another. He saw the instant before Herakles collided with Dionysus and slammed him onto the ground. The demigod roared with savagery to dwarf even the centaurs'. His fist connected with the bone mask, the sound like boulders slamming together. Again, again.

Rock-like fist met bone and cracked it. An antler splintered off.

As Theseus watched, Herakles pummelled Dionysus with relentless fury. The vise that had wrapt itself around Theseus's heart loosened. He could stand. He *did* stand. Impossible though it seemed, a Man now fought God. Herakles stood before the gathered camp and refused to kneel.

Sword hefted, Theseus closed in. He ought to have done this in the first place; until Herakles had shown him the way, he found no strength in his limbs. Now, now he—

Dionysus's hand shot up, caught Herakles by the head, and swung him behind himself in a parabolic arc. The demigod slammed into the ground with an *oof* that sent a cloud of dust billowing up.

Snarling, the God arose, half his mask dangling in loose shards intermixed with blood and pieces of what might have been his jaw. He plunged a fist into the ground. Of a sudden, a tangle of roots and vines burst from the earth. Fibrous tendrils lashed and bound Herakles.

Theseus took a single step forward, but the erupting plants snared his ankles and pulled him up short too.

Dionysus turned away from Theseus to look upon Herakles. "You ..." Though yet deep as the earth, his voice had grown slurred and mushy. "Little brother ... You, the direct son of Zeus. What say ... I make to him a present of your spine?"

7

———

KIRKE

1357 Silver Age

*T*he distortion seized Kirke for but a moment before she managed to shake it off, finding herself in a brine-reeking alley, huddled amid empty crates. Of course, Prometheus's words—his claim that his actions had been predicated upon her having revealed his future actions—had her reeling almost more than the reality-warping effects of the Box. Yeah, so the Titan had ignored their relation because she'd gone back in time and accused him of ignoring their relation?

Kirke wanted to get biliously drunk, retch it up, and punch the man in his stones. Or something along those lines.

Having given Ino the majority of her drachmae, Kirke couldn't afford much, but she could probably afford wine, and she happened to be in a city once more. The scent of fish mingled with the aroma of the sea and of unwashed bodies to create that special, unique stench one found only in harbour districts.

As Kirke made her way out from the alley, she soon recognised Argos, given that she'd come here oft enough in the past. The city lay upon the Bomycas river and proved a major port, though Kirke had sold Nectar here only on the rarest of occasions out of fear of discovery by the Krypteia. In theory, the Argosian secret police patrolled the countryside, not the city, but Kirke had little reason to take chances.

Still, she mused whilst hunting a wine merchant, she'd oft found welcome amid the ruling Tethid lines here and in particular had once—

"Kirke?" a woman called, voice rising in delight.

Kirke stiffened. She had once considered Princess Io, daughter of Inachus, a personal friend. Inachus was a demigod descendant of Tethys and Okeanus, through Thaumas, a son of Poseidon.

Though it flensed her soul, Kirke plastered a smile upon her face as she turned to take in Io an instant before the princess threw her arms around Kirke. Beyond Io, a pair of disinterested guards watched. Kirke thought she might have met one of them, but all this had been so long ago.

"I'd no idea you'd returned to Argos!" Io exclaimed. "I thought you had gone to Kronion?"

A pit opened in her stomach, a bottomless hole that swallowed light and life and sent Kirke tumbling ever downward until despair swallowed her. Of course the Box had brought her here, now, after the last time she'd ever seen Io. Of course it had.

"I think I forgot something," she said, the words coming out a mere wheeze.

"Well, come, come," Io cooed, locking her elbow in Kirke's and guiding her back toward the heart of the city and her father's palace.

Once in the Argosian palace lounge, plied with local wine and fresh olives, reclining upon downy pillows, Kirke found herself studying the contours of Io's face, whilst despair and rapture warred within her. The other woman carried on about the local gossip, though the palace was abuzz with the visit of the King of Olympus, come to discuss control of the archipelago off the coast. "I could hardly believe it when I heard he showed up," Io said.

"I could," Kirke said, voice trembling. Could she now spirit Io away and spare her Zeus's eye? The king would spot her, abduct her, rape her, and Io would then wander in atrabilious shame, a broken woman before at last coming to Phoenikia. Her tormented roaming had become the stuff of bards' tragedies, and Kirke had failed to find her friend, only learning her fate later. Io had become mother to Epaphus, a demigod who became king of Tyros and the ancestor of Europa.

For *centuries*, Zeus's abuse of Kirke's friend served as the capstone of Kirke's rage against Olympus, the very catalyst that ensured she began brewing Nectar with Kalypso. Those innocent, pellucid blue eyes looking at her—the thought of their pain fuelled Kirke's fire.

"Kirke?" Io asked. "Are you well?"

Kirke threw her arms around the princess, her weight bearing her down as she squeezed. No, no, no. She was not all right. She had to stop this, sneak Io out of here before she ever met Zeus. This was ... this would make all the madness she had endured with the Box worth it if she could change the past and thus the future.

"Whoa," Io said, wriggling around until they could both sit, then patting Kirke's back. "What happened?"

"I ... I need to ..." Why had Prometheus allowed Kirke's description of his future behaviour to govern it? Why had he felt compelled to maintain the course of history, even if that history was a bitter one?

Io was Europa's ancestor. Europa raised Pandora and their kidnapping—by *Mother*, for fuck's sake—had led Pandora to Prometheus, led her back in time to become Mother's mother. If Zeus did not rape Io, Europa would never be born. In which case, neither would Hekate or Kirke.

Prometheus ... Grandfather knew that if a single thread of time came unravelled, the whole Tapestry of it might begin to unwind. The thought, though logical, churned her stomach so violently that Kirke lurched away from Io, retching upon the mosaic floor, heaving up sour wine.

No choices …

When Kirke looked back at Io, her face haggard, the other princess watched her with such open concern Kirke wanted to weep. History had to play out, or Kirke would never exist. Nor Mother, nor Athene, for that matter, and who knew how many others.

And all Kirke could do was offer silent prayers to Gaia that she would open and swallow Kirke whole, saving her from bearing witness to this atrocity.

THAT SAME EVENING, Mother came to court, and though she conferred with Zeus in private, Kirke knew what she would tell him. Such things would become the talk of all Elládos soon. How Hades had breached the Mortal Realm and abducted Zeus's daughter Persephone, claiming her as his wife and dragging her bodily down to the Underworld. It was horror, and Thebes had seen it play out in perverse panoply, a dread violation of the natural order none could have before imagined.

Now, Zeus and Mother both stood in the court, whilst Inachus and Io beside him sat their thrones, speaking not of Persephone—they would learn that soon enough, Kirke knew—but of islands and trade and curbing the Pleiades' influence therein.

Kirke stood on the fringes, watching the scene unfold, powerless to stop what must transpire. Her gaze darted back to her hapless friend and again to Zeus, torn betwixt them as if each held an arm and they were ripping her in twain. If she allowed tragedy to befall her friend, was she not culpable for not having tried to stop it?

Zeus, though, had an empty look in his eyes as if he saw neither Inachus nor his raven-haired daughter. Perhaps the abduction of his daughter had shattered him—or affronted his pride—and all else paled before his gaze.

A sudden, sickening thought arose—though Kirke tried to push it down, for it constricted her bowels and sent bile scorching her throat —damned her utterly. Because of Kirke, Ino had tried to kill Phrixus and Helle. Her presence in the past had *created* the past she knew. What if ... what if Zeus was not about to do what he always did on his own?

No.

It was absurd. Unacceptable, unbelievable. Zeus was a lust-ridden cur, a bull without conscience, ruled by his stones and mercurial whims. He would ...

And yet Zeus and Hekate left the throne room, and the king had neither spoken nor once seemed to glance Io's way.

No.

By the fucking crotch of Nyx, no!

But history was not unfolding as it must. It wasn't ...

THOUGH SHE LACKED the moly to make Nectar—indeed, no one had yet begun making it at this point in history—still, a potion to inflame lust proved none too difficult, and within two hours, Kirke found herself clutching the draught to her chest, standing outside the chambers Inachus had granted to Mother.

Was she truly considering this? Could she be this person who betrayed her friend thus?

Though still bilious, she raised her hand and tapped on the door, soft enough part of her hoped Mother would not hear it. And yet, the door swung open to reveal those golden eyes and that auburn hair, the colour a shade softer now than it had been when Mother was a babe.

Shit, was that still *today* she had seen Hekate, a babe in Pandora's arms?

"Kirke?" Mother asked, ushering her inside and embracing her. "I thought you'd gone to see your sister in Kronion." A tremor ran through Mother, noticeable only because of their contact. A reminder that Persephone had been a close friend to Mother, even as Io was to Kirke.

And still Gaia refused to swallow Kirke. If she took her life, if she cast herself into the sea, could she abrogate this duty?

Her voice refused to work, but when Mother's gaze drifted to the phial, Kirke pressed it into her hand.

"What's this?"

"Yeah, um. It's a lust potion."

"I don't have need of—"

"You have to give it to Zeus and get him to lust after Io."

Mother glowered. "Why would I do such a thing? Is Helios behind this?"

Kirke wanted to laugh or weep or both. "Zeus will abduct her and rape Io, and she'll wander the world carrying his child before coming to Tyros where her bloodline forms a new dynasty, all right? And ..." Sobs wracked her. "And if she's not abducted, she won't do that and her descendant, Europa, won't exist to raise Pandora, who's actually your mother after she travels back in time, but that will only happen if you and Zeus abduct her and Europa, in uh, about two hundred years' time, repeating this whole thing. And if you don't, you and I and Athene and *everyone* just crumble!" Tears fell freely now, and she was clutching her mother's hands, blubbering, snot dribbling over her lip.

Mother pulled her hands free and wiped Kirke's lip with her sleeve, then took hold of her shoulders. "Travels through *time*?" The thoughtful look on her face held surprise, but perhaps not the total shock Kirke would have expected.

Drawing the Box from the satchel, Kirke held it out before her mother's face. "With this."

Mother took the Box, turning it around and round. Every time she poked at a panel, Kirke couldn't help but wince, though her mother made no attempt to solve the thing. Finally, she handed it back. "I know who Pandora is," her mother admitted.

Kirke wanted to ask how, to understand, but it all came out as another lachrymal wail and instead she collapsed, head into her hands, all the will blown out of her, scattered as though by a mountain gale. Damn the Moirai and damn them all.

When she at last tore her gaze from the fold of her fingers, Mother too looked apt to retch, rent asunder by the weight of destiny. But she would do it now, Kirke knew. History would unfold as it always had, and Kirke would, in the end, be the one behind some of Zeus's most egregious affronts.

Because she always had been.

8

———

PANDORA

400 Dark Age

The watery sphere collapsed, splashing down back into the basin around the device, even as the orrery's whirling arms slowly spun down. Pandora found herself on her hands and knees, gaping at the inside of the Time Chamber. She had to pop her ears twice to get her hearing back. Had her many uses of the Box left her better prepared for the shift than others would have been? She supposed she wouldn't know. Either way, it had been years since her last timewalk.

So then, where and when was she? The exit to the chamber looked nigh identical to the one she'd left, at least until she unsealed the metal hatch leading without. It opened out into a yellow-stoned tunnel that immediately made plain she had shifted to another location. Her only light came from the fading crackle of lightning within the Time Chamber, so Pandora ignited a flame upon her hand and moved forward. She had not gone more than a dozen paces when a second torchlight spilt around the corner.

She glanced over her shoulder, but save for retreating back whence she'd come, there was nowhere to hide. She had no weapon, either. A smouldering arose in her soul. The Phoenix reminding her that, free of orichalcum, she was never helpless, would never be again.

Then Prometheus strode around the corner, torch in hand, and flashed her his knowing smile. "You're here." Now he was the Titan she knew, she thought, though he wore not his Elládosi garb, but rather what she took for a Nusantaran sarong and little else. New tattoos ran up his arms, strange designs the likes of which she had not seen before.

Though she had just left him behind, an unexpected surge of relief at seeing him again rose in her breast. Because she had left behind *Amirani*, and now here was Prometheus. She sagged against the wall, steadying herself, then rushed forward to meet him.

His arms enwrapt her and all other concerns melted for a moment. A moment was all she could spare. Then she pulled away to stare into his face.

"You told me you would need my aid here," he explained in answer to her unspoken question. "That I would see you through this maze of ruins and to the surface."

She let the implication settle upon her before speaking. At some time in the future, then, she must travel once more into the past. "I have so many questions."

He shook his head. "We've not so much time, my love. The continent is in chaos. The ships of Babilim now close in, intent to claim all the world and bring it within their god-king's domain."

"The continent? Mu?" She inclined her head at his sarong.

"Yes." He took her hand and started to drag her through the tunnels, darting down one and the next without the least need to orient himself. "We're below the city Mugedang in Nusantara. These are the ruins of Murias, one of the cities of—"

"Dark Faerie." She jerked him to a stop and spun him around to face her. "I know that part. I want the other answers now, Prometheus, all of them. I saw you in the future, long past this Era, and you said I claimed I learnt more for having uncovered the truths myself. But every answer I have found thus far has spawned a dozen new questions. Much as I love puzzles and riddles, with insufficient clues such mysteries prove more vexing than intriguing. And I have smeared my blood across the ages in the name of your love. So tell me, *now*. Who are you? How have you been so many men through the vast mural of history?"

He winced, looked away, then visibly forced himself to meet her gaze, as if his sapphire eyes were not the most soul-piercing sight she had ever seen. As if he feared what she would see in him. At length, he sighed. "What do you know of the Archons?"

She shrugged. "The name means 'ruler.' Beyond that ...?"

"'Tis a title by which we referred to those more oft now named the Elder Gods. In the first days, when the World was new, they ... They came to us." He seemed, for once, at a loss for words, his unshakeable calm broken by crashing waves of emotion beneath his surface. The telling of this seemed apt to shatter him, and Pandora almost relented after seeing such pain in him.

But she needed to know. "You're saying you were there, in the first Era of the World?"

A pained nod. "They chose those of us who came first and tasked us to watch over Mankind, and thus called us their Watchers. They gave us power and immortality, the ability to roam between the Mortal Realm and beyond."

It took her a moment to catch up with the import of his words. "You are saying, you Watchers were the first people of the World."

A tear formed in his eye, but he blinked it away. "Oh, but you were one of us. I loved you, even then. Always, from the first days."

That claim caused the familiar tinge of pain in her chest to gnaw at her once more. In Vulgeth, Amirani had implied he had known her before. That she had lived before. But the full implication of it had not quite seized her then, in the tumult within which she had floundered. And now, now ... "I died."

It was a strange thing to voice aloud. Of course, life was inherently a finite thing for everyone—or everyone save these Watchers, perhaps—but to speak thus of one's mortality seemed surreal. The kind of statement one could apprehend intellectually, but still stumble upon when trying to grasp it with the disbelieving heart.

Prometheus might have reached across the gap betwixt them and steadied her, but instead he watched Pandora bring her own churning emotions to heel. She felt flushed, beset by trembles. Shaking, she leant against the wall hoping to ground herself.

"Souls are drawn to the Wheel of Life," he said, "spun out again and again, into new incarnations in an endless cycle. Maybe it ought not to have surprised me, then, to have seen your soul, long after I thought it lost, come around again." He touched her elbow and Pandora could not have said if the gesture was more for her benefit or his own, as if to reassure himself she was here, for a moment, once more.

Then something burgeoned in her mind and she cast a sharp look at him. "Other Watchers can die. *I* died. Given all I have learnt, I suspect Kronos was one of our kind, as well, and Kala murdered him. And yet you implied that death lies beyond your reach. There is something different about you, Prometheus, or whatever your original name was."

A moment, he shut his eyes, hiding those sapphires. "It was Matarśivan, and that's a tale for another time. As I said, the continent —the whole of this world—it lies in peril. Mithra, god-king of Babilim, closes in, and the Queens of Mu grow in desperation. Before the waves of chaos sweep over this place, I must see them."

Whilst she still sought more answers, worry creased his usually placid features, and she could not deny him. Besides, he had given her much and more to think on already. Reincarnations of the soul —*her* soul—over countless lifetimes in which, as must be, the past was ever forgotten. Or buried deep. Such things she mused on, trying to ignore the tightness in her chest, as Prometheus led her through the shadowed tunnels.

That, and Watchers. The Elder Gods—Archons—had created or chosen servants to act as guardians and messengers, but to what end? Why should they care about mortal souls?

The maze of tunnels at last let out through a narrow opening that Prometheus squeezed from, before they found themselves in the basin of an almost-dry canal. Debris from cyclopean blocks lay strewn about within the canal bed, clearly having fallen from one side that had crumbled. Creepers, roots, and tropical plants burst through the seams, overshadowing the gulley. The scents of flowers and petrichor could not cover the reek of human waste trickling in what remained of the waters, and Pandora covered her mouth with one hand.

Her other hand Prometheus claimed and led her up the slope, picking his careful way along fallen stones until they could reach street level. Though Pandora had, in her studies upon Atlantis, read of Nusantara and its glorious capital oft enough, those readings had not prepared her for the real sight. Many-tiered palaces capped with arcing saddle-roofs gave off the impression of a sea urchin's spines. Mountain-like temples, rising from the hills and carved with innumerable reliefs of celestial beings, turned Mugedang into a series of peaks and valleys. The city seemed haphazard and yet effortlessly sewn together.

Though she might have wanted to see the famed harbour where dhows would crowd the waters and bring trade from unknown eastern lands, Prometheus instead led her toward the heart of the city. He, of course, had his aims set upon finding the Queens of Mu, though Pandora had never heard tale of such people.

"I thought Mugedang was ruled by a cadre of sorcerers," she said as he guided her through the streets. They passed a throng of warriors, spears and shields in hands, rushing in the opposite direction. Most of the rest of the city folk seemed to be hiding within their homes and shops, fearing whatever threat now impended.

"It was and still is." Prometheus led her through claustrophobic alleyways, making clear he headed toward a mountainous stone palace set among lesser soaring temples. "As the threat of Babilim has grown in the past centuries, the sorcerers began to fear Kumari Kandam would claim their homeland. One of them regained some memories of her past life, a time when she had been a powerful Nymph who co-ruled Atlantis."

Pandora stubbed her toe on a loose cobble, so shocked was she when his meaning struck home. "You mean a reborn Pleiad!"

"Using forbidden Art, she called up the souls of her erstwhile sisters to be reborn into the next generation, and they established themselves as the Queens of Mu. Great sorceresses with power to rival the mightiest wielders of the Art in all the breadth of Gaia. They think to turn their powers against Mithra and his Magi, but they call upon forces not even they can control."

They had reached a wide stairway cut into the hillside, and Prometheus strode up it, forcing her to keep pace. "Have you come here to stop them from making a mistake, then? The Pleiades were your nieces, if not by blood, then by choice. Kelaino, your student, meant more still than the others. So, you will keep them from turning to the Art?"

He didn't look back. If aught, his pace only increased. "I doubt I can stop them from doing what they feel they must. But I must see her now, before it's too late."

How much of his interminably long life he had spent thus, chasing after moments, hoping to claim them before they slipped forever through his fingers? It was as if he knew doom crept in upon the horizon and, resigned to it, sought now only to seize what little joy lay in the space betwixt the darkness looming on either side.

Atop the stairs, they were met by a squadron of bare-chested, tattooed warriors. Indeed, these men bore tattoos very similar to those now gracing Prometheus's arms. The guards recognised Prometheus immediately and beckoned him inside with terse Nusantaran greetings, their tension palpable upon their faces. These were men who expected battle very soon, and they fair tingled with the anticipation of it.

A man met them inside and clasped Prometheus's arm.

"Nu'u," Pandora's lover said with a nod.

"Maui," the other answered, nodding in turn. Yet another name for her beloved ... "The queens are gathered in the Soul Hollow. But word reached us you would come, and they shan't make their final decisions until they've heard you speak."

"Then there is yet time," Prometheus said.

Nu'u shook his head. "Mithra's ships draw perilously close. My wife would see them loose the chains which Hekate placed upon Achlys and think perhaps the Elder Goddess will offer gratitude."

Wait, what? Hekate had done what now?

Pandora's lover grimaced. "Gratitude is not the nature of gods, the Elder Gods least of all."

Nu'u shrugged. "Desperation leads us down strange paths. They summon the Oracle of Tides to consult the Otherworldly powers. My wife objected, but Pokoharau has insisted, and Lilinoe cannot gainsay a fellow queen."

The rush of names befuddled, and Pandora had not the least idea what was going on here, save that the queens could not agree on how to meet the threat Mithra and the Kandamians presented to Mu. At Prometheus's bidding, Nu'u guided them through the heart of the palace and underground, down winding stair after stair until Pandora grew certain they had once more entered the tunnels beneath the city.

Those same ruins of Murias from which she had first emerged, though perhaps in a different segment. They came, at last, to a cavernous hall with a vaulted ceiling. Torches tall as she was stuck into a sandy floor, flickering and dancing. A sheet of water trickled along one side of the cavern, pouring into a vast pond at the back of the chamber.

Seven dark-haired women were down here, unclad, flinging their hips and in time to a rhythm that seven other young girls beat upon massive drums. A euphoric energy permeated the cavern and had the hair on Pandora's arms rising with anticipation.

One of the whirling women soon spotted them and broke away.

"Pandora," the woman called, nodding first at her, then her lover. "Maui."

Pandora struggled to keep the shock from her face whilst Prometheus took her proffered arm. "Mahuika."

Kelaino reborn?

"The Oracle of Tides draws nigh," Mahuika said. "We shall have our answers."

The waters within the pond rippled as something massive rose to the surface. Pandora had expected, perhaps, a mer, but the creature that breached the cavern was something else entirely. At first, she could not recognise the bulbous head. But as tentacle-like arms rose around, she knew it for what it was. An octopus, yes, but this one twice the size of an elephant, great arms thrashing the air as though it might well bring down the whole cavern if provoked.

"Behold," Mahuika said, "the great Oracle of Tides, Kanaloa!"

9

HEKATE

725 Bronze Age

"I think I can tell you how to use it now." Kirke's words came slow, seeming drawn out from a hollow core deep inside.

The pain there struck Hekate, had her enwrapping Kirke in an embrace as if she held the woman together. As if any of them could survive the scope of the Moirai's weavings.

That was what it came down to, was it not? That the Fates had cursed their family, and worse still, that Hekate and Kirke had damned themselves with the Art. At times, she dared to believe Kirke had used little enough sorcery she might avoid becoming a wraith in death, though Hekate could not be certain. For herself, though, every road led through agony and darkness. Becoming a wraith locked in eternal self-loathing now seemed almost a blessing compared to the unspeakable torments Aeshma would visit upon her. And of the warnings Pandora had given? Perhaps her mother spoke of Aeshma, perhaps something else. Hekate could not know.

Hekate awakened with a groan. Jolts of agony coursed through her thigh, her arm, her shoulder. A churning in her gut would have sent her retching had she taken more than water in the past few hours. Or longer; she didn't know how long she'd been unconscious.

With a start, she realised she no longer lay amid stone rubble, nor even in darkness. A mossy bed of leaves lay beneath her, redolent with the scents of loam and a hint of decay. A forest? She rolled over onto her back. And then she screamed.

A half dozen feet away, Dionysus hovered two feet off the ground, reaching for her, his visage a mask of wrath and consternation. Yet as Hekate scrambled away on her arse, the god remained floating, his hand advancing a mere hair forward with each passing breath.

"What in Nyx's dark bosom?" Hekate gasped.

Though waves of his puissance saturated the forest, Dionysus seemed *almost* frozen. The paroxysm in his eyes left no doubt he blamed her for his plight and would reap awful vengeance upon her once he broke free.

But then, she couldn't let such an opportunity pass, could she? It took more effort to summon Khione's ice in daylight, and more still in Hekate's current state, but she formed it around her good hand. Thrusting, she launched a shard of ice as big as a spear at the god's head. The frozen missile surged forward, only to slow to a crawl a few feet away from Dionysus.

Caught in the same effect as him?

So, fighting him was not like to avail her. She looked to her leg. A dagger-like sliver of stone was jammed into the back of her right thigh. Oh ... that would hurt. Gritting her teeth and pouring what Pneuma she could into Tolerance, she gripped the sliver. Its sharp edges dug into her palm, calling forth fresh ichor. With a hiss, Hekate yanked free and cast aside the impaling stone.

Judging how long this effect would contain Dionysus would prove impossible, she knew. Even with Tolerance, claiming her feet had her close to blacking out once more. If that happened, if she lost herself now, she might never again awake—at least not free of the god's hold upon her mind.

A look back revealed that Dionysus's lips had begun to part, the god intent on working his will upon her.

Offering him a rude gesture, Hekate hobbled away with as much haste as she could muster.

Titan resilience meant Hekate's wounds closed even before she left the forest. While she lost a lot of ichor, millennia of consuming Ambrosia meant she could handle injuries that would have crippled or even slain a mortal. By the time she reached a local polis—Delphi, she realised—she was famished and parched but able to walk without need of Pneumatikoi to fight off the pain.

She had only a few drachmae, but the local aristoi recognised her as a Titan, though they did not seem to know *who* she was. Curious. Hekate had thought her reputation would precede her in any polis in Elládos and many beyond. Either way, the king offered her food, a place to sleep, and wine. The last, Hekate found herself staring at in a churning mix of dubious distrust and mouth-watering desire.

Would a sip bring her mind back to Dionysus?

Before she could talk herself out of it, she grabbed the bowl and threw it back. Though watered, it retained a pleasant bite, warmth surging through her. When the bowl was emptied and a servant moved to refill it from a painted amphora, Hekate could not trust herself to speak. Instinct demanded she accept. An almost erotic desire for the draught wrapt its claws around her throat. It took the last of her faltering will to shake her head.

"What news of these lands?" She hoped her desperation to distract herself was not apparent to the mortal king.

"You have not heard?" The king rubbed at his brow, though he bore a barely concealed smirk. "A demigod seeks to atone for his crimes by slaying monsters. Rumour of *great* deeds abound." Something about the way he said it assured her he thought very little of the so-called hero's accomplishments.

In truth, Hekate cared even less for such things. She needed to find someone who could help her escape Dionysus. And now, to understand this Box. With Dionysus here now—and she had to assume he had somehow gotten caught in the flow of where the Box sent her—if she could find a way back, she might be able to reunite with Keuthos. When last she'd seen her friend, he was beset by far too many revenants to fight off. Perhaps they had left him be upon the arrival of Dionysus, fleeing as those pursuing her had scattered. Either way, Hekate had promised not to leave his side again, and breaking that promise sat ill with her.

Neither could she risk fiddling with a device she did not understand. The Box needed careful study before she activated it again, lest it send her to some other time entirely. Already, she knew precious little of the world in this time.

"Where can I find the Nymph Kirke?"

The king of Delphi shrugged as if such things were beneath him. Hekate fixed the mortal king with a pointed gaze in case he had forgotten he was in the presence of a Titan. First, he squirmed a bit, then he threw back a swig of wine.

"I, uh ..." He cleared his throat. "That's not a name I know, I'm afraid."

That, at least, she believed. The man had not the gall to lie to her.

KIRKE'S DREAMSCAPE had become a vast, empty chamber, faint echoes ringing in time with the padding of Hekate's sandals as she sought after her daughter. Arching windows in the vaulted ceiling allowed in a scattering of moonlight to break up a hall that extended much further than any space in reality. The sense of wandering for desolate miles pervaded until, at last, she came upon Kirke, sat in the middle of the floor, knees up around her chin.

A half circle of untouched amphorae rested before Hekate's daughter, the woman's gaze locked upon the wine vessels as though they offered some perverse mix of salvation and damnation. As if she loved and feared what lay within.

After so long under the thrall of Bacchic wine, Hekate knew that feeling to the depths of her bones. She felt it in the pith of her soul: an aching cry, a desperate reaching for that which she loathed and needed in equal measure.

Only when she knelt in front of Kirke did the glazed look pass from the other woman's eye. "Mother? Are you really here? I thought ... I thought you were dead." Kirke swallowed, paling. "Are you dead? Are you visiting me from the Underworld?"

How much time had passed? Her absence must have been prolonged for Kirke to conclude her mother had perished. In the interval, Ananke had ravaged Kirke with all the torments the Moirai could weave—that much stood plain.

"How long have I been away?"

"Um ... Seven hundred years, give or take a bit. Yeah, I mean, at first I thought you but wandering as was your wont, but as decades turned to centuries, I ..." Seven hundred years? Despite Kirke's long life, she seemed but a girl once more, face plaintive, imploring her mother for answers Hekate did not have.

Little wonder, given Hekate's momentary choice—her desperation in looking to the Box—had sent her to vanish from time for so very long. But if Kirke remembered her absence, did that mean Hekate failed to return to her own time? "I need to see you. Where are you?"

Kirke looked ready to burst. "Aiaíā."

Aiaíā ... As Kirke's father controlled the island, Hekate had to assume Kirke had gone there on some task for Helios. As the Titan rarely left Helion, Hekate hoped she would not have to see Kirke's father himself there.

"Why?"

"I am ... I was exiled here."

Her words lanced Hekate. The pain in them became blows against her body, a wonder, a shame. For had she been there, perhaps she could have spared Kirke whatever had led to this. "I'm coming to you."

FINDING passage to Atlantis from Delphi did not prove difficult, and from there, Hekate could take passage to Helion. Then she'd need to purchase a small ship to make for Aiaíā, given that no merchant had business there.

Seven hundred years. The very thought defied reason. The implication of it, of Hekate's removal from the doings of Elládos for an Age, they swept too broad for her to grasp. How fared Kirke and Athene? What had become of Pandora? Worse yet, without Hekate to limit his excesses, what obliquities would Zeus have wrought upon Mankind?

Kirke's words, the revelation that Hekate had *not* returned to the past, they had all but sundered her hope of reuniting with Keuthos moments after she had left. Still, she had to try, and Kirke might understand more of the Box than Hekate could.

Now, she had to try to save her daughter, yes, but at the same time hope Kirke could offer Hekate answers.

Hekate moored her small vessel at a village on Aiaíā's eastern shore, the only settlement she could see between the treacherous cliffs and mountains rimming the island's perimeter. Unless something had changed, Helios's sister Eos ruled this island and Hekate had not the least interest in encountering Kirke's aunt. She tossed the harbour-master a few drachmae, bid him tend to her ship, and hurried along the path to the manse where Kirke now dwelt.

The afternoon was setting when Hekate arrived at the estate given to Kirke and she faltered, for it was not Kirke walking down the path to meet her but Zeus. The platinum-maned King of Olympus caught sight of her, the widening of his pale blue eyes making plain he too had thought Hekate long dead by now.

Barely contained rage at his surprise washed over his face, his hands rising beside him as if in anticipation of a threat. "Where in Gaia's cavernous arsehole have you been?"

Beset by her fears of Dionysus and concern for Kirke, Hekate wanted naught to do with Zeus. She had neither the time to fondle his cosmic ego, nor the inclination to answer his questions. The desire to blurt that he would neither understand nor believe her if she told him rose upon her tongue, and only an effort of will pushed it back down before she made things even more uncomfortable for herself. "I wandered far seeking forgotten knowledge."

In the end, perhaps a half-truth would serve when she had not the energy left to lie.

Zeus sneered. "I expect you to attend me on Olympus within the month, witch." The menacing step he took toward her made it plain she had better have more explanation than that ready on arrival.

Oh, but then she could tell him about Zagreus, his misbegotten spawn sired on his daughter now reborn as Dionysus and come for vengeance. She could warn the king she had helped enthrone—at Enodia's behest—that his son came to do to him as he had done to Kronos. A word, an admonition of the things that must soon impend, it could prepare him. But then, though she loathed and feared Dionysus even more than Zeus, she would almost relish the brutal conflict that would unfold between them.

So she said naught, offering only a bow.

"I will have the Ontos," he snapped, his words coming out of nowhere. How did he even know of such a thing? "I will know all things, rule all things, witch." He pointed a thick finger back at the estate. "She will give me all I need. You *dare* not interfere with that."

What in Nyx's bosom?

Offering no further explanation for his ravings, Zeus tromped onward, leaving Hekate to approach her daughter's estate.

Upon the portico lay the broken forms of three dead wolves, skulls pulverised, bodies tossed aside like detritus in a storm. Gasping, Hekate rushed inside to find Kirke, curled in a foetal ball upon the floor, one hand between her legs, the other wrapt around her head. Groans of agony intermingled with weeping.

Her daughter's state struck Hekate as if Zeus had blasted her with lightning. A moment of rage—if that bastard had violated her, Hekate would have his stones as amulets—gave way to choking fear when she dropped down, hand upon Kirke's shoulder.

"Kirke, Kirke." Tenderly, she rolled her daughter over to looking into a face contorted with pain.

Her daughter coughed and sputtered but allowed Hekate to pull her into an embrace. The question she dare not speak died upon her lips.

"He hit me." Kirke's voice had become a wheezy whisper. Had she realised what Hekate would think and answered the unspoken query or merely needed to air her indignity at such a vulgar tactic? What man punched a woman in the groin?

Perhaps, instead of his testicles, Hekate would need to remove the offending hand. Unbidden, a vision of her *eating* the puissant flesh arose in her mind, gagging her. No! She would not become what Dionysus had tried to make her. She would not give in to such monstrous instinct.

When Kirke seemed able, Hekate eased her into a sitting position. "Why has he done this?"

A bitter scoff escaped Kirke. "He knows about the Nectar, Mother. He wants me to ... give him the Sight."

Most oft, the Sight awakened in one driven to the brink of death, so close they might glimpse the other side and be changed by the experience. In her younger days, she remembered a discussion in the Circle of Goetic Mysteries—one led by Damkina, the Circle's founder, in fact—about whether such experiences could awaken the Sight in any, or only those with latent psychic potential. In some cases, like Hekate's, the gift was so strong it came upon the young even without a brush against death.

For someone like Zeus, though? No, Hekate didn't think it apt to work, nor would she *want* Zeus having such abilities. The deranged megalomaniac was already a rampant typhoon venting its fury upon an unprotected land. The last thing anyone needed was him gaining true insight into the future or other aspects of the Ontos.

"Come," she said, easing Kirke to her feet, "let's get you cleaned up."

THOUGH KIRKE HAD OFFERED her wine—and indulged in far too much herself—Hekate limited herself to water. The Phoenikian red Kirke imbibed was not like to produce the effect of the Bacchic elixir, but Hekate felt little desire to take the chance.

The two of them sat before the hearth, filled with soup, talking of all the things that had brought Kirke to this bitter, lonely exile beneath Eos's disapproving eye. Perhaps it had been too much to dare hope that no one would ever uncover Kirke's guilt in brewing Nectar, and Hekate understood Helios's attempts to spare his daughter from Zeus by sending her here.

That, however, had clearly failed.

"I can speak to your father about having your exile lifted."

A brief smile flickered but it quickly faded. "And how do you think Zeus will react if I leave? He'd hunt me to the ends of Gaia, and we both know it. Maybe ... maybe if I can give him what he wants, he'll forget about me."

No, Hekate rather doubted it. Zeus was not the type to discard those useful to him. Men and women were tools for his ends, and he would not loosen his grip on one that could offer him aught. And those who proved no longer needful would find a yet worse fate.

"I'll do whatever I can for you, Kirke. But I do need something of you, now." Hekate pulled the Box from her satchel and proffered it. "I need to know how this works."

"Huh." Kirke took the device and turned it one way, then another. "What is this, a puzzle box?"

Her words—filled with innocent wonder and piqued curiosity— struck Hekate like a Cyclops's kick. They knocked her dumb, a dozen incipient thoughts arising and then discarded. A perverse causality now unfolded before her, one so twisted, so merciless she had never considered it possible.

"Yeah," Kirke said, "I'm sure I can figure this thing out. Heh, I mean, it'll take my mind off Zeus's absurd demands a bit. Any reprieve might help me come at it from a new angle. But why do you care about a toy, Mother?"

Maternal instinct demanded she snatch the Box now, bury it out of sight, and let Kirke never give it another thought. But ... but ... This must have already happened. Unwittingly, cruelly, had Hekate set Kirke upon the path that would lead to her prompting Zeus to kidnap Io, Kirke's beloved friend?

Words continued to elude Hekate, her mouth flapping like a beached fish. There had to be a way to take this back, to undo this insanity. But what consequence if she managed to do so? Besides which, she had no one else to explain the Box to her—and so very much riding upon her ability to harness it. Powerful enemies demanded one consider even the most desperate of tactics.

"Mother?"

"This small puzzle is a key to a greater puzzle, a piece I need to understand." Hekate hesitated, almost choking on her words. How could she allow her daughter to travel this road? How could she *not*? "Kirke ... I need to know how the Box works, but don't open it."

"Uh, sure, yeah. I can figure out a puzzle box without solving it. I was also thinking about reading a few scrolls without removing them from their cases. You know, after I sip some Phoenikian red before the grapes are plucked from the vine." Kirke set the box aside as if it was not the most valuable, most damning, taunting of all treasures. "There's something you could do for me in the meantime."

"You want me to speak to Zeus on your behalf."

Kirke rolled her eyes. "Sure, and after you convince him to change his mind, I'd like you to convince the land to rise up and make a bridge off this island. That, and maybe talk a pheasant into cooking itself for me. Ahem, no. Rather, I have a niece, which I assume you don't know because you've been wherever you've been, which was not *here*. My half-brother, Aeëtes, his daughter Medea. Before I was banished here, I was training her a bit in alchemy, but she always wanted more, and she keeps writing to me, as if I can explain aught about the Art in a letter."

As though teaching Kirke sorcery had not proved enough of a mistake already, now she wanted Hekate to train another. "You'd have me go to this Medea in ... Kolchis?" That was where Aeëtes lived, last she'd heard. "Teach her sorcery?"

"Sorcery ..." Kirke screwed up her face. "Some lesser arcana, perhaps. Surely you know the impotence a woman feels in the courts of men. Even a little knowledge might offer her a semblance of control over her own life."

If Kirke had witnessed even a glimpse of the Moirai's weavings that Hekate had now beheld, she would know that neither Man nor Titan held true control over their lives. The threads binding them allowed a veneer of freedom, a pretty self-delusion to cover the stifling truth.

And though it broke her heart, Hekate suspected Kirke would learn such things all too soon.

The effort of keeping self-loathing from her tone came nigh to breaking her. "I'll go to Kolchis."

INTERLUDE: ORPHEUS

728 Bronze Age

My story? Whatever your intent in asking, I find myself doubting you can imagine what it entails. Whence comes the stirring of our souls, dear Theseus? We are creatures of driving passions, Men, but do these passions come from some hidden depths within our flesh? Or is their genesis somehow in worlds beyond, unperceived by our paltry senses?

Yes, well, I am after all a bard. No, no. I shan't sing you the tale. Not this one. But if you truly wish to hear of it, of my katabasis, you must bear with me. Indulge a bard to tell his story as the muse moves him.

But are you certain you wish to know what lurks beyond the Veil sheltering this fragile world?

Ah.

Well, I was long in my preparations to make such a sojourn but determined beyond all dissuading for reasons I shall make plain soon enough. I had, by the time the conviction to make the trek moved my soul, already experience enough with the Realms beyond.

In my youth, I almost died. An accident upon a horse, of little matter to the rest of my story save for this: as life fled from me, I saw something. A squirming of the shadows, a welling of the darkness. Or mayhap the fevered fancy of a boy who'd broken three of his limbs in a single fall. That last was what I later told myself, for a time, when I sought sleep free of nightmares.

Unfortunately, such pretty self-delusions could not abide forever. In times of strain or terror—or on occasion, whilst I hovered on the threshold betwixt waking and dreaming—I would see the rise of those shadows once more. It was like peering through a gossamer shroud, and what lay beyond was a reality bereft of light and colour, save for countless greys and blues deep as the Axeinos Sea on a moonless night. Amid this shadowscape billowed a haze obscuring the distance.

And sometimes—only sometimes, mind—I would fancy I could perceive shapes out in those vapours. Man-like apparitions, though I did not think them Men, even back then.

Oh? Does it disquiet you to know that something else dwells *beside* our world, unseen, though they notice us? Would you have me stop here, Theseus? Walk away, then, and be freed before I drag you deeper than you've any wish to go.

You can't? Oh ... I see it, now. You too have seen something of the Realms beyond. You too have already bid farewell to restful nights and crossed a threshold from which one cannot return.

Well, then. Fetch us both some more wine, and I shall skip to the part you asked over.

❧

As I was saying, I spent years honing my mind to touch what lay beyond. In trances, I could visit the bleak, alien world across the Veil. But for all my training, I had neither the strength nor knowledge to venture so far as Hades's necropolis. To achieve such an aim, I had joined the Argo and ventured to far Kolchis, land of sorcerers. Maybe, had Jason not ensured we became so unwelcome, I would have lingered there and consulted other mediums about my ends. In some lands, they would have called men like me a shaman. Elsewhere, they term us wizards, witches, or any number of other names. We are those with psychic predilections, who possess secret lore unbeknownst to other Men. Our minds are warped, I suppose, and therein lies both blessing and curse. I felt certain a few others of my kind dwelt in Kolchis.

But you know well as I how poorly things went in the court of Aeëtes, and we fled. Perhaps the whole of my voyage might have proved in vain, had not Medea accompanied us back. But she was a witch herself, and well versed in the brewing of potent decoctions, the likes of which could aid in my mission.

When we returned to Phlegra, I consulted with Aeëtes's daughter. Though she tried to dissuade me from my course, I remained steadfast, stirred as I was by those foreign passions of which I earlier spoke. I pleaded with her to brew for me a draught that would allow me to delve deeper, much farther beyond this world of Man than I had ever before dared tread. She told me, too, of how the goddess Hekate had once made a sojourn to the domain of Hades. Using this knowledge, and my shamanic abilities, I bargained with spirits to learn the swiftest route to Hades's necropolis.

Still, it would prove no easy feat, reaching the needful state of mind.

So, I set myself away from the distractions of civilisation. Many in my position might have preferred finding a grove in the wood, but such little suited me. Instead, I found a seaside cave. I needed one deep enough I could venture into lightless depths. There I imbibed the witch's brew, I sat, and I beat my drum in hypnotic rhythm.

As the drugs began to take effect, it became increasingly difficult to maintain that song, but it served as a focus, so I managed as best I was able. In the past, my wife would have kept the beat for me, helping me cross and yet tethering me back to this world.

Oh, yes. Yes, I *was* married. Dear, dear Eurydike. She was a

Nymph, you know, with a wit quick as dragonfly wings, and laughter clear as a mountain spring. Oh, but it was her dancing that truly transfixed any who saw it. I am the son of a Muse, you know and ... Oh, you did not know that? Well, yes, the lovechild of the Muse Kalliope and the bard Linos. And I shared my mother's fondness for all expressions of the arts, dance included.

On the day Eurydike and I were wed, I sang for her and strummed my lyre, and such was my mastery of song that the trees bent and swayed for our joy. So when I tell you that her dancing outstripped even my artistry, I want you to fathom the full import of my meaning. Eurydike had a grace that would have driven swans and Kemetian leopards mad with envy. She did not so much move in the world as twirl it about her.

Well ...

No, I'm fine. It's the wine, now.

Yes, so I drummed such rhythm as I might keep whilst under the influence of the witch's brew. And slowly, like falling through a mire, my soul pitched from my mortal shell and out, into the sidereal spaces.

STEPPING into the shadows beyond our world is different than merely peering through the Veil at them. A chill saturates that place. Sourceless nether winds carry the moans of the damned to you as if in warning that you have trod into Realms in which no Man ought to tread. Yes, but too, the world is still our world, in a sense. The same place, but bent back on itself, as if writhing in pain.

I had walked here before, in my dealings with the dead and with spirits older still. Oh, Theseus, the land oft teems with tutelary spirits giving rise to the pulse of nature. You never know when a hill, a stream, or a forest might have its own life and will. In that shadow Realm, a shaman such as myself could communicate with those spirits, beg them boons to bring good harvests or ease the ailments of a village. With my songs, I would tame and soothe restless entities of the land, or animal spirits, or even put at ease the shades of the dead who remained trapped and wandering.

That was before, though. Before I lost Eurydike.

A pervasive melancholy seeps into that world, but it paled before the depths of the dolour that had wrapt itself about my throat since the death of my wife. The colourless expanse was indeed a mirror of the world in which I had long dwelt since she was stolen from me. Once, in earlier sojourns, I would have marvelled at the iridescent band that streaked across the firmament here, the only true vibrance in that Realm. Once, I'd have wondered what lay beyond our fragile Gaia.

Now, though, I pushed deeper into the shadows, caring naught for what lay above nor behind me. Medea's draught wormed through my core, hot and languid, but serving as a lodestone to guide my steps and keep true my path.

I wandered from the spectral mirror of my cave, along the shore, seeking a means of pushing beyond that Realm, into the further reaches of the cosmos. For this time, I had not come to bargain with the spirits of hills or plead aid from the trees, nor to set the stones to dancing or change the course of rivers, as once I had done in service to my people. Now, I sought after a prize on my behalf, though such selfish pursuits are frowned upon by most shamans, and not without reason.

Though I could hear, as if at a great distance, the lapping of waves, the ocean held no substance in that Realm. I followed its periphery for a time, paying no heed to the phantasmal images that I witnessed along the way. Oh, I saw them, sites of pain and loss, imprinted upon psychic currents like blood imbrued upon linens, never able to be made clean again. Here, a man murdered his friend over a meaningless dispute. There, a boy drowned in a sudden wave. Shades milled about listless, bemoaning the cruelties of Ananke.

Times past, I would have sought to ease their suffering, but not now. One finds it oft impossible to tend to the woes of others whilst crushed beneath the mountain of one's agonies. Besides, once you venture beyond the bounds of Gaia, there is ever the clutching grip of ennui eager to claim the heart of you.

As I said, Medea's draught gave me strength, but it would not last forever, and thus, upon reaching the designated spot, I headed into the empty expanses of the dry ocean. My first time venturing into those regions since leaving the Argo, and a voyage darker even than that one.

❧

THE ARGO ... Hmm, yes. Foredoomed vessel. Even then, before it made way, I felt a deep misgiving over the endeavour. Upon first spying that sleek hull and feeling those disquiet stirrings in my breast, perhaps I should have abandoned the hope of my vain quest. But then, Men are ever wont to delude themselves that they might have made different choices had they the chance to do over their pasts. The stirrings of our soul in those distant worlds prompt our choices, and as we cannot control our souls, we can hardly be expected to be Men other than ourselves.

Our choices define us, but they are made long ago. Or so I have heard the philosophers of Athenai muse, whiling away their days in blissful repose. It is easy for them to speculate on Fate's cruelties, having suffered so little of it firsthand.

After losing Eurydike, I learnt of a ship from my homeland bound for legendary Kolchis, and I could scarce pass such a chance, though I had to scramble to return to Phlegra in time. Before that? Well, a bit before, I was in Kalydon, much like yourself. Yes, I was there for the boar hunt, though I was no hunter, but merely a guest, along with Eurydike, of King Oeneus.

Well, you'll recall I arrived not long before the vessel was underway. I met Jason and convinced him without difficulty that a bard aboard would keep the crew in high spirits on their dangerous voyage. I suppose each of us had our reasons for being there. You as well, I'm certain.

The deeds of our days at sea hardly need recounting, my friend.

The murders, the sirens, Aeëtes himself—such things ought to have given me pause.

But Men obsessed see only the object of their desires. Those desperate needs hold us, fettered and blindfolded, unable to perceive aught save our consuming aims.

I suppose that's the same reason I pushed on, deeper into the dark.

OH, my friend, I think it meaningless to ascribe mortal geometries to non-physical locations. Huh. Well, if I had to try to herd the cosmos into something fathomable to Man, I would guess that the shadowy Echo beyond this one lies beside our world. In my mind—perhaps owing to the name alone—the Underworld lies beneath both our Realm and that shadow.

Leastwise, I made my way into its depths by descending through an undersea cave. I had no torch, but hints of sourceless starlight adumbrated the cavern, flickers reflecting off moist walls. At first, I traced my fingertips along those slick surfaces to help guide my passage. But as I delved deeper, I could not shake the sense the walls had taken on an almost sinewy aspect. Though chill, the very cavern had begun to intimate some alien life the likes of which had me trembling.

Bowel-clenching terror shot through me. All at once, the enormity of what I attempted settled upon my shoulders. I jerked my fingers from the wall and braced my hands upon my knees, standing there gasping, as if I had body or lungs in that state.

I could have turned back, then. I *should* have turned back, Theseus. Only the portrait of Eurydike in my mind steeled my frayed nerves. For the return of her soul, I had crossed the Axeinos with intent to make this very trek.

Yes ... I ventured deeper still. Razor-edged protuberances began to extrude from the cavern wall, pointed inward, like spikes warding against any who would try to escape. But I was not going back without her. The cavern sloped upward. My progress became slower, for at irregular intervals opened pits of weeping viscous fluid that reeked like pus. With one hand over my mouth and nose, I edged around these putrid holes and the thin streams that dribbled downslope out of them.

Eventually, the path narrowed, the walls now throbbing like convulsing muscles. The passage grew so tight I could no longer avoid brushing against the sides. Then, when I feared I would need to squeeze through, the path ended in an aperture, clenching and unclenching in rhythmic contractions. You can imagine how bile scorched my throat as I strove not to imagine what I had crawled through. Timing against the expansion, I hurled myself through the opening and tumbled along jagged-edged ground.

I lay upon onyx sands, suddenly aware of insectile creatures skittering over and beneath the surface. Gasping with fatigue and addled with terror, I looked up into a sky churning with smoke and ash that flowed like waves, rising and falling in obscene mockery of Gaia's seas.

Thunder rumbled overhead. I could not imagine what foulness might soon fall from those polluted clouds. But I had reached the Underworld, and, if my spirit familiars had spoken truth, I should have passed beyond the River Styx. Hades's necropolis would lie ahead.

Within that dark city, I dared to hope, I would find the soul of my beloved.

Oh, beloved Eurydike.

I ... Yes, forgive me. I may not ever be well again, but I've had enough wine to continue, I think. So long as you keep it flowing, Theseus. That is the implicit compact between bard and audience, you know. With words or music, I paint frescoes upon the halls of Men's minds to transport them to other places and times, to offer glimpses of lives not their own. For their part, they have but to see me adequately lubricated.

So. I was speaking of Eurydike.

You see, I awaked from one of my trances to find my drummer had fled from the grove in which I had begun. At dusk, I had sat upon a mossy stump, keenly aware of the burble of a creek down the slope and had listened to Eurydike's beaten rhythm as I pushed my soul from my body. We believed there was a spirit lurking in that hill, and I sought after its uncanny wisdom in the hopes of deepening my knowledge of the multitude of arcana. Things Men know not and ought not, in fact, even to seek after.

But I did not find a way to contact the hill dweller. The tether of Eurydike's drumming broke, and I was lost, wandering the Echo a time before I managed to find my way back to my body. When I woke, her drum stood idle, abandoned. My wife was gone. A full dark had settled upon the wood.

Panic was slow to rise.

I could not have imagined the truth. Rather, I grasped at mundane explanations for her absence. Perhaps she had gone to the creek for some water. Perhaps into the brush to relieve herself. Maybe she was foraging for some berries, beset by a late-night craving.

I called to her, lightly at first. But when met with silence, in such circumstances, urgency creeps in with snake-like stealth and speed. Unannounced, it raises its head, and you find yourself faced, of a sudden, with mortal dread. Now I was no longer calling for her, I was screaming her name as I raced like a madman through the darkened wood. I was shrieking with desperation I had not yet fully understood, though some part of me already knew something was sorely amiss.

There were others, not so far off, my companions, and I thought they could help me. Who? Ah ... Well, I ... I suppose I'll get to that, later. It does not overmuch matter at the present.

What matters is, in the darkness, something squelched beneath my sandal and I slipped, tumbling onto the forest floor. My cheek smacked against moist loam, my head against a root. There was something in front of my face, but it took time before my eyes could focus upon it, in the moonlight.

When I ... Ugh. When at last I realised on what I looked, a wail was ripped from my belly. There are ways men scream, Theseus. There are the screams of women. Perhaps, really, there is not so much difference between the two. Then, there are cries of anguish so primal as to seem born from something animalistic lurking beneath the veneer of humanity.

Such was the sound of horror that erupted from me upon seeing my wife's arm lying in front of my face. It was not severed. Not, naught so merciful as that had transpired here. Rather, a being of prodigious strength had torn it off, shredding sinew and yanking apart joints in the process.

How did I know it was Eurydike's arm?

I *knew*. You recall I mused about the stirring of our souls coming from Realms beyond? Intuition was born of such a place, then, and I knew my wife was stolen from me. Snarling and weeping, snot dribbling down over my lips, I crawled forth, following the trail of blood. I knew what I would find, though.

Pieces of her, rent asunder, limbs strewn along the hillside.

The Boar God had claimed his last victim, on the very day afore which you lot slew him. And like her body, my soul was rent into macabre ruin.

PART II

Much though they might wish to claim otherwise, not even the greatest Titans can outwit or outrun Ananke, that is, Fate. Some say it is woven by sisters out of time, the Moirai. That they draw the threads of all lives into a Tapestry. That they alone decide when the thread of a life should be severed. And most of all, that they alone can perceive the Tapestry of Fate.

— Urania, Analects of the Muses

10

HEKATE

726 Bronze Age

The door to Hekate's chamber creaked upon its hinges—she had to remember to the oil the damn thing—and Medea peeked her head within. Hekate suppressed the indulgent smile and beckoned the girl inside. She knew Kirke's niece worshipped her, and naught Hekate had ever told Medea seemed to shake it off. Not in six months of training her in the alchemical and enchantment lesser arcana. Nor even in the warnings Hekate had offered of the prices she had paid in pursuit of sorcery ... Never did Medea demure.

Those subtle abrasions of the soul ... that send one spiralling ever closer to the Dark ... Mormo rasped.

Yes. Hekate had refused to teach Athene the Art for that reason, but Kirke had begged her to train Medea, and she had started her down that road. Not the greater arcana, though, not that.

The path toward damnation, Khione mused.

Toward dread apprehension of greater Ontos ... Mormo countered.

No, Medea could master potions and poisons, salves, and charms.

She had the Voice and a hint of glamour. But Hekate would not make the mistake of teaching another of sorcery and the accompanying suicide of the soul.

Cradled like a babe in her arms, Medea bore something that had her beaming at Hekate. Was that ... moly?

Forcing a smile lest she drive the girl away, Hekate took the herb that had brought such troubles upon poor Kirke, turning it over in her hands as though the sight and fruity sweet scent of it were not carved into her memory. Kirke, while a middling sorceress at best, had become one of the greatest alchemists Hekate had ever known, with the greatest, direst, of her elixirs all born of this mercurial plant. Had Kirke shown Medea how to cultivate it, or had the young witch discovered it on her own?

In shadowed halls thick with oneiromantic portent, Hekate had seen intimations of Medea's future. Dark days of betrayal of the bonds of kinship. Whispers of pain and perfidy, and a life of misery from which Hekate could not spare her. With such desperate resolution had she sought not to care for Kirke's niece. With such fierce denial she had clung to the fraying of her emotions in hopes she would not need feel them, even as this girl wormed her way into Hekate's heart.

For who could disdain the genuine adoration of the young? Who could turn away from pleading eyes and the untrammelled yearning for wisdom and a desperate desire for approval?

If Hekate cast aside the moly, named it useless, would it have the least chance of diverting the course of Medea's life? No, the Moirai had wrapt their threads around the necks of every man and woman on Gaia, woven nooses with which all must invariably hang themselves.

"You have no idea how much pain this little herb has caused," she said, even knowing the warning would pass unheeded. Medea would do as she wished ... because it wasn't really *wisdom* the young sought from their elders, but knowledge.

In a mirror of the future Hekate had imagined, Medea's face fell, the girl offering a veneer of chagrin while no doubt exhilarated, drunk on the thrill of the power inherent in something capable of inflicting such damage.

With no other option, Hekate stroked Medea's cheek. "You've made such progress." The truth, for certain. "Soon, I must return to check on Kirke." And pray to Nyx and Gaia she had made even more.

The young witch's lips trembled, eyes hooded. Perhaps she considered begging Hekate to linger but knew better. There was, in truth, only but so much more Hekate could teach of alchemy. If Aeëtes would have consented to allow Kirke to visit Medea, she might have learnt enough to fill a library of papyrus scrolls, but the king scarce granted his daughter the chance to leave the Qulha Palace.

"I had a dream." Medea's voice had become a distant whisper. "A man came to me ..." A flush coloured her cheeks, making plain the content of this dream.

"Sometimes dreams are but the blooming of wild seeds sown in the mind."

But, of course, for a witch, they might well be more.

FIELDS OF IRISES had begun to sprout along the hills outside of Qulha Palace, and Hekate took to roaming in twilight, ostensibly hunting roots for Medea, though her mind more oft flitted back to her real daughter. All too soon, Zeus would return for Kirke, and Hekate ought to be there to ensure he did not harm her if her efforts proved fruitless.

Then, of course, she needed to check in on Athene. Papa had promised to help her through the difficulties she had faced in the wake of the Gigantomachy, and Hekate had trusted him to do so, but that had been an age ago. She had visited Athene in a dream and found her daughter much changed, obsessed even with pursuit of her visions on behalf of Mankind. And unforgiving of the mother who had abandoned her for centuries—yet how could Hekate burden Athene with knowledge of her jaunt through time and the implications of such circular weavings of Ananke? Since learning of such things from Kirke long back, the knowledge had proved a constant burden upon Hekate, an onus straining her already sleepless nights.

"Pyrrha," someone said, and Hekate spun to see her mother trudging up the hill, pensive and worn.

"Pandora ..." Even now, even understanding the weight that had crushed and bludgeoned the other woman, even seeing the scope of the fate that had seized her, still Hekate could not bring herself to call her *Mama*. Understanding ought to carry with it forgiveness, she knew. And yet ... yet ...

Pandora rushed forward and embraced her. Hekate wanted to return the gesture. She wanted to. But she couldn't. Her arms refused to lift, refused to respond at all, until her mother broke away, face betraying the pain of that tiny rejection. "There are so many things I have to tell you."

Unable to speak, Hekate nodded.

SHE BROUGHT her mother back to the chamber Aeëtes had granted her, and, after servants had brought wine—a local draught Pandora sipped but Hekate did not touch—and a fragrant bean soup, she settled upon a divan to stare at the other woman.

The delicious ... unbridgeable gulf that forever ... separates ... Mormo taunted. *Do you think ... Kirke feels it ...*

It took an effort of will to not snap at the wraith, even knowing it would have made her seem a madwoman to Pandora.

After savouring the soup as though she'd not had hot food in days, Pandora swallowed. She sat on the floor before the divan, legs folded beneath her in a way Papa too so oft sat. The gold of her eyes glinted in the wan light of Hekate's small brazier, further reminder of the connection they shared.

A desperate, choking need to tell her she *understood* welled in Hekate. To say that she ... felt ... Her mouth worked, but she could not form the words. Could not apologise for the things she had been forced to inflict upon Pandora. Could not offer the feeble condolence that she had watched her in dreams, that she had seen Tantalus punished for his deeds. All she found herself capable of was a looming silence.

"The path you're on ends in darkness," Pandora said, staring at her wine.

"What?" The abruptness of her mother's words had drawn her from herself with the force of an unexpected slap.

"You will …" Her mother looked up now, face ravaged with such agony even Hekate winced. "If you continue the sorcerous road, you will become a *curse* upon the lips of Man. A blight, an incarnation of death itself, hated and feared, Pyrrha."

"My *name* is Hekate, Pandora."

"I am your mother!" Wine sloshed as Pandora shoved her bowl aside.

"And yet I am your elder." And had granted Pandora more sheltering than her mother had ever provided to Hekate. Pandora glowered, and Hekate gagged on the bout of self-loathing that clogged her throat and pinched inside her chest. Why must she hurt her mother over and over? Why could she not bring herself to forgive?

But then, all those lonely millennia offered gaping, empty answer, writ large across the cloth of history.

With a sigh, Pandora let her face fall into her hands, remaining thus for so long Hekate considered rising to check on her. Before she could make up her mind, Pandora looked up. "Somewhere in the dark of all this, I have to believe I could find the words to reach you, bridge the gap, and save you from the end I've beheld."

That throbbing, damning frustration Hekate knew all too well. The unattainable third option that none of them had yet stumbled upon. "To thwart the weavings of the Fates without unmaking ourselves and all we hold dear."

The look Pandora shot her ran so deep it pierced Hekate to the pith. In her mother's eyes lurked the desperation of one who had striven, over and over, for such. Who *knew*, in her very core, the struggle Hekate choked upon. In her mother's visage, in her drive,

Hekate might have at last found someone that could apprehend the iniquities of the World.

A chance to share the burden. With wary hands, Hekate withdrew her grimoire from its hiding place in a crevice behind the hearth. "You fear I will damn myself with the Art only because you have not seen enough of the Ontos to realise what lurks beyond your perception." As Pandora crawled over to peer at the tome, Hekate flipped through the pages until she came upon a sketch scrawled amid the text. At a glance, one might mistake it for mere ornamentation, the strokes random and abortive, amounting to naught. Yet, staring at it long enough, with the eyes relaxed just so, intimations of tendrils crept up of the empty spaces between lines. Blanks left a hair too wide in the script melded with the margins and the abstract swirls until they formed something profane, odious beyond words. A living darkness behind the sky, worming toward Gaia, unperceived only because Man could not look upon it and remain sane.

From the dawning horror creasing Pandora's face, she saw it. With trembling fingers, Hekate's mother turned the book toward her, her other hand going to her lips. A single, no doubt unbidden, tear dribbled down her left cheek. "Is that ... a demon?" Pandora at last rasped. "Or is this supposed to be an Elder God?"

Hekate shuddered. Never had she given voice to the thought, but if she was to truly have an ally against the future, perhaps the time had come ... "I am no longer certain ... there is a difference."

With a suddenness that had Hekate starting, Pandora slammed the grimoire shut. "Turn from this, Hekate! This thing, wherever you got it, it reeks of the darkness in tales of the Nyxlands."

Frowning, Hekate yanked away the book her mother had abused. While experience had proved the tome thus far indestructible, she didn't appreciate such treatment of her treasure. "I have been to the Nyxlands," she admitted. "There is a dark city there, a ruin built upon yet older ruins. They—those inhabitants—I think they understood more of the World than those of our Era. I think they realised something, tried to harness it, perhaps. And I think they *failed*."

"Vulgeth ..."

"What?"

"A ruin upon ruin." Pandora tapped a finger on her lip.

Hekate scoffed, shaking her head. "You cannot think to go there. Despite whatever power you wield as Nike, you are woefully unprepared for the Dark."

"I have to, Hekate. Kronos told me this began in Vulgeth, and if there is *any* chance at escaping from beneath the heel of Ananke, it must lie within the origin of these circles of madness."

Of all the arrogant, heedless ... Why? Why could Pandora not *listen*? Why could she not join Hekate? Indeed, the Art held terrible danger, but only through it did Hekate or any of them have a chance against the predators lurking just beyond sight. And her mother refused to even consider staying here, with Hekate, finding the answers together. "I found the Box there!" Hekate blurted before she could think better of it. "I found it buried amid millennia of rubble!"

"What?" But from the widening of her eyes, the rapid breaths that escaped her, already understanding had dawned. If Hekate had found the Box there, it followed Pandora would one day lose it. Somehow, the device had wound up in the distant past.

Unless ... unless it had been made there in the first place?

"Where did the Box come from?" Hekate demanded.

For a bare instant, so fast she *might* have mistaken it, Hekate saw recognition writ upon Pandora's visage. She knew the answer, but still she refused to trust Hekate with all her secrets. A mask settled over Pandora's features, a shake of her head the only answer Hekate would receive now.

Ire rose in Hekate, so hot her flesh felt aflame with it. A fury at the small betrayal, that, though she knew it had grown far beyond its source, she still could not smother.

"Get out," Hekate commanded. "There is naught for you in Kolchis."

In fact, there was naught even for Hekate. Her only hope now lay with Kirke, upon Aiaíā.

11

PANDORA

400 Dark Age

Mahuika broke away from Pandora and Prometheus—or Maui as the Muians called him—and moved to the water's edge, joining her sister in paying homage to the Oracle of Tides. Given all Pandora had seen, the fact that the creature was a giant octopus ought not to have so shocked her, and yet she found herself struck speechless, gaping at the half-submerged mass of muscle and writhing arms.

The seven Queens of Mu each took a knee at the pond's banks, pressing their palms upon the shore such that their fingertips brushed the water's surface.

"We queens greet you, great Oracle," one said, daring to raise her head.

"That's Pokoharau," Prometheus whispered into Pandora's ear, his fingers twining with hers, steadying her. "Her affinity lies with the sea, and thus it was through her influence they turn to this denizen of the Eternal Depths."

When the octopus spoke, its flesh muffled its words, and yet they boomed, filling the cavern with an almost physical presence. "Whilst floundering in the chasms of despair, one must, should one seek survival, turn toward the merest light. Imagine then, should the light come from yet further depths, the only means of egress might, in fact, lay in plumbing the hidden recesses of said crevasse. Wandering, dreamlike, in murky depths, there to perceive the glorious incandescence of the Leviathan, long slumbering."

"What in Hades's gloomy arsehole was that about?" Pandora whispered to Prometheus.

"Kanaloa is a child of the Elder Deep. That is, an Elder God, whom the Elládosi call Echidna. The Babilimians term the entity Tiamat and think creation rises from her salt. Elsewhere in Kumari Kandam, they call it the Leviathan. Here, they would name it Vari and think it might offer salvation."

A chill seized her at his words. As if the mere mention of dread intellects whose vastness defied mortal ken might somehow draw the eyes of such inimical entities down upon them. Once the thought generated, she could not shake the awful sense that now, from far worlds unknown, something momentous turned its attention toward her.

The pain in her chest returned, redoubled and crushing. Never could she recall feeling smaller than she felt in this chamber, witnessing the queens debate the efficacy of calling upon deities they could never hope to control or understand. "The same Elder Gods the Watchers served, in times past?"

A grim nod answered her. "We were each assigned to the authority of a particular Elder God."

"We have to stop them." Even as the words left her mouth, she knew them for absolute truth.

Swallowing it all came a looming wave, rising above the land like the arm of a god, intent to sweep the Earth clean. The shadows of the impending waters darkened cities the agonised instant before the wave broke. Lurking within the surging tide, a deeper shadow, a hint of incandescent eyes of such enormity as to defy all sanity.

The memory of the Well of Mimir's vision threatened to send her to her knees. "Oh, Gaia," she moaned. This was it, wasn't it? This was the ending of the World? Already it unfolded before her very eyes. In vain desperation to thwart the advance of this Mithra, the Queens of Mu would unleash calamity unlike aught the Earth had seen before. In her mind's eye, she beheld the rising of that wave, closing, closing in upon Mu.

Not only Mu, however, for the surging seas would rip asunder Atlantis, as well. She had seen it, what seemed so long ago now, when her future self had saved her from death. It all traced back to this singular moment. The tightness above her heart twisted afresh.

Already, the queens had begun dancing once more, and this time, to more fervent drumbeats. The percussive energy filling the cavern had grown more urgent, perhaps, though it could have well been her perceptions about what must now impend. To save *their* World, they imperilled *all* the world. Such acts, no matter how understandable, could not be borne.

The queens whooped and whirled, their dance fluid and somehow blasphemous. A foul tang crept into the air, offering fore-warning of things soon to follow.

Pandora had taken a single step toward the queens, hands curled into fists, when Prometheus grabbed her arm. She looked to him, but he was staring into the shadows limning the cavern beyond the reach of the torch poles. From that gloom, in the space where none ought to have stood, stepped a figure, firelight glinting off aureate plates, eyes blue as Prometheus's and luminous in the darkness. Though Pandora could not explain it, Nemesis seemed to melt up from the shadows, as though she had walked from somewhere beyond the Earth.

The realisation she was unarmed hit Pandora, even as she forced herself to stride forward to meet Nemesis anyway. Too many times, the agent of the Fates had thwarted her. Always there, always preventing Pandora from altering the pitiless course of history.

"Stop the queens," Pandora begged Prometheus.

Nemesis raised her arms as if commanding the shadows. The darkness responded, uncoiling in mist-like eddies that flowed around the torches, creating scattered islands of light around the cavern. From the tenebrous depths emerged five further figures, not golden plated like Nemesis but clad head to toe in robes dark as midnight. The formfitting garb made plain two were female and three male, but otherwise, Pandora could guess little of the nature of these newcomers. They bore strange weapons—curved swords and bladed chains and razors jutting from their hands like claws.

"Vinata!" Prometheus shouted, though at whom, Pandora did not know. "Leave this! Forsake the Unseen and leave in peace."

Nemesis dared a step toward the Firebringer, sapphire eyes still gleaming beneath her golden helm. "You, twice over the traitor, would think to give commands to the servants of Ananke itself?"

Prometheus spread his hands, palms upward, and flames leapt from two torch poles into his grasp, dancing around his forearms. "I have not betrayed the Moirai. I remain bound in service to Fate. Still, I serve in my way and will not permit you to strike down Pandora."

Pandora's gnawing apprehensions warred with the wakening fury of the Phoenix within her soul. Of their accord, the flames burst along her arms, incinerating the fringes of her shirt. She cast a single, desperate glance over her shoulder at the queens. The Phoenix bid her hurl fire at them and disrupt the vile ceremony they enacted— their voices already straining against the air and seeming to permeate the World with discordant lamentations—but Prometheus did not want them slain. Instead, she pointed a flaming hand at Nemesis. "I tire of this."

"But it has only begun," the armoured woman mocked.

"I will attend to her minions," Prometheus said. "I cannot bring myself to strike down Vinata so long as an alternative exists." His sudden leap sent him bounding into the shadows. He landed amid the dark-clad figures, and they burst into explosive action. Pandora caught but a glimpse of their struggle.

On the surface, Prometheus's manoeuvres resembled throws and punches from Pankration, but his movements were unlike any style she knew. With bare hands—bare save the flames, she supposed—he danced amid his attackers, turning their skilful blows against them.

She heard the impact of his blocks and it left little doubt that these foes, like Prometheus himself, had strong Pneumatikoi. He held his own for now, but she could expect little help from his quarter.

She had time to gauge little else before a beat of Nemesis's wings hurled the woman toward her. Pandora danced aside before an armoured fist collided with the stone where she'd stood, unleashing a spiderweb of cracks. Using a move Themis had taught her, she caught Nemesis's next blow upon her forearm and twisted, going for a grapple. The assassin reversed her hold and slammed a fist into Pandora's face, sending her stumbling backward.

Pneuma flooded to Steadfastness had kept her skull from crunching, but still, Pandora staggered. Nemesis leapt forward, wings flapping, fist descending once more. This time, Pandora evaded. They fell into jabs and blocks, dodges and a dozen near misses. Pandora ducked a blow and punched Nemesis's breastplate, the impact resounding through the cavern. Nemesis's elbow caught her in the face, hefted her off the ground, and sent her spinning around.

Before Pandora could recover, the assassin caught her shoulder, twisted her back to face her once more, and kicked Pandora in the midriff.

Pandora had an instant to send more Pneuma into Steadfastness before the blow landed, otherwise, the impact might have crushed her spine. The kick sent her hurtling fifty feet backward, arms flailing in a vain, breathless attempt to slow herself. Abruptly, a meaty slab snatched her from the air and sent her plunging into cold watery depths. It happened so fast it took her a moment to realise Kanaloa now held her beneath the water.

The Oracle wanted the queens to summon the Elder God. And it knew Pandora had come to stop the process. A mountain of muscle bore her down, holding her against the underwater bowl. Squeezing. Pressing. Air slipped from her lungs, replaced with water. Replaced with terror. Absolute.

The Phoenix lurched up from her soul, but underwater, its flames turned to steam that only blinded her. Even her Pneuma-infused bones began to creak beneath the octopus's horrific strength.

Her bubbles slowed.

Even the pounding dread that closed in around her grew quieter.

Everything started to dim.

Peace welcomed her into its silent embrace.

§

Sulphurous clouds twisted in choking whorls across an ashen sky, illumined by sporadic flashes of volcanic lightning. Rumbling quakes shook the rocky landscape beneath her, trembling with magma flows beneath the surface, seeking egress.

Just as the burning within her soul sought an escape from its fleshy prison.

Death had returned her to the flaming netherworld whence came the Phoenix. This place called to her. It offered her reprieve … in the ceaseless burning of her soul for the temerity of trying to tame a piece of itself.

Billows of smoke rolled across the land, converging upon her. The smoke watched, lit by hints of fiery eyes. Denizens of Phlegethon, so very eager to claim her in the name of their furious deity. In the distance, unseen, she could feel it too. The Elder God. The Archon of Flame. It knew she was here. It waited for her, dripping naphtha like salivation before its feast upon her soul.

They were coming for her.

Fire is life.

The voice cut through the clouds, a whisper. An imploring call from something beyond this dark flame.

§

Fire is life.

A spark flashed, somewhere in the deep recesses of the soul, hidden in a place where only darkness remained. A flare of light, of heat, shimmering and refusing that final stillness that ever crept in upon it. Defiance of the cold emptiness.

Hope.

An inferno erupted within Pandora's breast, flames bursting from her as she lurched upward. The Phoenix, a bird of wildfire, shrieked skyward, burning pinions singeing the tenebrous depths of the cavern, if only for an instant.

Then the flames winked out and Pandora was on her side—naked, for her clothes had become ash—retching seawater. Prometheus was shaking her, screaming her name from some distant place, his auburn hair plastered against his face.

Reality crashed back in with hateful violence, an onslaught of sensory inputs. The awesome roaring of Gaia as the world trembled in agonised quakes. Sporadic screams cutting through the clamour of tremors. High above, stalactites ruptured, sending streams of dust and stone tumbling down in damning curtains. The promise of impending cataclysm.

"We have to go now!" Prometheus shouted, yanking her to her feet.

"I died. I died! I died!" The thought crashed upon her as surely as the collapsing cavern.

Prometheus grabbed the sides of her face. "The Phoenix is a manifestation of pure Pneuma, enough to rekindle the spark of your life even when it had been reduced to ashes. I ... I saw you rise from your pyre, Pandora. I begin to hope, perhaps, like myself, you might have moved beyond the constraints of death."

Her limbs trembled, scarce obeying her commands. Whatever the Phoenix had done, it had drained her to the point she could no longer control her body. "I ... we failed. They summoned the Elder Deep."

His grim nod answered her. Prometheus draped her arm around his shoulders and ushered her out. Before they had gone a dozen paces, he swept her into his arms and pulled her aside. The next instant, a stalactite the size of a small house ripped from the ceiling and plummeted to the Soul Hollow floor. The colossal roar of its crashing drowned her screams as her lover shielded her from flying debris with his body.

Next she knew, he broke into a mad dash outside. With great

bounds, Prometheus cleared the stairs from the palace dozens at a time. All around, cacophony masking the shrieking of those they passed. The city burst apart at the seams. The land recoiled as though turned into a turbulent sea itself, rippling and flowing, collapsing inward. Yawning fissures swallowed sprawling manses and towering civic buildings in churning masses of stone.

In the distance, the ocean rose. Not a wave so much as a wall of water, miles high. A mountain formed of the sea itself.

And within those murky depths lurked incandescent eyes and a shadow fit to engulf the world and consume all Gaia with its fathomless appetite. The sense of a fell, unspeakable intellect crashed in upon her.

Pandora screamed.

Not looking at the surging doom, still bearing her in his arms, Prometheus leapt amid the cataclysm, hurdling gulfs and debris as he jumped from one cyclopean block to the next. The city rushed by in a blur, but she soon had no doubt where he intended to take her. He retraced their steps from the Time Chamber, even as Mugedang collapsed all around them.

Before her eyes, the city's great plaza was rent in twain, half of it jutting skyward whilst the other side slid beneath the shelf. Everywhere, men and women and children were tossed about and crushed, vanishing into rifts that swiftly filled with churning waters. The colonnade collapsed in succession, like children's blocks kicked over, and Pandora watched, with utter horror, as the stoa's roof tumbled down upon a shrieking family.

She felt Prometheus tense as he saw it too, but he did not stop to try to save anyone besides her. Maybe he could not.

Again she looked at the rising wave, and now the abomination within had become more than shadow. Instead, she could make out hints of saurian features amid that incandescent gleam, as if some drakon lurked in the depths, but one of a scale to make even Python seem but a garden worm. Not two eyes but dozens gleamed behind the veil of water. Within the wave, reaching for the city, rose a mass of tentacles, any one of which might have encircled a palace and ripped it clean off the face of the Earth.

Then Prometheus hopped to a lower level and her view of the looming horror was, mercifully, obscured. The next instant, he jumped again, landing shoulder high in surging waters. The sea slapped her, brine and chill reminding her of her present peril. Only when he shoved her through the tight opening into the half-flooded tunnel did she realise they jumped into the same once-dry canal she'd emerged from.

"Can you find your way back to the Chamber?" he shouted. Or she thought that was what he had said, though she could make out little over the roaring collapse around her.

"Come with me!"

He shook his head, still at the tunnel's threshold. "I cannot! I am needed elsewhere! You must go, Pandora!" The waters were rising upon her. She had moments only to escape through the tunnel before this route would be closed to her. But she could not leave him.

Not *again*.

He cupped her cheek with his palm, then took off, vanishing into the canal, stealing her choice from her.

Dammit! Prometheus!

She hesitated for a heartbeat, then spun. Already, the rising water made navigating these tunnels a hundred times more difficult than before. She had so little Pneuma left, but she managed to ignite a tiny candle-flame in her palm to light the way. For another moment, she reconstructed the map of this place in her mind, retracing the steps by which Prometheus had led her free earlier. He had counted upon her having an eidetic memory. She wanted to snap at him for making such an assumption—that she might rely upon that gift even whilst beyond the bounds of all exhaustion—but there was no one here to chide.

So she pressed forward, back through the tunnels.

Back until she found the sealed Chamber. Pulling open the metal hatch with so much water pressure—now shoulder high—forced her to burn through more Pneuma. Even as she cracked it open, the water began to pour into the spherical room. Would excess fluid in the hold below interfere with the device? She hoped not.

After slipping through, Pandora yanked the hatch closed behind her, then fell to her hands and knees, gasping. Her sodden hair hung like a dark mop around her face.

The metal grates beneath her creaked and trembled. Would the whole continent of Mu be ripped apart by the advance of Tiamat?

Lacking the strength to rise, she instead crawled to the centre of the orrery. She had neither the time nor the energy to make precise calculations, so she spun the dials backward. She needed to try again, before the collapse of the world. She needed to find a way to stop this.

With both hands, Pandora grasped the lever to the great machine. And, gasping, she activated it once more.

Sparks of lightning coruscated along the orrery arms as they again began their frightful spinning.

12

ARTEMIS

728 Bronze Age

From the woods around Mount Pelion, Artemis watched the centaurs run rampant over the Lapith wedding celebration. The beasts slaughtered and stole. They abducted girls, throwing them over their shoulders and tromping off into the woodlands with blatant, stomach-churning intent. With the fragment of free will Artemis could manage, she imagined launching arrows into the throats of the rapacious marauders. That idle fancy, carried out as a mental shadow play, was all God permitted her.

Dionysus stood before her upon the wood's threshold, watching the carnage. Though he said naught, she knew he was aware of the blasphemous bent of her thoughts. Too, she knew he exulted in the chaos. He stood naked, phallus erect, moaning as if in the throes of one of his unbounded orgies.

In the eyes of God, rape, cannibalism, murder were acts of nature. He would have called it manifestations of the cycle of life and death. Any atrocity was permitted, so long as he received his worship. So long as Men lived and died and reproduced and remained ever upon their knees.

With Perspicacity drawn, Artemis heard every scream, every agonised, terrified cry. She heard the shrieks of Orpheus as the centaurs rent him limb from limb, and she grieved for the death of one she had known in Dionysus's endless train. The only one to ever escape, and then, not for long.

She might have released the Pneumatikoi. She might have shut her eyes to the suffering. But however deep her grief and fathomless her desperation over Orion had been, she had willingly sworn herself to Dionysus. In serving God, she remained culpable for all done in his name. So, jaw set, she forced herself to take in all that unfolded within the river camp.

Through the moil of battle—if battle was an apt name for an unprovoked assault upon guests largely unarmed—Dionysus saw something that had his hands balling into fists. "An heir of Zeus," God said, voice thick with Otherworldly malice. "Linger here and bear witness as I smite this befouled specimen of Man."

God's commands rooted Artemis in place. Unbidden, her head swivelled to watch, and she found herself powerless to so much as blink. She saw it as Nessus murdered the bride at her own wedding. And too, she watched Dionysus approach the subject of his fury.

"The blood of Zeus," Dionysus said, the sound reaching Artemis's Pneuma-enhanced senses with crystal clarity. She could not look away, though she did not want to see what must soon unfold. Her unblinking eyes stung, dry and irritated by the smoke. A moment before, she had tortured herself, watching the carnage in penance for her part in it. Now, with God demanding she see, all she longed for was to shut her eyes against the spectacle.

The man turned, looked to his doom. His sword dipped in terror, his posturing making plain he foresaw the horror before him. "Dionysus ..."

"A prince of Athenai, and thus a descendant of Athene." It was Theseus, Artemis realised. This boy was of the line of Pandion, Athene's son of long back. "The blood of *Zeus* must be drained away to the last blighted drop, the World cleansed of its stain in ichorous cataracts pouring from dying Titans."

Even from the distance between them, she saw the dread that wrapt itself around the Man's heart.

God took another step toward Theseus. "I shall rip your soul from its tainted vessel."

Theseus fell to his knees before the approach of the God. Dionysus closed in upon him with vicious languor, a cat toying with its prey.

From the tree line, Artemis waited for Athene's heir to weep and plead for his life. Instead, he bellowed defiance at the approaching God, the force of his fury a slap upon her face. A second roar joined Theseus's, and Herakles was racing forward—blighted, damnable Herakles!—then Zeus's bastard son ploughed into Dionysus, and the pair of them were on the ground.

It was impossible.

A Man—a demigod, yes, but Man still—had tackled the God?

Still roaring, Herakles struck Dionysus in the face. Over and over his blows rained.

With each impact, the fetters upon Artemis's soul eased. A hair at a time, a weakening of the links as God's will faltered beneath the momentous impacts of Herakles's fists.

Artemis blinked.

The hateful mask cracked, antlers breaking away. God trembled beneath those blows.

Artemis took a step toward the melee. No strength of limb, no Pneuma was enough to strain the chains that bound her. But her will, her *choice*, focused with all she was upon a single desire ... The chains binding her snapped in twain, and she spilt to her hands and knees from the sudden release.

Was it possible? After three years enslaved to Dionysus, was she free? A lightness settled upon her shoulders, a full breath filling her lungs for the first time in ever so long.

When she looked up, Dionysus had seized Herakles by the head and swung him around in a rainbow arc. Zeus's son lay there, unmoving.

Teeth gritted, Artemis gained her feet.

Dionysus too stood and drove his fist into Gaia's flesh, his power surging into the earth and summoning forth an explosion of vegetation. Plants erupted to bind Herakles and Theseus both.

Unshouldering her bow, Artemis pulled an arrow from her quiver.

Artemis's erstwhile master looked to Zeus's bastard. "You ..." he slurred. "Little brother ... You the direct son of Zeus. What say ... I make to him a present of your spine?"

As Dionysus approached Herakles, Artemis drew back on her bow. She let fly, and at the last instant, Dionysus looked to her, the weight of his regard crashing into her like a club. He knew he had lost her. He tried to twist aside, but her arrow took him in the chest, and he shuddered, falling back a step.

His will slithered over Artemis's once more. It wrapt around her soul and mired her limbs. But she was no longer bound to this creature. No longer his puppet. Growling, she shrugged away his hold, and even his colossal will sloughed from her like so much muck washed clean at long last. She nocked another arrow.

A trio of centaurs raced at her then, summoned by their master who must have at last realised his peril. Letting fly at the closest of her attackers, Artemis immediately sent Pneuma into Alacrity. Her perception of the charging horse-men dilated. She danced to the side of a hurled javelin. Pneuma in Lightness allowed her to manage an aerial cartwheel over a centaur and land on his back, drawing a knife even as she fell.

Standing astride her foe, she slit his throat with a single motion. Even with her Potency, the centaurs might have matched her strength. But Alacrity made her faster than any of them, and Artemis danced between the monsters with ease, swipes of her dagger severing hamstrings, spilling guts, or opening throats. In a matter of heartbeats, seven of Dionysus's minions lay dead or dying at her feet.

But of the chief of the abominations, no sign remained. Frantic,

Artemis cast about, hair whipping as she spun. The roots had withdrawn from Herakles and Theseus, which told her that the fell God had withdrawn his power. Fled into the woods?

Perhaps he had never imagined she could break his hold upon her. Even that had only transpired because he had underestimated the sheer might of Herakles. In truth, had Artemis not seen it with her own eyes, she'd not have credited that anyone could overpower Dionysus thus, even for a moment.

She looked to him now, Zeus's bastard, and he watched her, wary, no doubt wondering if she intended to slay him for the blood and pain mingled in their past. Maybe once, she would have. But this night had seen death aplenty already, and they had fought together against a common foe.

As she took a step away from the demigod, her legs wobbled. Burning through so much Pneuma drained one; more, her contest of wills against Dionysus had sapped her reserves. It would not do for the mortals to see her stumble, so Artemis made her way back into the wood.

It was his place, of course. Satyrs and centaurs and perhaps the trees themselves would watch her every move and report back to him. Maybe he would come for her again.

Artemis slumped against an elm and rubbed her temples. Dionysus could not abide any of his disciples ever turning from him. Such choices would have bruised his colossal ego beyond endurance, and thus the God would punish that crime above all others. Even this very night, his vengeance against Orpheus was at last sated, and Artemis knew he'd planned it long, stewing in rank ire at the bard who'd dared to leave his side.

He would come for Artemis, too. She knew he was, in the end, an avatar of Pan, the Elder God of the Wood. The entity dwelt far beyond the bounds of Gaia, and if a being so timeless and unfathomable hunted her, she was truly lost. Her only solace might come in the fragile Veil separating those cosmic entities from the Mortal Realm, and even that would not protect her forever. But Dionysus was not just Pan; he, too, was the rejected spawn of Zeus, and mingled within the unplumbed depths of divinity of an Elder God lay the petty sensibilities of a Man.

Was it then Pan or Dionysus who sought such bitter retribution against those who turned their backs upon him? All Artemis knew of the Elder Gods implied that an individual Man—even a Titan— usually lay beneath their notice. If so, Pan exerted its influence and wrath against her only through Dionysus.

He would come for her ... unless she found him first.

Idly, Artemis stroked a finger along the span of her bow. This so-called deity had taken advantage of her in her moment of grief and weakness. It had used her pain and her fears to enslave her, body and soul. Much though she agreed with Dionysus over the need to bring down Olympus, for the moment, he had earned her wrath to a yet deeper level.

She did not know where he had fled.

But Artemis—well, Men had always called her the Goddess of the Hunt.

THE CRUNCH OF LEAVES UNDERFOOT, faint though it was, startled Artemis to wakefulness, and she lurched up, one hand clutched around her dagger, the other up in defence. A few paces away, Athene raised her hands in warding. Her khiton was torn and stained brown with dried blood and other filth. "I came to talk, Sister."

Sister? Maybe when they stood together as Olympians. But Athene had been cast out long back, and though Zeus may have allowed her back into his graces now, Artemis was no longer certain she considered herself among the Olympian Order. Sheathing her knife, Artemis rose, watching Zeus's daughter with a wary eye. She could not be certain of the other woman's allegiance. Though Athene oft sought the righteous path, she could not tear herself away from the need for her father's affection, and Zeus saw it, using the with-holding or doling out his attention to pluck her strings.

"So many things have happened in recent years," Athene said.

Artemis bit her lip. She did not *want* to make an enemy of Athene. Whatever her misgivings about Zeus and the others, she had considered Athene a friend, once. She had trained her in the arts of stealth and the hunt. They had shared wine and bread and a thousand, thousand nights of quiet laughter.

In Athenai, she had gone with the other woman to the theatre to watch the performance of tragedies written by the Muses of Themiskyra. One night, they had lain awake until the first lavender streaks of dawn, debating the merits of various playwrights and whether tragedy alone could serve as its own point. Artemis had claimed it self-indulgent of the playwright to punish the characters for choices not their own. Athene had called it a commentary on the inherent inequities of life.

In her mind, Artemis could see herself spilling Zeus's golden ichor across his mountaintop throne. She could kill Hera for her callous cruelty and think she had done the World a favour. Ares was as twisted as his father, and Hermes only a few steps better. Others, she would find it harder to murder. Men and women she had known for Ages, and—in her rage and grief, stoked by Dionysus—she had been ready to see them all dead.

Not Athene ... Nor did she have personal grief with Hebe or Hestia. Even Poseidon, in truth, had done *her* no great wrong. Of them all, though, Athene she had liked best.

"Many things," Artemis agreed, uncertain what to say to the woman now. Whatever they had shared, she was Zeus's daughter, and her words might get back to the king.

"Father wants you back upon Olympus," Athene said, reserved enough it made plain she feared to speak such, and with good reason.

Artemis glowered. "I'm certain he does."

"Artemis ... please ..."

"I'm going to hunt down Dionysus. I'm going to destroy the monstrosity responsible for all this."

Athene nodded, making plain she knew more than enough of what had transpired.

Once more, Artemis bit her lip. "Do you know where Dionysus has fled?"

"No." Athene shook her head. "But if I did, I would help you."

Oh. "You know he's your brother, don't you? That he intends to bring down your father."

The other Olympian frowned and leant against a tree. "I know what he intends. We could work together, Artemis, to stop him from destroying our world."

So very, very tempting. "I cannot." Much though she longed for a companion. Much though she needed an ally against Dionysus. Stark realisation settled upon her. There was no going back to Olympus. There had never been any going back. "So long as you swear loyalty to your father, I cannot trust you."

"Trust me?" Athene scoffed. "You are the one that helped that monster unleash the accursed Boar of Kalydon."

Artemis crossed her arms. As if she did not know what she had done already. "So quick to chastise me over the boar, as if your hands were clean, Sister. As if Medusa did not writhe in torment at the curse you wrought upon her."

Her erstwhile sister shut her eyes as if in pain. Maybe she too saw the wretches they had all become. Ananke did not permit Titans to live moral lives. The price of ruling the world was one's conscience. Power corrupted, for only in corruption could it ensure its continuance.

"In the end," Artemis said, "we are not so different from Man."

"We are gluttonous beasts, grown corpulent on feasts of power, whilst looking upon our fellows as lions look upon prey."

So Athene did understand. "I dare hope ..." Artemis swallowed. "One day, my friend, you will have to pick a side. You cannot serve both Olympus and Mankind. I hope you make the right choice before it is too late."

"Artemis ..."

"Goodbye, Athene."

13

ATHENE

728 Bronze Age

Another centaur lay dead at Athene's feet. With a rag, she cleaned the blood from her sword before sheathing it. A half dozen beasts had fallen to Apollon's arrows further from the village. She had to admit, the Titan had uncanny skill with that bow, rivalling even his sister.

"They yet run rampant," he warned. "I can see more of them farther off, haranguing other villages." His eyes were damn acute, too. "We cannot hope to thwart their advance unless we split up."

He had the right of it. There were too many of these creatures, swift as their horse kin and savage enough they could not afford to let a single one loose in Elládos. But they were also driven to this, she was certain of it. Apollon had claimed Dionysus sent the centaurs forth, and perhaps, should he fall, their assault would break as well. "Protect the villages. I'll hunt for their master."

The Heliad nodded, nocking another arrow. Then he took off at a dead sprint, fast as any centaur, a blur of motion racing over the hill.

BY THE TIME Athene reached the camp of the Lapiths, along the Pineios River, the dead were beyond counting. She could see where tents had burnt down to smoulders, and even by the silver gleam of moonlight, the land was imbrued crimson with so much spilt blood.

Athene came to a girl, perhaps ten years old, curled up by the river, arms about her knees, rocking herself slowly, eyes rimmed red. Already she knew too well what tale the child would tell, even before she knelt before the girl and laid a hand upon her shoulder. She had no need to ask where the parents were, for, if they had survived, they would never have let the girl out of their sight.

"What's your name?" she asked instead.

The girl turned toward her, eyes empty, looking for a moment too shocked to form an answer. Then she sputtered and swallowed. "Kressida."

Athene squeezed her shoulder. "Kressida, can I bring you to someone?"

"Uh ... um ... My aunt and uncle, in Oikhalia."

"Good." Athene beckoned, and the girl clambered into her arms. She weighed very little. With Kressida's head resting upon her shoulder, Athene passed among the camp, directing survivors to the wounded where she could.

"Mama," Herakles said, and she turned to see her son, blood-spattered and wounded.

"This girl is Kressida. She has kin in Oikhalia," she said.

Something about the name had Herakles curling his lip, but then he nodded. "The prince of Oikhalia is alive and well. I'll see the child to his care." He hesitated. "Theseus is here, and overwrought in his desperation to seek out a woman he believes may have been with Dionysus."

"All right. I'll lend what aid I may." She found Theseus wandering the woods beside the camp, heedless of the danger of centaurs still present as he screamed over and over for Ariadne. A wild frenzy had seized him, and he cast about, rushing through the night-darkened woods at random.

"Theseus," Athene called, and he spun on her.

"G-goddess Athene?"

Though she had long watched over him, even spoken to him whilst glamoured, she supposed she had never presented herself to her descendant as herself. Rather than stand upon propriety, she drew him into a sympathetic embrace. "I'll help you look."

THEY FOUND NOT the lost princess of Knosós but Artemis, asleep in the woods, exhausted as from an extraordinary ordeal. And Athene could guess how the woman had gone missing for so long. She bid Theseus return to camp, and that she would aid him more later, and alone approached Artemis.

Attempting to walk gently, still her presence woke keen-eared Artemis, who started awake and snatched a dagger. Athene held up her hands for peace. "I came to talk only, Sister."

The other Olympian rose and sheathed her knife, but from the way she stared at Athene, she had little trust at the moment.

"So many things have happened in recent years," Athene said.

Artemis bit her lip. "Many things," she agreed, after a moment.

The raw tension strung so deep within the other woman tugged at Athene's heart. Part of her wanted to reach over and offer a comforting hand, but Artemis no longer seemed like the woman who had, in years long gone, trained Athene in stealth and woodcraft. Something deep inside had changed in her erstwhile mentor, and it stung that Athene could not seem to fathom what or how. Surely, there was some way to restore their relationship. She could not even say what had begun to let it fray, unless it was the long absence Athene had made from Olympus after the Gigantomachy. Still, she had seen Artemis on occasion since her exile, and she had not been this way.

Before the events of a few years ago, Athene would never have believed the Phoebid capable of her part in the horror of Kalydon. But that, at least, Athene had seen clear as day in the Oracle Mirrors.

"Father wants you back upon Olympus," Athene said, though she knew Artemis chafed whenever compelled to return to the mountain.

Now her old friend glowered. "I'm certain he does."

"Artemis ... please ..."

"I'm going to hunt down Dionysus. I'm going to destroy the monstrosity responsible for all this."

Good. That was good. She nodded.

Artemis bit her lip again. "Do you ... know where Dionysus fled?"

"No." Unfortunately. "But if I did, I would help you." The Titan intended to destroy them all, and Athene needed to see him slain.

"You know he's your brother, don't you? That he intends to bring down your father."

It was Athene's turn to glower. She knew only too well. She leant back against a tree. "I know what he intends. We could work together, Artemis, to stop him from destroying our world."

"I cannot." There was a war going on behind Artemis's eyes but no warmth in her posture. Not anymore. "So long as you swear loyalty to your father, I cannot fully trust you."

"Trust me?" Athene scoffed. "You are the one that helped that monster unleash the accursed Boar of Kalydon." She knew, of course, castigating the other woman for her mistakes would avail her little. Pointing out another's failings served only when that person remained unaware and primed to repeat those errors. She could not stop herself, though.

Athene's loyalty to her father was not a failing. It could not be.

Artemis huffed, arms folded over her chest like a petulant child despite having millennia of life behind her. "So quick to chastise me over the boar, as if your hands were clean, Sister. As if Medusa did not writhe in torment at the curse you wrought upon her."

Athene shut her eyes in acknowledgment. Blood and ichor stained her fingers, such that they might never wash clean. Was the pettiness, the wrath, the all-consuming vitriol a side effect of the Ambrosia they all so craved? Did the very source of Titan immortality and puissance corrupt even as it fortified, thus sending them spiralling into depravity?

Over the centuries, she had seen many of her kind fall thus, wrecking suffering upon mortals and Nymphs because they could. Or rather did she, in seeking to blame the Ambrosia, simply seek to abrogate her culpability for a faulty character?

"In the end," Artemis said, perhaps following her line of thought, "we are not so different from Man."

"We are gluttonous beasts, grown corpulent on feasts of power, whilst looking upon our fellows as lions look upon prey."

"I dare hope ..." Artemis swallowed. "One day, my friend, you will have to pick a side. You cannot serve both Olympus and Mankind. And I hope you make the right choice before it is too late."

"Artemis ..."

"Goodbye, Athene."

No, it ought not to end this way. Artemis was her friend, her sister on Olympus. But her words held a sense of terrible finality Athene could not shake free from, and she found herself watching the shadowed wood long after Artemis had disappeared into the dark of the tree line.

✿

THEY HAD NOT FOUND ARIADNE. For Theseus's benefit, Athene had gone into the wood, found a small, calm pool of water, and stared. She had tossed a pebble in and watched the ripples against the surface, letting the patterns serve as catalyst for her hydromantic trances.

And she had found an answer for the prince of Athenai, though not one he would welcome or which she was eager to deliver.

It was not Theseus's approach that drew her from her trances, though, but far heavier footfalls.

"Hello, little sister," Ares said, voice deep and eyes wild in the moonlight. He stood, palm resting upon the pommel of his sword.

Was that an intentional threat or merely his ever-present belligerence rising to the surface?

Athene rose to meet her half-brother, careful to keep her hands away from her weapons. Apollon's vision had exonerated Ares, at least from charges of treason, and Father wanted him back upon Olympus.

"We discovered the son of Zeus who intends to overthrow Father," she said. "He knows it was not you."

Ares sneered. "Oh, now he knows. When neither blood nor even my oath served to convince him. And I suppose he intends to offer me formal apology?" Her brother drummed fingers upon his sword hilt now. Surely, he did not intend to attack her ... "Will he come to me to upon his knees and beg forgiveness for ever having doubted my loyalty?"

No. No, Athene could not see her father apologising. Thinking back, in truth, she did not think she had ever heard him apologise for aught in her life. "You know better than that."

"Yes." Ares's laugh held not the least mirth. "Father can do no wrong, can he?" Another bitter chuckle. "I imagine I must now be, simultaneously, innocent of the crime, and yet somehow this is still my fault, as well?"

His assessment fell uncomfortably close to Father's words.

"You must return to Olympus, Brother. We must make this right." She could already see bitterness settling in him, but surely he could not surrender his birthright over it.

"Ha!" Ares took a threatening step forward then. "When, and if, I ever return to that mountain, it will be not to kneel once more at our father's feet, but to claim the throne it is my right to inherit."

No. "Ares ..."

"I am the God of War! Did he think he could dishonour me without consequence? Did he think I would bear every insult, every snub, every belittlement down through eternity? There are ... *limits*, Athene. Why should I not follow the example he set forth when he cast down his own father for lesser crimes?"

Athene stood aghast, hand going not to her sword as she knew duty bid her, but to her mouth, somehow hoping to deny his words. "You cannot mean to invoke a second Titanomachy. The World scarce survived the first one. Brother, please. *Please*, do not do this."

"You must choose a side."

The echo of Artemis's words left her sputtering and numb. He could not mean it. He could not truly intend such carnage as would follow any attempt he made at rebellion.

But then, Ares thrived on carnage.

14

THESEUS

728 Bronze Age

"But you saw no sign of Ariadne?" Phaidra asked when Theseus had related all that had transpired at Pirithous's wedding. They sat now in a shadow-drenched room of the Athenian royal palace, peering at one another over the dwindling flame of an oil lamp. Neither had touched the bowls of wine set before them.

He had, some months back—in a fit of masochistic melancholy, perhaps hoping she would curse him—told her the truth of why he had abandoned her sister on Naxos. Phaidra had turned inside before insisting they return and search the island for Ariadne.

It had taken every drop of courage he could muster, however meagre it proved, for him to venture upon that shore once more. And they found no sign of Ariadne and assumed whatever wretched god had called for her had dragged her away to some far-off world. Phaidra had slapped him then—twice—before collapsing against his chest and weeping and sniffling and begging him to undo what had transpired.

But time had blunted the edge of her anger, he thought, for it was not directed at him. Grief had joined them rather than driven a wedge betwixt them, and Theseus had taken to confiding his recurring nightmares in her. Phaidra would sing sweet arias of the blessed Golden Age, when Men lived freer lives, and Theseus would imagine a life where never had he laid eyes upon the offended deity that had so wronged the both of them.

Some nights, whilst she hummed beneath the stars, she would pull his head to her lap, stroke his temples, and soothe his worn nerves.

And he had allowed himself to think it all behind them. Until the wedding. Until the centaurs attacked and Theseus saw again the face of the one who had stolen both his betrothed and his mettle in one fell swoop: Dionysus. The god had rendered him a sham of a man, trembling at his dreams, lost in drunken sorrows.

"I searched everywhere for her," Theseus said. "Athene was there, and I sought her aid. The Olympian helped me to scour the woods first, and upon finding naught therein, she turned to her Oracular gift. She told me ..." Theseus struggled to keep his voice from breaking. "The goddess told me that Ariadne is lost to us forever. That neither you nor I shall ever look upon her face again in this life, and all striving to recover her will prove in vain." The Olympian had returned from her divination pale and bitter; it seemed relating such a dire prophecy took its toll upon her.

Now, Phaidra traced a lazy finger in her wine bowl, drawing crimson patterns that reminded him of the hateful Labyrinth. Abruptly, she slapped the bowl aside, splattering wine and sending the ceramic shattering upon the floor. Moaning, Phaidra pressed her palms against her brow. "Why ... why ..."

Both of them, he knew, had held out the unspoken hope they would one day make right what had gone so wrong upon Naxos. Hopes so oft died the longest of deaths, buried long after the people to whom they were bound were dust.

Should he leave her be? Would solitude balm the anguish that squeezed her heart now? But the thought of abandoning her as he had done to her sister had bile scorching his throat. Never again would he make that mistake. Theseus scooted around the low table between them and wrapt his arm around her shoulders. "I am so sorry. I will never ... not be sorry for this."

She let him draw her into an embrace. Or rather, she fell into him as if unable to support herself to sit a moment longer. Now he held her, stroking her head as she had oft done for him.

He had lingered long upon the slopes of Mount Pelion, trying to comfort the equally inconsolable Pirithous. But Theseus's dearest friend had fallen for Hippodamia, and his had been a marriage as much of the heart as for the alliance Oikhalia had presented. Theseus had sought to help his beloved Pirithous drown his sorrows in rich Theban wines, but his friend refused drink. Even getting him to take food had become a labour in and of itself, and Pirithous slept but in fits. In the night, he would wake, moaning, haunted by the agonised death he'd witnessed.

After days of it, having stayed waking by Pirithous's side much of the time, Theseus found his patience had worn thin. A shameful part of him longed to point out to Pirithous that he, too, had lost a woman he'd intended to marry. And all he wanted now was to return to Athenai and tell Phaidra of what he'd learnt. All he could see was her face. Duty compelled him to tend to Phaidra, and so, before many more days had passed, he had embraced Pirithous and told him he would check back with him soon enough.

Now here was Phaidra, weeping in his arms, and he had no more idea how to comfort her than he had how to aid Pirithous. Theseus was, in the end, of use to no one. All he could do was hold her and hope that alone proved enough.

❦

With wine and bitter reminiscence, Theseus and Phaidra made nightly memorial to Ariadne, slowly circling the empty hollow left by her absence and the awful realisation they would never have the full truth. They would bury no body, erect no tomb, and mostlike, avenge no wrong done to her. She was just ... gone. Like Io, she was stolen from Man by a god, and neither the will of her kith and kin nor of herself had mattered a whit.

He had not expected it—though he had imagined it, ever and anon, whilst trying to sleep—when his and Phaidra's lips had first met. Wine-drunk and fevered in their emotions, parting lips had soon led to clothes strewn across the marble floor. To moaning desperation and longings fulfilled and to a faraway fear they might regret this, come the morn.

BUT IT WAS NOT for regretting, leastwise not to him, and it had left him with a single incessant answer. The only route, really, and the one he must follow.

"How could we wed?" she asked when he offered to make her the future queen of Athenai. "How could I take your hand knowing I would forever be but the shadow of my sister in your eyes? I am ..." Phaidra huffed and steadied herself. "I am but the treasure claimed because it was all that was left behind."

Maybe, he might have once deluded himself into thinking such and thus had not considered Phaidra as a wife. "When I first brought you here, I saw you as my betrothed's sister and naught more. But now I ... The truth is, I know you far better than ever I knew Ariadne. For two years we have comforted one another. We have supported each other in our sorrows and, also, shared a few laughs, I seem to recall."

She snorted, and he wondered if she dwelt upon the same memories as him. Oft, she had entertained with tales of court at Knosós or fanciful accounts of the many manuscripts she had read in her father's library. Phaidra had a swift mind and a sharper wit, well capable of eviscerating pompous courtiers with her tongue.

"I love her," Phaidra said. "I love my sister more than even you can know. But I ... I need you to swear to me you do not do this because of her. Because much though I love her, I cannot be her imitation."

"No ... I want only for you to be yourself, Phaidra. Always."

A wry smile crept over her face. "Of that, you can rest assured."

⁊

IN THE SPRING, at year's end, word came to Theseus of a visitor come to Athenai, blind and impoverished, yet of kingly aspect. Thus he searched out the man in question and found him, resting in the shadow of the Colonnades, tended by a girl child, who took offerings from people whose sympathies the pair had stirred.

Theseus sat upon the bench beside the blind man, and a hush settled around the stoa, the populace waiting with bated breath to see how their prince would treat the stranger. Except, this man was no stranger, and the tale of the recent fall of the king of Thebes had already come to Theseus's ears.

"Unhappy Oedipus," Theseus said and laid his hand upon the erstwhile king's own. "I know the sad tale of your fate and how you yourself pierced those blinded eyes. I have not forgotten the similarities of our childhood hardships, raised in foreign lands. What would you have of me?"

Oedipus wheezed, the phlegmy sound of his lungs soul destroying. "My body fails me, and I cannot say I much regret leaving this wretched life behind me. Not much, save a fear for my children. I need someone to swear to look after their interests in the days that come. Though Kreon sits the throne of Thebes, one day, it ought to come to my sons."

Theseus folded his arms over his chest. "My hearth is open to all, and sheltering yourself and your daughter offers no burden. But your request might well have me embroil Athenai in a potential Theban civil war."

"And yet, it is their birthright. I cannot die in peace knowing my sons denied such."

Theseus rubbed his brow. Once, he'd have considered his troubles too many already and might have demurred. But with his wedding to Phaidra looming on the horizon, it felt an ill omen to refuse the last request of a dying king. So Theseus squeezed Oedipus's hand, made his promises, and when the man passed some days later, held for him a stately funeral worthy of his station.

For Antigone, Phaidra agreed to take the girl under her care, at least until such time as a fitting home was located for her. There was a strangeness in having a child wander the palace halls, but Theseus found himself oft driven to try to pry a smile from the girl. With flowers and gifts and kind words, he and Phaidra sought to blunt the edge of her grief.

He was never certain they succeeded, of course. For grief was a knife with a thousand razored sides, ever keen, ever eager to cut when one least expected. Theseus knew it all too well.

HE AND PHAIDRA were wed in the summer, before the new year. The sky rumbled with thunder; the clouds thick with unshed drops when the priestess sacrificed a bull. The procession moved from the temple back to the palace. Theseus's father stood behind him, and, so far as Theseus knew, the man had not stopped grinning in the past three days. So wide was his smile, Theseus had to imagine his jaw must ache from it by this point, and yet the man's hand closed on his shoulder in encouragement whilst Theseus awaited the arrival of his bride.

It was a strange wedding, in a way, for Phaidra already lived in the same home as Theseus, and thus she was escorted not down the street, but down the hall to his chambers. Palace servants—and Antigone, after Phaidra insisted the girl be included—rather than her kin, had performed her ritual bath. They had brushed her hair, he was told, and cut a lock of it to cast into the sea, dedicated to Aphrodite.

Outside Theseus's chambers, a throng of witnesses watched Phaidra's approach, and he caught himself wondering if the gathered courtiers would have paid the moment such solemnity had they known he and Phaidra had already shared one flesh oft enough. Indeed, she had confided, last night, she thought she might be with child already. Such joyous news meant, he supposed, it was well they had settled on today after all, rather than waiting until the solstice in a fortnight. Less chance of wagging tongues later when she began to show.

Behind the procession of court ladies and little Antigone, Phaidra walked, her face concealed by a veil. Thanks to her Nymph heritage, Phaidra stood half a head taller than most of the women around her, and from the sly crane of her neck, Theseus imagined she had stolen a glance at him. Though the veil hid her expression, he could picture the mischievous upturn of her mouth, the hint of that smile in her eyes.

Outside his chambers, the women ushered Phaidra forward, and she paused before Theseus. He clasped her fingers with one hand. With the other, he lifted the veil, making her his wife in name as well as in his heart.

All the darkness that had passed before his eyes melted like frost beneath the spring sun. Life was new again.

THEY SAT IN THE COURTYARD, basking in the afternoon sunlight in what promised to be one of the last warm days of the season. Already, a crisp autumn breeze ruffled Theseus's hair, and beneath his fingers, Phaidra's arm had pimpled with gooseflesh. She leant back against him and he rubbed his hands over her biceps to warm them, watching the geese upon the pond. Soon, they would fly from here. Soon, there would be no sitting in gardens for hours at a time.

Anyway, Phaidra was thick with child, and already her ladies fussed and harrumphed over her, chiding the future queen for being up and about too much. Theseus and Phaidra had agreed the clucking hens made much over very little. It was not as if the babe would come before spring, or the tail end of winter at the soonest, and she could hardly sit on her arse for all months in between.

Once, when Phaidra sat upon the ground, playing dolls with Antigone, the head woman had tried to instruct Phaidra on the matter, insisting upon what was proper for a future queen. At which point Phaidra pointed out that she'd grown up "a princess of Knosós, daughter of a queen, and I'll thank you to remember it." And that had been the end of that.

There was peace here, Theseus reflected. It made him wonder why he had sought, with violent fervour, for fame and glory as though such things held in them joy. In the name of ambition, he'd sailed to Kolchis and ventured the dark of the Labyrinth, but the only happiness he had found came from quieter worlds. It dwelt in moments free of strife, with murmured conversations barely audible over the chirping of birds prancing along the rooftops. Contentment more lay in the caress of Phaidra's finger along his wrist than in all the skilful cuts with a blade ever struck.

He supposed that Herakles had tried to tell him such a thing, some years back.

The messenger's sandals squelched upon the garden loam, soft yet intrusive, nonetheless, shattering Theseus's illusion that he and Phaidra were the only people in his serene world. He looked up at him, bit back his ire, and accepted the papyrus scroll the man had brought.

It bore Oikhalia's seal. Eurytos sending word he yet hunted more centaurs? Over the summer, Theseus had heard of more of those creatures raiding and rampaging around Mount Pelion, some reaching as far as the outskirts of Thebes. But no true invasion had come, and they all dared to hope the defeat of Dionysus meant the end of such chaos. To break the seal, Theseus would need to disentangle his other arm from Phaidra, and as that did not much appeal, he instead let the message drop beside him.

"What is it?" Phaidra asked.

Didn't leave him much choice, then, tempted though he was to ignore the missive. Grunting, he eased free his arm and popped the seal.

Dear Theseus, it read. *With heavy heart I write you knowing of what import you held in the life of our Pirithous. I wish there would be some easier way to inform you of what has happened, but I can think of none. Our friend has succumbed in the battle he waged against despair and chosen to end his life. By the time this reaches you, Pirithous's body will have been interred with all possible honours in the tombs of his ancestors within the mountain.*

"No," Theseus mouthed the word more than spoke it, for words seemed impossible in the face of what he'd just read. *It* was impossible. He read it again. "No." His voice broke. His *World* broke.

"What happened?" Phaidra asked, frantic now, snatching up the missive.

Tears blinded him. His heart withered, his insides turned to dust. A wail ripped from his lungs, erupting like a long-dormant volcano, burying him in the colourless ash of misery. Though some dim part of his mind knew Phaidra cradled him in her arms, tried to soothe him, all Theseus could manage was an endless moan.

It was a lie!

It was a lie.

It was ...

15

HERAKLES

729 Bronze Age

Standing in Eurystheus's chambers in the palace of Mykenai, arms folded over his chest, Herakles wondered if he had heard the king correctly. If so, he could see why the man had not proclaimed this next labour in the open throne room, before the greedy ears of gathered courtiers. The rumour alone of such an intent would see Eurystheus torn apart by the Olympian Order.

"You want a golden apple from the garden of the Hesperides?" He did not know whether to laugh or shake his head at the king's temerity. Were he to turn the man in for such a request, he could be rid of Eurystheus forever. But then, how could he complete his labours if he turned against the one Ananke had decreed must assign them?

From the corner of his eye, Herakles espied the shade of Deikoon, watching him. His boy waited to see what his father would do, given the chance to throw down his enemy at last. All Herakles need do was inform a priest or priestess of the Olympians and then watch his cousin dragged screaming from his palace toward his well-deserved end. That, and give up his chance to appease his boys with but two labours remaining.

"Yes. Bring me an apple from the great tree of Atlantis."

Maybe Herakles having but two labours remaining was the very point of this. Eurystheus grew more desperate to see his cousin dead. He saw now that Herakles could and would succeed in every impossible task laid out before him. Now, at last, he turned toward a quest that would not only mostlike prove suicide but would, if discovered, ensure Herakles a place in Tartarus. Of course, if he stole an apple on Eurystheus's behalf, the king could not well turn him in without implicating himself.

"Why would you want it? It won't be Ambrosia." No Man knew by what method the goddess Hebe fermented the apples to brew the tonic of the gods. Stories claimed, without that process, the apples themselves were useless. Of course, tales could be wrong. Bards were wont to spout off whatever sounded good to a half-drunk audience, about as concerned with keeping to facts as they were with staying sober.

Herakles's vile cousin shrugged, a cruel smile curling his lips. "What I intend with the apple little concerns you. Are you refusing the labour, then?"

Dour, Herakles cast another look at Deikoon. The boy nodded. How could he deny any chance to appease his sons? "I shan't refuse."

And really, there was naught more to say.

HAD he a way to reach her, Herakles would have called upon Athene. His adoptive mother must know where upon the massive island of Atlantis the Garden of the Hesperides lay, and her advice could save him days or weeks of searching the wilds. But Athene had returned to Olympus at their common father's behest, and Herakles dare not climb the mountain, much less voice his intentions to steal from the garden before the very seat of the Olympian Order. Instead, he made sail alone for the island at the heart of the Thalassa.

The polis of Atlantis lay on the southern shore, with Knosós to the north and a handful of villages scattered about the coastline. The island's mountainous interior remained wild, dominated by the towering Mount Evenor. Lesser peaks surrounded the great mountain, and, Herakles thought, the Garden would lie in a valley somewhere amid that imposing range.

As he broke from the polis and moved beyond the encircling farmlands, he saw fewer and fewer people. No one questioned him, though he had heard trekking to the valleys was forbidden to Man. Perhaps, given his height, the locals took him for a Titan in the employ of the Olympian Hebe, who now ruled here. She was his half-sister, he supposed, though Herakles had not met her.

Passing beyond the lands of civilisation, he kept to the woods. If a Titan should spot him, he did not fancy answering questions about his reason for heading that direction. He could not well claim he intended a mere stroll in the mountains, after all.

As dusk fell, Herakles picked out a spot amid the trees to rest. Wandering the woods in the dark might well earn him a sprained ankle or worse. Still, he doubted he would sleep much in this place, knowing he came here intent on violating the sacred laws of Olympus. His father would have destroyed him for attempting such a thing ... but Zeus had not deigned to take much interest in his son over the years. Herakles alone must see to the releasing of his children's souls from their torment, and so he alone could decide how far he must go.

In the wood around him, nightjars chirped, cicadas buzzed, and somewhere distant a frog croaked. Shutting his eyes, he massaged the back of his neck. Almost finished. Almost done with these labours. Was it a betrayal of his sons that he had, at long last, begun to think of an *after*? In truth, he ought to remain focused upon the task at hand. Legend claimed a many-headed drakon called Ladon protected the Garden.

Another hydra?

Either way, Herakles found his thoughts drifting to Iole. Eurytos ought not have done as he had. The girl herself had asked him to shoot for her hand, keen enough for their wedding. Contest aside, a father ought to have considered his daughter's wishes. And Herakles *had* won the godsdamned contest on her behalf. Only the most wretched of all Men broke their words. A word, once given, was the most precious of all gifts, and the violation of it among the worst of all crimes.

A twig snapped in the direction Herakles had come from. His eyes shot open, his fingers wrapping around the hilt of his xiphos. The tall man that approached flashed a wolf-like grin. With teeth so pointed, he had likely tasted the flesh of Man. Herakles had fought Gigantes aplenty during the battle on Olympus. This one, he was halfway down that road already.

"Who are you?" Herakles asked, rising without either drawing his blade or releasing his grip upon it.

"Kyknus, Son of Ares, and thus I suppose your nephew, Son of Zeus."

"Better, Nephew, had you not given in to the temptation to feast so freely."

The other man shrugged as if they spoke of sheep or goat meat. "Got to eat when the craving arises. You could try it. However powerful you are now, champion, imagine your might when fortified by the strength imbued within the flesh of Man. You could, Uncle, join me. Father won't abide you remaining in service to his sister any longer. Swear to him and we can be allies. The alternative ..." Kyknus flicked a too-long tongue over his canines.

Herakles could not help but scoff at the obscene offer. "You'd have me break faith with the woman who raised me. Not only that, but feast upon Man-flesh and give in to the bestial taint that lurks within Titan blood." Wise men claimed that, for a Titan or even a demigod, one taste was all it took to spark perennial cravings. There could never be enough to sate such prodigious needs. And sooner or later, monstrous appetites would lead to monstrous transformations. He eased forth his adamantine xiphos, holding the blade between himself and his nephew. "Get gone from here, Gígas."

That feral grin returned. Kyknus leapt, kicked off a tree and flew at Herakles with uncanny speed. A blade appeared in his hand as he soared, and Herakles barely deflected a blow that would have cleft his head from his shoulders. Next he knew, Kyknus had passed him. The Gígas bounded onto a lower tree branch, making leaps higher and higher until he'd vanished into the dark of the canopy.

The Man-eater seemed almost able to fly. Herakles growled in frustration, turning about, sword before him as he scanned the branches above. Where had the bastard gone?

A crunch of leaves overhead, and he turned. Kyknus soared toward him, blade-first, gliding across the air as though hefted upon non-existent winds. Herakles beat aside the blade with his own, then caught up his nephew's tunic as the man passed. The fist that struck his chest blew the breath from his lungs and sent him hurtling through the air, his momentum only stopped by a tree trunk.

Gasping, Herakles dropped to his knees. He'd not had time to focus his Pneuma into Steadfastness and the blow had almost caved in his chest. Kyknus hooted and cackled, gone mad with sadistic pleasure at Herakles's pain. Had consuming Man-flesh so fortified Kyknus's Pneuma, or had the demigod tasted Ambrosia?

Either way, cautious, Herakles rose, one hand to his chest, the other keeping his xiphos out ahead of him. Each breath sent liquid fire scorching through his lungs. His vision had hazed over. Flooding Pneuma into Tolerance let him suppress the pain enough to keep his footing.

With another wild howl, Kyknus sprang, kicking off trees and bounding about Herakles in a blur of motion, bouncing one way and the next. His blade would dart in, sometimes scoring a bite against Herakles's now Pneuma-hardened flesh, sometimes deflected upon his xiphos. But his foe's speed and agility made it hard to corner him or bring Herakles's strength to bear.

After parrying another flying lunge, Herakles swung backhanded with his other fist. Kyknus twisted aside like a leaf caught in a summer gale and Herakles's blow cracked a tree trunk. His nephew's counter kick snapped into Herakles's knee and sent him crashing to the forest floor.

Like a scorpion's sting, Kyknus's xiphos darted in. It struck Herakles's Pneuma-infused flesh like a gong. The blow was strong enough to punch through, and the xiphos bit into his thigh, though the force of the blow split the blade in twain. Still suppressing his pain with Tolerance, Herakles lunged forward, catching both of Kyknus's legs about his shins. With Potency drawn, he heaved, his own roar almost drowning out the sound of Kyknus's pained screams. He bent the man's legs backwards until his knees popped out the wrong way.

His nephew collapsed, clutching at his ruined limbs and shrieking.

Grimacing, Herakles drew the shard of Kyknus's blade from his own thigh and cast it aside. So, Ares planned to move against Athene, did he? Well, if the God of War and his son thought to hurt Mama, he'd have to go through Herakles. With another growl, Herakles fell upon his nephew and swiped his blade over the man's throat.

Once he finished upon Atlantis, Herakles would need a way to get word to Athene. She must know what Ares planned.

16

HEKATE

726 Bronze Age

*A*long the desolate path to Kirke's estate, Hekate found her eye twitched with anticipation, her pulse pounding and irregular. There was a breach of maternal instinct, she knew, in placing the sum of her hopes for herself in her daughter's hands. In placing, with such crushing desperation, the burden upon Kirke to save Hekate from the woes before her.

In a fair World, in a *better* World, the mother would have worked to shoulder the burdens of the daughter. But neither had Pandora done so for Hekate, nor could Hekate manage it for Kirke. Or maybe, if her daughter solved the mysteries of that Box, Hekate could find a way to save them all from the depredations of Ananke and the consuming hunger of the Dark.

Besides that small village, Aiaíā was home but to birds and beasts —those grizzled wolves watching her, the wrens chirping in the trees —such that, though Kirke's estate might have seemed a quiet refuge for those visiting, to the imprisoned it would have turned desolate. A crushing loneliness that might consume the weak, and Helios had inflicted it upon his daughter in his faltering attempts to spare her from Zeus. And he had failed even at that.

If the King of Olympus had not already come calling upon Kirke, he soon would. Hekate could only hope she was not too late, that she could protect her daughter from the mad king.

The oppressive sense of bleakness only deepened as Hekate reached the manse. The animals that had once frequented the place had vanished. No smoke rose from the hearth. No sound issued from within, even when Hekate stood upon the threshold.

"Kirke?" Had she gone out? Or—though Hekate refused to countenance the thought—had something befallen her daughter? "Kirke?"

With quickening strides, Hekate ploughed through Kirke's home, each room dark and empty. Until, checking the kitchen, she nigh stumbled over the woman. Hands folded in her lap, her daughter sat upon the floor, legs stretched out, eyes staring into the deep shadows. The only hint of light came from the half-shuttered window, its intruding beam far from Kirke's still form.

Horrible, chest-tightening doubt raced through Hekate, a physical pain at the thought she had come upon Kirke's corpse. But as she dropped beside her daughter, her hand falling to her head, Kirke turned a hollow gaze upon her. The dark circles framing her eyes had grown so deep Hekate might have mistaken them for black eyes. The woman drew a shuddering breath before collapsing against Hekate, her hand seizing Hekate's with a grip at once tentative and so desperate it seemed she might drown if she lost hold.

A small flood of Pneuma into Potency allowed Hekate to heft the woman in her arms and carry her out into her chambers. There, Hekate set her daughter upon a divan, sought about until she found a blanket, and wrapt it around Kirke.

That done, she settled down beside the couch to wait. Perhaps Kirke would never speak of what had passed, or perhaps she needed time. Was the pain in her due to Zeus? Or rather, had she, despite Hekate's useless warnings, used the Box?

So like you, Khione whispered.

But then, Hekate had always known Kirke would open it. *Must* open it. Kirke herself had come to her in the distant past, had shown her the damned thing. And three generations of Hekate's family had become snared in the endless, circular depths of this Box.

WHEN DAWN BROKE, Hekate cast wide the shutters, allowing the burning light to spill upon Kirke's face. The girl didn't start or stir and, in fact, Hekate realised, her eyes were already open. Perhaps had she had not slept in the least.

Now—almost certain that this Kirke had been the one to visit her centuries back, had forced Hekate to engineer the abductions and rapes of Io and Europa, the years of tribulation that fell upon Pandora, and the whole blighted course of their family history—temptation arose, bitter and selfish. An irresistible need to confront Kirke over things she had done, though surely she had found no more choice in front of her than Hekate herself had. To blame her, to even ask her, would be petty and cruel.

Mostlike they both knew where the woman had been, and Kirke would have not the least desire to speak on it, and Hekate could not stand to inflict further pain upon her.

"I think I can tell you how to use it now." Kirke's words came slow, seeming drawn out from some hollow core deep inside her.

The pain there struck Hekate, had her enwrapping Kirke in an embrace as if she held the woman together. As if any of them could survive the scope of the Moirai's weavings.

That was what it came down to, was it not? That the Fates had cursed their family, and worse still, that Hekate and Kirke had damned themselves with the Art. At times, she dared to believe Kirke had used little enough sorcery she might avoid becoming a wraith in death, though Hekate could not be certain. For herself, though, every road led through agony and darkness. Becoming a wraith locked in eternal self-loathing now seemed almost a blessing compared to the unspeakable torments Aeshma would visit upon her. And of the warnings Pandora had given? Perhaps her mother spoke of Aeshma, perhaps something else. Hekate could not know.

Only that there had to be some way, no matter how concealed, how reckless, that might break her free of her fate. The third option —neither to surrender to Ananke nor to destroy herself and her daughters by trying to unravel the whole of the Moirai's design.

And if any such option existed, if any chance of finding succour was out there for Hekate and her kin, it must surely lie within that Box. The power to move through time meant she had to be able to change the course of history, if she could but find the right moment, the right choice.

"Show me," Hekate said.

It was the last, only choice yet before her.

KIRKE HAD LEFT the Box sitting upon the kitchen floor, but in the dark, Hekate had not seen it. After her daughter rose and retrieved it, the woman beckoned Hekate to kindle a flame in the hearth. Before its flickering light and warmth, Kirke spoke, explaining how every panel, every twisting gear must align just so to locate a particular moment in time or space.

"Space?" Hekate asked.

"It can move you across both with equal ease, though predicting an exact location has no ease about it whatsoever."

When Hekate was fair certain she understood the instructions— as certain as she could be, given the infinite complexity of a device meant to encompass all time and locations upon Gaia—she bid Kirke a bitter farewell, kissing her daughter's brow. If she could, she would save both her daughters from their onerous burdens, all the anguish they had suffered in their long lives, and those worries yet to come. Maybe, maybe even she could find a way to help Pandora, to obviate the need for her bitter past and uncertain future.

Hekate's road to damnation, to the consumptive Dark, had begun long ago, as a child, when she'd met Enodia. That ghost sorceress in whom Hekate had placed so much trust had fed her lust for knowledge and power with enough tinder to ensnare a young mind.

Mormo cackled in her mind. *How delicious ... how you abrogate responsibility ... for your insatiable need for answers ...*

"But then, maybe you'd be free, too."

If she could convince her impressionable self to listen to her father, to turn from that path, maybe she could save her own soul from damnation as well as Kirke's. A fear lingered, of course, that if she never went to the Circle of Goetic Mysteries, neither Kirke nor Athene would ever be conceived. Too, if her choices prevented Pandora from encountering Prometheus, Hekate herself could never be born. But maybe even oblivion, for all of them, was better than eternal torment.

Besides, if risk stopped her from even trying to spare herself, she had left only the option of surrender. A choice she would not make, *could* not make. Not when the Box was here, presenting her this one hope.

Outside Kirke's manse, kneeling in the dirt beneath the light of a waning moon, Hekate activated the Box.

"I WAS TOLD," Rhea said, drifting close enough Hekate had to look up at the taller woman, "that my beloved gave to you a cloak he had procured for me, and yet I find you clad in plain travelling clothes."

"I met with misfortune and the cloak was stolen."

"Hmm, most unfortunate indeed." The Titan lady tilted her head to one side, a silent prompt for Hekate to state her purpose here.

"Lord Kronos once bid me attend him, that he would teach me of the Ontos."

The lady's smile curled with a hint of vicious satisfaction. "What would we want with one who walked away from such an offer? Which mentor would welcome back a pupil who spurned their lessons when offered freely?"

THE HARSH LIGHT of the setting sun bored into Hekate's eyes, even as a chill breeze ruffled her khiton. Wet cloth clung to her flesh. It took a moment to recognise the cause: she lay upon snow-caked rock, a mere foot from spilling off a mountain peak. The rock upon which she lay jutted from a tiny plateau, offering a pulse-quickening view of a precipitous drop that fell away for hundreds of feet. The howling wind rustled below, stirring up snow drifts whilst evoking thoughts of predators stalking these expanses at nightfall.

After easing herself into a sitting position, she peered around, hand raised over her eyes to block out the sun's glare. While she couldn't say for certain, the peak looked an awful lot like Olympus. If the Box had brought her to a time after the Ambrosial War as she had hoped, it would make sense that no buildings would yet limn the slopes.

Still looking around, Hekate sought a means of descent that didn't involve plummeting into the ravine. There was a path a few dozen feet away, but she'd have to scramble over rime-slicked boulders to reach it.

With no better option, she crawled from the plateau toward the nearest rock. As she'd feared, it had grown slippery. Potency could lend her strength to cling to rocks, but she was no expert climber. Still, it seemed her only choice.

With a deep breath, Hekate heaved herself onto the next rock.

AS HEKATE CLAMBERED from the last of the rocks onto the rough-hewn path, a calloused hand seized the back of her neck. With a single motion her accoster sent her sprawling into the frozen dirt, then tumbling over on her shoulder. Dazed and groaning, her vision came back into focus, and she turned to look at the Titan who had snared and flung her.

"Who are you?" Kronos demanded. "What business have you upon this forsaken slope?"

For a moment that stretched so long the Titan lord's face grew darker still, Hekate could only gape at one she had last seen millennia ago when his son had cast him into Tartarus. Whether or not Kronos had been a just ruler, he was surely leagues better than his offspring.

Glowering, Kronos withdrew his infamous adamantine sickle from behind his back. Hekate's heart leapt into her throat. She had not come this far to die like this!

"Dwellers in rock be stirred," she sang in Supernal, voice resounding over the peaks, "hold fast one who dares trespass so far beyond the lands given to Man."

The ground beneath Kronos turned quaggy, sucking at the other Titan's sandals, giving Hekate time to scramble away on her arse, then find her feet.

"A Kandamian spellsong." The lord's voice held a new note of respect now, though his brows knitted as he slopped his way free of the muddy mess the land spirit had created beneath him. "A sorceress belongs here even less than an ordinary Titan."

If Kronos resolved to murder her, Hekate doubted calling upon the spirits dwelling in the land here would save her from his wrath. She could run, but he would mostlike catch her before she made it halfway down the mountain.

"You're here researching the Tartarian Gate, aren't you?" she blurted. "Or have you come for those Seeing Pools?"

Though he ceased his struggles with the mud, something about his posture warned she had trod into greater peril now. One day, thousands of years hence, Kronos would, in utter desperation, pull forth an Old One from that gate and unleash it upon Gaia. She had to assume that now, in this time, he'd have not indulged even a thought along such lines.

"I know about the Hekatónkheir," she said.

The lord's expression did not change, though he resumed his plodding toward her. A few more lurching steps, and he'd be free.

Flee or linger, she must choose, and choose now. Hardly a choice at all. "You know the power hidden deep in this mountain, yet you didn't build Kronion here. In fact, the island upon which your polis flourishes lies almost as far from Olympus as one can get and yet remain in Elládos. Legend claims you founded Byblos, too, and that sits even farther off, in Phoenikia."

"You know a great deal, sorceress. If you can tell me why I would never raise a settlement upon these mountains, I will consent to talk with you rather than strike you down for the hubris of daring this place."

Why had he not chosen Olympus as his home? Zeus had done so, had demanded they built his great abode here the moment he learnt of the terrible puissance lurking in the deep places below their feet. And in the intervening centuries, his madness had redoubled. Obsessed with the Ontos, he had demanded Kirke give him the Sight.

"Because ..." Hekate found it hard to breathe for admitting what she ought to have known for so long. "Because there is a taint here, seeping through the stones, polluting those who dare linger. Because to peer overlong into the secrets buried beneath this mountain is to invite aberrations of thought into one's mind."

Zeus was a tyrant, a madman. Maybe he had always been such. But even the other Olympians, those who dwelt long here, they had surrendered pieces of their humanity sure as a sorceress. Self-obsessed, some even solipsistic, they had become parasitic rulers over Man. Such was the order of the Elládosi world that, when Zeus had banished Athene, Hekate had first considered it a *blessing*, a reprieve for her daughter.

Sloshing free at last, Kronos replaced his sickle behind his belt, face an unreadable mask. "You know more than you ought to, sorceress, and despite your kind's predilection for seeking forbidden knowledge at any cost, I sense a nascent wisdom waiting to burgeon." He took a step toward her, not threatening but with an open hand. "There is a power here Men cannot fathom, and the direst of perils accompanies it. If you wish *true* wisdom, if you wish to strive to free your will from the chains that ensnare us all, come with me. Long have I sought one with the calibre to question."

Something in his words bespoke a different kind of madness. An obsession with truth she knew all too well. Was not that ceaseless need for answers its own form of peril? Either way, she had little time to find her past self.

"I have my way free of the chains. My answers lie not on Olympus but in Thebes."

The lord's hand fell like a weight, resignation in his eyes. "Then go and let me not catch you hunting for ingress here. I do not know how you know of the ... pools ... but they are meant for us alone, and we tolerate no rivals."

Us? Kronos worked with someone?

"Wait," he said, then withdrew something from his satchel. "I purchased this cloak for my wife in Delphi—but you will catch your death of the chill up here." He tossed her a beautifully embroidered garment in a style that, though ancient now, seemed oddly comforting like something out of her childhood.

Grateful, she slung it over her shoulders and offered Kronos a bow. Tempted though she was to linger, to question, her road lay elsewhere. She had to hope it was not already too late.

17

PANDORA

399 Dark Age

*S*carce able to stand without leaning on the wall for support, naked and alone, Pandora exited the Time Chamber and emerged into new tunnels. Her knees wobbled, threatening to give out beneath her. These halls bore enough resemblance to those beneath Mugedang to make plain a connection between the builders. Under which of the frightful cities of Dark Faerie did she now find herself? The Gnostic Cabal had built these Time Chambers to try to challenge Fate, even as she herself strove against Ananke.

And they had failed.

No, best not dwell upon such things and risk allowing her mind to smother hope. Instead, she expended her faltering Pneuma to spark a flame in her palm, just enough light to see by as she wandered these unfamiliar tunnels. The air had grown chokingly stale here, heavy, as though no living being had been here in thousands of years. Perhaps none had, though insects and arachnids skittered away from the pale light of her makeshift torch. Its flame illuminated curtains of spiderwebs strung between corners, so thick Pandora oft needed to duck to avoid tangling them in her hair.

At last, she could make it no further and found herself forced to slump down against a wall, heedless of centuries of grime that rubbed off on her bare skin. Her paltry torch flickered out. She wanted to weep in horror and frustration at the destruction of Mu—not only Atlantis, but even the continent of Mu was being ripped apart—but exhaustion left her unable to muster the strength even to grieve for so many lives lost. Instead, she let her head fall into her hand. Shudders wracked her. Every which way she turned, Ananke loomed, monstrous as the abomination she'd beheld beneath the waves, and equally implacable. The ouroboros encircled *everything*.

It had killed her, even. And still it wrapt itself around her and refused to leave her be.

A twinge of pain pinched inside her chest, above her heart.

No, no, no. She was not giving in to this. She wrapt her arms about her knees and rocked herself, alone in the utter darkness, willing away the rising panic.

No.

She had to force herself to breathe.

Just breathe ...

She must have fallen asleep, for she awakened lying upon her side, arm numb from being tucked under her body. Not even being a Phoenix avatar protected one from sleeping wrong. Tingles of lightning shot through her fingers as feeling returned to her arm once she sat.

Her stomach growled. About now, she would have paid her last drachmae for a bowl of olives. Her hunger made it harder to replenish her Pneuma. There would be, she supposed, a certain perverse irony if—after all she had endured—she met her end in these sepulchral halls, lost and starving to death. Before the panic could rise again, Pandora rubbed her palms together, then snapped her fingers to summon a tiny spark. A flame, no larger than the nub of her finger, arose. Concentrating, she guided its course from her fingertip to her palm and cradled it there like a precious babe. The resurgence of light had more pests scrambling away from her, no doubt vexed at the intrusion into their domain.

"Don't worry," she murmured. "I wish to be gone from here even more than you want me out."

Still weak, she rose. The hurried flight from Mugedang after … after her *death* … it had jumbled her thoughts, and she had not made a mental map of these tunnels thus far. Doing so now would serve to keep her from dwelling on all that had transpired. Moving with care, protecting her fragile candle, Pandora made her way forward, noting each passageway in her mind.

She could not have said how long finding a way out took her. Many hours, at least, but time became hard to judge in such circumstances. Eventually, she emerged into a great stone hall centred around a massive fire pit. Her candle failed to illuminate the vaulting ceiling, but cracks in the ceiling allowed bands of moonlight to spill in, crisscrossing the complex.

A layer of sand caked the stone floor, gathered in mounds beneath the openings above, as if the entire chamber lay under a desert. When the wind howled above, a fresh curtain of sand streamed down in a crinkling rain, confirming her suspicions. The ruin lay at least partially buried.

Through a massive expenditure of Pneuma, she could manifest her flaming wings and launch herself up to that opening and escape. Of course, that would leave her to wander a desert with no knowledge of which way to walk and no protection for her skin from the sun. The Phoenix stopped her from burning by fire … would it prevent her bare flesh from baking beneath Hyperion's merciless heat?

Delaying, she instead wandered the cyclopean ruins. More chambers centred around fire pits adjoined the one she'd entered from. Had the denizens of this city worshipped fire in some distant Era?

Fire is life.

The voice sounded like Prometheus. Had he somehow spoken to her whilst her mind wandered in death? Or was her addled brain rearranging the order of events? No, this was not the place to relive her death, lest she risk it becoming real and permanent.

She found a staircase, but sand had flooded it. In the end, she decided digging herself out would use more of her energy than manifesting enough Pneuma to fly for a moment. Thus she returned to the first chamber and peered at the cracks in the great, buttressed ceiling. Pandora shook her head. Was this what Prometheus had intended for her?

He knew so many things, but it seemed plain enough he never knew *everything*.

They chose those of us who came first and tasked us to watch over Mankind, and thus called us their Watchers. His words, which she had, up to now, had little time to work over in her mind, chilled. The enormity of the burden thrust upon his shoulders would have broken most Men. And she had, in another life, been one of those Watchers, as well. How had she died? Did it even matter now?

Such thoughts but delayed her need to escape from here.

Pandora dropped into a crouch and gathered her Pneuma into her legs and back. She felt it welling, barely contained, like a volcano aching to burst. She leapt into the air, flames surging from her feet and stretching from her back in great pinions that sent her soaring up amid the buttresses.

She caught the lip of one, kicked off it, and wedged herself into one of the cracks letting in the moonlight. The manoeuvre earned her a mouthful of sand, but sputtering, still she emerged from the side of a dune. With Pneuma-enhanced strength, she heaved herself free. Then her energy faltered and she slipped, tumbling down the slope, end over end.

Rough sand scraped her face and bare skin. The World spun. Impact after impact. Followed by a final, breath-stealing blow. It took her a moment to even manage the strength to groan.

Lying on her back, she stared up at the night sky. As her senses came back, constellations took shape before her eyes. For a time she studied them, comparing them to charts she had read in the past. Despite subtle differences, she suspected it meant she was somewhere on Kumari Kandam. Which meant, she was probably in the Empty Desert south of the Badian Steppes of Neshia.

And with that knowledge, she could, maybe, navigate her way free of this place and find civilisation. Maybe.

AFTER HAVING SNUCK into an oasis town and stolen some clothes—the twinge of guilt she felt lasted but a moment given her pressing need —Pandora learnt that the great armies of all Kumari Kandam had begun to gather. The god-king Mithra, the self-same ruler the Queens of Mu had so feared, had called to himself all his countless vassal states. His empire encompassed nigh the whole continent of Kumari Kandam and, too, Phoenikia, Lydia, and Kemet. Rumours claimed the god-king would march soon upon defiant Elládos and Nusantara on Mu, as well, as if Mithra thought he could expand his empire in all directions at once.

From the endless streams of soldiers she witnessed heeding his call, perhaps he could.

She trekked across mile after mile, watching the billowing clouds of dust bestirred by millions of sandalled feet. In towns she passed through—most settlements deprived of their young men—every lip uttered the name of the god-king. They believed him when he said he would claim the whole of Gaia, and Pandora found herself shuddering at the looks of fanatic devotion she saw upon visage after visage.

Mayhap he could do it, for the threat of him had prompted the mighty Queens of Mu to summon fell Tiamat, even knowing the risk. Therein lay her true objective. If Pandora could find Mithra, could somehow convince him to give over this mad dream of conquest, then the queens would not, in desperation, take the steps that led to such cataclysm.

History is merciless.

The words played in her mind in unending, damning refrain, making mockery of her efforts. Still, she had to *try*. If she could divert the course of the future, even a little, perhaps the World could be made better. Mithra sought an empire, but the inundation of the world would leave him naught to rule at all. Atlantis need not be rent in twain. Mu not sundered. And maybe, if she could save them all, maybe then Pyrrha would not one day unleash the frozen nightmare Pandora had witnessed in an Era yet to come.

So she made for Babilim. In Pandora's time, the polis had been young and of little import compared to the great Neshian cities like Ugart and Nineveh. Time changes all things, and the mighty slide into obscurity whilst those who once knelt in the dust rise to grind down others beneath them. In her sojourns across time, Pandora had begun to see the whole of human edifice as a fragile, cyclical thing. How transitory it all must seem then to those few remaining Watchers—they who had beheld everything since the dawn of time.

Such were her dark musings when she at last beheld the sprawling city of Babilim. It sat upon a great plain, with both the land and the city sliced through by the knife of a swift river. Sandy brick walls enclosed both halves of the city, all of it surrounded by a moat that would make assaulting the imperial capital a nightmare. Beyond the defensive wall, she could make out an even taller bulwark segmenting the city. A gated bridge joined the two halves, and other gates followed the roads into Babilim. Men streamed in and out through those gates as if caught in the currents of history, swept along by events beyond their ken. The guards eyed Pandora with suspicion as she entered but did not bar her passage, perhaps judging a lone woman no threat to their grand empire.

Beyond the walls she beheld whitewashed colonnades and opulent palaces that might have shamed most aristoi of Atlantis. Wide streets and stairways—cut from the same stones—bustled with traffic, much of which seemed bent on arming and supplying the soldiers marshalling outside the city. The clatter of iron echoed as carts of spears and shields struggled down busy streets. Porters bore wrapt packets of goods. Wagons laden with barrels of—the scent told her—beer creaked under the weight of their cargo. In market stalls, vendors shouted in Neshian about amulets said to offer luck and protection from the perils of war.

As she moved, Pandora noted an intricate system of canals brought water to small fields and gardens within the city, creating a sense of greenery despite the urban sprawl. A third wall sectioned off the heart of the district she had entered, perhaps separating the local aristoi from the common people. There was chaos here, yes, but also an order in the construction and running of this city. A clever mind had planned these streets and plotted these defences.

Pandora paused to admire both the cunning and the beauty inherent here. In fact, she had to remind herself that the god-king here would, on some level, be responsible for the ending of the World. However majestic his kingdom, the whole of Gaia would suffer because of this place, unless she could change his course. Of course, given the heretofore unheard-of military buildup, she doubted anyone would turn back from war now. Once Men had invested in a direction, be it an investment of drachmae or of pride, they were loath to back down. They saw, then, only what they would lose of that investment, never what more they might still be forced to part with should they stay the course.

"They told me a Heliad woman had come here," a woman said behind her, and Pandora spun and beheld Artemis, a wary look upon her face. The Phoebid had a single finger resting upon the pommel of a knife at her belt. "Of all those I imagined might have come, I never guessed it would be you."

Nor had Pandora imagined finding an Olympian here, in the camp of the enemies of Olympus. For a moment, she stared stupidly at Artemis. In that time, the other woman released her knife, strode forward, and drew Pandora into a tentative embrace, uncertain how welcome it would prove.

"After Ilium, I did not know where you had gone. I looked for you, though. I guess ... I should have known you only ever seem to show up in the midst of great conflicts." She quirked a half smile and shook her head. "Goddess of Victory, indeed. Damn, but I'm glad you're here."

"You are?"

Artemis nodded. "Of course. You've come to help me bring down Zeus, have you not?"

Pandora reeled, trying to parse what must have happened—for Artemis—since she had last seen the woman after the Kalydonian Boar Hunt. "I never held much love for the tyrant of Olympus," she said, deciding it best to remain cautious. She had no idea what Artemis was saying about Ilium. Pandora had been outside the city when Herakles and the others had sacked it, and she had not seen Artemis there. Which meant, mostlike, she would encounter the woman in that city again in the future.

"Come, then," Artemis said. "We've much to discuss. I'm only recently back from the war in Elládos, and I cannot long linger here. Before I return, I should introduce you to the god-king. And, of course, to my betrothed."

Betrothed? And the war had already begun? Were the soldiers marshalling beyond the gates not the first wave of an army but rather reinforcements?

Artemis grabbed her hand and dragged a befuddled Pandora along behind her.

18

KIRKE

1357 Silver Age

$\mathscr{N}$estled within the same alley—or similar enough, for it was laden with crates and nets—in which she'd appeared in Argos, Kirke watched Zeus speaking to Io. The princess's guards had fallen back to allow the King of Olympus to converse with relative privacy, more was the pity, and though her friend remained out of earshot, Kirke imagined Zeus demanding she become his pallake.

Imagined, too, Io refusing with more civility than Kirke could have mustered, almost obsequious as she claimed Zeus honoured her.

In her mind, she saw herself shoving Zeus into the sea, allowing Io the time to escape back to her father's hall. Of course, Kirke would do no such thing, and anyway, were she to try, not even fleeing to her father would save Io from the Kroniad now.

Overhead, the sky darkened, clouds gathering at Zeus's growing ire. Kirke shut her eyes as the crackle of energies in the air set her hair on end.

A deafening roar of thunder and a flash of white so bright it seared her vision even through her eyelids. The sound swallowed up the screams Kirke knew must follow, and when next she looked, Zeus had hurled Io over the withers of his pegasus and taken flight.

Like a wretch, Kirke reached a lame, useless hand up toward them. "Io ..." As if she had not wrought this herself, all for the self-important excuse of ensuring she and her bloodline came into being.

With a hiss of self-loathing, she sank onto her arse. Her satchel wedged against her back. Glowering, she dug the hateful Box out and stared at the thing. Should she toss it into the sea? Eh. Soon, Men would name the archipelago here the Ionian Isles in Io's honour.

What had Kirke become? Could she blame the Fates for it?

Shuddering, she clutched the Box back to her breast. If she cast it aside now, she'd find herself stranded, what, some nine hundred years in the past? In fact, another Kirke, her younger self, already lived here now. Soon, she would learn of her friend's fate and begin an ill-conceived attempt to trail Io, though without success. Was she to spend the next centuries avoiding her prior self and preventing anyone else from knowing two Kirkes roamed the Thalassa world?

No, she had to try again, find a way to reach the time she'd left.

Well, she'd watched Prometheus work this and felt fair certain she could guess how to move *forward* in time now. So, if she ... The top cracked open and the World bent back into itself.

In silence, her niece sipped at her wine, her Kroniad companion shifting in obvious unease beside her. Did sitting in the manse of an exiled Nymph discomfit him, or was it rather being here in the presence of a sorceress?

"This is my husband, Jason," Medea said. "Husband-to-be, I mean, though our betrothal is fixed and our love a tale for the ages."

Hyperion's fiery arse, she was in earnest, wasn't she? Kirke ran her forefinger over her brow, sipped her wine, and chose not to answer Medea's comment. All too oft Kirke herself had thrown herself into even pale hopes for love and companionship. She'd tried, more than once, to make some connection, to find someone who could understand her and make her feel as though she at last had a place.

In Medea, she saw all that same desperate pain and longing. Maybe, once she had the girl alone, she'd warn her about the dangers of clinging to another with such fervour. Too many men—and women—had disappointed Kirke over her long life for her to believe such things still possible for her. Perhaps Medea's love story would fare better than Kirke's ever had.

THE COLUMN-SUPPORTED lounge looked into a familiar courtyard, a wide green that served as a gymnasium used not by men, as was always the case elsewhere, but by women clad in naught save linen loin cloths or sometimes naked completely. Some raced around the green while others caught one another in pankration holds, shifting and twisting, going for a lock.

This time, the distortion hadn't fazed her, and Kirke got her feet back under her in a heartbeat. This was the Muses College in Themiskyra. Long ago—assuming it had already happened—she had attended lectures here with Kalypso, maybe in this very lounge.

"Who are you?" a woman demanded behind her. The speaker, a young girl really, had lain on the floor, studying some scroll, hair tied up in a tight bun. No one Kirke recognised. "When did you get here?"

"I, uh … Well, yeah, I was visiting. I mean visiting because I came here before and I wanted to visit again and I, uh … Do you know where Themis is?"

The woman pointed off into the green, where, sure enough, the dark-haired Titan was among the pankration students, unclad as the others, body glistening in oil. And her immediate student was the raven-haired Heliad, Pandora, her too wearing naught save a linen tied around her nethers. Themis hurled her to the ground with comical ease, then stood, hands on hips, staring down at her pupil, while Kirke approached.

A person was meant to have a bitter response to someone who shoulder-threw her grandmother, Kirke imagined, but she found life had become so unruly, no answer suited.

All she could see was the slim chance Pandora could help her. "I would speak with you … Grandmother."

Staring at her from her prone position, Pandora gaped.

WHILE PANDORA CLEANED HERSELF, Kirke walked the green with Themis, glad to see her former mentor. She dared not reveal the truth about where she'd come from, but from a single askance look Themis had cast her way, Kirke had to wonder how much the foreign Oracle knew. She had heard Themis had been, in days long past, a compatriot of Prometheus whom he had brought to the Thalassa from far-off lands to the east. But Themis did not speak of her past, instead choosing to reminisce upon Kirke's time as a student here, in the school's early days.

Simpler days. Yeah, Kirke longed for them so fervently she caught herself considering, for a brief moment, using the Box to try to reach them. But such would never work. That time already had the past Kirke, and the woman she was now had no more place there than she did here. She needed to return to her own time.

Snow began to fall whilst they walked, and Kirke tried to ground herself in the easy pleasure of it. There was no snow upon Aiaíā. Sometimes, the simplest of things, once lost, mattered more than one would have ever imagined.

Pandora was not long away and returned cleansed and dressed, drawing Kirke to walk with her along the colonnades past the College. Snow painted the whole city white by now. Oh, Gaia, how many times she had revelled in fresh powder here with Kalypso. Nostalgia could have reduced her to tears if she let it. Instead, she focused only upon the present, leading Pandora down a path she and Kalypso had walked oh-so-many times before. She hopped up to catch the eave of the east dorms and pulled herself up to the roof.

From there, she jumped across the alley and onto the entablature of the bouleuterion. This space she followed until she could scale the roof and sit upon the flattened crown of the civic building.

She offered her grandmother a hand, which the other woman accepted, and Pandora soon settled down beside Kirke.

"I used to come up here with Kalypso and watch the stars," Kirke said, her words slow. It was hard to put her thoughts into order. Pandora's presence here was both shock and balm, and a fragile hope she could help Kirke escape her maddened circumstances. She could not bring herself to look into Pandora's Heliad eyes—so like Kirke's. "I'm afraid to ask how much you already know."

"I know you are Hekate's daughter by Helios. I know you are my granddaughter."

Now, Kirke did glance the other woman's way. "Yeah, I think we established that." From her satchel, she produced the Box and held it up before Pandora. Prometheus had claimed the woman had her own version of this.

Her grandmother gasped, then began tapping a finger against her lip. "You too?"

Kirke snorted. "Sums it up, I guess." She could no longer stop a single sob from escaping her. "I can't ... I can't ... do *this*. How the fuck did we get here?"

Pandora's hand landed on her shoulder, squeezed. "We've always been here."

Kirke scrubbed at her eyes and sniffled. "What does that even mean?"

"These tangled paths of past and future are predicated upon themselves. They created us, created everything we've ever loved. It's why we cannot simply cut through the threads, no matter how they wear at us, how raw they scrape our flesh as they slide by."

Oh, wonderful. "Yeah, Ananke cannot be denied, right? So, we just line up for the whipping, wipe off the blood, and wait for our turn to come round again."

"There's still hope."

"Oh, yeah?"

Pandora's smile, wan though it was, carried forward Kirke's fragile hope. "Always."

"Psh. I wanted to *hate* you. First, I thought maybe you were Nike's bastard child. Then, I realised you must be Nike and I couldn't fathom what Prometheus was doing with you. But I kept thinking, you made Father surrender to that despot. You and Artemis, you built this wretched future." This was all apt to cleave Kirke in half. She could not take much more. She'd come here, way back then, when Themis founded Themiskyra, and thought for a time to escape Zeus's blighted domain. "And here I go, betraying my own friends to uphold the same appalling timeline you crafted."

"I didn't craft it. I cannot escape it."

"Yeah, well, I have to blame someone, don't I? Blaming myself appeals about as much swimming in a latrine, which I try to avoid."

"You should."

Huh, yeah. Kirke found herself playing with the snow, letting it trail through her fingers. "I, uh ... I never *fit*, you know? Sometimes I talk too much, without hardly knowing what I'm saying, or what I'm supposed to say, so I just ramble." She traced patterns in the snow as if she might so chart the course of her life. "Yeah. Like, other people have this sense of people, where they can catch all the whispers that are supposed to lurk between words, and I feel like I need these things shouted at me. Only, if you shout at me, it feels like stones hurled against my skin. But all this time, I just thought, sure, I'm lonely because Mother barely acknowledged me for, maybe, the first five decades of my life. In the throes of melancholy, my heart blamed her, too. And now ... now, come to find out, even if I didn't *cause* that, I had a hand in some of the worst things she's ever done."

Saying naught, Pandora clutched her hand, putting a stop to Kirke's drawing.

Kirke sighed. "Our whole family is wrapt up in this tangled weave, I think. Blame. Right? We want someone to blame, but how can anyone be held culpable for events without beginning or end?"

"Time is an ouroboros."

A serpent eating its own tail? Kirke had heard of such creatures, though Thalia called them more metaphor than flesh. An eternal cycle ...

Oh, damn it. Too apt, too painful. A shiver ran through Kirke. "Urania said, uh ..." She sniffled. "She said in this lecture that well-being is a product of well-living. Our happiness predicated upon our goodness. I wanted to save Mankind, to save Nymphs, to save *women* from the fuck-awful rule of self-righteous men. I thought that was good, but I don't think I've ever been happy. Now, I think I might even be close to my own time, but if I go back to my island and they realise I ever left, I'm dead."

"What do you mean?"

"Yeah." Her despairing laugh maybe concealed her further sobs. Maybe. "Father exiled me to Aiaíā for brewing the Nectar. Among ... other things. And Zeus, he knows. I mean, I don't know how he found out, but he knows about it. So, if I defy my imprisonment, one of them would take it amiss. It means, if I wind up back even a year or two after I left, they'll know I was gone. I guess I could hide in the past, but isn't that kind of like denying myself a future? And if I live long enough to reach the point of my own exile, then what, hop back again?"

Her grandmother sighed and held silent a moment. "I believe the Box has a kind of memory to it. If we can backtrace your steps, we can find the moment you left and, with luck, send you back within a few days of then."

Kirke whirled on her. "You understand its workings."

"I'm starting to. Together, we can find a way to get you back to Aiaíā. If that's what you truly desire for yourself ... Granddaughter."

Kirke wriggled, but Pandora did not let go of her hand. As if to say, she would not abandon Kirke. With a trembling sigh, Kirke clapt her free hand over Pandora's and squeezed to reassure the both of them. Yeah, their plights were, perhaps, not dissimilar after all. "I can't do this anymore. Even now, I'm afraid to tell you all the things I've seen and done for fear of rupturing our family line. I cannot know which of those events have already unfolded for you, and which are still to come. If I ... If I were to ask, even ..."

"We can solve the Box together," Pandora promised.

They spent days working the intricacies of Pandora's Box. Until, at last, they could progress no further without Kirke trying the device.

It was the only choice left to her. She cast a final look at Pandora, and her grandmother nodded in solidarity.

She could do this.

Kirke activated the Box.

INTERLUDE: PROMETHEUS

Asura Era, Golden Age

A flock of hornbills had alighted in the boughs of the Tree of Life, their beaks the colour of flame as they watched the vibrant sunset. The tallest of its branches pierced the clouds and scraped the firmament, binding heaven and earth, even as it reached the height of the surrounding mountains. Its canopy shaded the better part of the valley.

As the gloaming set in, the last glint of sunlight highlighted the curve of Aditi where she lay beside Matarśivan. It limned her flesh in radiance and, though they had sated themselves already, he couldn't restrain himself from tracing a languid finger over her nipple.

They had claimed this glade beneath the Tree as their own, while the others explored the rest of the valley. Arundhati had set about constructing some shelter against the rains that so oft inundated the vale in the afternoon, no doubt conscripting Kratu as well, for he seemed tied to her by the same gossamer strands that bound

Matarśivan to Aditi. He could not guess where the other eight of them had wandered.

Perhaps they swam in the river or danced upon the mountainside or made love themselves in one of the innumerable glens. He'd even heard Kadru mention caves that ran beneath the valley, where she'd spied the great roots of the Tree boring into the Earth. Mitra thought the Tree had birthed the twelve of them, and thus dubbed it the Tree of Life. Whether he had the right of it or no, Matarśivan could not deny a pull back toward the towering Tree.

It was Aditi who had first climbed into the boughs and plucked the golden apples. One for each of them. When they had eaten the fruit, a rush had passed through them, as though they stood within a cataract of sheer life. Power had galvanised their flesh and, more, had demanded they sate that flesh, over and over. He could not say how many times he'd lain with Aditi that day, caught in throes of passion that had folded ever inward.

The gentle plod of feet upon wet grass had him rising to sit, followed by Aditi, who immediately pointed to Danu. The woman led others toward them.

Others not among the twelve of them.

Matarśivan leapt to his feet. While they debated if more people might live in the world beyond the valley, never had they seen evidence of it, and none of them wished to venture far from here. This was home, and it called to them. Or perhaps they called to each other. Either way, though some of them had made the trek down to the sea, they had found it impossible to stay long away and had returned to the valley with all possible haste.

But now Danu brought others here. Nine others he saw, five males and four females. As they drew nigh, Aditi clasped his hand, her fingers tightening in apprehension. He could see why. They had about them a presence, a *deepness* as if the World swelled in their wake.

Perhaps drawn by their arrival, others of Matarśivan's brethren began to stream back into the glade, gaping at the newcomers. Where had these beings come from? Were they Men at all?

Some of those Danu had brought watched the Tree with guarded gazes, their expressions unreadable. Among them, one strode forward and Matarśivan realised the rest of his people had fallen in behind himself and Aditi, as if he knew aught more of the situation. The rest save Danu.

"The gods reveal themselves to us at last."

"Gods?" Matarśivan asked.

"Our true creators," she said, her voice so thick with reverence Matarśivan felt the sudden urge to prostrate himself before the newcomers. Looking behind, he realised the others had done just that. "The Archons."

Gods ... At last, they would have knowledge bestowed upon them. In gratitude, he too slumped to his knees.

One of the deities stepped forward, his skin lambent. Light poured from effulgent eyes, coalesced around his hands, and even seemed to pulse faintly from his phallus. His voice, when he spoke, sounded hollow and echoing, emanating not merely from something so mundane as a throat but from the very World. These beings were deeper than Men indeed.

"You are chosen to become guardians and guides for nascent Mankind."

The power of his words hit before their import, and it took Matarśivan a heartbeat to parse them. "There are others?" he at last managed to ask.

"Few, but their numbers grow, born from the seeds of this Tree." And the gods would have Matarśivan and his ilk guide them. "The fruit has slowed your ageing to a crawl and made you different than your lesser kin. You will leave this island and see to their tutelage. But first, you shall bind yourselves to the gods, that we may use you as our emissaries." The radiant figure paused. "Your bondage comes in flesh-sworn oaths as our power flows into you."

As the lucent god spoke, he advanced upon them, his phallus growing erect in confirmation of his meaning. Aditi's fingers squeezed Matarśivan's the instant before the god grasped her cheek. All the gods had moved around them now, hands stroking skin. Not with the caress of lovers but with the seizing demands of insatiable need.

No conscious thought began it.

A roil of flesh, and they were all of them, Man and god, enmeshed in a sea of moans and penetration and cries of ecstasy, as if the very hillside pulsed with their lascivious cravings. Twisting, and groaning, and grinding.

He moved to enter one of the female deities—her rich skin tone deeper even than Aditi's own—but Latsatian was already between her legs. Before Matarśivan could turn away, find some other flesh, the goddess's skin shivered, and a second vulva opened between her shoulder blades. Dimly, he saw some of the gods had multiple phalluses now, too. Their forms moved to encompass and subsume those of Matarśivan and his kin.

Without any intent to do so, his hands were on the goddess's shoulders as he pumped his hips against her incipient sex.

Everything was one. The World itself throbbed and he was inside them and it inside him. Tendrils of power writhed about in his soul, scraping over it even as his hips pumped.

A vision of fathomless, roiling darkness bombarded him as though he witnessed a convulsing mass slithering behind the stars. It shredded his consciousness and left him gasping, tears welling in his eyes.

When the orgy finally abated, he lay on his back, body and soul aching as if some vital part of himself had been drawn out through his seed.

His hands trembled.

He felt enervated, torn in half.

From the look of the moon overhead, this bonding must have stretched on well past midnight.

A god settled upon his knees before Matarśivan, his skin black but lit by incandescent striations beneath his skin. Flames swirled inside his eyes. Between two fingers he clutched a metal band of rosy gold. Matarśivan did not resist as the god slipped the ring upon his finger.

"YOU SHALL BE OUR WATCHERS," the lambent god said. "The twelve of you, a Dodecadic Circle who will forever guide Mankind on the righteous path. You watch, you guide, and you bear our message."

Matarśivan and the others stood beneath the Tree of Life, gathered before their gods, spent and weak and leaning upon one another. At the deity's words, he felt the ring constrict his finger, a weight binding him.

"Swear it," the god said.

"We swear to serve as Watchers of the Dodecadic Circle," they said in unison, though Matarśivan could not say even how he knew the words. "We watch, we guide. We bear the message."

On speaking, a convulsion wracked his back muscles, doubling him over. As he caught sight of the others, he knew the same had befallen each of them. Several dropped to their knees, shuddering.

Something erupted from his back. Seeing it upon the others, he knew what it was. They had each sprouted great, birdlike wings, the unfamiliar appendages flapping and stretching in the night air.

When the sun rose, the gods vanished, leaving their Watchers behind.

PART III

Though the most well known, Nyx was never the only Primordial deity. Called also Elder Gods, these beings arose before time and, during the Golden Age—before Zeus declared the Olympians themselves gods— received the worship of Men. Even to this day, some cults remain, offering prayers to the ineffable powers that no doubt gave rise to the World.

— Polyhymnia, Analects of the Muses

19

HEKATE

216 Golden Age

Flooding Pneuma into Tolerance allowed Hekate to go days without rest if need be, though she would pay for such excesses with the exhaustion that must follow when her reserves became depleted. It would take time to replenish her Pneuma, but still, she pushed herself, all the trek from Olympus to Thebes, almost three days without pause for sleep or sustenance. When she came to streams, she drank but allowed herself no other indulgences of mortality, not whilst time moved against her.

Her only chance lay in reaching her younger self before Enodia inducted her into the Art in the first place. Maybe then, she could save her soul and avoid the cruel spirals of Fate.

Through rugged mountains and wooded hills she pressed on, heedless of the dark or the pattering of rain upon her himation. Even oblivion—should that result from her choices—must prove better than the agonies she had and would still endure if she failed.

Now twilight had given way to the deepening indigo of night, and, as Hekate descended the cliff, a cool mist wafted in from the sea, coating Thebes's harbour like a diaphanous blanket. A sense of dreamlike familiarity gripped her, and Hekate found, despite her intent to press forward, her footsteps slowed as she took in this place as it had looked millennia ago. Stricken by inexplicable instinct, she embraced the Sight and beheld, across the river, the processions of ghosts and phantoms, tickling her memory. The vestiges of their pain twisted their faces into masks of torment as they played out their last moments over and over. In her time, most if not all of the shades would have faded, consumed by the Roil. But here, now, they yet lamented their deaths ... inflicted when Kronos had attacked Thebes when Hekate was yet a babe.

The battle she had, for so long, thought her mother lost in.

This mist ... this procession ... this moment. Was it possible she had reached the genesis of her descent into the Dark? Breathless and trembling, she broke into a mad dash for the wood beyond the harbour.

Too late! Was she already too late?

The muted roar of the waterfall north of the polis was all she could hear of the Mortal Realm, drawing forth so many memories half forgotten. If she was right, if but moments remained to her ...

"Did Kronos do that to you?" she heard a young person ask, their voice carrying through the Ethereal currents of the Penumbra.

A whispering rasp answered and Hekate flooded what Pneuma she could spare into Alacrity, desperate to close in faster. Her teenage self had come upon the ghost of Okeanus, and that meant, this very night, she would meet Enodia. She had to get across the river, protect herself from Okeanus.

"I want to help, but don't know how. If you help me, though, I'll try. I want to find out what happened to my mother that day. Can you tell me if you saw—"

As Hekate raced forward, a feral scream—a shriek of defiance and pain—caught her off guard an instant before someone slammed shoulder-first into her chest. The impact blew the breath from her lungs, sending her sprawling to the ground amid roots and grasses.

"Hope is but the delusion with which we poison our souls," a woman said. "Like the apparition that is free will, we chase it because we cannot abide that our very thoughts arise not from our desires but from the chains of fate."

Sucking in a painful breath, Hekate pushed onto her arms and looked at her accoster. To find *herself*. Her left eye was missing, a gaping wound where it ought to have been. Yet no doubt could remain that the figure glaring at Hekate with some perverse mix of loathing and resignation was, in fact, another Hekate.

Each breath burnt against her abused lungs, and Hekate had not the Pneuma to spare to push down the pain. Instead, she gritted her teeth, rising slowly to stare at the woman who thought to attack her.

"So you would defy Ananke by killing your past self?" Hekate demanded.

"As close as you draw, still apprehension escapes you." Ice crystals formed shifting fractals along the other woman's hands. "If only we could have seen more, seen farther, maybe this could have been avoided. Now, it is the last choice—or illusion thereof—yet left to us."

As her future self swung her arm, shards of ice arising and launching in a hail of missiles, Hekate twisted to the side, a Potency-enhanced blow aimed at the other woman's ribs. Frozen projectiles surged overhead, but her foe caught her wrist, sending waves of cold jolting up Hekate's arm, drawing a gasp from her. Before she could react, before she could pull away, the future Hekate called forth a lance of ice over her fist and punched up at Hekate's jaw.

The weapon punched through her cheek, ruptured her sinuses, and out of Hekate's left eye. The pain that ravaged Hekate was not cold but burning. Searing. A mountain of torment that had her prone once more, a torrent of ichor gushing through the fingers Hekate pressed to her face in a vain attempt to hold back the vital fluid.

"Maybe, if I allow Mormo to feast upon your soul, this can be ended," the other Hekate said.

Sucked under by waves of torment, the mere mention of the wraith, the wretched thought Hekate turned toward the hateful creature, proved enough to let the ghost rise.

Its hissing rasp echoed in her mind as its tattered tendrils constricted around her heart, its shroud flitting before Hekate's eyes. Using her body, Mormo turned, looked at the other Hekate with such illimitable hunger as to defy all reason. The future Hekate's fingers had become skeletal claws, extensions of a wraith ready to savour its feast. The Mormo within Hekate lunged up faster, the wraith caring naught for her agony, even as its claws sank into her future self's gut.

Hekate felt as Mormo used her hand to tear out her attacker's viscera. The brutal, sadistic attack sent the future Hekate stumbling backward, onto her arse, and Mormo used the moment to surge forward.

"None of this matters," Hekate's attacker gurgled, ichor dribbling down her mouth. Her remaining eye had turned black, a miasma of wraith-possession swirling in her iris.

Mormo cackled with laughter for a bare instant before burying Hekate's face in the fallen woman's wound, teeth gnawing, churning through the stomach, biting up toward the heart. Slurping, sucking, it filled Hekate's mind with delicious nourishment. Mormo gorged itself on the tattered vestiges of an abraded soul housed within wretched Hekate.

Retribution long denied ... The wraith cackled.

The bloodlust that had seized the ghost faded to a trickle, a sudden silence in which Hekate abruptly found herself able to move once more. That, and again beset by the consuming throes of misery that ravaged her body, surpassed only by the woes of her soul.

Oblivion ... Mormo's voice sounded broken, distant.

And Hekate could imagine why. Though the wraith had sought after Hekate's soul, it had feasted not upon her, but upon the soul which the future Hekate had brought to the forefront. Mormo had devoured *its own* future soul.

Rising, Hekate stared at her future self, the woman gagging on ichor, bleeding from too many wounds for any amount of Pneuma to staunch. "I will not become you," Hekate swore.

"Pyrrha!" The voice of her father cut through all other sound, pierced the night like a hurled javelin and froze Hekate to her core.

Struck by such innominate horror she could not form a thought, much less a word, all she could do was look to Papa as he shoved her away from her dying future self.

"No!" Papa shrieked. "Not this! I cannot bear *this!*"

As Hekate rose, she saw him, ancient, perdurable Prometheus cradling the broken body in his arms, tears streaming from his stricken face. A single, gutted look he cast her way, more ravaged than Hekate had ever imagined her father could look.

Even as the other Hekate stilled. As she faded.

"I won't let this be the future," Hekate managed, her voice a whisper that no one could have heard over Papa's inconsolable sobs.

At last he laid the corpse down, the reverence in his movements so profound Hekate dare not speak. He seemed not to see the Hekate of now, though, instead burying his face in the dirt, wracked by fresh lachrymal convulsions. Then, without warning, he rose, growling, to his knees. Flames burst along his fist as he pounded it into the rock before him, again and again, giving in to bestial snarls.

Stone chipped and shattered under his relentless, fiery blows. The very earth was primed to give way beneath the weight of his grief and accompanying rage. A conflagration burst around him, igniting the nearby grasses, flash burning them away to dust in an instant.

"Atropos!" Papa bellowed. "Moirai! I will *destroy* you for this! I will burn down the whole of your abominable Tapestry for such an affront! If it takes me a thousand lifetimes, I swear—"

His words broke off as the future Hekate's corpse lurched upward, gagging, retching up a torrent in putrescence. Before Hekate's eyes, her future self's face mouldered, the half of it around her ruined eye sloughing off to reveal skull beneath. A fell, rubescent gleam arose into that empty socket, the glint of the damned. Of a revenant arisen, possessing its own corpse.

The future Hekate convulsed, clutching her ruined insides, as more pieces of her—the whole of her left side decomposing—pulled free.

Papa gaped at the abomination his daughter had—*would*— become, falling onto his arse and scrambling several steps backward.

"Pyrrha ... what have you *done*?" Now, he looked to her once more, seeming no more than so many shards of broken ostraka scattered across the floor, beyond all repair.

But Hekate could not spare him her attention, for the dead Hekate advanced upon her and knelt before her. This was it. Her future self would succeed in killing her at last and put an end to the circle of madness. Everything would be over.

Instead, the revenant snatched the clasp of Hekate's cloak and tore it free, then settled it around her shoulders. At last, she drew the hood up over her head, concealing her face, save for the golden glint of her good eye. The revenant waved a hand in front of her face, and a glamour settled in, creating the illusion of a second golden eye.

"I told you," the revenant said. "Hope is an illusion, and we would not want little Pyrrha to guess at the truth beneath Enodia's hood, would we?"

Her words shattered Hekate's perception. She did not remember falling, but she lay on her back, her remaining eye staring up at stars and scarce seeing them. The seams of the World shot through the firmament, visible in this moment of abject horror, even as they began to fray.

20

—————

PANDORA

399 Dark Age

Artemis had guided Pandora inside the sanctum on the near side of the river, to a castle-ziggurat she called Etemenanki, which doubled as both a temple to the sky gods and the palace of their living god-king. Verdant terraces along lesser—but still grandiose—ziggurats ringed Etemenanki as if the royals had tried to create their own dangling jungle in the midst of their city. Waterfalls pitched over sculpted facades into aqueducts, and down again and again in beauteous cascades that those on the far side of the wall would hear but never lay eyes upon. A riot of colour bloomed among the tropical flowers, the foliage attracting birds and other wildlife. A sense of familiarity settled on Pandora at the sight, and she feared she knew why.

In her vision induced by the Well of Mimir, Pandora had seen this place of wonder. Here she had looked into the wrath-limned visage of her friend and saw murder in those silver eyes as Artemis closed on her, daggers in hand. And it would happen, unless Pandora could at last find the means to slay the ouroboros that strangled them all.

But for the nonce, Artemis chattered amicably, treating her as a beloved companion long absent, and Pandora could scarce bear the thought of the rift that might open betwixt them. The Phoebid escorted Pandora through the gardens, introduced her to her half-sister Phaethusa who had come here with her sister to join Artemis after some unpleasantness with their common father—or so Artemis whispered behind her hand—and called for servants to bring wine and lamb stew. After having eaten only what she could catch in the desert with her bare hands or sometimes steal from those who seemed able to afford it, the food Artemis offered represented the finest of luxuries. Pandora savoured each bite as though it were spiced with Ambrosia itself, suppressing small shudders that threatened to run through her with every exquisite sip of the wine.

Phaethusa, for her part, drank but did not eat, forever watching Pandora as though she saw in her a dire threat but would never speak against her sister. Pandora could not blame her. As Nike, she had helped put Zeus on his accursed throne and she could never explain to the Heliad what perverse reasons had compelled her to that cause. Then again, Artemis had been chosen as one of Zeus's Olympians herself, so Pandora hoped Phaethusa would get over it.

Pandora's host must have seen the weight of prolonged fatigue and hardship and insisted that Pandora accompany her to the royal baths in the palace. These halls were among the most ornate Pandora had ever beheld. Gold trim capped walls adorned with frescoes depicting strange celestial courts Pandora knew little about. Beyond the corridors, vaulting ceilings soared up to painted domes, with handsome courtiers in silken robes mulling about those chambers. The marmoreal floor was polished until it gleamed, reflecting the light of countless braziers set amid the great halls and along the corridors. Many of the wider chambers centred around fire pits, not unlike those found in the buried city of Dark Faerie whence she'd emerged into this time.

Before she knew it, Artemis was guiding them into a steaming bath hall, decorated with cerulean tiles in a patterned mosaic. The steam rose from a great tub—a small pool, really—set within a raised platform. Servants, or perhaps slaves, appeared, took their clothes, and escorted them to the waters. The girl that claimed Pandora's stolen, travel-worn garments pulled an affronted face on looking at them, but Artemis waved her off. "New clothes for my dear friend."

"This must be ... disposed of." Before Pandora could make comment about the servant's scorn of her attire, another slave girl was guiding her into the bath. The heat soothed at once, quickening the Phoenix inside her soul, and Pandora allowed herself to sink neck-deep into the waters.

Artemis, on the other hand, eased herself in, allowing her body temperature to adjust a moment before settling in. The Phoebid quirked an eyebrow at Pandora but did not question why the heat had no effect on her. Perhaps, having seen her powers, she could guess well enough at Pandora's connection to flames.

Phaethusa tossed aside her clothes and slipped in more quickly than Artemis, though she winced. Perhaps she had sought to prove she could tolerate the heat as easily as Pandora, without realising the reason for Pandora's resistance.

"Nice to hear you are betrothed," Pandora said to Artemis, pointedly not looking to Phaethusa as the woman grimaced. Artemis had lost someone, Pandora knew. In grief and rage, she'd had a hand in the Boar that ravaged Kalydon. But so far as she could tell, many years had passed for Artemis since then, and more had transpired between herself and the Phoebid, in the interim. "I always ... wished happiness for you."

"And one could do worse than the son of the god-king," Phaethusa interjected.

Pandora struggled not to gape. "Is that ... how you came into the service of Mithra? Through his son?"

Artemis shot Phaethusa an exasperated look. "No, I met Marduk later. After the fall of Ilium, I was ... lost. I gave my loyalty to Mithra and he swore one day Olympus would pay for its myriad crimes."

And afterward Artemis bound herself to the god-king's flesh and blood. Pandora would need to tread with utmost care here. As his future daughter-in-law, Artemis would have Mithra's ear, yes, and perhaps could help sway him. But she would also be firmly lodged on his side, and the both of them wanted Zeus overthrown. In truth, so did Pandora, but she could not allow it at the cost of unleashing Tiamat to destroy the whole of Gaia.

"Tell me about this Marduk," Pandora said, glancing at Phaethusa, though she addressed the question to either woman.

"He commands the Immortals," Artemis said. "I would call him the finest of warriors. His mother was a great sorceress, though she died in childbirth, long back. Mithra will, of course, rule for all eternity, and he has groomed Marduk to serve forever as his right hand and general. Where Zeus would have regarded Ares in such a position with unabating suspicion, Marduk holds Mithra's complete trust."

"All good things," Pandora said. The heat and a full belly were so soothing she grew groggy. "But I meant to ask, rather, about *him*. In what, five thousand years or so, you never showed inclination towards marriage. Now I learn you are engaged. I doubt it is because the man is good with a sword."

Phaethusa snickered. "Maybe he is good with another type of sword."

Artemis splashed water at her sister without looking. "He's ... introspective. Others have called him brooding, but it is more they do not perceive the depth of his ever-churning soul. He has a fierce intellect that challenges me at every turn without ever crossing the line into arrogance."

"Oh, he's prideful enough," Phaethusa mumbled.

"On the battlefield, perhaps," Artemis begrudgingly admitted. "And not without some justification. I recall him knocking you upon your arse whenever you tested his mettle. But I meant to say he respects the intellects of others."

Phaethusa huffed again. "Of you, anyway."

"And his father?" Pandora asked.

Artemis sank deeper in the water, the movement so slight

Pandora wondered if the other woman realised she had done so. "I thought I had taken more than my fill of men claiming divinity." The words, almost a whisper, seemed a painful admission from her, her eyes creasing. "But Mithra ... When you hear his words and finally sound the depth of his meaning, only then will you begin to question if a man might, indeed, be also a deity." Maybe Artemis believed her words, at least in part, but Pandora felt something else, thrumming inside the woman, eager to burst forth.

"Or mayhap," Pandora said, "Mithra serves more as the means by which you might claim the vengeance you so desire against Zeus."

Artemis frowned but made no denials. "You seem exhausted, Nike. I can arrange chambers for you to rest before you meet the god-king."

Pandora swallowed. "Yes. Thank you." Rest sounded most needful before she confronted one who could induce such frightful ardour in so many. Pandora had borne witness to the rise of an Elder God. Even next to that, there remained something horrific about those with such charisma as to become living guideposts for the lives of others. It was not Truth that blinded but devotion itself that could burn away intellect and make slaves of the masses.

Hollow dread began to grow inside her core. A fear of what such a leader might be capable.

AFTER PANDORA HAD SLEPT and taken another light repast, Artemis took her once more to the gardens. "It's my favourite place in the city," the Titan said by way of answering the unasked question. "I wanted to introduce you to the god-king, but he sits now in council with his advisors. Though we sacked Kronion, our losses at Salamis and Thermopylae proved greater than anyone expected."

Pandora frowned. "Why did Mithra strike them in the first place?"

"Word came from Elládos that some of the poleis had refused the tribute of earth and water. It made war inevitable, but in truth, Zeus would mostlike have forced the issue no matter what the poleis said. Either way, Argos and Kronion refused to join the empire."

Pandora frowned at that, pausing to examine a jasmine bloom sprouting along the wall. "So asking for submission was but formality, as if to give justification for the slaughter that would invariably follow."

"No." Artemis leant against a tree and folded her arms over her chest. "Mithra has no intention of harming those who offered the tribute and thus became his vassals." But the half-truth was writ plain upon her face.

"Even if he doesn't harm them, Zeus will name them traitors and visit a worse still fate upon them. You have left the common people caught between two damnations with no means to save themselves."

The other woman huffed and shook her head. "There is a corruption riving through the core of Elládos, and it spawns from Olympus itself. I will see it burnt out."

Pandora tore the jasmine flower free of its branch and crushed it before letting it fall. "And those whose lives are cut short may take comfort in the world being made better for others."

Artemis winced, then abruptly jerked her head to one side. Pandora followed her gaze to see a Neshian Titan approaching. He was heavily muscled, his exposed arms bearing strange tattoos. His black hair was woven into braids, as was his thick beard. The man moved like a predator, yet the hint of a smile creased his lips as he looked upon them. Or, rather, upon Artemis, for his gaze lingered on Pandora for a heartbeat before settling on the other woman.

"Marduk," Artemis said, and Pandora could have sworn relief had crept into her voice at the reprieve from their debate. "This is my old friend, Nike."

Now Artemis's betrothed turned to Pandora, sweeping into an old-fashioned bow before her. "I would count any friend of yours as my friend." He looked back to Artemis. "Father commands you attend him in the war council. He would speak of the ships."

Artemis nodded. "I was giving Nike a tour of the palace. Perhaps you could fill in for me." So eager for an escape from

Pandora's judgments. And had Pandora, in fact, judged Artemis too harshly? She could not forget the vision she had beheld, the battle that might still come between them, and had to wonder if that knowledge had soured her and diminished her sympathy for her friend's plight. And too, she could understand Artemis's fervent need to see Zeus and his order at last thrown down. But Pandora had to think of the preservation of the whole of Gaia, now, and Artemis had no idea of the chaos Mithra's actions would soon unleash.

Marduk dropped into another bow. "It would be my pleasure. Lady Nike."

Pandora shot Artemis a look to say, "*we are not yet finished*," and from the grimace the other woman adopted, Artemis took her meaning well enough. Though Pandora did not much appreciate Artemis foisting her off on Marduk, perhaps Mithra's son would provide an opportunity to learn more about this Age and how Pandora might avert its end. So she fell in step beside her new escort, and the man guided her first through more of the gardens, saying little.

At first, she thought Marduk perhaps sullen, but as she watched him from the corner of her eye, she decided his posture was more reserved than brooding. Did he mistrust her as a stranger, or did a certain aloofness lie in his base nature? Those whose thoughts roamed into deep places others could not see oft held themselves apart from the masses who would never understand them.

"I've been away from these lands for many years," she said. "Perhaps you could tell me some of the history of your city. I had the chance to see the architecture and it sparked my curiosity."

Mithra cast her a quizzical look, then decided little harm would come in relating tales she could have learnt from any educated person in the city. "You must mean long away indeed, if you don't know of the rise of Babilim." He guided her down a staircase cut alongside the sandy-coloured wall, and they passed behind a small waterfall that misted her face. "My father's tutors drove home such lessons when I was a child, and though I've not much thought on them in a few centuries, I cannot have forgotten *everything*. Bahar's bamboo rod made certain of that!"

He chuckled, though not with much mirth. "The city is old, dating back to the late Silver Age. But the story of its rise to power starts much later. Some years before the war between Ilium and Elládos, King Kurus I ruled in Kissatu, which was, at the time, a tributary of great Nineveh. With Kurus's aid, King Ashur of Nineveh claimed Ugart for his empire, and Ashur rewarded Kurus with ample land and power. Two generations later, Ashur's descendants would regret it. A prophecy of the Magi claimed a Babilimian would seize control of the Nineveh dynasty.

"Kurus's grandson, Kurus II, was, as it happened, half-Babilimian. I shan't bore you with the details of the actions the king of Nineveh took against him, but it ended with Kurus II seizing control of Neshia, Babilim, and even Nysa and parts of Phoenikia across the sea. That is, he now held control of the whole of the Ninevehan Empire." He cast her a wary look. "Is this news to you?"

Pandora forced a wan smile. "You have no idea."

"Hmm." Marduk now led her back through into the palace's vestibule and paused to let her ogle some mosaics depicting battles up in the clouds.

Much though she might have liked to inquire about their meaning, Pandora didn't want to lose her chance to understand the situation. Somehow, in this Age, Babilim had become the most powerful empire in the world. A power so frightful, the Queens of Mu would turn to madness in fear of it. "You were telling me of the reign of Kurus II."

"Ah." Marduk raked his fingers over his beard, adopting the faraway look of one trying to recall things heard long ago. "Yes. Well, at this time, King Priam of Ilium had become powerful, and since Kurus now controlled Phoenikia, this was a matter of some concern." Priam ... that was the son of Laomedon whom Herakles had spared when the Argo landed at Ilium, meaning now she had at least some idea when all these events had unfolded. "Before Kurus could move against Priam, King Kroisus of Phoeba launched an invasion of Tyros, with help from some Elládosi poleis. Kurus defeated and captured the king, forcing him to swear fealty to Babilim. At which point Kroisus admitted Zeus had prompted the invasion in an effort to curb Babilim's growing influence without provoking direct war. You can imagine how well the king took this news, but he was not prepared to move against Elládos at that time. Whatever he might have intended, he died." Marduk hesitated. "I think he went into the desert for something and never came out. I don't recall.

"His son was Kabujiya, an Oracle. He reigned but a few years before his visions drove him to madness and his death. His brother, Smerdis, took the throne. Or so it seemed." Marduk pursed his lips. "My father was among those who discovered the Smerdis who sat the throne was an imposter, a Magus who had usurped the true Kurus dynasty. Together with the loyal Magi, he ousted the traitor. Father's allies then proclaimed him the true king of Babilim. Not long thereafter, my mother died giving birth to me. It was a dark time, full of bloodshed."

"As opposed to now," Pandora said, unable to help herself. "When Babilim's star rises, an empire built upon warm embraces and the dreams of baby unicorns."

Marduk looked not to her but to the mosaic that she'd been staring at whilst he spoke. "My father told me, before time really began, there was a war betwixt two races of gods. Elder Races, he called them, and they nigh destroyed this world. They fought again and again until, at last, one side won and cast the other off the face of Gaia. Maybe that was the dawn of history." The man shook his head. "We enter this world birthed in blood. Small wonder blood should define our existence and eventual escape from this life."

There was a depth to him that unnerved, though Pandora could not quite name what it was that so vexed her. Perhaps that air of intensity—of danger—was the very thing that had attracted Artemis to him. She wanted to be happy for her friend, but, even apart from the fear of Marduk's father, she found herself wary of this man.

She was saved from needing to offer him an answer by the reappearance of Artemis, who looked somewhat more haggard than when Pandora had last seen her. Still, there was a terrible eagerness in her eye now. She wanted this war. She needed it, and Pandora could see how things must turn sour between her and Artemis all too soon, no matter how much she might wish to deny it.

Artemis looked at her, eyes lit with fervour. "The god-king will see you now."

21

ARTEMIS

729 Bronze Age

Another summer had come and gone, bringing with it the new year, and though Artemis had seen sign of her prey, still she had not closed with Dionysus. Alone, she had crossed the wilds of Phlegra and risked chimeras and centaurs. She had passed on, into Kimmeria, land of the Amazons.

Dionysus was a god of the wood, and the Hylean Woods north of Themiskyra were known for their dense, trackless expanses forbidden to Man. If the god sought a place to lick his wounds and rebuild his forces, it would explain why his trail led east.

So Artemis came to Themiskyra. Her first sojourn here, long years back, after Themis had fled from Elládos and raised this polis, had been fraught with anxieties. To win the Titanomachy, Artemis had slain her grandfather, Koios, Themis's lover, and banished the Oracle from Elládos. She had only spared the woman because Prometheus begged it of her. Themis had come here, bitter and lonely. Perhaps it was that loneliness that enticed her to summon women from Phlegra and Phoenikia, offering them the chance to throw off the shackles of patriarchal oppression and build a society where they ruled.

Word of this supposed paradise had reached Artemis, and pensive and cautious, she had travelled the vast distances to reach Themis and see how the other Titan would receive her. Those initial tensions melted with time, however, and Themis made her welcome in exchange for Artemis helping train Themis's daughters in woodcraft.

"I took a mortal lover," Themis had explained then. "A kind man named Targitaus, and we had three daughters." So Artemis had agreed, teaching the girls all she could of the hunt, the bow, and the spear. It was the youngest and bravest of those girls, Kolaxa, who claimed the throne of Themiskyra, for Themis had little desire to rule aught anymore.

"Why did you never return to Dangun?" Artemis had asked Themis, once.

"Because all I left behind there is dust."

It had taken Artemis time to apprehend the depth of her meaning. So far from Atlantis and the flow of Ambrosia, Titans would not live as immortals. Indeed, only those in lands in and around the Thalassa could petition the ruler of Atlantis for their allotments. Themis's kin in the distant east would have perished millennia ago. She had come here with Prometheus and taken the Ambrosia, and for her, there was no going back. And Themiskyra, in Kimmeria, probably represented the furthest reaches Themis could settle in and still maintain her supply of the life-sustaining elixir.

Now, the dark-haired Oracle met Artemis at the gates of Themiskyra, no doubt having foreseen her coming. How far back did an Oracle's vision stretch? Had Themis learnt of this moment only this morn? A fortnight back? A century?

Themis opened her arms in welcome, and Artemis clasped them. Every time she returned here, some small part of her expected to face the woman's wrath for what Artemis had done during that ancient war. Each time, she envisaged scorn creasing Themis's brow, or perhaps hordes of archers aiming at her. But Themis had never, in all these centuries, brought up the past, and Artemis admired her capacity for forgiveness.

"I know why you've come," Themis said softly, her voice pitched so as not to carry even to any of the warriors up in the watchtowers above.

"Then you can tell me where to find him. Is he in the Hylean Woods?"

"Yes ... Sometimes, in the night, a handful of women go out without permission. They wander, as if compelled by some hypnogogic summons. And if no one spots them in time and restrains them, they go, off into the deep of that forest. We sent scouts in to bring them back, but they too have never returned. There is a presence that has settled in that wood, ancient and terrible. Hungry."

Artemis nodded. Dionysus was collecting a new flock of Maenads. The sheer ferocity of Herakles had caught the god off guard—it had taken her by surprise as well, she had to admit—but she did not think it was a mistake he was mostlike to repeat. If she allowed him the chance to rebuild his force, his next push into Elládos would prove far bloodier. "That presence shall feast soon enough upon my arrows."

Themis's frown only deepened at that. "Come and rest yourself first. I would speak with you. Perhaps a hot meal and some wine would not prove amiss?"

Artemis quirked a smile. Did Themis not already know the answer before posing the question?

Themis escorted Artemis to her modest palace beyond the College of the Muses. The architecture bore unusual flourishes Artemis took to be styles out of Dangun adapted to the local constructions, though in truth, she had never ventured east beyond the Kunlun Mountains and knew little of the lands there.

They sat at a low table and a serving girl brought them bowls of hot wine and steaming dishes of fish and cabbage. In the shadows of columns beyond, a child played, skipping and hopping. Artemis watched the toddler a moment before starting, her wine sloshing in its bowl. "That's a boy."

Amazons kept men around only for menial labour and as breeding stock. They sometimes exposed their male children. Those they kept remained tightly controlled, reared to serve their purposes. They did not roam palaces, playing and snickering.

Themis nodded once, watching Artemis over her bowl of wine. "*Your* boy?"

The Oracle sipped her bowl before setting it down. "No. The child belonged to Queen Hippolyta."

Artemis found words escaped her. Kolaxa's ancient laws forbade the rearing of royal males. If Hippolyta had borne a boy, the law demanded she sacrifice him to the wood before the sun set on the third day. Yet this boy looked to have at least two years behind him.

"The queen refused the sacrifice," Themis confirmed, in answer to Artemis's unspoken question. "Even knowing it would mean taking the boy's place."

Artemis winced. She had trained Hippolyta herself, years back, and remained fond of the woman. She hardly knew what to say to such news. Kolaxa's laws struck her as savage beyond need, more interested in vengeance upon males for the way women suffered around the world than in creating ideal lives for women here. Or perhaps Themis's daughter had feared, if a prince of Themiskyra lived, one day the city would have a king instead of a queen.

"Hippolyta named him Hippolytus, after herself, and she went willingly to her death."

"Is this why you brought me inside?" Artemis demanded. To hear about this tragedy?

"I thought you might like a warm meal and a comfortable bed before you go hunting for your prey." Themis helped herself to fish from the serving bowl. "But, yes, in part, I wanted you to meet the child."

"Why?"

"Because he is also of Elládosi royal blood. And despite Hippolyta's sacrifice, he cannot well stay here. As he grows to manhood, the others will begin to think him a threat. Sooner or later, he will meet with an accident. At best."

Artemis chewed her lip. She did not need this responsibility foisted upon her. She had come here to hunt down a dark god, not play nursemaid to a brat. "Which genos?"

"Kroniad. You know Prince Theseus of Athenai?"

"I know of him." A hated foe of Dionysus, and thus an unwitting ally in Artemis's own liberation. And this was his son. "How came he to have a son with the queen of Themiskyra?"

Themis shrugged. "A casual liaison along a riverbank, when the Elládosi sailed away from Kolchis."

"Mayhap she ought to have controlled her urges a smidge," Artemis mumbled under her breath.

"Life holds grief enough without denying the natural inclinations of hearts and bodies." Themis had clearly caught Artemis's words and was having none of it.

"I know, I know, dammit." Nor did she disagree. "Should I survive this hunt, I'll see the prince's son to him in Athenai. That's what you wish to hear, isn't it?"

"That." Themis nodded. "And more. I see growing disquiet in you, waiting to erupt. Should you kindle this wrath, I fear the ends it would lead to."

"I was wrong," Artemis said. It was the first time she had stated it aloud, brazen and plain as the morning sun. "I ought never to have supported Zeus." Despite how Hekate's pleas had swayed her. She shook her head, grimacing. The Ouranid League had its faults too, but a deeper rot had crept into the Olympian Order. That putrescence had seeped forth from the king and infected all of them, her included. "So, yes, I live with that regret. And even Dionysus spawns from Zeus. Had I not abandoned the hunt my father sent me on long ago, had I slain that degenerate when first he raised arms against Kronos, how many women would have been spared his hateful embraces? For so long, in the name of my pride, I tolerated the corruption that had seized our order. I refused to see truth because I could not stand the thought of admitting my error."

"Be that as it may, to turn against them now may come at an even higher cost. Who do you imagine shall suffer the most when Titans go to war?"

The answer was obvious. "Mankind." Artemis huffed and took up her food once more. "So you think," she said around a mouth of fish, "I ought to let the rot fester for fear of cutting loose healthy skin in the process of excising it."

"I think when you conceal people's lives behind the guise of a metaphor, you can forget the import of those lives. For the mother who buries her son, cut down in war, the healthy flesh cut away is not tissue but the sum of her World."

Artemis picked a tiny fishbone from between her teeth. "At the moment, I shall content myself with bringing justice upon Dionysus."

"You mean vengeance."

She shrugged. "I am no philosopher to idle upon the steps of the Muses College and debate semantics. I will see him dead for what he's done, Themis. That, and for what I know he will do, given a chance. I need not concern myself with details beyond that."

THE WOOD CLOSED in around Artemis, the trees watching her skulking progress in tracking its master. In the boughs, ravens stared with unblinking eyes. The eventide had settled in, and though Artemis counted upon the gathering gloom to conceal her, still it brought this forest closer to the Otherworld. Birds and beasts and plants were bent toward Dionysus's will, and he would know soon enough she was about.

Perhaps she had miscalculated in favouring stealth over a brute rush into the wood. It was too late to change the course now, though. If she withdrew, it would give her foe too much chance to set his defences against her, dooming her assault before it even began.

So onward she crept until, at last, she heard the telltale reverberations of the drums. The Maenads would welcome the night with wild dancing, unbridled music, and the offering of blood to their hungry god. Perhaps, as it spilt into the greedy earth, Dionysus absorbed some portion of the Pneuma that would seep into the dirt. Or perhaps violence and pain aroused him. She had never been certain.

Either way, she followed the drumbeats to a glade that, as expected, stank of terror and blood. Two dozen masked, naked women danced about an altar upon which they had slit the throat of a black bear. The sight of the dead ursine set the spirit inside Artemis growling. Dionysus had, mostlike, chosen the bear to spite Artemis, perhaps having compelled the innocent creature to lie down, meek and accepting of its own murder.

Well, if he wanted a bear ...

Artemis laid down her bow and stripped out of her khiton. The animal rose in her. Her back arched and she dropped to all fours, unable to suppress the feral growl that built in her throat. Those Maenads closest to her looked in her direction. Perhaps they saw as her face elongated to a snout or as dark, matted fur sprang from her hide. Perhaps, somewhere behind the befuddling haze of Bacchic wine that clouded their minds, they felt a twinge of terror.

With great bounds, Artemis closed the distance to the circle and waded into their midst. Her powerful paws swiped aside one Maenad after another, sending the women sprawling. She tried to avoid using her claws, but the animal rage was on her, and the bear had a will of its own. Some of the fallen might not rise again.

A shrieking woman rushed her with a knife.

Artemis roared, the sound so deep, so powerful, it drove even the madness-seized Maenad to a staggering halt. Artemis rammed shoulder-first into the stunned woman, sending her hurtling through the air.

She spun, saw another masked woman staring at her, hand upon the gigantic bulge of her belly. Another roar had the woman falling back several steps. Since she could not well bowl over a woman carrying a babe, Artemis turned again, finding more Maenads to lay out.

One attacked with a spear. Bestial instinct seized Artemis then, and that hapless woman felt the fullness of her fury as ursine claws cleft great rents in her torso.

"So ..." Dionysus drawled, emerging from the trees, naked as ever and bearing those whirling pigments. His mask was replaced—or healed?—the damage Herakles had inflicted gone. "My champion returns."

Drawing her Pneumatikoi, Artemis leapt. Lightness meant her mass hurtled faster and farther, her leap carrying her thirty feet across the clearing to collide with Dionysus. The pair of them went down in a tumbling heap, Artemis snapping and clawing, intent on ripping to shreds the god who had enslaved her.

Her claws found purchase upon his abdomen and tore. The reek of loosed bowels struck her snout. Her jaws closed upon his throat. Flesh and bone crunched beneath her teeth. Hot ichor spilt down her throat. She jerked her head back and ripped away his windpipe, then spit the grisly mess aside.

Whilst her head was turned, Dionysus punched a fist inside her chest. His other hand seized her head and she looked into the gaping ruination of his neck. Cataracts of golden blood tumbled from the mess, behind which she could see bits of his shredded spine. How the fuck was he yet standing? His breaths wheezed through a tattered neck and his guts dangled from the holes in his belly.

His hand closed upon her heart and squeezed, latched onto something deep inside her. Deeper than flesh. Some Etheric piece of her very soul. Absolute terror gripped her. The foe she had hunted was not mere Titan but something Primordial. Her fury seemed only to have incensed its own.

How, how had he not fallen with the wounds she had inflicted?

Dionysus ripped his hand from her chest and something was torn from her. Artemis collapsed to the ground, a sharp pain in her chest. Her heart had stopped. The realisation slammed into her an instant before a second epiphany. She lay naked, in human form.

Within the god's hand, bent around his arms in Etheric, shifting colours, he held the bear spirit that had for so long been fused to her very soul. Dionysus raised that hand to his face and, with a macabre, wet sucking sound, drew the soul inside himself. Those colours—that intangible piece of *her*—vanished into the abomination looming over her.

Lurching shadows crept in upon her vision. She could not draw breath. Her blood no longer pumped.

All at once, Dionysus collapsed into a heap. His desiccated flesh turned to bubbling, reeking goo, popping like pustules.

Agony ripped through Artemis's core as her heart beat again.

Behind her, the pregnant woman shrieked and collapsed. Her screams rent the night, inhuman in their agony and terror. Artemis had witnessed many births in her time, but never had she heard a woman cry out in the throes of such unearthly horror.

Though she could not breathe herself, though crushing oceans of pain had settled upon her chest, she crawled toward the woman. That mask had fallen away when the woman pitched over.

Ariadne ...

Aura.

An infant hand reached from the woman's nethers, flailing. It braced against Ariadne's thigh. Artemis's vision was still hazed. Surely, her delirium must be making her see apparitions. Surely, such madness could not exist. But that hand clung to Ariadne and an infant yanked itself free and splattered upon the ground amid clumps of blood and afterbirth.

The babe shook itself, then rose and *stood*. It swayed upon unsteady legs a moment before making abortive strides to where Artemis lay upon the ground, clutching her chest and begging to Thoth to make this but a nightmare.

But the infant walked to her, dragging its placenta behind it. "Behold the living and dying God ..." it said.

Unable to bear what unfolded, Artemis welcomed the darkness rising to claim her.

22

———

HERAKLES

729 Bronze Age

*A*s Herakles crested Evenor Mountain, a valley unfolded before him in verdant panoply. An explosion of vegetation arose here, at the heart of which lay the colossal Tree of Life, tall as a mountain itself. The branches and leaves of that Tree alone created a canopy overshadowing the valley.

He supposed he no longer need wonder which path to take from here. Now the question was, once he reached that far-off tree, how would he manage to climb such a behemoth? In truth, he could scarce imagine pulling off such a feat. Would he find protrusions in the bark that might allow him to scale it like a rugged cliff face? Certainly none of the branches drooped low enough for him to snare them and climb the tree as he would a lesser specimen.

Working his jaw at the thought, he descended into the valley. The lesser trees soon obscured his view of the great one, but he felt fair certain his course remained true. Before long, the sound of running water came to him, and he followed it to a river snaking through the valley's centre. Through the break in the forest the river provided, he could once more catch glimpses of his destination. It looked like the waters might well run close enough to the Tree he could follow the river upstream to reach it.

He had not gone far when an aberrant sense set his skin atingle, as if the air convulsed and thrummed with the presence of something vast and ancient stirring. Bards' tales of this place crept back in upon him, reminding him of dangers he had not given thought to since his encounter with Kyknus. Stories said a timeless drakon watched over the Tree, warding against all thieves. According to one legend, the creature had clawed its way up from the bowels of Gaia long before Ouranos had banished Nyx. Before even time was time, already the drakon had lurked in the depths of the wild.

Or perhaps Herakles's mind played tricks upon him now as he violated the most sacrosanct of Olympian laws. He trespassed where no mortal was ever allowed to walk, and for such a transgression, even his father would make a bitter example of him. Were he caught, Men would whisper of his fate for centuries in warning.

The further in he pushed, the heavier the presence around him grew until he could no longer attribute it to nerves. A nameless dread coiled about his chest. He plodded now into spaces far beyond the ken of Man and could not help but feel he had more to lose here than mere life and limb. Would this entity feast not only upon his flesh but upon his very soul, should it corner him?

A hundred probing, burrowing tendrils seemed to brush against his awareness, digging into his mind and promising agonies unlike aught he had known before. It grew harder and harder to press onward, as if coils bound his limbs and every step—every breath—required an exertion of strength and will.

At a bend in the river, a jutting rock arose, oddly carved, in the aspect of a bird. A Kroniad woman leant against it, watching him with a wary gaze. On her hip, she bore a xiphos, but she made no move to reach for the blade. Instead, she heaved an affected sigh at his approach and shook her head. "You are not meant to be here, little brother."

Brother? So this was Zeus's daughter Hebe, the guardian of the apples from which Ambrosia was brewed. He had heard she alone knew the secret recipe for its creation, a mystery guarded even more jealously than the Ambrosia itself.

"Gaia's breadth, do we *have* to do this?" his Olympian half-sister moaned when he failed to answer, sounding more akin to a teenager irate with her irredeemably dense parents than a millennia-old goddess. "Look, it knows you're here. So get you gone from here and you won't have to, you know ..." She flapped a hand around to indicate whatever awful fate would befall him should he disobey.

Herakles allowed himself a moment to gather his wits. The cyclopean will trying to burrow into his mind remained. It was a profane violation, enough to choke a man and leave him gasping for reprieve. The last thing he needed in the midst of such a struggle was to deal with Hebe, too. If he stole an apple now, she'd report him to their father. "Given the choice," he grated, "I'd take your advice in a heartbeat, Sister." If she was to refer to him by their kinship, perhaps he could use that, too. Perhaps he could avoid making an enemy of her. "But in truth, I've sworn an oath upon the souls of my dead children. To appease their suffering, I am forced to submit myself to the onerous will of a petty king and fulfil his vain demands."

"Ugh ... Dead children." Hebe managed to shake both her head and her eyes at the same time. "Fuck. What am I to say to that, then, huh?" She pointed an accusing finger at his chest. "If I refuse to sympathise, I'm just a queen bitch of this island, right? A foul blow, invoking that, Brother." She clucked her tongue. "Ill done."

Herakles glowered at the Titan in indignation. "Forgive me for the imposition of having suffered an unspeakable tragedy. I'm sure my anguish must represent quite the inconvenience upon you."

"Psh. Yeah, at least you've the wit to realise that much."

So self-absorbed she could not fathom the irony of his words. Herakles found himself nigh tempted to roll his own eyes at Hebe. Why had their father given her this task? Did he trust her because she lacked either the ambition or the inertia to betray him?

He folded his arms over his chest. "You need not do aught, Sister. Pretend you never saw me."

"Fine." She groaned more than spoke the word. "But I cannot call off Ladon. You can try to sneak past it, but the Old One sees with many eyes." A shrug. "If you can get past the drakon, I won't stop you from claiming a single apple."

"Or speak of my presence here."

She waved it away as if reporting him would have represented more trouble than it was worth. He supposed he ought to be grateful for her indolence.

Unshouldering his bow, he looked across the bank of the river. In the shadows there, behind the trunks of thick trees, he saw something massive and squamous slithering. The crunch of underbrush came to him even over the burble of the river.

He doubted he would do any sneaking past such a creature. Well, it would not grow easier if he lost the daylight. With cautious steps, Herakles plodded into the river, slowly wading across. It must have poured down from a mountain, for despite the heat of Atlantis, the waters had an icy bite. At its greatest depth, the river reached almost to his shoulders but soon receded as he drew nigh to the opposite bank.

Rustling filtered through the treetops when he reached the shore, and Herakles peered up, gazing into the incandescent eyes of a saurian head as large as his torso. Its sinuous neck arced down above the leaves, watching him with malevolence unlike aught Man saw upon the face of Gaia. Its horn reminded him of tales of Hy-Brasilian rhinoceroses. Its fangs dripped acidic venom. Its scales glistened with black virescence.

Such dire intellect as now pressed upon him Herakles had felt only once before, in the very pits of Tartarus. The serpent whose gaze bombarded his soul had the aspect of foulness beyond reckoning, and its assault upon his senses turned now from probing intrusions to a full attack.

Under the weight of its regard, he could scarce move. Every step forward required a battle of will. Every motion became an uphill charge. Teeth gritted, Herakles nocked a black-fletched arrow to his bow. The Old One watched him with disdain as if daring him to keep his feet. Cyclopean will pressed upon his shoulders and demanded he take his knees before the calamitous enormity whose ire he had drawn. A thousand pleas for mercy would not prove enough to sway this demonic abomination, and yet it demanded he plead, nonetheless.

Arms trembling, Herakles raised his bow instead. Confronted with absolute malice, the only viable answer came through responding in kind. Incredulous, as if unable to believe any mortal could have such temerity as to raise arms against it, Ladon peered at him, unmoving and unblinking.

"Uhh ... little brother ..." Hebe whined from across the river. "Stealth has failed you ..."

Herakles loosed, his poison-laced arrow streaking through the late-afternoon air. Such force had he instilled in his bow, the missile punched even through draconic scales and landed with a crunching sound. Ladon recoiled, shaking its head one way or the next. Would the hydra venom fell even another drakon?

All at once, Ladon convulsed, its head cutting a collapsing arc through the wood. It pitched through the treetops, shattering branches as it plummeted sideways, the sound of its fall a series of crashes. The corpse slapped down on the shore not far from where Herakles stood. An earthy reek of snakes and decay wafted off the carcass.

Strange. He had heard tales Ladon had many heads, like the hydra, and he had thought ...

More rustling in the trees drew his gaze skyward. Another head peered at him now. Another, and another. Dozens upon dozens of serpents, all glaring at him from different angles. They enclosed him, some watching from left or right or behind, some from above. He could not see where flesh joined or if Ladon was, in fact, a nest of serpents rather than any singular entity.

Either way, a hundred scathing, colossal minds now scraped across his mind. They glared at him with terrible wrath for what he had done. Any time in which he might have begged for mercy had now passed.

"Shit." It seemed the only appropriate thing to say. He let the bow slip from his fingers, avoiding sudden moves as he withdrew his shield from his back and then eased his sword from its sheath.

Turning about, keeping the hundred serpents in view, Herakles flooded Pneuma into his Pneumatikoi, for he would need them all. What matter if he destroyed himself by using too much of his own life energy, considering the consequence of failure? Potency for strength and Alacrity for speed. Steadfastness to blunt the inevitable impacts he would suffer.

A chorus of voices murmured in the distant mists of his mind. The voices offered half-understood advice. Warnings and instincts, as if any Man might fight against an army of drakons.

There is an army within us …

Herakles did not know the voice that rose to prominence from amid the chorus. Surely it was but one more sign of the madness within. Surely. And yet … if he was to be an army, then he and Ladon would have not an execution, but a *war*.

As if in response to the thought, a black-scaled serpent lunged at him, lightning fast, smashing the forest as it moved. Reflexes enhanced by Alacrity, Herakles dodged to the side and rammed his xiphos through its reeking scales. He gripped the blade with both hands as it passed, the serpent's momentum shooting him through the wood. Another head surged at him, even stuck as he was on one of its brethren. Herakles kicked off the hide and passed under the new threat, whose jaws closed upon the neck Herakles had ridden. His xiphos tore a six-feet-long gouge from the throat of his newest attacker.

They surged at him, a mass of slithering serpents crawling atop one another, ever closing in with intent to chomp him in half. He ran up the length of one serpent, hacking and slashing, Potency-infused leaps carrying him from perch to perch. His blade darted faster than he'd ever moved, faster than he'd ever believed possible. Instincts beyond all ken settled upon his muscles, turning them toward manoeuvres he did not know and could not have imagined.

A haze of red clouded his vision.

A kick off scaled hide, and he flipped in the air to land upside down beneath another head, ramming his adamantine xiphos hilt deep into saurian guts. Mounds of squamous muscle slammed him, over and over, tossing him about the battlefield. More than once, he found himself knocked into the treetops, only to have that chorus of voices—instincts—send him leaping away before he even knew another head closed in upon him.

As the war raged, he apprehended the dread shape of the drakon. Its heads were joined to a colossal serpent's body wrapt around the base of the Tree of Life, entangled with and emerging from its roots.

When he had slain a dozen heads—and was himself bleeding from as many wounds, certain venom now coursed through his veins —he managed to carry the fight to the base of that Tree. Those roots burst from the ground in a nest-like maze. Ladon's sinuous bulk slithered through the extruded roots, but it could not with ease reach many of its heads into the confined spaces. Herakles dove within the maze, heedless of the fibrous tendrils dangling from the roots, and scrambled away from the edge.

Despite his Pneumatikoi, he gasped for breath. His vision blurred from fatigue and poison. Woozy, he closed in upon the slithering serpent's trunk. With a bellow, he drove his blade into its bulk, then jerked it sideways, opening a gouge that split scales and sinew and sent cataracts of dark blood spilling down amid the roots. The serpent recoiled, trying to slither away, but its movements only served to further skin its tail.

Herakles stood ankle-deep in mud formed from loam and acidic blood, trying to ignore the stench and the agony of his burning feet. He could afford but little Pneuma for Tolerance. Just enough to keep from collapsing from the pain.

A saurian head burst through the cage of roots. Herakles spun, but not fast enough. Fangs sank into his thigh, punching even through his reinforced skin. The serpent reared, yanking Herakles's legs out from under him. He was jerked through the roots, splintering wood.

A blur of concussions.

Battered body. Whirling skyward. Sword gone. He looked down. That maw held him above the lower trees, amid the branches of the great Tree. With a flick of its neck, it tossed him up, gaping maw intent to catch him as he fell. Herakles twisted, caught the edge of a nostril with his shield arm. With the other, he swung around, grabbed the flesh, and, roaring, ripped the serpent's nasal passage in twain.

The creature convulsed in agony and Herakles's blood-soaked fingers slipped, sending him free-falling, limbs careening. He snared a branch of the Tree as he fell, the impact jarring even his Pneuma-reinforced shoulders.

Another black head surged forth, leaving him no choice save to release his grip and plummet further. As he fell, he infused as much Pneuma into Steadfastness as he could. With an *oof*, he landed in a crouch, cracking the dirt with his momentum.

Gasping, limbs trembling, he tried to rise. His knees refused to obey, and he slumped back into the loam.

Even indomitable Vritra was cast down, the chorus in his head sang. A shadow of an inchoate memory assailed, befuddling and damning in its lack of substance, as though he ought to know it. As though he had forgotten some profound impression upon his soul and was made lesser for it.

Again, he managed his feet. Barely.

Ladon's remaining heads flailed, grown sluggish from blood loss, and yet driven by pain toward greater depths of malice than even before. A head surged in. Herakles swept his shield at it. The adamantine disc collided with fangs, shattering enamel. The head lurched back in agony an instant before a second head came chomping at him. A swaying, drunken sidestep carried him free of the maw. The serpent's sinews slapped him even as his shield smacked into the side of its head. The impact sent him staggering backward, uncertain what effect he'd had upon the monster.

A septic reek emanated from the adjacent root cage. Ladon's thrashing had ruptured its bowels which now spilt from the enormous gouge he'd ripped along the length of its middle. Its every attempt to close with him was literally tearing it apart.

Another lunging head. Another sweep of his shield, this one wild and awkward. A gong-like clang as he struck the hardened scales. Not waiting to see the result, Herakles half ran, half fell toward the roots. He ducked beneath the arch of one, stumbled against another, and turned in time to raise his shield against another snapping maw.

His lungs burnt. His veins were aflame with the serpent's venom. Blood streamed from the wounds in his legs, and he had no Pneuma to spare to begin thinking of healing. Death would come for him now.

Ladon would follow him to the grave, though. Not even the ancient drakon could survive such wounds as Herakles had inflicted upon it.

Another painful breath.

Another.

Herakles slumped to his knees. He had no more in him.

A series of crashes roared through the jungle, sending successive tremors shaking the whole valley. Trees crunched. Debris flew in all directions. The great, timeless drakon had fallen.

The Old One, at last, perished.

Herakles wheezed a final, agonised breath. Empty, he pitched over sideways and let the dark claim him.

GOSSAMER STRANDS CAUGHT distant torchlight and reflected in an otherwise darkened cavern. He was on his knees, loam squelching beneath them. Somewhere out of sight, water dripped, splashing down on a pond or well. With his gaze he traced the line of the spiderwebs as they crisscrossed the cavern, spanning the space betwixt stalactites.

No, not stalactites—those were fibrous strands of root protruding from the ceiling in a dangling maze. Along one of the strands, against a root, a shrouded figure crouched, still as a corpse. For a moment, he thought the body suspended by the web.

Then a woman's voice issued from that otherwise motionless form. "The blackened blood comes round again."

"An end crafted by thine own hands," a second voice called, echoing from further dark recesses above him. This woman sounded ancient, her words raspy and strained. "The beast slain gives rise to more of the same."

"A world sows what it has reaped," said a third woman, this one younger. Herakles turned his gaze and spied her behind him, perched upon one of those shimmering strands that ought not to have borne her weight.

"The circle goes round and round," the first woman said. "The choice made upon the first turning must ever revolve."

"The Wheel turns," the old woman added.

"Fire must drive back dark," the youngest said.

Herakles swallowed. "I don't understand."

"Time comes for that," the young one said. "Always, time comes round."

23

ATHENE

729 Bronze Age

*T*he sense of palpable urgency that had driven Athene's steps—driving her to break into occasional trotting—across Atlantis turned tenfold upon the macabre, ruined corpse of Ladon. The impossibility of what her son had done slapped her in the face and she raced forward, dodging around trees and vaulting the draconic necks where they lay sprawled across the paths.

Athene did not know by what means Hebe controlled Ladon. Whatever the method, it seemed tied to the secret recipe of the Ambrosia. A forbidden knowledge possessed once by Atlas, then by his daughters, and at last, gained by Father and given to his elder daughter. Sometimes, she thought Father having gained that secret was the real reason he executed the Pleiades all those years ago.

"Fuuuck," a woman groaned, and Athene caught sight of Hebe, as if the thought of her had summoned her sister. The woman walked the length of one great fallen neck of the serpent, studying its hideous wounds. "I mean, come *on*, little brother. How am I to explain this shit? 'What's that, Papa? That Old One drakon who guarded the Tree since before the arse-end of time? Uh, yeah, it tripped and fell. And died and stuff.' Pshaw. You can't go around slaying monsters, all right. Sometimes they *belong* to people." Hebe kept shaking her head, apparently oblivious to Athene's presence. "Well, somebody has to take the blame for this steaming donkey turd. And somebody shan't be me."

Athene surged forward, seized her sister by the bicep, and spun her around. Her vision had made plain that her son lay dying and Athene could not abide it. "Where is Herakles?" she shrieked at the vexing woman. Athene had never known Hebe well, had never cared to, considering her a witless simpleton more given to preening before a mirror than bothering with politics or power. Athene had not missed the woman when Father had sent her to oversee Atlantis after the fall of the Pleiades.

"Heh." Hebe shrugged free of Athene's grasp. "Mostlike marinating in his own bodily fluids, if even one of Ladon's many maws pierced his flesh. Which, you know, one must have. Odds, and such. Ladon had a great many—"

Athene barely restrained the urge to throttle the woman. "Where is my *son*?"

"Uh ... pretty sure he can't be your brother and your son. I mean, I guess he could, but that's icky and I'd need to scrub my brain on a washboard should I dwell upon it. So, um ..."

"My *adopted* son, you fatuous buffoon." Now Athene did grab the woman and shove her against the husk of Ladon's neck. In case her point was not well made, she eased forth her xiphos and placed it against Hebe's throat.

She had spent the last months hunting both Dionysus and Ares and found precious little success in either. Nor was she even certain she had wanted success. Whichever of them she found, it could well mean a battle, to the death, with one of her brothers. And when at last she had, in desperation to save Father, turned to the Sight, she had instead seen her son dying upon Atlantis. So what did it matter, really, if she had to turn upon a sister as well?

No matter which path she took, her family was destined to be rent asunder, and she could not save them all. But if she had to choose between a sister and a son, she knew what choice she would make.

"You're going to take me to my son. You're going to give me an extra draught of Ambrosia to treat him with. And you are never going to mention a word of this to anyone, least of all Father. I will have your oath, sworn upon the dark waters of the River Styx, Hebe. Or else I shall have your life."

"Uh ... You know, I met Styx, whilst she lived, and she was—"

"I don't care!" Herakles could be dead already. He could be bleeding out or, as Hebe had surmised, succumbing to draconic venom. Every moment wasted increased the chance she would lose him. Athene could not bear that loss. Not that. "Swear it now."

"Y-yeah, all right. I swear. I swear on the River Styx I shan't speak of this. All, right." As Athene withdrew her blade, Hebe rubbed her neck. "Shit. Coulda asked nice or something."

As if the woman would have agreed to share Ambrosia with a mortal, much less keep quiet about it. "Take me. *Now*."

HERAKLES'S BODY had grown chill beneath the roots of the great Tree, half-submerged in muddy loam. Only the faintest of breath fell upon her finger as Athene placed it beneath his nose. "Come on," she whispered, tilting his head back and pouring the Ambrosia down his throat.

Father would rage against them—her, Hebe, and Herakles too—for this crime. But Athene had given Herakles a taste of Ambrosia once before to fortify his Pneuma and might have done so again, had she thought she could get away with it. He was her boy. Naught would ever bring Pandion back. She would not lose another son. Oh, she knew one day time would catch him, wrap its necrotic fingers about his throat, and slow his steps. It would bring the ache to his bones, the stiffness to the joints that plagued mortals as their time upon Gaia waned. But she had always refused to dwell upon that, had oft even considered if she could divide her own allotment of Ambrosia with him. Doing so would have meant she would age, albeit slowly, as would he.

It seemed better than watching him grow old whilst she endured.

But how to explain her crime—all Men knew it the most sacred law of Olympus that no Man should taste Ambrosia—to him? Such had long given her pause. A single draught he believed a gift from their common father. More than that, and he would have grown suspicious.

"Come on," she repeated. "Drink."

Amber liquid trickled into his mouth, and he, blessedly, sputtered on it. A rasping breath moved his chest, Gaia be praised. Then she eased more of the life-saving tonic over his tongue. She had heard that a draught of Ambrosia could heal almost any wound or ailment.

There was speculation made in the Muses College—blasphemous in the eyes of Olympus, but she had heard it in her wanderings—that if an apple was left to ripen long enough, one might derive from it more lasting benefits than even those of Ambrosia. Fermenting the apples into the tonic of immortality took time and a secret recipe, but from what she understood, a single apple could thus be made to sustain many Titans. Were they to halt the process and begin letting individuals eat the apples—assuming one could wait for this theoretical supreme ripening—hundreds of Titans across the Thalassa would be left without their age-aborting draughts.

From all she had heard, letting Herakles eat one now would have proved less potent than a draught of Ambrosia. Elsewise, she'd have climbed the damn Tree and seized an apple to feed her son.

With agonising slowness, his breathing eased, at last falling into something resembling regularity. Tears of relief burst from Athene and she laid her head upon her boy's chest. "You are my World," she whispered to his unconscious form amid her sniffles. "I'll not let aught befall you. Not ever."

She should never have allowed him the mad quest of his labours. He had been so very desperate for something to *do* to make up for the crime he had committed whilst under the influence of Nectar. What mother could ignore the earnest, broken pleas of her child? But she had made things worse for him. How many times now had these missions nigh claimed his life? And there was yet one more.

"If I asked you to abandon this quest, would you?" she asked, knowing full well that were he awake to hear the question, he would have refused. Of course he would. Because, even as she would have done aught for her child, so too would he take any risk for even the chance of aiding his sons.

Athene forced herself to sit up. With a dirty rag, she scrubbed away the snot and tears that marred her face. When Herakles woke, he would not see a bereaved and trembling mother watching over him with terror but an ally who was by his side, helping him achieve his aims. "Families are ever so difficult, are they not?" she whispered.

Not an hour before, she'd threatened to murder her sister to protect her son—who, as Hebe had pointed out, was, yes, actually her half-brother—from their common father. She groaned. Now, she wished she knew where to find her grandfather, and that he might offer her some answers about how to move forward.

Dionysus—another brother—was out there, actively planning to destroy Olympus. It was easier to stomach the idea of bringing battle to a brother she had never met than of hunting down Ares because he might make good upon his threat. Oh, she loathed Ares, of course. So far as she knew, anyone who ever stood in the same room as Ares despised the sadist. Shit, most people who saw his statue probably took an instant dislike to his arrogant visage. But she had also known him her whole life, stood on Olympus at his side, and ruled the world together with him.

If he came for their father, she would fight him. But Athene didn't think she could bring herself to seek out a conflict with him.

With a sigh, she scooted over to where she could stroke Herakles's brow. Too many situations all called for her attentions, and she could not divide them well enough. She knew, too, other mortal heroes and demigods suffered. Names flitted up to her, reminders she ought to check in upon them. Jason and Oedipus and Theseus and Laertes and so many others. They could have used her guidance and aid, but she had so little time to spare. She had to deal first with her son, and then with her wayward brothers.

How did Prometheus manage to find the time to tend so many fires at once? How did he, wandering the world, know where best to allocate his time? He had his share of failures, he had once told her. He had striven and fallen short, time and again, but saw that as no excuse to cease trying.

So Athene would do the same. She would manage her fires as best she could and hope to keep the World from burning down around her. What else was she to do?

HERAKLES HAD LAIN in his torpor for a long time, sometimes muttering in his sleep but more oft lying so frightfully still as to seem he had succumbed to his injuries. As for what beset his dreams when he slept, Athene could not guess. Whatever it was, he strove against it, again and again.

Did he communicate with the spirits of his slain children? Did he battle with the endless plethora of monsters which his life had set against him? Or did he behold some darker still dreams she could not imagine?

When at last he woke, Athene moved to his side once more and mopped his brow.

"Mama?"

She stroked his cheek. "You're safe now."

Her son huffed, pushing himself up to a sitting position with a weighty groan. "I am not certain that is the case." Though she had cleaned the blood, gore, and other filth from his face and chest, he looked a mess and Athene could not help but remember all those times he'd stumbled in from play in the woods, twigs in his hair and seven layers of grime caking every bit of his flesh. "I dreamt I saw the Fates themselves, and they ... they spoke to me as though I had agreed to some burden. But their words were riddles, and fleeting ones at that. The details flit away from my mind like sand through my fingers."

There was something Otherworldly about this place. Athene had felt it the moment she'd approached the Tree of Life, and sitting here, for so many days beneath its roots, the sense of lingering upon the threshold of the cosmos had only deepened. Was that why, caught betwixt living and dying, Herakles could witness the Moirai in this place? Or had his fever dreams conjured up the notorious sisters who wove Ananke? Athene did not know, for certain, that even existed.

"You must rest more," she said in answer. "Eat and regain your strength before you pursue this labour further."

He must have noted that she did not ask to what purpose he had come here. That seemed plain enough, and she had debated turning Eurystheus in to her father for making such a demand. But Zeus would see not only the king of Mykenai as guilty but Herakles as complicit for not turning on him the moment he spoke of such a crime. Besides, it might well come out that Athene had forced Hebe to give Herakles a draught of Ambrosia, and then Gaia alone knew what Father would do.

Leaning against the root cage, after arranging some food for them, Athene watched Herakles once more dozing, recovering his strength. This labour had nigh ended him. Had she come a moment later, she didn't know that he would have lived. And if that had happened ... No, she could not bear to dwell upon such thoughts.

When he had slept more, and another day had broken, Herakles rose, stretched, and prepared to make the long climb up into the boughs. It would be like scaling a mountain, and Athene wished he would allow her to accompany him but knew better than to ask.

"There's some sort of platform high above," he said, shielding his eyes with one hand whilst staring skyward. "Maybe a massive knot in the trunk, but it would make a fair resting point."

A premonition struck her like a sharp prick of a needle, and Athene worked her mouth soundlessly before she could orient herself. "Should you see a hollow in the Tree, do not enter." Why there should be any such opening, she didn't know. Had she dreamt that? Seen it in a vision? She could not shake the sensation that, were one to delve within the Tree, one would enter a liminal space that could lead anywhere. "What you seek lies in the upper branches."

With a grunt of acknowledgment, Herakles moved to test handholds and footholds upon the roots. Soon he was high above her, hundreds of feet up.

And still climbing.

He would live through this labour; she was certain now. But she dreaded to think what Eurystheus would come up with next.

24

THESEUS

730 Bronze Age

I should have done more. It was the thought that skulked the corners of Theseus's mind. Just when he thought himself done with the guilt and melancholy of it, the thought would creep up and pounce from the shadows. It would seize him in a stranglehold and leave him breathless.

Listless, he wandered the grounds outside the palace. In such moods, he could not stomach the innocence in little Akamas's eyes or the comfort Phaidra would try to offer him. He ignored Antigone's every attempt to draw him into her childish games. The bite of winter winds chapped his bare arms and exposed legs, and he welcomed the discomfort.

I ought to have tried harder. I should have gone back to check in upon him. I never should have left him alone at all!

Had he abandoned Pirithous to drown beneath his grief over Hippodamia? Had Theseus, in his desperation to tell Phaidra of Dionysus, let his dearest friend sink into the mire of his despair, slowly vanishing, alone? He had been so godsdamned wrapt up in his own life, he'd forgotten to attend back to one who had needed him.

I failed him.

A chorus of self-recriminations would rise up to fill the silences that otherwise punctuated his life. He should have his joy with his babe and his wife and his beloved Athenai. He should live and laugh and love.

I should have done more.

Always, that thought came slinking back to him. It would ambush him when he was alone, sometimes even in the midst of happiness. Then his guilt would redouble, for he stayed here enjoying all the wonders of life Pirithous had missed out on. His beloved Pirithous had almost had a wife, almost gotten to live his dreams, *almost* had the time he should have had. Almost—a hairsbreadth or a league away.

And Theseus found that same *almost* now stole his joys. For how could one exult in one's life whilst buried beneath mountains of crushing guilt? How could he live out all his remaining days, knowing Pirithous's life had been cut so mercilessly short?

I should have done more.

Such wounds could never heal.

THE MASK of consternation Phaidra wore had Theseus almost questioning whether her countless hours of empathy had been but feigned. But no, that was bitter and unfair of him. She leant against the wall beside the window in their rooms, arms folded over her chest, eyes stealing glances at Akamas's crib where their babe slept. "You have to let this go. You allow it to eat at you until Pirithous may as well have dragged you down into the Underworld alongside him."

Theseus bit back his sullen retort that he would have, had his friend asked, chosen to walk beside him on such a journey. Such was childish fancy; he had no desire to die.

"If I had but lingered there a few days longer—"

"Then he might have delayed his choice a few days." She pushed off the wall and moved to grip his elbows. "But you cannot save someone from their own choices, no matter how much you love them. It was his *choice*, and he alone bears responsibility for that. You may circle round these what-if questions in endless permutations, but they lead to nowhere save despair. You have a family *here*, now, and Pirithous has gone where you cannot yet follow."

Mustering his courage, he forced himself to meet her fervent gaze. A thought had begun to form of late, a wondering oft suppressed for it seemed madness or blasphemy. And yet the shadows of that question ever crept into his periphery. What if he could reach that place whilst still alive?

What if he could follow?

Phaidra would not have understood. Or perhaps she would have, but she would certainly not have approved. Lying to her, even by omission, left a sour taste upon his tongue and set a bilious churning within his gut. Still, he could not share his intent with his wife, for she would have done almost aught to stop him from following through upon this plan.

Such musings plagued him as he trod the beaten path back to Troezen, ostensibly to visit his mother and maternal grandfather. In truth, he could not bear the warmth of comfort they would try to shower him with. In the depths of the bitterest melancholies, even a mother's sympathies could prove another burden. Out of love, his kin would seek to shake him from his dolour. But Theseus did not want his sorrows washed from him or his guilt assuaged; would not allowing such be a violation of Pirithous's memory?

His shame over his friend's unkind fate was precious coin to be hoarded, not cast aside as a burden.

Thus, he came to the manor Jason had raised, upon the lands Theseus's grandfather had granted him. The Iolkan received him warmly, plying him with olives from his most recent crop, spiced wine, and idle chatter. Putting up with the latter proved a feat almost as onerous as slaying the godsdamned Minotaur. Theseus feigned interest whilst Jason droned on about planting seasons. He pretended to listen as the man hinted—only hinted, of course—at how Theseus might help him secure better trade terms in Athenai.

When he could endure the gossip that followed no longer, Theseus set his wine bowl on the table. "In truth, Jason, I've a need to speak with Medea."

The Iolkan's face darkened. Only a hair, but it was there. The pursing of his lips making plain his displeasure. "What has she done?" he asked after the silence had stretched to the edge of rudeness.

"Naught." Not yet, leastwise. "But I need consult her about some matters of the sort men would rather not dwell upon, given the choice." Theseus had no choice.

Given that Jason lived here through the graces of Theseus's grandfather—which Theseus himself had arranged after the fool got himself exiled from Iolkos for Medea's foul Art—the man could not refuse Theseus the chance to speak with his wife. Such was not done, Jason might have said, true. A man did not take private council with another man's wife. He could have objected. But Theseus held him with a level gaze that promised things would go ill if Jason tried to deny his request on grounds of propriety. Jason and Medea, they had, both of them, violated all propriety on more than one occasion.

"I'll send her to meet you on the portico."

Theseus nodded and made his way from the house, then settled upon the stoop. Winter's chill stung his skin until he had to rub his arms to get the blood flowing.

"What are you doing here?" Medea asked after Theseus sat long enough he'd had time to imagine a heated debate between husband and wife on the upper level of the manse. Though Theseus could not recall expressing outward rudeness to Medea, neither had he ever pretended to hold her in high regard. Everything about her Art screamed of foulness. To be in her presence gave one the feeling of passing through a cemetery at night. There was always a sensation one could not shake, that something unnatural lurked out of sight.

He had not heard her approach, and it took an effort not to start at her words. Instead, after a steadying breath, he rose to meet her. She stood with a hand upon the slight bulge of her belly. The witch spared him no time for pleasantries. Just as well. He had the patience for none, either. "After Kolchis, you spoke with Orpheus. You gave him drugs that helped him reach the Underworld."

He might have imagined the faint, indrawn breath she took at his words. "Orpheus is dead. He failed."

Theseus nodded, not bothering to admit he'd witnessed the unhappy bard's murder. "He failed to retrieve the soul he sought, yes. But he reached the Underworld. So must I."

Medea quirked her wicked smile. "There are easier ways to find yourself at Hades's gates."

"Do not test my patience today. Is it in your power to help me reach my desire? I can see you well compensated with drachmae for your trouble."

The witch sighed and shook her head, a few of her dark locks spilling from her braid. "Orpheus was a medium. He had an innate connection with the Penumbra which you, I can only assume, lack. To reach across the worlds, you would need not only the drugs I could brew but to find a liminal space where the Veil is more permeable."

"Where?"

With a grimace, she cast a look toward the house. When next she spoke, her voice dropped even lower, as if she could not bear to voice such things aloud in proximity to her husband or children. "I've heard of caves in Mount Tainaros. Places were foul deeds were done in Ages past. I do not know if such wicked tales are mere fancy, but it's the closest such place I can think of."

"Then make your drugs."

She hesitated. "If you do this, you shan't return."

Feigned concern? For surely she had no care for his wellbeing. "I've no choice in the matter. Make the godsdamned drugs."

§

A LONELY PEAK jutting out over the sea, Mount Tainaros lay betwixt Argos and Korinth. It had taken Medea time to prepare the draught she said he would need to eject his soul from his body—a turn of phrase that had given him pause but not broken his will. When next he returned to Troezen to claim his potion, she warned him once more against his course.

Not that she seemed to care for him, but she'd spoken as though terror beyond his ken unnerved her. Still, he had to make this right for Pirithous. He had to find a way to bring back his friend's soul and return him to life. If he could but speak with him one more time, he knew he could convince the Lapith that life, however tumultuous, remained worth living.

So, in his small vessel, he'd sailed the coast of Troezen, skirted the Korinthian peninsula, and anchored off the shore of Tainaros. Shards of rocks poked from the waves, forbidding him to draw his ship too close. It meant swimming. Beyond the rocks, he thought he could see a break in the cliffside. A sea cave, and perhaps the point of ingress he needed to reach the Underworld.

After checking the phial Medea had prepared was secured to his belt—and too, his sword—Theseus unstrapped his sandals and vaulted the side of his boat. Winter had not quite broken, and the icy waters slapped him like a blow. It took all he had to keep from losing his breath and sucking down a lungful of seawater. Then he burst to the surface, caught a sputtering breath, and at last swam toward the cliff. Harsh waves battered, ever threatening to hurl him against the exposed rocks.

The edifices served as a breakwater against the sea's fury once he'd slipped past them. Made it easier to work his way within the cave. By the time he found a shelf of rock to climb upon, his teeth had started chattering, his limbs trembling. All he wanted to do was curl into a ball. Instead, he yanked off his sodden tunic and tossed it aside. The wet clothes would only deepen the chill. Ought to have left them in the boat in the first place.

He had neither means nor fuel to start a fire here, so all else he could do was try to massage feeling back into his arms. Would Medea's potion do aught if he died of the chills before finding the way to Pirithous?

She'd told him to await nightfall, claiming the darkness sympathetic to the Realms beyond Gaia. Theseus didn't much understand such things, but he had to assume Medea spoke the truth. Between now and then, he needed to get warm and stay awake.

THE CAVE'S angle was wrong to catch the sunset's flame reflected upon the sea, but Theseus imagined it would have been vibrant. Still, he saw the barest glint of orange winking out before the gloom within the cave deepened to an almost total darkness. He could scarce make out more than a foot in front of his face.

Almost the moment he lost his vision, a sense crept over him; a feeling of something in here with him. Moving beyond the range of his perception. Whispering things he could not quite hear but felt as susurrations in the air. Flitting from place to place. Watching his every moment. Listening to the beat of his heart with ardent attention.

Now.

Movement had become an impossibility. His gaze darted one way and the next, certain something malicious lurked close enough he could reach out and touch it.

Drink it now, Theseus told himself.

But moments more passed before he could force his quivering limbs to crawl to where he'd left his clothes and retrieve the phial from its strap on his belt. This draught would let him enter the Underworld. Assuming Medea had not sent him here to die. The witch could have poisoned the brew. She knew no one would ever find his body here. By Zeus's beard, she'd told him plainly he would not return from this.

And now he was tormenting himself with such paranoid fancies.

Theseus uncorked the phial and raised it to his lips.

Drink it, he told himself, *or these regrets will haunt you the rest of your days.*

He downed the bitter draught, then let the empty ceramic container slip to the ground. Orpheus had claimed he used a hypnotic drumbeat to help focus his mind. But Theseus knew no such rhythms.

Instead, he sat there, blind in the darkness, waiting for something to happen. His gut churned, dancing as though he ought to have had a shit before attempting this.

Such thoughts fled his mind as fast as they formed. The sensation of presences had redoubled now. The intimation of whispers had become a real murmuring of nonsense. Moans and laments, cries and weeping all melded into a distant dirge, carried to his ears upon a sourceless wind that ought not have pierced so deep within the cavern.

Theseus turned, looking back into the recesses of the sea cave. Where once had stood an alcove now yawned an open maw, the stones warped as though contorted in pain. And he could see, for a faint luminance now adumbrated the cavern, allowing him to make out almost as much as he had before dusk.

That opening beckoned. It taunted and mocked, daring him to make good on his blasphemous intent. Theseus rose and found himself clad now in his tunic, no longer wet, though his discarded garment lay where he'd thrown it. He looked back. His body was slumped over, as though he'd fallen asleep whilst sitting.

Once more, he looked into the gap that had made way for his passage. Madness, yes. But he had no choice.

So, Theseus ventured into the darkness.

THE NARROW PASSAGE forced him to scrunch in upon himself. His shoulders scraped against the ceiling, bruised oft upon irregular angles in the stone. No ... this was all too much like being back in the

Labyrinth. Dark and cold and cramped, the way carved by madmen whose minds wrought spirals where others saw straight lines. Here, at least, he saw no branching paths. No fear of getting lost this time, whatever small mercy that offered.

A cave like this, water ought to have slickened the surfaces, but they remained dry and harsh. Even the faint light in the air seemed to dim, and Theseus had to move forward by feel, his fingers reaching into the gloom, hoping to thus avoid smacking his head upon any oddly protruding stones.

As he delved deeper, the wails and moans of the damned became more distant. Should not have the passage to the Underworld brought him closer to the cries of the dead? Or perhaps his frantic mind sought reason to turn back. No. *No turning back, Theseus.*

At the end of his journey, Pirithous awaited, desperate and alone. Theseus would save him. Had to save him, even if he must wrestle Hades himself to accomplish the task.

Without warning, the ground gave way beneath him, pitching him onto a steep slope or chute. It wasn't wet, but the stone was so slick he skidded, collapsed onto his arse, and hurtled downward. On instinct, he reached out, slapping all four limbs against the walls to slow his fall. His sandals squeaked over the stone a moment before he jerked himself to a stop.

Heart in his throat and ready to piss himself, Theseus stared down into the blackness below. He had no way to know how far down the passage went. For all he knew, it might well have no bottom, and he could have fallen for all eternity. Pleasant thought, that. Would his body starve back in the real world?

And yet, even could he climb back the way he'd come, it only led toward that body. Toward rejection of his last hope and acceptance that Phaidra was right and Pirithous was gone. That he must let go the anguish. How could he betray his friend in such a way? How could he choose to release his grip upon the man, when he saw his eyes in the glint of every star? Death was a perversity that stole loved ones from one another, and Theseus would not abide it.

The path backward was darker still than the one ahead.

So, after a steadying breath, he eased off his hold and let his fall continue.

Until, at last, light surged up to meet him. Not the warm light of the sun or clean, pure moonlight, but a lurid gleam sparking in the air. The slide pitched him out from a shaft into the open air, and for a sickening moment Theseus was free-falling without even the slide beneath him. Burgundy clouds billowed and hiccupped. Theseus fell through one and smacked hard into a floating rock island drifting from it. The impact rang through his skull and echoed in his very bones.

For a time he lay, groaning in pain.

Having left his body behind, how could it hurt so very much?

When at last he managed to turn, he saw the chute he'd fallen from emptied out from another flying isle, all obsidian glinting in the fell light, as was the island on which he lay. Dozens of these strange islands soared about. As he sat, he saw a pair crash together. A ripple ran between them, then black shards exploded in all directions.

Including toward him.

"Oh, fuck." Half running, half crawling, Theseus scrambled to take cover behind an obelisk-like outcropping. Razor-edged projectiles crashed onto his isle the next instant. It was a cacophony, as though a thousand ceramic amphorae had all shattered at once. Debris whizzed past him. Some of the shards struck the ground and carved out new missiles which burst in random patterns. Blades lacerated his arms. A hundred tiny cuts shredded his tunic. Blood dribbled down his brow, his neck, his limbs.

When at last the madness abated, Theseus dared to stand. Blood streamed from too many tiny wounds for him to count. He looked about, seeking aid or shelter. Instead, he saw another of those islets heading right for the one upon which he stood.

The Moirai were having a jest with him.

The bitter thought was all the time he could spare, then he dashed like mad for the edge. Blood squelched between his toes and in the space under the arch of his foot. Weak and wounded, he stumbled twice before he managed the ledge. Another soaring rock passed below, and Theseus leapt from his perch.

All flailing limbs and terror.

Then another heavy impact.

It was worse. So much worse than he had ever imagined the Underworld might prove. A world of burbling Khaos. Dread made manifest.

He pushed himself up onto his elbows. In the rock before his face, an eye opened, revealing two overlapping irises each as big as his head.

Theseus shrieked, scrambling away.

The moment he reached the precipice, he jumped once more. Surely anywhere was better than this mound of living obsidian. Surely an escape from this nightmare lay ahead. He need but find the path Orpheus had described and follow it to Hades's necropolis.

He was soaring in the air once more, then dark waters surged up to claim him. He splashed down hard, sunk into unknown depths. So dark it took him a moment to even judge up from down. A swift current had him. He managed the surface, caught a breath.

The flow was too strong. Ahead, the stream pitched over a cliff in a misty waterfall. Theseus had neither the time nor energy to scream. Frantic, he swam for the side, but the current refused to release him. He was drawn beneath the surface once more. Tossed and shoved, then shot free. Screaming, he soon learnt, was in fact, still possible.

He fell a dozen feet, smacked his back against a rock, and rolled off into further rivers. Before he knew what was happening, hands had seized him and dragged him ashore.

Ashen-faced and wan, Ariadne stared down at him. Abrasions marred her delicate neck, making too plain how she'd reached the Underworld. All this, Theseus absorbed in a single glance. The next moment, tears welled in his eyes. "I'm so sorry. I'm so, so sorry, Ariadne."

"You should not have come here ..."

"I ... I had to try."

Something passed over her face. Despair? Resignation? Did she believe he had come for her? Maybe he ought to have, but he had not, in fact, known for certain she had died.

A howl ruptured the stillness. Followed by another. And a third. Awful, soul-flensing sounds.

"He knows you are here," Ariadne said. "He knows you carry the blood of Zeus in your veins."

The howls rang out again, closer. A sense came over Theseus, a feeling of something momentous drawing nigh. Racing toward him. He managed his knees and pulled his sword.

Pity limned Ariadne's face as she shook her head. "You ought not to have come here. Now, there is no escape. It comes for you."

"What comes?"

Again, a trio of howls, this time, over the rise of a hill. Theseus turned to look up. In the darkness gleamed six incandescent eyes.

25

HEKATE

216 Golden Age

The gulf between lucidity and utter madness had never before seemed so very narrow. Lying upon her back, watching the unsteady heavens, Hekate felt she teetered on the edge, that the slightest shift of her balance would send her spilling downward into a drowning abyss from which she might never emerge.

That she had killed her future self to create—to *become* Enodia— boggled the mind, yes, but worse, it affronted all sensibility, flying in the face of reason and decency. To imagine that she would knowingly walk such a path both horrified and bemused. With each wild revolution of her thoughts, she flailed further out over that gulf, ready to pitch into whatever meagre escape insanity offered.

She could not have guessed how long she remained prone. Being so untethered, with naught left onto which she might cling, she could find no reason even to move. Surely some path must lie ahead, some route by which she could avert the future she had just witnessed.

Yet her mental question prompted neither answer nor jibe from the silent spirits coiled within her core, as if even they, timeless and Etheric, were struck dumb by the sheer weight of Ananke.

"You must find another way," her father said, drawing Hekate from her daze.

Bit by bit, her vision focused on his face hovering over her own, abject and yet somehow still daring to commit the fallacy of hope that Hekate's own future self had sought to disprove.

Papa eased her into a sitting position. "How are you here?" Never had she heard his voice so raw. "I ..." The man swallowed, visibly composing himself. Hekate watched as he tried and failed to replace the mask of serenity that always lay over his visage. "In the flames I saw a shadow, a fear, that some peril would fall upon my daughter this night, down by the river." Papa cocked his head in disbelief, voice breaking. "*Sorcery*, Pyrrha? *Sorcery*? This is the future before you? Have I so failed you?" Her father choked on the emotion, seemed ready to weep once more for the death of his child. For her damnation. The cool brush of his finger over the rawness of the wound on her face stung.

Her Pneuma, weakened though it was, would keep her from bleeding to death, though she could not regrow the eye.

"You must find another way," Papa repeated, his sapphire eyes imploring her to break a cycle of Fate that Hekate had begun to think must prove immutable.

Why else, after all, would she have allowed herself to come to this moment, to become Enodia?

"I ..." Her mouth still tasted of pooled ichor.

"There are things that must happen," Papa said, hand cupping her cheek now. "Things to ensure your birth, precious daughter." A rugged breath shuddered through him. "I have a course I have to follow, for all our sakes. But you *must* find a way around this end."

"I thought I could stop myself from ever learning of the Art." A bitter, futile attempt to spite the Moirai who, even now, must be laughing at them. But ... Papa had addressed the Fates as if he knew them personally, had threatened them as though he might reach them, harm them. Was such possible? "I can try again." With the Box she could take as many chances as need be to find her third alternative, to discover some path the Moirai had not accounted for.

Even if it was a fool's hope, it was all she had.

"I have ... time. But I ... If I am to unwrite my own history, this"— she waved a hand over her ruined face—"might make it hard to pass unnoticed."

A resigned sigh billowed out of Papa. "I can teach you to glamour that away." The way Enodia had? Perhaps the same thought had given Papa pause, or perhaps he had not realised what Enodia had done. Either way, Hekate could not turn from knowledge or power freely offered. "First, I'll make a poultice to help with the wound and dull the pain. Pyrrha oft sleeps well past noon, so you must find me each morn, when I will await you outside Okeanus's Gate. Given your intellect, I imagine you can master the arcana in less than a fortnight."

Nice to know he thought so well of her. Nice, and strange, for never had she imagined Papa becoming her co-conspirator in her attempt to unmake her own life.

❧

In the end, when she learnt the glamour from Papa, she found herself with no choice but to leave Thebes behind. Despite it all, despite everything, he *still* knew more than he revealed, and Hekate had grown so very tired of playing out the same arguments they'd had since her childhood. She needed to know everything, especially if she was to have any chance of saving herself.

"It is easy to claim the truth cannot harm you whilst nuzzled in the sheltering embrace of blissful ignorance."

His words carried in them a rebuke all the more striking, for indeed, her same thirst for knowledge had first led her into the dark that now wrapt itself around her soul. That Papa had a point did little to change the fact that, if he would not tell her all he knew, she must seize those answers elsewhere.

Thus they had parted once again, neither able to bend far enough for the other. Besides, Hekate did know of another ancient Titan who might offer her the secrets she sought after. Perhaps Papa had the right of it, and the more of the Ontos she uncovered the more bitter her life would grow. She had gone too far down the path now to turn back. Even if she demurred, ahead lay damnation and the cruel games of Fate.

She came to Kronion, having taken passage out of Korinth. The place seemed strangely empty, a simple, open-air shrine to Dyaus standing where the Temple of Athene would later dominate the plateau.

For an Ouranid lord, Kronos's palace hinted at subtle tastes, relying upon intricate architectural flourishes over ostentation or grandiose size. Marble reliefs rimming the entablature depicted the fall of Nyx, with the Elder Goddess seeming more a void in the sky than any fixed shape. The Titan holding the light against her must have been Ouranos himself.

A steward greeted her on arrival, clearly having recognised her genos, if not herself. The man swept a bow. "Be welcome, Heliad. Whom may I announce to the lord and lady of Kronion?"

"A woman the lord met in the mountains, not long back."

Her obscure answer earned her a raised eyebrow, but the steward did disappear inside to announce her.

When he returned after long enough Hekate had begun to suspect Kronos now ignored her, it was not the Ouranid lord who accompanied the steward but Rhea, Kronos's lover. Gentle brown curls fell about the Titan woman's face. Her robes, dyed in the richest of Phoenikian purple, her golden circlet, her wan smile—all bespoke a softness Hekate knew lay over a core of stone. If there was kindness in Rhea, there was cunning too. For millennia, she had wandered— or would wander, Hekate supposed—the Thalassa world, pursuing ends of her own or those of her lover. Up until Zeus, her own child, had murdered her in his paroxysmal rage.

"I was told," Rhea said, drifting close enough Hekate had to look up at the taller woman, "that my beloved gave to you a cloak he had procured for me, and yet I find you clad in plain travelling clothes."

The memory of Enodia yanking the cloak off her sent a fresh jab of pain rushing through Hekate. "I met with misfortune and had the cloak stolen."

"Hmm, most unfortunate indeed." The Titan lady tilted her head to one side, a silent prompt for Hekate to state her purpose.

"Lord Kronos once bid me attend him, that he would teach me of the Ontos."

The lady's smile curled with a hint of vicious satisfaction. "What would we want with one who walked away from such an offer? Which mentor would welcome back a pupil who spurned their lessons when offered freely?"

It took an effort to keep frustration—or desperation—from seeping into her posture or tone. "One who recognises the value of a student who has seen the other paths and knows the price of ignorance."

"But does she know the price of knowledge?"

It is easy to claim the truth cannot harm you whilst nuzzled in the sheltering embrace of blissful ignorance. Her father's words of warning rang through her mind like a clarion. But she had already ventured into the Dark, and the Ontos had its claws lodged firmly in the depths of her soul.

Hekate shook her head. "No one can know that until knowledge is gained. But I have to believe even the most painful of truths should be preferable to alluring lies."

Eyes glinting with mischief, Rhea twined a finger in her ochre locks. "Then follow me, sorceress, and be tested."

RHEA BROUGHT her around the back of the acropolis where they took a narrow path to descend the cliff. One hand on the rough rock kept Hekate steady, so long as she did not stare too hard at the precipitous drop into the city two hundred feet below.

Strange, but in all the years Athene had ruled this polis, never had Hekate imagined this route lay here. When they had climbed down perhaps a third of the way, Rhea paused, turning sideways so as to slip within a passage open inside the mountain. From above or below, the numerous rocks would have concealed this cave, and even descending the path, Hekate had not seen it until Rhea had turned back. An almost invisible sanctum, into which Rhea and Kronos could seemingly disappear, unbeknownst to even their own servants.

Very little light filtered in from outside, so Hekate had to navigate by keeping her hands on either side of the cramped passage. Were she much larger, her shoulders might have scraped against the coarse rock walls. As it was, she faltered when at last the tunnel opened out into some sort of chamber, a place saturated with a faint reek of decay.

Rhea knelt upon the ground and struck flint to light an oil lamp. Flames wakened, casting a moil of dancing shadows about the room. It was not a cave, for large bricks formed the walls. Layers of dust caked the perimeter outside of the area where Rhea sat, beckoning to Hekate, while armies of spiders scrambled over a maze of cobwebs spanning the corners. A hint of a black, sinuous form slithered into some gap in the wall, driven off by the sudden light.

The Titan had led her into a tomb, a place that must have waited within this mountain even from the Time of Nyx. If Rhea thought guiding Hekate into a musty grave would intimidate her, the other Titan had grossly underestimated Hekate. She, who walked through Python's sepulchral tunnels and braved the Stygian depths of the Underworld, did not find overmuch to fear in these dark chambers.

The Titan lady's face revealed no hint of whether or not she had sought any response. Once Hekate settled before her, Rhea withdrew a bowl from her satchel, followed by a tiny amphora. Uncorking the latter, she poured a milky fluid into the bowl, then sprinkled it with some powder.

"What is it?"

"Death." Rhea let the word linger, filling up the space between, a more effective threat than the crawling denizens of this tomb. "Or awakening, depending on your ability to maintain a hold on your soul." The Titan turned her hand over, motioning to the bowl before Hekate.

Could Kronos have arranged all this as means of killing her? He had tried to strike at her with his sickle before her words—and spell-song—had given him pause. Hekate had thought she had won him over, but what if his change of heart had been a ploy? Even if so, she had already beheld her own future; she'd not die here.

From the steady gaze Rhea levelled on her, Hekate had two choices now: drink and endure whatever risk lurked within the draught, or demure and give over any chance of getting answers from Kronos and his fellows.

Hekate had never been one to turn aside from danger. Not even when she should have.

With a steady hand, she took up the bowl and raised it to her lips. The woody flavour of cinnamon only slightly masked the acrid bite of a viscous tonic that, unless she missed her guess, had some sort of serpent venom in it. Perhaps even something akin to the fluid she had taken from Python's lair, long ago.

Rapid convulsions shot through her gut. Only force of will kept her sitting. Hekate closed her eyes and let the darkness seep in.

Silken strands of night brushed over Hekate's face, teasing her one way and the next, drawing her in a circuitous route through the pitch-black space engulfing her. A caress upon her chin guided her to the left until a hint of a nudge on her shoulder turned her to the right. Tugging upon her legs— so faint she might have imagined it—carried her forward. Though she raised a hand before her face, she could make out not a single finger.

The further she walked, the more the inky darkness seemed to take on substance of its own until she felt herself wading through it. No longer gentle caresses, unseen forms, bands of sinew and scale, brushed against her.

A nameless dread arose in her, a tremble in her core. The ground sucked at her heels, a ruthless tar trying to claim her, to deny her even one more step. Bands of thick fluid lashed up, entangling her shins, pulling her downward, demanding she melt into the black.

A shape slithered around her, pinning her arms to her sides, coarse, and reeking of old earth. Slowly, muscles knotted around her, constricting her torso, driving breath out. A chorus of hisses replaced all other sounds, drowning out even Hekate's grunting struggles against the crushing force. Bones strained. She felt them beginning to crunch. As the last of her air escaped her lungs, she felt something else filling up the space it had occupied.

The darkness was inside her, seeping, swirling. Transmogrifying her until she was one with it.

A darkness she had willingly imbibed.

This was a nightmare born of poison she'd downed in her desperate search for Ontos.

But a nightmare was, in the end, a dream. And Hekate was an oneiromancer. She had the Sight. She had, long ago, survived imbibing the Python's liquid puissance.

If she wished light, she would have it. A pale blue flame arose, first from her fingertips, but then shooting up her arms and engulfing the whole of her torso. The caliginous shape encircling her abruptly loosened, a saurian form slithering off into the darkness.

Though Hekate had sought to cast back the expanse of shadows, all she had managed was to illume her own person, as if this dream were not entirely her own. As if it had a will of its own, one that strove against her.

In the distance, adumbrated by the flicker of fragile light, mammoth saurian bulks slithered one atop the next, each vast enough to encircle and devour an entire city. Like living masses of writhing darkness, here squirmed eldritch abominations on a scale that defied all comprehension. Or worse, Hekate began to suspect in rising dread: not numerous abominations, but rather a singular, multifaceted, cosmic bane. A horror fit and primed to feast upon the World itself.

The scream that refused to pass her lips choked her, rendered her insensate and immobile.

To look upon the infinite Dark was to let it consume her mind.

So she turned inward, heedless of the bits of herself that had already *frayed and been lost. She looked instead at the pieces of scathing Khaos roiling in her core. And those, she would make her own.*

❧

EVEN THE DWINDLING illumination of the oil lamp pierced her eyes like an arrow, forcing Hekate to blink against its sudden intrusion. A moment before, a part of her had not expected to behold light again. Had felt, in the very depths of her soul, that she had sunk so deep into the yawning dark that not even a flicker of brightness could ever touch her.

Across from her, Rhea sat, legs folded beneath herself, so still she must have fallen into a meditative trance of her own. Yet, as Hekate lifted her head, Rhea's eyes popped open, fixing Hekate with a look weighty as the mountain in which they sheltered.

"There is a question even the shrewdest of sorcerers dance about, the place even the most far wandering of shamans dare neither to look nor even contemplate. A fear we do not voice, for visceral dread of such lies ingrained within our souls, writ there in the time before time." Rhea cocked her head. "Do you know of what I speak?"

She could neither swallow nor tear her gaze from Rhea's piercing eyes. "What lies beyond the walls of Tartarus ... and whence did it come?"

Rather than answer, Rhea quirked a smile, then rose, drifting to the shadowed recesses of the tomb. When she followed, Hekate realised, where the Titan lady stood, the dust had not gathered as thick, nor did the cobwebs connect here. Rhea pushed against a slight protrusion in the bricks.

An instant later, the grinding of stone upon stone filled the chamber. A rumbling sent curtains of dust showering down from above and thrummed through the ground, even as a previously unde-tectable seam in the wall opened. A segment of it slid back, then disappeared into a hidden alcove off to the side, creating a doorway from which spilt distant torchlight, perceptible only because of the extreme gloom in which Hekate stood.

Without so much as a glance her way, Rhea strode down a corridor leading deeper within the mountain. Set perhaps every thirty feet in sconces on alternating walls, torches offered enough illumination to keep from tripping over their own feet, but not nigh enough to shake the sense that Hekate plodded into some subterranean dungeon from which she might never emerge. Had Kronos and Rhea co-opted a tomb to create this very effect? If so, the effort was wasted upon a sorceress. Those who plied the Art, those who dared the greater arcana, did so with dread as their perennial companion. Every time one looked beyond the Veil, one risked drawing the eye and ire of its denizens. Every time one evoked spirits, stripping them of will in order to enforce one's own, one walked knowingly into damnation.

When every night became a nightmare, when foreknowledge of the eternal torment of one's soul lingered ever upon one's thoughts, what was mortal darkness in comparison?

At last, after wandering several hundred feet, they came to a door wrought from dark metal and engraved with designs that seemed like a maze of concentric diamonds. Before Hekate could ask how, in this time before Man or Titan began to work with iron, there could be an ancient door of it, Rhea threw the portal wide.

The sepulchral shadows engulfing them were cast back by a pair of crackling braziers just inside. A large chamber was supported by four columns, each too wide to encircle with her arms, and each engraved with geometric designs not unlike that upon the door. Past the braziers, within a depression two steps down, two men and two women reclined on silken pillows. Hekate had the sense they had been deep in some conversation that the door's groan had cut short, and now all eyes settled upon her and Rhea.

Oil lamps in the midst of this group added extra illumination, dancing about their features. Platinum-haired Kronos was there, thumb and forefinger massaging his brow. Hekate could not stop the widening of her eyes when she saw, to his left, Themis, whom she had not seen in millennia. Though young Pyrrha would not meet

Themis for several more years yet, the Oracle of Delphi looked at her now as though she knew her. Perhaps she did.

Beside Themis sat another woman, her dark skin and hair indicating Kandamian heritage. A viper coiled around her raised arm, the snake also having turned to stare at Hekate.

The last man's gaze darted back and forth between Hekate and the venomous creature, giving off the sense he might have scooted farther away from the animal if he could have done so without being obvious about it. Dark curls fell about his face, at odds with the intense green of his eyes.

Moving in beside her, Rhea pointed at each of the waiting men and women in turn. "Kronos you have already met, and Themis is out of Delphi." She indicated the dark-haired man. "Laran comes to us from Rassenia."

"Illyris," Laran corrected.

Rhea ignored him, motioning instead to the Kandamian with the snake. "And this is Ningal."

Introductions made, Rhea settled down beside her lover, looking to him to continue whatever ... this was.

Kronos motioned Hekate to sit upon an empty pillow, one between Ningal and Laran, and no doubt positioned close enough to the serpent to test her nerves. Did they know of the nest of such creatures she had seen in her trance? Did they hope to engender panic because of it?

Having not the least intention of offering them such satisfaction, Hekate settled upon the pillow and fixed the Ouranid with her gaze. "Who are these people, Kronos?"

The lord folded his hands in his lap and drew in a long, pensive breath. "The World is not what you think." Though he did not raise his voice, it filled the whole of the chamber, making her wonder if he had *the* Voice. "It is older than Man or Titan imagines. It was birthed, it died, it was born again, over and over, in a vicious cycle of Eschatons." He paused, letting his words settle against her, letting inchoate images of cataclysms rise and fade from her mind unbidden. "And watching it all unfold, there were some few first immortals. Though they fancied themselves guides of Man, they lacked all the answers. Realising, at long last, their ignorance, and having caught glimpses of the Ontos, a cadre of these immortals formed a secret coterie in search of the Truth. We called ourselves the Gnostic Cabal."

"Gnostic?" Hekate's voice had become a whisper, faint and childish against the all-consuming bombardment of Kronos's words. Yet so enraptured did she find herself she could scarce manage even a hint of embarrassment at the timid sound.

"Those who seek Gnosis"—Kronos tapped a finger against his temple—"the hidden knowledge, the forbidden Truth. It is the personal insight into the Ontos. The pursuit of it, the desire for liberation from the Wheel of Fate. It is the very Enthymesis of Light, the purpose of souls in the World, or so we posit."

His words conjured a panoply of images dancing within her mind, a shadow play that threatened to destroy her with its sheer immensity. The implication she had drawn was that, if even these first immortals of which he spoke felt life concealed some fateful lie, all her fears about what lay in the Dark beyond their world had not begun to scratch the surface of the true empty horror surrounding them.

The scope of what lay before her threatened to swallow her, devour her mind and leave behind a quivering, weeping wreck. How oft had she heard that the pursuit of Ontos was the road to madness? If she was to walk that road and yet avoid such an end, she must keep her vision narrow, focus upon one revelation at a time. "You were one of the first immortals?" She almost laughed. "The legends say you fought alongside Ouranos to end the Time of Nyx."

Kronos folded his arms, leaning back. "That ... is a corruption of the name I used in those days."

On any other day she might have gaped at him, to hear him name *himself* the legendary Ouranos. She might have sat here in awe, struggling to mouth the thousand questions such a revelation engendered. Now, in the wake of her apparent induction into this Gnostic Cabal, even this claim became but one more ripple upon a sea of wonder.

"When we realised the nature of Fate, we sought with *such*

frightful desperation for a means to escape it. We harnessed the dark powers of Falias to create the Oracle Mirrors, seeking ever for some vision we could behold, some means to prove the existence of free will. You cannot begin to imagine the defiance with which we met the dawning knowledge that all our choices were already made. How we strove, again and again, to avert aught we beheld. But we saw only the things we could not change.

"Yet hope dies the slowest of deaths. When we found a time-walker, one who defied causality and sought to unmake history, we thought we had the answer. In the ruins of Dark Faerie, we crafted the Time Chambers. If we could not *see* a means of altering the future, of breaking through Fate, we thought we would control time itself and thus achieve our aims of shattering the Wheel of Fate."

The bitter, haunted chuckle that poured from him bespoke a despair she knew all too well. The utter despondency of one who has foreseen their own damnation.

"What is the Wheel of Fate?" She had to ask, though she feared the answer. Though she *knew* the answer.

"It is the unabating procession of time, locking us in causal chains. It is the twin spinning wheels of history and reincarnation that bind us to Fate. And what is Fate?" Even Kronos shuddered now, his voice trembling. "That the Dark ever encroaches, despite all our faltering hopes and dreams, and that it will, one day, rise and reclaim the souls of Man. That it is not only you, sorceress, who is doomed. We are, all of us, *the whole of Mankind*, damned."

26

KIRKE

726 Bronze Age

"It's not soldiers we fear," Jason said, the first he'd dared speak in her presence. "We are warriors and would not back down from any foe which might be challenged with spear or blade, Lady."

"Some years back," Medea said, "Father turned to sorcery."

"What?" The madness of it cut through even the dolour that had seized Kirke's heart. Aeëtes had long disdained the Art, even to the point of insulting Kirke over it a time or two. He'd barely consented to allow her to train Medea in alchemy and would have raged had she deigned to teach her of the greater arcana. "How? When? No! Better yet, who did he pull from Nyx's arsehole to train him in such dire pursuits?"

Now Medea paused to nurse her own wine. "The when of it … After what happened to your common sister, Pasiphaë, he took a dark turn. He began cloistering himself in private meetings with the sorceress Damkina."

⸙

As Kirke shook herself free of the disorientation the Box produced, she realised she now knelt in her palace-prison on Aiaíā. She would have recognised this place even in her sleep, so many years had she spent here.

"What the—" a voice called from her work desk.

An instant later, another collapsing bubble burst, sweeping another Kirke into it. For a heartbeat, she'd been in the presence of her past self.

Her hand went to her mouth, and Kirke gaped. She had just witnessed the moment when she'd been sucked back in time. It meant Pandora had been right about the Box having memory, and her grandmother had managed to send Kirke to precisely the right juncture.

Kirke ought to have rejoiced to have found herself free of her maddened sojourn through time. It was what she had wanted, after all. Save that now, now she had returned to her banishment. Loneliness crept upon her like a stalking predator.

Too late, she wondered if she might have instead chosen to remain by her grandmother's side. If she might have, in so doing, found a place with *someone* in the ambit of the World, who could have, at last, understood her. Fresh tears streaked unbidden down her face as she slapped an impotent palm against the marble floor. Not even Titan strength could spare her from such a plight.

Time is an ouroboros, Pandora had said, and they were all of them caught in its coils.

Kirke wailed. As if her cries might somehow sway the apathetic Moirai to change the fate they had woven for her. As if anyone, anywhere, would hear her anguish and spare her the least dollop of empathy.

But, of course, there was no one.

There was, always, no one.

"KIRKE?" someone asked, breaching the darkness that suffocated her. All sense of time had slipped from Kirke and she could not say whether hours or days had passed. Thought, even, had flitted through her trembling grasp, allowing her to form but inchoate musings upon the nature of the universe and of herself.

Broken, helpless. Wretched.

Kirke had not risen from the floor where the Box had left her, though she had scooted up against the wall and folded her hands in her lap. Somewhere betwixt meditation and sleep, she had lingered in the gloom and thought it the expanse of the World, for a time.

"Kirke?" the voice called once more, violating the quietude Kirke sought.

Crashing footfalls. Sandals slapping marble. She did not want to note it, so she chose not to.

Her mother dropped down beside her. A dream? A memory?

It didn't matter.

Kirke allowed herself to collapse against Hekate, clutching her in desperation. The hope for something real. A moment later, she was hefted in her mother's arms.

Through the dark manse, Mother carried her. Her head upon a warm shoulder, Kirke knew no more.

IN THE PREDAWN DARK, Kirke woke but found she could not bring herself to move. To gaze so fully upon the Moirai's accursed Tapestry was to behold the impotence with which she had lived her life. To know the ambit of time was woven upon that loom served as incontrovertible evidence that, in the end, free will was but an illusion. All Kirke had ever done, all she would ever do, even this very moment, it was all decided long before her birth.

As Hyperion's rise streaked the sky aflame, Mother threw wide the shutters and let the harsh light pour onto Kirke's face. She had not the strength to curse the over-bright sunrise, nor to move, nor act, nor care. For none of it would matter.

Time is an ouroboros.

The serpent was the real loom, Fate woven between its constricting coils.

Or she could fight against that colossal drakon. She could refuse to help her mother understand the Box and hope doing so thwarted Ananke. Which thread should she pluck? Which to cut, and risk the unravelling of the whole of time?

Had Kirke the strength, the *cruelty*, to decide to unmake herself, her mother, her grandmother, and their whole line? No, she had neither.

"I think," she forced herself to say, her words slow and painful, "I can tell you how to use it now."

For a moment, her mother stood there, lost in her own dark musings and personal pains. Kirke saw them and wanted to care. She wanted to rise and offer empathy, but the winds of Fate had stolen from her any such capacity.

"Show me," her mother said.

Kirke blew out a breath and forced herself to rise and make her way back to where she'd left the Box upon the kitchen floor. She motioned for her mother to light the hearth, and Hekate did so. The pair of them settled before the warmth, though Kirke imagined neither found overmuch comfort in those flames.

The tortures of Ananke deprived even simple pleasures from the joys they once had held.

Solemn and despairing, Kirke demonstrated the usage of the Box, careful not to activate it in the process. "In theory, you can reach any moment in time or space," Kirke explained.

"Space?" Mother asked.

"It can move you across both with ease, though predicting an exact location has no ease about it."

Kirke had paid heed to all Pandora had done, but still, she could not operate the device with that level of precision, much less teach her mother to do so. Or maybe such mattered little. For the ouroboros already accounted for the Box, so it would deposit Mother when and where it had always taken her. She would play at attempting to escape the coils, clinging to her persistent fantasy of free will until, in the end, the final, crushing revelation destroyed her last hopes.

And Kirke could not save her.

Was *this* what Prometheus had felt? Was this powerlessness in the face of history what drove him to slavishly follow the course set before him?

In the end, Hekate took the Box, kissed Kirke upon the brow, and left.

She would go where she, in self-delusion, believed her own will carried her. And in so doing, she followed the weave of the Moirai. It was all any of them could do, pulled along by puppet strings.

Alone, Kirke lacked the strength to rise from her place before the hearth. She had no energy left inside to follow her mother and see her off. No tears remained for her to weep. No hopes left to pursue. The sum of her life added up only to empty despair and a desolate island.

That, and the fear that one day Zeus would return and demand more of her. He would take and take and take.

Until the last vestiges of Kirke were used up.

27

PANDORA

399 Dark Age

*I*n his great, vaulted hall, the god-king sat upon his throne, face half in darkness, the light of his numerous braziers not quite reaching his dais. Before his great seat, halfway down the steps, another figure watched her. With a suppressed start, Pandora recognised that man, for she had seen him in Zeus's camp during the Titanomachy. Morpheus, the oneiromancer, the one so many of Zeus's own allies had so feared. His words had sealed Arke's fate, though Pandora had been the one to implicate the poor, blasted woman of treason.

It took a concerted effort to tear her gaze from the oneiromancer and focus instead upon his new master. This god-king had earned the loyalty of at least two of Zeus's former allies, and Pandora caught herself wondering what it was about him that drew so many to his banner.

"The Goddess of Victory," Mithra said at length, his voice soft yet somehow filling up the vaulting spaces of his great hall. He sat unnaturally still, as though chiselled from the same rock as his throne. "The Oracles foretold your coming, but even they quibble and prevaricate over its import. You, champion once of Zeus, stand now before us, and every breath catches in every throat, hanging upon your words. We dangle in desperate wonder over whether you will act for us or for the tyrant king of Elládos."

Pandora felt herself beginning to flush. Mithra claimed everyone here hung upon her words, and, if true, then so too did the fate of the World. Her incessant anxieties, ever-present in the shadows beyond her periphery, threatened to burst forth into the light and engulf her in their crushing embrace. Her eyelid had begun to flutter with such fervour she feared that, even up on his dais, the king and his sorcerer would have noticed the twitching. A mis-chosen word here could earn not only her death, but those of thousands—of millions—of others.

She strove not against a mere Man or Titan but against the aligned will of Ananke. And history was merciless. She had seen the future on Atlantis, on Mu, in the distant, Mist-choked Era claimed by Hekate. That future existed and would not give way without a struggle, if at all.

"I come here not on behalf of any king but to offer a final entreaty for peace on behalf of all peoples. The World watches as the might of Babilim stirs, and none can deny it. But if you grasp ever further, sooner or later, history shall judge you rapacious and cruel. They will not name you great but an overreaching tyrant no better than those he claimed to oppose."

A faint chuckle emanated from the throne. "History ..." Mithra stretched the word out to momentous import. "Do you believe you are in a position to measure the scope of so vast a conceit as history? We are all servants of history, threads woven into the Tapestry of Fate, destined to play out our roles, great and small, over the course of our lives." Water-like, he flowed from his throne, inhuman in grace, possessed of that disquieting stillness even in the midst of movement. When he strode forward, into the light, Pandora gasped. For she knew that face, too, had beheld it, oh so long ago, in what had once felt like the darkest moment of her life.

Here now, before her, stood the boatman who had ferried her back to Ogygia after Zeus had bound Prometheus.

"You know him?" she had asked.

"Off and on, as his wanderings and mine cross. The name's Enki, and I can take you back, if you wish."

And now, more than a thousand years later, Enki sat upon the throne of Babilim. Off and on he had known Prometheus. Two Titans of long acquaintance, and Pandora could no longer believe it a coincidence Mithra had awaited her that day. He had *known*, even as Prometheus had known what would happen within Olympus when Prometheus defied Zeus. Damning revelations slammed into her like successive blows.

Mithra had not emerged as some minor Babilimian aristos, taking advantage of the fall of Smerdis. He had plotted, quietly and behind the scenes, for centuries. For millennia, perhaps. Layer upon layer of machination to bring himself into this position. Had he intended, even back then, to rise to such lofty heights? Her World reeled as she struggled to parse the realisations that refused to slacken. She could not state such things openly, not before Morpheus and this small army of Immortals gathered here.

"If you press the Queens of Mu, it could lead to the very end of the world." But already she knew such a plea would move him little, if at all. He was no dupe, swept up in events he could not understand, but rather an ancient schemer who had planned this for longer than anyone else had realised. He spoke of history as of a well-worn book, its every page committed to memory, creased and crinkling from a thousand perusings.

"History shall not be denied," Mithra said with an air of royal decree. "Destiny drives our steps."

Pandora scowled. She was so damn sick of everyone being so enthralled to Ananke. The god-king's obsession with Fate almost reminded her of Prometheus. But whereas Pandora's lover had settled into a resigned fatalism that espoused that time could not be changed, Mithra almost seemed to imply time *ought* not be changed. And was that not the very ideal of the Unseen Order? At least, she gauged it thus if Nemesis was their chief assassin of Fate.

Did that make Mithra an agent of theirs, or a mere puppet? She needed to understand the depth of his role in this, and she needed to understand the Unseen Order itself. The answers were here, of that she was certain.

Mithra moved closer still, peering at her from the bottom step of his landing, beside Morpheus. "Think over what I have said. Come the dawn, I will have an answer of you, Pandora. The time swiftly approaches when you must choose a side."

He had called her not Nike but Pandora. Of course he had known her, back then, when he called himself Enki. But to have it announced to the whole court felt like something precious had been stolen from her, her secrets stripped bare and exposed to sunlight. On his dismissal of her, Pandora was taken to guest quarters, and there she sat on the floor, legs crossed.

For the maze of her thoughts had grown dense and impenetrable.

A LONG TIME, well into the night, Pandora sat motionless, running it all over in her mind. Even had she not feared Morpheus probing her dreams, she doubted she could have slept. So much had changed in so little time, and she had scarce had any chance to arrange it mentally. Kronos and his allies had, in the days of Vulgeth, formed the Gnostic Cabal and created the Time Chambers in a seemingly vain struggle against the Wheel of Fate. This would place them in direct opposition to the Fates and their assassin, Nemesis, who had hunted them across time. As did Kala, though he appeared to be no ally of Nemesis, rather pursuing his own agenda.

The Unseen Order strove to keep history lodged in its well-worn tracks. Mithra, too, seemed bound in service to the chains of Fate. He had to be involved in the Order, one way or another. Did that mean reaching him with reason would prove impossible? She needed to see him alone, without the court observing their interactions. If she was to have the least chance of swaying him from this path, it must come from an earnest appeal to his humanity, or whatever vestiges of it remained after millennia of Ambrosia-derived immortality.

His Immortals would never allow her to reach his private chambers, though. In touring the palace with Marduk, she had seen a verdant terrace rimming the highest tier of the palace. It stood to reason the god-king would dwell literally above the rest of his people and must be there.

Slowly, Pandora rose and drifted to the window. Outside, off to the left, she could make out that distant level, a hundred feet away and several dozen feet above. Could she make that leap? If she did, her burning wings would immolate the top of the silken dress Artemis had provided her.

"Godsdamn it." She shook her head. She had grown weary of destroying her clothes this way. Maybe it meant she relied upon the fiery wings overmuch since becoming the Phoenix avatar. Still, it seemed her best option here. She doffed the dress from her shoulders, wrapt the top of it around her waist and hoped that would stop it from catching fire. Then she climbed onto the windowsill and braced, hands on either rim of the wall.

The lives of millions depended on her convincing Mithra to change his course, to abandon the Unseen Order and let history be altered. She had to do this. Thus, when her eyelid began to twitch, she squeezed it shut a moment. If naught changed, the Era would end in cataclysmic floods and the rise of an unspeakable abomination.

She leapt, flames surging from her bare feet, wings erupting from her back, hurtling her across the empty space betwixt her room and the palace summit. For an instant she was flying, soaring, wind whipping her hair. Then she closed upon the stone terrace and slammed against its edge with an *ouph*. Her Phoenix-enhanced strength allowed her to dangle there, even breathless.

From within the god-king's chamber, words reached her.

"Yes, Unseen One," a woman said in answer to some question Pandora had not caught.

"Then receive the gift of time itself, that you might trace its ambit and perceive the streams that flow about us. Fulfil your destiny."

Pandora heaved herself up onto the terrace and beheld Nemesis, down on one knee, cerulean eyes flashing beneath her aureate helm. She watched as this woman accepted an object from the god-king. Pandora's precious *Box*.

"No!" the words burst from her, even as Nemesis turned the Box over in her hand. Even as she, though casting Pandora a wary glance, popped the top. Mithra stepped back before the bubble engulfed Nemesis, tearing her out of time. Despite herself, despite her determination and rage, Pandora raised a hand to her mouth in silent objection of what she'd just seen. To have come so close to reclaiming her Box and lose it again thus, it filled her breast with a hollow ache so akin to grief as to become indistinguishable from having had a loved one torn from her life.

Dazed, she turned to regard Mithra. His gaze raked her, and belatedly, Pandora realised she had not re-donned her dress. Without taking her eyes off the god-king—and hardly self-conscious after the life she'd led—she slipped her arms back into the sleeves. The movements gave her reeling mind time to slow its whirls and parse what she had seen. And heard.

"You are not a mere agent of the Unseen Order, but its leader." When she was clad, she forced her hands to her sides, though a rising fury balled them into trembling fists. "Enki, Mithra, whatever you true name is." Here, before her, stood one who rode the very ouroboros of time.

The bare hint of a wry smile creased his lips, though he remained, otherwise, in that statue-like stillness, hands held behind his back. "Oh, but you ought to know by now a person can hold a great many names. Pandora or Nike ... or perhaps, as you were once known in a lost life, Aditi." He took a single step toward her now, more flowing than walking. "Those of us who were first, we have held so very many names in the intervening centuries. We don them like local raiments to suit the needs of the present and discard those that have grown worn by time's ravages. Surely

Matarsivan has intimated as much in the time you have spent together."

The import of his words drove her backward as though he'd shoved her. Wide eyed and struck speechless, she gaped at him. He was like Prometheus. He was a Watcher. And, too, a servant of the Fates.

"You ..." She sucked in a breath to steady nerves that threatened to revolt from her control. "You already knew your actions would end this Era. You knew ... everything."

Despite the unnerving stillness with which he held himself, part of her had still expected a visible reaction on his features. Instead, he remained expressionless, features chiselled to impassiveness. "No one knows everything, and yet, to those of us who follow the true path, we are given to know enough to fulfil our roles."

She shook her head in fervent denial of all of it. He was—in ways that churned her gut—too much like Prometheus. And yet, this man possessed none of the simmering passions of her lover. Perhaps they both served history in their own way, but one did so with remorse, the other with self-righteous resolve that permitted none of the faltering doubts that must define one's humanity. Another thought rose to the surface, one she had oft considered in regard to Nemesis. "If Fate is so immutable, why then would the Fates have need of the Unseen Order to maintain it?"

"For the simplest of reasons imaginable. Because we, too, have always been part of the weave of the Tapestry. Our struggle against the Gnostic Cabal and those their misguided views have swayed was, from the beginning, accounted for. Some wills would forever strive against the inevitable, and they must have foes against which to direct their ire."

No. His words knifed through her heart, a sudden impact for which the full pain had not yet reached her brain. She refused to believe it. For if what Mithra claimed were the truth, it meant her struggle, too, was but mummery. This war across and over time, it had to be more real than that. It had to mean something.

"I know one way to change the future," she said, raising her fists and igniting torches from them. "You will lead no invasion if you never leave this room."

She had not come here to murder anyone. The thought of approaching a man with such intent had bile rising in her throat. She had never wanted to be that kind of person. She had seen such wretched violence in so many others, but she had thought it always a last resort. Now ... now she *had* reached her final resort to save this world.

"You have seen the future. You already know you fail."

She shook her head. "Not this time. Tonight, I write a new future."

Blank faced, he watched her, making no answer. The arrogance of that impassive gaze sparked the Phoenix's fury in her breast, and flames erupted all along her arms, her hair, her torso. She leapt forward, intent on sweeping him into a pankration grapple Themis had taught her.

Rather than rise to meet her, he stepped back, out of the way of her assault, hands still clasped behind his back. Again and again, he evaded her with a maddening efficiency of movement, as if in mockery of her rage. She lunged, and Mithra bent backward, thrusting out a foot that she tripped over and stumbled out onto the terrace.

"How do you aim to overcome one with tens of thousands of years of experience?"

Burning energy surged within her and she poured it into her feet. "Sheer fucking tenacity." Flames burst beneath her heels, hurtling her forwards like an arrow from a bow. She slammed into Mithra and bore him down.

Her flames ignited his clothes and beard. Shrieking, she rained blows upon him. Some he blocked, possessed of uncanny strength himself. But he could not quite match the raw power of the Phoenix. She heard his shoulder snap beneath the force of her assault, and even that statuesque visage creased in pain. Seeing it gave her a moment's pause; a weighty realisation she intended to beat a man to death with her bare hands.

Mithra got a foot under her and kicked, sending her flying. Her back slammed into the ceiling, knocking the wind from her lungs. Then she was falling, only to smack hard into the floor once more.

When she managed, groaning, to lift her head, she saw Mithra had moved out onto the terrace and stood upon the rim as if he imagined jumping. Perhaps he, an immortal Watcher, could hop down to the next level without risk of injury. But so could she. And she would not hesitate a second time. Pandora pushed herself up on her arms.

"There was never chance here for you," Mithra said. He leapt into the air. But he did not fall. Ebony-feathered wings burst from his back. The wind of their beating washed over her, billowing her hair and Mithra flew up, vanishing over the building.

"Shit," Pandora moaned, scrambling to her feet. She paced onto the terrace and peered into the night sky but saw naught save stars and moon.

Somewhere below, voices rose in alarm. "The god-king is under attack!"

INTERLUDE: ORPHEUS

So, I lost my Eurydike. Mayhap I ought to have joined the hunters, when first you gathered. But I did not do so. I have oft enough proved craven in my life—and I am well enough into my cups to admit it now. But it was not cowardice that stayed my hand from joining the hunt back then. No, it was selfish apathy. I thought the plight of Kalydon of no consequence. I thought myself and Eurydike safe amid our companions, powerful as they were. A fool, I spent my time seeking after hidden lore whilst a monster terrorised the countryside.

I paid the price for ignoring the looming threat.

I forgot, I suppose, that I too was a Man in the World, and bound thus to share the fate of those living in it. We are, all of us, tied to one another, Theseus. It is only in arrogance we may think the threads of our lives' existence separate from others.

With gross violence, Eurydike's death ripped the shroud from eyes and forced me to gape into the mirror of my many inequities. I had seen my failings and resolved that they would not hold me back. Not again.

Thus I crossed the tenebrous expanses of the Underworld, climbed the dark mountains. Before Hades's gates I came face-to-face with his horrific watchdog—a massive, snarling monster of three fiendish heads—and only through the greatest of my songs did I lull the beast into slumber.

Beyond, I reached Hades's necropolis. Of the wretched city of the dead, I will say little. If my tale thus far has not instilled in you enough dread of what lies beyond this world, then you've failed to heed aught I wished to impart.

No, what mattered now to me was this. Hades's servants came for me, but with my music I charmed even the dead and convinced them to escort me into the king's sepulchral halls. My songs, you see, are not *mere* music. They are the lost art of old days in Kumari Kandam, when gods and great Men could sing the World into what shapes suited them. And when sung with clarity and confidence, by one with the gift, even a wraith must harken to the music's allure.

In the dead king's throne room, pale fires smouldered in iron braziers, serving more to deepen the oppressive shadows than cast them back. Columns supported a vaulted ceiling that hung over a vast hall. I could make out little upon the fringes, save that shades or wraiths drifted about, waiting to see what their master would make of me: a living Man with the temerity to intrude into his domain.

And Hades ... was twice, *thrice* the height of most Titans. Even upon his throne, he towered over me like a mountain of necrotic flesh and bleached bone. Almost vanishing into the shadows behind his throne stood the pale figure of his abducted wife, Persephone.

The King of the Dead leered at me, baring fang-like teeth, his eyes glinting red. Beneath his withering gaze, all my planned entreaties died upon my tongue. I stood there, trembling and wretched, a facile simpleton forced to confront the scope of his colossal blunder. Hades turned up his palm, and the air shimmered as if illumined by blue flame. The burning currents writhed and twisted, taking shape until I beheld an apparition of my beloved.

Though I had yet to utter a word in his presence, Hades knew who I was and why I had come. I cannot fathom whence comes his power and knowledge, but it was vast, deep as the very sea into which I'd trod to reach that forsaken world.

"I would hear his song, husband," Persephone said. Her voice had a hollow quality to it, as though she was not entirely there in the room with us. "Let us sample the delicacy of music said to stir the dreams of stones and trees and soothe the abraded souls even of your wraiths."

What? You do not believe my reputation might stretch even into the gloomy depths of the Underworld? Perhaps you underestimate the power of ancient songs, friend.

Hades chuckled, then, a foul sound, as of a thousand last wheezing gasps of dying Men.

"Release my wife from the Underworld, and I shall play for you a song the likes of which has not been heard since before the Time of Nyx. Harken to the lay of the Fall of Gorias. Quiver before the tale of the untrammelled fury of Moccus, who smote the very stones of the great city-state."

"I like deals, mortal." Hades leant forward upon his throne and curled his fingers about my wife's image as though they were bars of a cage. "Allow me to stipulate my condition. Impress me with your song, and her soul shall follow you. But." He raised his other hand and extended a single digit in warning. "You must not look back at what you leave behind here. You must flee from my domain without so much as a second glance, mortal."

It sounded strange but simple enough. And so, I sang.

And the stones of the hall thrummed and swayed in time. The pale fires danced. And the shadows joined my chorus.

As I said, my songs are the lost art of Kumari Kandam. I had long sought to perfect them, and before Eurydike's death, I had a mentor. One who helped me reach the Realms beyond and pull from them all the arcana Men cannot know. From spirits that slumbered within the flesh of Gaia for uncounted eons I learnt, and I grew, and I perfected my craft.

When I tell you my mentor was a God, do not mistake me or think I refer to the self-styled deities of Olympus. No, for the one who tutored me was so far beyond their ilk as to make them seem but children mumming their parents.

No, the one under whom I trained was older by far, if not in flesh, then in soul. There are entities out there in the cosmos, friend, existing beyond mortal conceptions of time, beyond the fragile paradigms upon which we base our lives and our very thoughts. Oh ... Oh, Theseus, perhaps you know somewhat of what I speak. If you have been so unfortunate as to touch minds from the far ranges beyond our world, you have my pity. What little, at least, I have left to spare.

So, then.

The God bore many names. Most oft, however, he went by Dionysus. Yes, the very same deity who rent asunder King Pentheus in days gone. Such deeds brought him infamy, but he has done far more, and worse. No Man nor Titan holds immunity to the seductive touch of his power, of that I can assure you.

Those of us in his inner circle he taught, and taught well. Beneath silver moonlight, in sylvan glades, he would expound upon mysteries of the World you cannot imagine. Time would melt away from us like snow held too tight in your palm, hours becoming days. He spoke of the lost lore of the fallen cities of Dark Faerie, of a time *before* the Time of Nyx. No, no ... the details matter not, nor would you find yourself better off for being subjected to darker truths. He showed us how to train our minds in a multitude of the lesser arcana. And me, who already had a foundation in the spellsongs of Kumari Kandam ... Me, he took under special tutelage.

When God penetrates you, friend, it is not mere flesh he enters, but mind and soul. Oh, please spare me your sputtering facade of sexual mores. The soul is stirred as the soul is stirred, and regardless, I know no one who could turn away from God's embrace.

With caresses and whispered intimations, Dionysus guided me to depths of knowledge the likes of which Man has not known in long Eras of the World. My spellsongs became compounded upon themselves. They reached deeper, beyond space or time, until I could sing the chords whose vibrations held together the cosmos.

So, when I tell you I drank the knowledge he offered in equal portion to the rivers of wine Dionysus called forth, I hope you grasp the depths of my meaning. Were I so inclined, with a song I could split the heavens and call forth storms to inundate the land. I could set Gaia herself to trembling and bring toppling down the towering palaces of aristoi. I could sway the mind of Man or beast. I could induce warriors into killing frenzies, heedless of their own safety. Or I could lull a drakon into blissful slumber.

But not even I could bring back the dead.

I TELL you these things so you will understand that even Hades, dark God of the Dead, sat moved by the songs I sang. Such was the power of the music of creation. When at last the final echoes of my song faded from his dark hall, Hades slumped back into his throne, his massive fingers tracing obscure patterns upon its armrests.

I will not claim to know the mind of one so unfathomable as Hades. I cannot guess what strange calculus unfolded within his soul. After a time, Persephone moved to his side and whispered something to him, and the dire god nodded, once.

"Abide the terms I gave you," he said, voice at once booming and somehow stifled, as if directed inward.

A moment, I awaited, thinking someone would bring Eurydike to my side. All that time, Hades held me with his red-tinged gaze until I was left quivering and forced to acknowledge the razor edge of his bargain. He would not present my wife to me at all. He had bidden me to depart the Underworld without looking back, and thus I would have to leave his court clutching to naught save trust.

Would he have deceived me? Could he break our agreement?

Shamans held that, whilst eidolons delighted in lies and decep-tions, they held at the very least to the letter of their deals, if not the intent. But did any such rules apply to a being of such unbridled power as Hades?

Yes, his bargain would cut deep, such was its cruelty.

And I knew better than to argue with a god.

ъ

OH, yes. Dionysus, the one we knew not as a god, but as the God.

Before we met him, Eurydike and I had come to the wilds south of Delphi. We swam in the mountain lakes, made love beneath the stars, and she danced to my songs. Then, one night, as I sought the wisdom of spirits in a shamanic trance, I felt a colossal will. An intellect beyond aught I had ever imagined brushed against my mind and tickled my soul.

With honey-sweet promise, it called to me.

COME, ORPHEUS …

Like a fool, I heeded its summons. As I said, we Men long cling to the delusion that, given another chance, we might have made better choices. Or maybe choice itself was denied me, for that foreign mind was in my head, its song more entrancing than even those of the sirens that later sought to drown all aboard the Argo.

The voice promised all knowledge, all answers. It promised, even then, the depths of the song I had so long sought. Everything would be mine—if I but harkened and followed.

So, follow I did.

In the depths of the woods, I found the God. In fear for Eurydike, I had bid her stay behind, but God had sensed her as well, and she trailed close at my heels. We stumbled into a small glade and there, for the first time, I beheld Dionysus. The God was suspended in midair by some inexplicable force, as if held in a bubble of collapsed space. I know not even how to describe such a strange phenomenon.

LET MUSIC SOOTHE THE SWOLLEN BANDS OF TIME …

I cannot say I grasped the whole meaning of the voice in my

head, but I understood enough to know the God called upon my music to aid him. Can you imagine the honour of such? To think God needed me, a Man, to aid him. He sought for *my* songs to sing his worship.

Perhaps it might have behooved me to ask why a true God would ever have need of a mortal.

But I saw the depth of the entity before me, and that depth imprinted upon my soul.

And so I sang. I sang of the easing of fetters and the soothing of an abraded World. And with languorous movements, Dionysus eased himself free of the space that imprisoned him. Like a popped bubble, the contorted space burst, flowing back into normal reality.

"Come," a voice deep as the mountains said.

And with him, we went.

OH, escaping from the Underworld? Yes ... I felt the eyes of the uncounted dead watching me as I made my way down the shadow-drenched streets of Hades's necropolis. Like a chill breath upon the back of my neck, their regard brushed over me. Yet, save for the jangling clatter of chains over stone, my departure from that place was met with silence.

Ever and anon, I had to fight the overwhelming urge to call to Eurydike. Were her eyes among the many watching my slow retreat from Hades's domain? Did she, as the king had promised, follow me, out of his grasp, back toward the life so cruelly rent from her? Each time, something like a constricting serpent wrapt itself around my throat and forbade me from violating the quiet that had settled over me.

At least, until we had passed through osseous gates of the foul city and I could no longer bear the weight of the silence crushing me. "We'll be home soon," I promised.

Eurydike did not answer me.

The awful fear that I had suppressed all this time reared its viperous head now. Had Hades betrayed me? Had I left that city trusting my wife followed, when, in fact, I walked alone?

"I ... I gathered your limbs. With my songs, I staved off decay and restored your body, my love."

Only stillness and dead air.

No, I would not breach the terms the god had set before me. I would *not* look back. Onward, I pushed, further down the mountain paths and back toward the passage that could return us to Gaia.

Moments stretched so thin I feared they would snap.

A clammy sweat ran over what passed for my flesh in that existence.

"Eurydike?"

Some will say there is bliss in the quiet. But there are few things more horrible than to speak and be met with silence. Without someone to listen and acknowledge them, our words lose substance and become mere animal grunts.

Upon the onyx sands, my resolve cracked. "My love," I cried, daring a glance over my shoulder, certain already that I was alone.

She was there. Arms bound behind her back, gagged. Her eyes met mine and widened, love washed out by the dawning horror of what we—what *I* had done.

Then the Khaos rose. The sands danced along the ground a heartbeat before something worked itself up through those grains. Tenebrous fingers like so many breaching worms. Arms, bifurcated at the elbows, followed. Too many grasping hands seized Eurydike. She railed against her captors, even as they began to drag her down into those sharp sands.

Never will I erase from my mind the utter terror I beheld in her eyes then.

I lunged, catching her hands. But the entity that had seized her had strength beyond the ken of Man. With inexorable progress, it dragged her beneath the surface. When the last vestige of her hand vanished, I wailed, scrambling away on my arse.

What had I done?

Had I come so far only for my resolve to fail me at the last?

What had I done? *Why*, oh why could I not still the impulse to look back and assure myself she was with me?

These questions have no answer, I think.

❧

OH, fuck, Theseus.

Had I the courage, I would have sought to join her in death. Ah, fine, say what you will of the taking of one's own life. It is not always so easy as it sounds. Believe me, I longed to see her again. To beg her forgiveness for my mistake.

Is it not cruelty beyond measure that, for a transitory error, one might suffer eternal torments?

Heh. But I was always the architect of my own damnation, friend. I had set Dionysus free, yes, and more than that. I was there, by his side, when he claimed the first of his new Maenads. The Olympian Artemis ... Did you know that? It was through her that Dionysus called forth the Boar God to ravage the countryside. I do not know his aim in doing so.

But I watched him approach Artemis at her weakest, most broken moment, when she proved Olympians were every bit as fragile as mortals. I watched him call forth the beast that had rent the stones of Gorias. Oh, yes, the self-same Boar God you hunters slew.

Mayhap I could have dissuaded him. I could have tried. But in my fascination with the worlds he showed me, I revelled in the chance to witness such timeless glory. I thought myself blessed to see dread Moccus walk the world once more.

Eurydike, though, she had a doubt. Somehow, despite the lure of Dionysus's supremely intoxicating wine and even more enthralling presence, she managed to voice dissent. A worry, about the price of unleashing such chaos.

So, God offered a bargain. If Men could slay this incarnation of Moccus, Dionysus swore he would prevent the Boar God from taking another immediate host. That he would force the progenitor soul to reincarnate within mortals like any other being, and thus, Men would have the chance to contain its fury.

Dionysus gave her that promise.

But I ask you, old friend. Do you think, after she demanded concessions from God, it mere coincidence that the boar's next victim proved Eurydike herself?

I ran from my God, then. I had seen too much of his callous plan to mistake it, or him, for beneficent any longer. And yet, even now, I feel him, calling back to me. He calls for his wayward disciple.

God tolerates none to leave him.

For my craven heart, I run from him. Yet I wonder, when at last he finds and finishes with me, will I then behold my beloved once more?

What do you think, friend? Do I deserve a second chance?

PART IV

<hr>

Much has been written of the Sight, yes, never with a fully accepted definition. That is a sixth sense, a gift from the Moirai, an awakened awareness anyone can achieve, or even an aspect of the Art. I would argue the difficulty in framing the exact nature of the Sight lies in the fact that the term is applied to several distinct, if interrelated, phenomena: mediumship, prescience, retrocognition, or even—and this remains disputed—telepathy. I would further posit the defining characteristic of the Sight is that it allows one to apprehend what philosophers term the Ontos—the truer reality behind reality.

    — Second Chronicle of the Circle of Goetic Mysteries

28

HEKATE

219 Golden Age

For three years, the Gnostic Cabal had tutored Hekate, instructing her in their secrets, even as they plumbed the depths of her knowledge for answers of which they too might make use. She had ventured farther, delved deeper than any sorceress or medium of which they knew, and their thirst for ever deeper insights matched her own. Their desperate need to find some means to strive against the bitter realities of the Ontos sent them all down so many winding paths, so many false leads, so many aborted schemes that all ended with the abhorrent conclusion: that Fate was immutable.

So many times now she had climbed the slopes of Olympus and descended down to gaze unto the Oracle Mirrors, within beholding vision after vision, each reaffirming history as it had always played out for her. The future was her past, twisting upon itself in sick spirals of depravity that had her wondering how the Moirai could even dream of such convoluted knots.

*W*HEN *P*YRRHA *finally reached the shore, another woman was there, wrapt
in an embroidered cloak, with only a few strands of hair dangling down
from her hood. The woman offered her a hand up and pulled Pyrrha to her
feet. "I saw that," the woman said.*

*Pyrrha took a moment to wring out her hair, then wrapt her arms
about her shivering chest. The second time tonight she'd wound up going for
a swim in waters too cold for it. "He mistakes his simply being present for
wooing and a lack of revulsion for interest."*

*The woman shrugged. "The powerful cannot conceive of their so-called
lessers not worshipping them."*

Damn if that wasn't the truth. "I'm Pyrrha."

*Now, the woman nodded. "And I am Enodia, a sorceress formerly of the
Circle of Goetic Mysteries. I have felt you, Pyrrha, and sensed your potential from long back. I can help you open your mind and reach that potential
if you so desire."*

*All Pyrrha could do was stand there, mouth agape, peering at the hooded
woman. What exactly the Circle-of-whatever was, she had no idea ... But a
sorceress! Oh, there were always rumours about that sort of thing. Women on
the fringes who balked at the hierarchy of the World, who took to forbidden
studies for the chance, for any chance to not have to bend their wills and
bodies to the whims of men. "You're offering to teach me sorcery? It's real?"*

*Enodia snorted, then clucked her tongue. "Mmm. It is real, but your
bumbling around in the Penumbra will not give you such power. If you ever
managed to confront a spirit thus, it would mostlike slip inside your body
and ride you like a horse, sating its perverse desires using your flesh. It
would feast upon your soul and leave you an empty husk, perhaps after
enduring centuries of slavery."*

*The sorceress's words only intensified the chill that had seized Pyrrha.
"Why?"*

*"Why then would people like me dare hold concert with the denizens of
the Ether? Why would any save madmen touch the Otherworld?" Enodia
took a step forward and seized Pyrrha by the arms. "I offer you more power*

and knowledge than you could ever have imagined. Is that not what you have sought after, combing through the dark? Did you imagine such would come with neither risk nor price?"

And there was only one thing to say to that. One answer appropriate for a woman who might be like Pyrrha, who could understand her. Who could see the umbral horrors that had forever haunted her. "Teach me."

Memory bled into foreboding until the two became as hopelessly entwined as Hekate's past and future. It all spread out before her, but she could not trace its circuitous path, save to judge the loops had neither beginning nor end.

"I'm fine," Pyrrha said, snatching her hand away from her father. "Thank you for asking."

He sighed. "You are not fine. You deepen your studies in the Art."

"Yes." Of course she did. What else was there for her?

"Pyrrha, sorcery abrades the soul. You cannot practice the Art without it destroying the person you are inside."

Pyrrha scoffed and stared at him, disdaining his ignorance. "Sorcery abrades the soul? Well, so does life, Father. It scours and scourges and takes and takes until we are but nubs. Shells of our former selves. Does sorcery harm us? Perhaps, but so does training as a warrior, and you do not dissuade any from that course. We pay for power in pain and blood, but at least we gain some semblance of control over our lives!"

"Pyrrha, you cannot—"

"My name," she interrupted, "is the sorceress Hekate."

"I want to help," Hekate heard the young girl saying, *"but don't know how. If you help me, though, I'll try. I want to find out what happened to my mother that day. Can you tell me if you saw—"*

It was time. Hekate shrieked, letting all the pain of tortured millennia pour forth. All the bitter self-loathing her abraded soul deserved, all the unspeakable vexation the Fates had inflicted upon her, they mingled into a scream so inhuman she could scarce believe it had ushered from her. A moment of defiance, and then, enhanced by Potency, she shoulder-slammed into the younger Hekate. The impact hurtled the other woman away, sending her tumbling several times before coming to rest amid a maze of roots.

All choices, all her life had been illusory. Her self-deception of free will had cast her unerringly down this path. Or maybe this, now, was her first true choice. She walked willingly into the Dark.

She stalked closer, coming to pause just before the other Hekate, hovering over the fallen woman.

How those words rang in her ears, unforgettable. "Hope is but the delusion with which we poison our souls. Like the apparition that is free will, we chase it because we cannot abide that our very thoughts arise not from our desires but from the chains of fate."

Her younger self pushed herself up on her arms, turning to look at her. Hekate watched as gaping, mind-numbing shock washed over the woman whilst she strove to regain the breath blown out of her lungs. With gritted teeth, the other woman stood, making her vain attempt to stare down the Hekate of now.

The one who, even now, must become Enodia.

And Enodia could not allow pity to stay her hand. The World admitted no room for such indulgences as mercy. "So you would defy Ananke by killing your own past self?" A pause. "As close as you draw, still apprehension escapes you." Summoning Khione's power, she coalesced ice crystals around her fingers. "If only we could have seen more, seen farther, maybe this could have been avoided. Now, it is the last choice—or illusion thereof —yet left to us."

❧

WHEN THEY EMERGED from the depths of Olympus after another fruitless stretch of scouring the Oracle Mirrors for answers, Kronos led Hekate not toward the crumbling steps that would descend the mountain but rather onto a side path that wrapt around the peak. Unless Hekate missed her guess, Apollon's temple would later obscure this route, for she had never seen this path before.

"What are we about now?" she demanded, unable to infuse her words with the bite of bitterness she'd hoped for. Three years the Gnostic Cabal had instructed and prodded her, and neither she nor they seemed a hair closer to breaking free of the designs of Ananke. Despite the Cabal's refusal to surrender to inevitability, all they learnt served to reinforce a single conclusion: that time had unfolded, complete and entire, at the very inception of the cosmos. That, though they forded its currents, they could not redirect its flow.

"Long ago I discovered something, a relic of the first Era of the World. A record, if you will, of destiny itself."

Their path forced them to press up against the cliff, gazing down at a sheer drop plunging for hundreds of feet. The view sent Hekate's heart racing and sweat slicked the same palms with which she steadied herself against the rock wall.

At last they reached a wider shelf, then had to squeeze through a narrow crevasse separating the mountainside. From the look, a quake had opened this rent, albeit one long back, given how wind and rain had eroded the outer edges.

Wedged within the tight confines, stuck—given that Kronos's bulkier form scarce fit at all and his progress had become a crawl— Hekate grunted in discomfort. "Do not the Oracle Mirrors already serve as records of Fate?"

Kronos's answer came as a growl. When at last he broke into open space, the Titan lord gasped and panted. As Hekate eased her own way from the crevasse, she spotted a steep decline ahead. The path descended a few hundred feet before twisting down to a cave, a gap bridged by an arch of stairs of dubious integrity. Indeed, when they reached the bridge, mortar crunched beneath Kronos's weight, showers of dust raining in a cataract beneath the stairway.

The route held, if barely, and when Kronos had crossed and reached the cave, Hekate followed. The Titan lord, she had found, served as the informal leader of the Gnostic Cabal, reinforcing her suspicion he was one of the immortal founders. Laran was a demigod born not thirty years prior, so she had ruled him out as one of the others. As for the women, none offered her a straight answer, so she could not guess whether any of them had lived so long as Kronos. Regardless, Kronos had served as her direct mentor, her connection to the others much more sporadic as they pursued their own ends.

Crumbling columns flanked the cave's entrance, adjoining to an arch carved with elaborate geometric designs, all sweeping arcs and curves evoking the glory of nature. Inside, the fading daylight limned further architectural embellishments. The recesses of a vaulted ceiling vanished into the gloom, making it impossible to gauge the true size of the holding.

"This was built by the same people who constructed Vulgeth, in the Nyxlands," she observed.

Offering only a nod in answer, Kronos plodded through the darkened chamber with confident ease, leaving her no choice save to follow. Upon reaching a much larger chamber, he set to igniting lamps attached to the walls, using a wick set upon a long pole. With each flame that sprang to life, more shadows danced about the inner vault.

As she edged forward, the brickwork upon the floor groaned and shifted, drawing her eyes down to cracks that had shot through the once-fine workmanship. Though this place may have endured for centuries or millennia, it did not go untouched by time. One day, Gaia's restless shifting would sunder the ancient hold, burying whatever secrets lay within forever.

When he had finished with the lamps, Kronos strode toward the heart of the chamber, at which stood a stone pedestal. Atop the pedestal rested a simple stone tablet, engraved with glyphs that, whilst similar to Supernal, differed in flourishes. Upon closer inspection, Hekate began to think it a list of eight names, though she could but guess at what those were.

"Behold the Tablet of Destiny," Kronos intoned, arms spread in grand gesture, as if his mere words ought to have awed a great mass spread out before him.

"What is it?"

"A foretelling of cycles of destruction and rebirth. A circular prophecy, binding us to the cataclysmic ends of Eras and the fragile hope that some vestige of Man will crawl from the dust after each termination of our world. Herein lie the names of the Destroyer, the catalyst that keeps the Wheel forever spinning."

Hekate leant closer, fingers brushing engravings that radiated an aura of timeless antiquity. A psychic echo resided within this thing, something she could perceive but lacked the psychometric ability to interpret as more than a sensation. "The world has ended eight times already."

"Not ... yet." Kronos's words filled up the empty space in the chamber, thick with import, choking as they settled in her mind. Some of the Eschatons had yet to unfold. And still the future lay before her, carved in stone. Herein lay the proof that the Cabal's bumbling attempts to alter time or Fate were naught but a farce, even if they themselves could not see it.

Idamdra? Naresa? Othinn? Rudra? The others she was even less certain of. All of them Destroyers of Eras, heralds of destruction.

The weight of it all set her to trembling. The enormity of this stone bit at her fingers and she jerked her hand back as if burnt.

"You see," Kronos continued, lost in his own self-important expounding and oblivious to its real import, "if we can but learn to understand the Tablet, we might uncover the means of averting destiny. A single nudge might lead the whole of the Wheel of Fate to crumble. We can still become the lords of time, Hekate."

A bitter mix of chortling and weeping spilt from her, a tear welling in her remaining eye. "You told me the Time Chamber beneath Vulgeth was destroyed when the city collapsed."

"Indeed," he admitted. "We have not yet found a way to thwart Fate. Every crossroads we see, every chance we might have to prove the future mutable seems to come at untenable, impossible cost. But if—"

"Of course it fucking does! That's why you *don't* make those choices, which is why you can see those futures in the damn mirrors!" Her shrieks sounded like those of a madwoman, she knew, reverberating through the ancient chamber. It didn't matter. She couldn't stop herself from railing at him for all the Cabal's failures. "You never changed a fucking thing, not even with the ability to timewalk. The names of those on this Tablet are already written."

"What is written may change." Kronos folded his arms, not the least perturbed by her outburst. "The better question is, what if we *have* changed something? Would we even know?"

Hekate's next tirade died upon her tongue. Kronos implied that, if time could flow, if its course could alter, would not their memories of past visions change to account for the new timeline? What if she had *already* altered Fate and made it worse and now remembered it always unfolding in the new way? Surely to tread down such paths of thought was to court madness.

Struck speechless, she allowed Kronos to lead her from the accursed vault and its damning contents.

ALL THE LONG route down Olympus, Hekate found her thoughts too moiled to bother with conversation, and Kronos, with his uncanny perception, seemed to know it well enough. Indeed, that was but another question she mused many a time since coming to the Gnostic Cabal: how keen a mind would one have after uncounted thousands of years of life? Astute, perhaps, to the point that one could take in others in a moment and judge the sum of their thoughts, of their lives?

In four thousand years of life, Hekate had accumulated such an ability already, and could oft gauge the minds of those around her. Kronos's abilities went further, almost as keen, Hekate thought, as those of another she knew, with whom she had spent *far* more time than she had with Kronos.

And watching it all unfold, there were some few first immortals. Though they fancied themselves guides of Man, still they too lacked all the answers.

Whilst Kronos had almost certainly been including himself in that description, his words, then and later, had implied a number of other immortals, not all of whom ever joined his impotent little Cabal.

Along the long route, she considered—almost every night after Kronos slept—how she might still find a way to unmake her past to alter her future. Her future self had stopped her from interfering with her meeting with Enodia, but still, there had to be a way, a nexus in history where will alone might defy the tyranny of Fate. A dozen times she set the Box, considering each point in the vast span of her life where it might have taken another turn. Surely, given enough tries, enough throws of the die, a new future could yet be cut loose from the weave of the Tapestry. Kronos had claimed that any action they might have taken to change the future would have come with an unbearable price.

Maybe, then, those were the prices Hekate must pay.

When at last they returned to Kronion, and to the Cabal's sanctum beneath the acropolis, they found Themis waiting there for them.

The Oracle Titan sat staring at a pool of water, no doubt lost in hydromantic trance, oblivious to their entrance.

Upon taking a seat across from her and bidding Hekate to join him, Kronos cleared his throat. "Why have you come here unbidden, Themis?"

The glaze that coated her eyes faded. "Not long ago I fulfilled a vision." Her gaze, heavy-lidded and yet still oppressive, fell upon Hekate. "In the ancient catacombs beneath Delphi I awaited the coming of a girl I knew I must guide. Though I saw her a fortnight ago there, here she sits, a woman grown."

Hekate drew a sharp breath. So her past self had drank of Python's puissance and refined the visions in her dreams.

Kronos caught Themis's implication with alarming swiftness, spinning upon Hekate. "You are already a timewalker."

Hekate turned to glower upon the Titan lord. How tired she had become of their ineptitude. "You have *failed*, time and again. Had you shown me a morsel of hope against the chains of Ananke, I would have shared the whole of my knowledge with you." She rose then, backing away from the two Cabalists, reaching into her satchel, fingers searching out the grooves of the Box. "You are not willing to do what is needful to defy Fate or escape from the yawning maw of Khaos closing in upon the World. You have, despite your immortality, not the strength to take the darkest path." When had she last set the Box for? Oh, yes, she remembered. A time when she might unravel *everything*. "I will do what you never could. I will put a stop to the sick cycle that fetters us."

"Hekate ..." Kronos said, rising with hands lifted in warding, the look upon his face making plain he had realised at least something of what she intended.

Casting her would-be mentor a last, bitter smirk, Hekate activated the Box.

❦

"Maybe, if I allow Mormo to feast upon your soul, this can be ended," *Hekate said. For she had to provoke both incarnations of the wraith. She saw it when Mormo seized control of the other Hekate.*

A moment of indecision, of doubt, crippled her. And in that moment, Hekate-Mormo lunged, its skeletal claws ripping through Hekate's guts. A tidal wave of agony blinded her, stole vision and thought, filling her sight with red haze and screaming without apparent source.

Next she knew, Mormo had yanked out her intestines, sending Hekate pitching over backward. She sat on her arse, looking up at the half-possessed Hekate.

"None of this matters," Hekate gurgled, ichor spilling over her lips and

down her chin. She felt Mormo rising in her now, taking control, seized by some animal moil of dread and fury and hunger. Mormo had her now, but it didn't matter, because this had all happened before. She already knew how this ended, and thus, her mind grasped for somewhere else, some other thought, some distant memory that might serve to block the ravaging pain.

VERTIGINOUS WAVES RIPPLED THROUGH HEKATE, her clearing vision only increased the urge to retch. She lay slumped against a wall, inside a courtyard, the warm evening seeking to lull her back into the escape of unconsciousness. The plucking of a lyre mingled with laughter, filling a space saturated with the bouquet of fine wine and an underlying hint of vomit.

As she looked around, she realised a party or symposium unfolded within this courtyard, the finery the locals wore announcing them as Phoenikian, albeit Phoenikians with antiquated tastes.

It had worked.

Pushing herself up and stifling a groan, Hekate gaped around the courtyard. She stood in a shadowed corner within the courtyard of Epaphus Palace in Tyros. Had she truly reached that very night?

Nervous jitters thrummed through her chest. It felt as though the shaking might send her crumbling apart, as though the weight of the moment would crush her to pulp. The impossibility of both Fate and her intent to thwart it formed a thought of such enormity she feared to linger upon it lest it consume her.

Dazed, she wandered a moment as though meandering through the nebulous corridors of a dream, in control of her own actions only through a direct exertion of will. Then, in the shadow of a stretching cedar tree, she saw them: Pandora and Kirke, locked in what seemed a weighty debate.

Here? Now? Had Kirke been here that night?

Her daughter glanced in her direction and Hekate stepped amid a passing crowd. No matter if Kirke had been in Tyros on this night, if

Pandora was here as an adult, *she* had clearly timewalked to this moment. Yet the woman made no attempt to avert her own kidnapping?

No, Hekate could not afford to risk either of them seeing her. She could not risk that they might try to keep her from doing what she must. The Gnostic Cabal said they could not change time because any action that might do so always proved onerous beyond endurance. Hekate would make the choice they never could. She would free herself from Ananke—and her impending damnation— by erasing herself.

That such a course would cost Kirke and Athene their existence was a thought she pushed down, as she had in every consideration of this course. It was a needle worming its way through her heart—one that would have killed her, had she not plotted her own oblivion— and all she could do was pretend it did not trouble her. To dwell on such would shatter her resolve and leave her as powerless as Kronos and the others.

Even as she hid from her mother and daughter, a commotion arose within the palace vestibule. It was starting. She was almost too late.

Threading her way among the guests, Hekate raced into the building, where Zeus ploughed through the crowd like a bull, a much younger Hekate following in his wake. Guests scrambled out of the way, but in the rush, many did not move fast enough for the king's liking, and Zeus hurled them to either side in the frenzied, tonic-induced lust Hekate had inflicted upon him. Nyx's bosom, what had she done? How had she let Kirke convince her to follow this obscene route of Fate?

Wending through the crowd, Hekate closed in on her past self. Zeus would prove beyond reason, but maybe, if she could reach *herself*, she could find the strength to stop the king. Or if not, all she needed was to prevent herself from insisting he take Pandora, for without Hekate, Zeus would otherwise have ignored Europa's child.

But the past Hekate, her gaze drifted away from Zeus, fixating upon a column supporting the vestibule. Upon the cloaked woman standing in its shadow. Wondering if she had just seen … Enodia.

Fuck.

Hekate had forgotten about that, and Enodia would never let her carry out her plan.

Desperate, Hekate surged through the crowd, shoving her younger self and sending her stumbling. In the distraction, Enodia slipped away, and Hekate raced after her, trusting that by the time her past self rose, she'd have no idea what had happened. She had to first stop the revenant sorceress from interfering, *then* she could see about sparing young Pandora this fate.

She'd seen the swirl of Enodia's cloak as the woman disappeared back out into the courtyard. Yet when Hekate emerged into the open night, she caught no sight of the interloper. Where had the damn ghost gone? Should Hekate go back to the throne room? A glimpse of swishing fabric caught her eye the instant before Enodia vanished through an open archway.

She had no choice. She could catch Pandora on the boat if needs be, but she had to stop Enodia first, or the revenant would undo aught Hekate managed to accomplish. Flooding Pneuma into Potency and Alacrity, Hekate broke off into a mad dash across the courtyard. She burst into the room and found it empty, though doorways opened off to either side. A set of stairs descended into a cellar, and a wooden door there hung ajar, swinging slightly.

Damn that wretched ghost. After pooling a bit of Pneuma into Steadfastness, Hekate leapt to the bottom of the stairs and burst into the shadowed cellar. Within stood row after row of giant amphorae. The whole cellar, lit only by a single oil lamp on the wall, was redolent with the scents of wine and stored lamp oil. Some careless servant, in a rush to keep the guests drunk and happy, had knocked over one of the amphorae, spilling oil and cracked shards of pottery across the floor.

Heedless of it soaking her peplos, Hekate pushed inward, gaze darting one way or the next in search of Enodia.

"This mad circle of our history must end," Hekate said,

summoning Khione's ice to her fingertips. She pushed deeper into the cellar, but the shadows loomed so thick the ghost could have lurked in any corner, all but invisible. "You cannot believe the course of our past and future behoves us." The only sound came from the sloshing of her sandals through mingled oil and wine, the cracking of ceramic shards beneath her heels. "Enodia, answer me!"

"How many men and women have deluded themselves in the throes of desperation?" The ghost's voice came not from the cellar's tenebrous recesses but from behind Hekate. She spun to find Enodia standing on the threshold of the doorway. "Still you believe you could find some way free of Fate, forgetting your opponent is *yourself*. Your every thought has already flitted through my mind. Your every scheme, every machination is doomed to fail against me, for I have already lived them all."

"Listen to me—" Hekate pleaded.

"But I never do ..." Enodia slapped the oil lamp free from its shelf.

It toppled, the instant of its flight enough for Hekate to realise her error. No servant had broken the amphora. Enodia had shattered it on purpose, and no doubt cracked many others before luring Hekate inside.

It was the only thought she had time for before the flames struck the ground. The sudden whoosh of fire devouring air stole her breath even as heat and light erupted, great chains of exploding amphorae, lamp oil bursting aflame. A consuming, devouring conflagration shot through the cellar, the roar deafening, leaving a ringing in her ears that drowned out even the sound of her own screams. Scalding heat washed over her, flames racing up her oil-soaked garments, bubbling flesh.

She fell, hands flailing in vain attempts to extinguish the spreading inferno. But fire was everything. There was no sight, no sound. Only a cyclone of consuming agonies.

In utter desperation, she reached inward, caught Mormo. The wraith's power yanked her across the Veil. Passing through the Etheric membrane somehow snuffed out the flames engulfing her, leaving her a smouldering, weeping mass of torment.

Relying on the wraith in such a state had opened her up to it. Its claws burst from her fingers. Its seething darkness rasped from her lips. Ephemeral coils wrapt around her heart, about her neck. They burrowed inside her mind as the wraith pushed itself up using her body.

Vision returned, the fire's light in the Mortal Realm a pale flicker in the Penumbra. The ringing continued, and yet she could hear Mormo's hateful voice.

Your path ... will see us ... consumed ...

With the sum of all her will, Hekate raged against the wraith. Invisible claws lacerated her charred flesh, the ghost desperate to tear its way out of her. In fear of its very existence, Mormo strove to take advantage of Hekate's weakened state.

Shrieking, wailing, Hekate willed the wraith back inside. She would not lose herself.

She would not lose herself.

She would not ...

Compounding agonies threatened to swallow her whole.

Then, at last, the wraith receded, umbral vestiges of it slithering up inside Hekate's form once more, claws retracting.

I will ... have you ...

Not this day. It was the last thought she managed before unconsciousness rose up to claim her.

29

PANDORA

399 Dark Age

There were few wounds that stung so viciously as having the scales of one's own gross ignorance ripped from one's eyes. Crouched in the shadows of ferns, hidden from the Immortals now scouring the royal district for her, Pandora nursed worse injuries than those of her pride or her body. Rather, her assurance in her own abilities to assess the situation had crumbled, leaving her doubting and inept.

So gravely had she misjudged Mithra, in every respect. She had thought him a Titan, sought to reason with him as a Man and yet found in him one whose strings the Elder Gods had plied since the dawn of time. The sharp pain in her chest served as reminder of her inequities, her utter unpreparedness to tackle such situations. She needed Prometheus. His strength, his wisdom, his unwavering conviction. And yes, how she burnt at the thought she alone should not be enough, that she should have to rely upon another to serve as a bulwark on which she might steady herself. It chafed and rubbed raw her nerves. It sliced away the last vestiges of her self-respect and left her wretched.

And now men cried through the city that one sent by the Queens of Mu had striven to assassinate their god. That she had failed only made it worse. She had served up all the pretence they would need, if pretence they had ever sought, for an invasion of Mu at the same time as Elládos. That the queens themselves had no knowledge of her mattered little to anyone, least of all the Babilimians swept up in the currents of their righteous fury. They drank their wrath like fine wine and, drunken, cast aside the inhibitions of morality.

Wanting to weep—to *scream*—Pandora slapped a silent fist against her brow in frustration. How far astray this had flown. Whilst she knew wallowing here in self-pity served no one, she had not a clue about what to do *now*. Nemesis was gone with the Box—and was that how the gold-armoured woman had appeared over and over at the most inopportune moments to haunt Pandora's steps?—and Mithra was now on alert. She would not find herself with another chance to bring down the god-king before his invasion of Mu began.

What then? She knew, sooner or later Prometheus would be on Mu, as Maui. But she also already knew how those events would play out. Were she to go there, to strive again to stop the rise of Tiamat, she doubted the outcome would be any different than the first time. So, where could she go and still have hope of—

"You betrayed my trust," a woman's voice said. Artemis's sandals produced only the faintest of slap upon the garden's yellow-stoned ground. The woman bore a pair of daggers—akinakai—each like those carried by Babilimian soldiers. Utter wrath limned her face, an anger beyond any Pandora had ever seen in the woman.

Hands raised in warding, Pandora stood and stepped free of the bushes. She ought to have known she could not long hide from such a skilled tracker as the so-called Goddess of the Hunt. "I sought not to betray, but to save. I am trying to save the *World*."

"So am I!" Artemis bellowed, taking a threatening step toward her. "For two and half millennia, Zeus has ruled as the greatest tyrant in history! His death will free the whole of the Thalassa from his megalomania and oppression! It is through Mithra the land has the chance to be free of him."

"You don't understand—" Pandora began.

"I understand well enough! You serve him still."

"No! Never! I despise Zeus with every breath. But Mithra will destroy Gaia in the process of bringing low the one you loathe. How hollow shall your vengeance ring when enjoyed upon continents piled high with corpses?"

Artemis snarled. "Lies!" She lunged, coming in with speed that, even as Pandora flooded Pneuma in Alacrity, remained nigh blinding. The blades surged in, and though she managed to block one of Artemis's wrists on her forearm, the other akinakes ripped a hot gouge along her abdomen.

Pneuma alone pushed down the pain and kept Pandora fighting. She wrapt her hand around Artemis's wrist. Before Pandora knew what was happening, Artemis had leapt onto the wall and run around behind Pandora. The moment carried Pandora around, too, and next she realised, she was flipping through the air, thrown over Artemis's head, and slammed hard into the ground. When she tried to stand, the Titan's fist crashed into Pandora's temple like a hammer upon an anvil, the blow sending her sprawling onto the stones.

The next instant, Artemis's sandal connected with her ribs. The blow sent Pandora airborne and she tumbled off the terrace, breathless and unable to shriek. She fell a storey, crashed through the leaves of a palm tree, and smacked hard onto another stone floor. Even as she struggled to rise, Artemis appeared over her. Pandora dodged one dagger slash and the next, but the third opened a cut along her forearm. Another on her thigh. One on her hip. A dozen wounds, none fatal.

Artemis was trying to leave her weak from blood loss without actually ending her. Not having caught her breath much less her thoughts, Pandora couldn't begin to know how to feel about Artemis's mercy. When Pandora mistimed a dodge, Artemis impaled an akinakes through Pandora's thigh. Red-hot pain burnt even through the protection of her Pneuma, blinding in its agony. Artemis snared

Pandora's arm with her now free hand and smacked the pommel of her other dagger into Pandora's lip.

The Phoenix surged, a burning inferno in her breast. Pneuma poured into Potency of its own accord. Artemis herself had locked them into a grapple, and Pandora seized the woman, using holds Themis had taught her to ensure Artemis could not escape again. Spitting blood and snarling, Pandora swung Artemis around sideways, slapping the woman's spine into the palm tree's trunk. Again hefting the Titan, Pandora smacked her into the tree a second time.

Artemis was faster, more experienced, and a better fighter. But, given the Phoenix inside her soul, Pandora could be stronger and more resilient than most Titans. A third time, she slammed Artemis against the tree. Before she knew what she was doing, Pandora's flaming fist smacked into the woman's skull. Once. Twice. The trunk cracked and splintered beneath the blows. A third strike.

The Titan staggered, fell to one knee, supported only by Pandora's grip. Pandora's fist was her pyre, smouldering death held a hairsbreadth from Artemis's face. All she had to do was close that gap, and the flames would devour the Phoebid and deprive Mithra of one of his greatest assets. But Artemis had been her *friend*, at times even a mentor. Pandora had liked her, had cared about her. And now ... now she had given truth to the Titan's accusations of her betrayal.

Maybe slaying Artemis here could change the course of the future. But would such murder not prove too high a cost for her hope?

She wrung her hand, extinguishing the flames. "I pray you open your eyes and see your master for the lie he is." She released Artemis and staggered backward, the pain of her wounds rising up and seizing her with fresh force.

Then she wrapt a hand around the akinakes still embedded in her thigh. This would hurt, she knew. She yanked it free and let it fall, stifling a shriek but unable to keep from toppling over. Heat welled over her thigh as if flames burnt beneath her skin. The sizzling, sickly sweet aroma of roasting flesh came to her, carried up by wisps of smoke rising from the wound. Was she directing her Pneuma thus without realising it? The gouge seemed to burn itself closed, and Pandora lay on the ground, groaning, unable to resist the tides of pain threatening to drown her.

She had to keep moving though. Someone would have heard her struggle with Artemis and the Immortals might already be on their way up to these gardens. Through gritted teeth, Pandora managed her knees.

Abruptly, Marduk leapt up from a lower tier and landed before Pandora. His gaze settled upon his betrothed slumped where Pandora had left her against a palm tree. "Artemis!" Perhaps he had assured himself the Titan would live, for Marduk's regard lanced back to Pandora now, even as she struggled to her feet, wobbly and bleeding, though she had swept up Artemis's fallen knife as she stood.

"Fuck the godsdamned Moirai," she mumbled. She did not need this now. She raised the Babilimian knife in warding. "Your beloved will live."

His face was grim as the grave. "Thus shall you arrive before my father in chains rather than beneath a burial shroud." His akinakes, longer than those Artemis bore, eased free of its sheath, the rasp upon leather whispering all the wicked intent of a viper ready to strike.

"Don't—" she began but got no further before he lunged, forcing her to parry.

His blade twisted against hers, and in two moves, he'd sent her dagger flying. Before she had time to cry out, his sword flashed, gouging her arm, then her leg. Her shriek of pain escaped the same instant she hit the ground, and only then did her mind catch up to what had just happened. Against a master warrior like Artemis, Pandora had barely held up. But Marduk turned battle into art, his strokes sublime and unrivalled.

All she could do was kneel there, fighting with the pain, gaping at the man who had so effortlessly overcome her. She had seen such skill once before, in Kala, the future incarnation of the Destroyer. So, who in Tartarus was this Marduk to demonstrate comparable prowess?

Whilst she knelt stupidly, Marduk withdrew rose-gold fetters from a bag tied to his waist. Orichalcum chains. Pandora tried to rise, to object, but the gouge he'd dealt her thigh—close to where Artemis had stabbed her—stole her strength, and her leg gave out beneath her, sending her sprawling face-first onto the garden's golden stone floor.

"I have seen the future!" she blurted as Marduk yanked her arm up. The first manacle clapt around her wrist. "I have beheld a world inundated by waves that rise like flowing mountains, drowning the whole of Mankind's civilisation." He spun her so he could pin her hands together before her. As the other fetter clanked closed, she felt her access to her Pneuma shuttered away as if a sluice gate had cut it off. "Your father's invasions will spark the end of our world!"

Marduk jerked her around until her face was a hairsbreadth from his own. "Why should I believe a word that comes from the mouth of a woman who, though a guest beneath our roof, tried to murder her host? Your imprecations mean less than the mewling of a newborn lamb, for at least those are earnest."

It was hard to deny she had mis-stepped, however certain her reasons had seemed at the time. "I acted thus *because* I am in earnest. Because I have spoken the truth, and I know what the end of all this must invariably be!"

He wrapt a fist in her hair and yanked her head until she yelped. "Perhaps you recall, I told you of Kabujiya? He was an Oracle, and his visions drove him to a madness that nigh ruined our great polis. Even if I believed that you believed the drivel you spew about this war leading to flooding, still I would not give credence to the words of an Oracle."

But she was no Oracle. Still, were she to claim to be a timewalker, it would only confirm his impression of her possible madness. She had to hope that, somehow, in the depths of his soul, he had taken heed of her words.

It was a shallow, useless hope.

It was all she had.

30

ARTEMIS

729 Bronze Age

The harsh glare of dawn streaming in through a crack in the shutters woke Artemis, and she groaned. "I'm a Moon Titan," she groaned, in that space betwixt dreams and full alertness.

Then she remembered.

Clutching a hand to her chest, she sat up in the bed. No sign of visible wounds, though her insides ached. She was still naked, save for a linen sheet draped over her legs, but now she lay upon a plush divan in what looked to be Themis's palace.

"Oh, fuck," she moaned. It seemed the only viable thing to say if even half of what she had witnessed last night proved the truth.

Her days enthralled to Dionysus had revealed some of the most twisted revelations she could have ever imagined. All of them paled before what had transpired with Ariadne's son. Was that ... had Dionysus somehow reincarnated himself into his son's body? Had Artemis slain the god, only to find him, in the end, unkillable?

Behold the living and dying god ...

A shudder wracked her, and she hugged her arms, trying to steady herself against the surge of nameless dread. What she had seen defied reason. Dionysus called himself an aspect of nature, but in her eyes, what he had done mocked nature with its obscenity.

Suddenly, she craved the harsh light of Hyperion and fair leapt from the bed to throw wide the shutters. The sun's warmth tickled her bare flesh, and she closed her eyes, letting it wash over her. Imagining, for a moment, sunlight was all there was. Profane rituals in the darkness were but the stuff of twisted dreams. Or so she wished she could believe.

When she had dressed and taken time to steady herself, Artemis stepped from the chambers in which she'd lain and wandered Themis's palace. The Titan employed few servants, and Artemis saw no one as she walked the halls. At last, she came to the gardens where Themis sat on a stone bench, watching vibrant orange fish swim one way or the next. Their pattern looked like chaos, yet they managed to avoid running into one another.

Was Themis a hydromancer? Come to think of it, she had never inquired how the Oracle harnessed her gift. The other Titan looked up at her approach, so definitely not lost in any vision trance at the moment. Concern washed over Themis's face, and she rose to take Artemis's elbows. "I had begun to fear you'd not wake at all."

"What? How long was I out?"

"More than a fortnight."

As if to prove the Oracle's words, Artemis's stomach growled. She gaped, still wishing she could deny the impossible events of that night. "I ..."

It was impossible to separate an animal spirit fused with a human soul, Hekate had sworn it. Such mergings created shifters; dividing them would kill the host. In fact, every sorcerer and witch Artemis had ever consulted had told her the same. And yet, Dionysus had torn the bear spirit from her soul, though he'd damn nigh killed her in the process. Perhaps her Ambrosia-fortified Pneuma alone had allowed her to survive the violent extraction. The more she examined herself, the more it felt as though some piece of her basic nature had been torn from her.

The bear's senses were gone. Its rage too. In place of that lay her own simmering anger. Her wrath had not come merely from the spirit. It had never been only the bear.

"Terrible things have happened," Artemis said, watching the fish rather than the other Titan.

"Some of them I know from the survivors. You spared many of the Amazons, for which you have my gratitude. Some were broken beyond all mending and left us, but others we nurture back toward a semblance of life. It is a weighty thing, to have one's will stolen."

Artemis knew it only too well. "Ariadne?"

Themis sighed and clucked her tongue. "It was too much for her to bear."

No. No, not *again*. Aura. Aura! Artemis clenched shut her eyes as though she might thus block out the truth.

"Ariadne went into the wood that next day, alone. She ..."

"She hung herself," Artemis finished. Even as Aura had done all those years ago. As Dionysus had driven her to back then, as well. Maybe it was fatigue or hunger, but her legs could no longer support her, and she slumped down on the bench.

The Oracle sat beside her and patted her knee in whatever tiny, vain comfort she could offer. She made no attempt at platitudes, and for that, Artemis was grateful. For no words could assuage the pain or guilt or that terrible, growing wrath in her breast.

Dionysus. Zeus. The whole benighted Olympian Order.

Naught but rot.

Artemis spent several months convalescing in Themiskyra. In that time, she saw how the Amazons looked upon Hippolytus, watching the boy with mistrust and no little loathing. Themis was right. If he remained in this polis, sooner or later his enemies would find a way to eliminate him.

She could not allow the child to suffer thus, and so, with the boy in tow, she began the long trek back through the wilds toward the hills of Phlegra. There, amid oak and elm, they camped, the boy by her side, watching the sunset. All those years of paying homage to Thoth, sacrificing to the moon, and now dusk evoked in her a primal dread she could never suppress. Rather than hide from it, Artemis forced herself to stare ever into the face of her terror.

She refused to accept fear.

"I wanna be a hunter too," Hippolytus said by her side. "I wanna grow up strong."

His words sliced through her malaise like a knife but left her raw and bleeding. So like Atalanta. The girl had once uttered almost the same words and left Artemis and Orion beaming with pride in their adopted daughter. And now both the man and the child were gone forever.

Gone, but *this* child was right here, looking to her as if she could replace the mother stolen from him. Sweet Hippolyta had deserved a better end than she had received. She had given her life for this boy, and Artemis had to honour her sacrifice.

Artemis choked down a silent sob. "If you wish it ..." It took all she had to keep her voice steady. Thoth, she could not do this. To open her heart again would mean carving off another piece of it, and she had so few slivers left to her. "Then one day I shall teach you."

So she would serve up one more bloody chunk of her soul.

"THESEUS IS GONE, I know not where," Phaidra said, when Artemis at last called upon the royal couple in Athenai. She had taken the long road by land. What had begun as a burden to transport a child across half a world had become something else, and soon she had found herself loathe to fulfil her oath and deliver him to his father. So she had lingered first in Phlegra, then in the regions around Mount Pelion.

They had passed the winter in the farmlands around Thebes and, when a carpet of flowers announced the return of spring, had headed not south toward Korinth but instead toward Delphi to see her brother.

But Apollon had warned her that trouble brewed within the halls of Olympus, and Artemis knew it only too well. She knew from the way he looked at the child that Apollon realised she had kept the boy more as balm for her own lonely soul than for his benefit. A boy his age needed a home and toys and stability, not this vagrant lifestyle which forever called her.

Besides, sooner or later, Zeus would learn of her presence in Elládos and would take it amiss that she had not returned to Olympus as per his commands. If he found her with the child, he would, at best, use Hippolytus to control her or, at worst, murder the boy out of sheer spite. That, she could not allow.

So, come another winter, she arrived in Athenai and found she had waited too long, and Theseus, burdened by the suicide of his best friend, had headed off into unknown lands where Phaidra could not follow.

"Who is the child?" the Knosósian princess asked with a nod toward Hippolytus.

Artemis bit her lip, wondering whether it was wise to tell Theseus's wife that, before he met her, he had sired a son with another woman. A queen, no less. But Phaidra would become Hippolytus's stepmother. Besides, given what had happened to Phaidra's sister, Artemis owed her every sympathy. "There are ... a great many things I need to tell you. Things about the child and about your sister, both."

31

KIRKE

726 Bronze Age

*S*ome weeks after Hekate left, new visitors came to Aiaíā. Once, Kirke would have danced with joy at the reprieve from solitude the presence of anyone here with her represented. She'd have opened the best vintages of her imported wines and drank the night away in camaraderie and taletelling.

Oh, yeah, still she drank her nights away, true enough. But no longer could she bring herself to care that anyone came calling. At least, so she told herself until she recognised her beloved niece Medea. She did not know the Kroniad with her, though any of his genos served as a reminder of accursed Zeus and was thus somewhat unwelcome to look upon.

Medea, though, Kirke embraced with as much warmth as she could muster. Pulling even that much care from the ruination of her soul took its toll, and Kirke, on escorting them inside and serving them wine, collapsed onto a divan with a tremendous huff.

Even sitting here, a realisation dawned upon her. There was ever a strangeness in seeing the fulfilment of oneiromantic foretelling, like the sense of dream, once half-forgotten, but not leaping back into startling clarity.

In silence, her niece sipped at her wine, her Kroniad companion shifting in obvious unease beside her. Did sitting in the manse of an exiled Nymph discomfit him, or was it rather being here in the presence of a sorceress?

"This is my husband, Jason," Medea said. "Husband-to-be, I mean, though our betrothal is fixed and our love a tale for the ages."

Hyperion's fiery arse, she was in earnest, wasn't she? Kirke ran her forefinger over her brow, sipped her wine, and chose not to answer Medea's comment. All too oft Kirke herself had thrown herself into pale hopes for love and companionship. She'd tried, more than once, to make a connection, to find someone who could understand her and make her feel as though she at last had a place.

In Medea, she saw that same desperate pain and longing. Maybe, once she had the girl alone, she'd warn her about the dangers of clinging to another with such fervour. Too many men—and women —had disappointed Kirke over her long life for her to believe such things still possible for her. Perhaps Medea's love story would fare better than Kirke's ever had.

Kirke set her empty goblet down on the low table beside her divan. "I had not thought Aeëtes would allow you to leave Kolchis, much less come here." Nor had she expected her brother would allow his daughter to leave whilst only betrothed to the Kroniad, rather than wed. Aeëtes guarded his daughters like tokens to be bargained, saving Medea for the best possible match. Who was this Jason, that Kirke's brother would allow Medea to go off with him *before* marriage?

But she would not voice such things, she resolved. Doing so would make her sound a bit too much like petulant Eos, and Kirke would *not* become her aunt, no matter what cruelties the Moirai had woven for her.

Her guests glanced first at one another, then abashedly back at Kirke.

"Oh, yeah." This was brilliant, wasn't it? She needed another amphora of wine. She needed several more amphorae. "He didn't permit you to leave at all. You two eloped. You bolted like fuck-starved rabbits, didn't you?"

"That's not why we're here, Aunt," Medea said. "We need your help."

Kirke's face tightened. Even her? Even Medea came to see Kirke only when she needed something? She did not sail to Aiaíā to visit her aunt, imprisoned here for two and a half decades. Not because she missed her or held the least concern for Kirke's wellbeing. No, she came seeking remedy for whatever plight she found herself in. As so oft Kirke's siblings had come to her in times of distress, so too now did their children.

A bitter laugh escaped her. "What, Medea? Wrought some chaos and now you seek a potion to deal with it? Or perhaps you seek to forward some political ambitions? I have heard it all, you know."

Another sidelong glance passed between the illicit lovers. "Aunt, we came here on my husband's ship, which sailed from Kolchis after an altercation with my father and my brother."

Their plight resolved in pellucid clarity before her eyes. "My brother hunts you, now." Another time, Kirke might have exploded in temper at them for it. She might have mocked or laughed or taunted or had some reaction. Now she found she could muster only the same apathy as had infected the whole of her life since her jaunt through time. Everything felt small beneath the enormity of the Tapestry she had beheld. Medea's concerns seemed petty, almost beneath notice. "You hope I'll shelter you from his soldiers?"

"It's not soldiers we fear," Jason said, the first he'd dared speak in her presence. "We are warriors and would not back down from any foe which might be challenged with spear or blade, Lady."

"Some years back," Medea said, "Father turned to sorcery."

"*What?*" The madness of it cut through even the dolour that had seized Kirke's heart. Aeëtes had long disdained the Art, even to the point of insulting Kirke over it a time or two. He'd barely consented to allow her to train Medea in alchemy and would have raged had she deigned to teach her of the greater arcana. "How? When? No! Better yet, *who* did he pull from Nyx's arsehole to train him in such dire pursuits?"

Now Medea paused to nurse her own wine. "The when of it ... After what happened to your common sister, Pasiphaë, he took a dark turn. He began cloistering himself in private meetings with the sorceress Damkina." That name sounded familiar, but Kirke could not quite place it. Something from long ago, she thought. "He changed, grew darker, and the palace changed with him. I think, perhaps, he blamed you for Pasiphaë." Well, that was fair. "Mayhap he feared you might come for him next, no matter how I and Mother assured him otherwise."

As if Kirke had ever sought after a throne at all, much less the throne held by her brother.

She shook her head. Too much Ambrosia seemed to have fermented rampant paranoia in the man. She pitied him, though Kirke had long ago drifted away from Aeëtes. Kingship had not suited him; power turned a naïve boy cruel. Or maybe a throne would forever have that effect on even the best of Men and Titans.

"To escape, I ..." Medea faltered and Jason clutched her hand. Genuine support or mutual desperation? "I found myself pursued by my own brother, who refused to let me leave."

"Absyrtus?" Kirke nodded. "Men so oft think they need to control their female relatives. Even and especially men without the wit to tell their own arses from a hole in the ground."

"To escape ..."

Oh. Well, dammit. "You killed your brother." Had she been holding something, Kirke might have thrown it. Picking up her goblet only to hurl it felt juvenile, so instead she fixed the pair of them with a glare. With her ire up, her golden eyes would have glowed with white radiance. The look had both of her guests inspecting their sandals for the slightest imperfection. "You murdered your own kin. Now you don't know if you've got a curse upon you for doing so, or if my brother justifiably called something foul to punish you for your crimes. You don't know what hounds you, but ill fortune trails in your wake like a shark freneized with the scent of blood."

Medea managed a shamed nod without actually lifting her gaze to meet Kirke's own.

And she'd been right. They had come to her because they needed her Art. Not her company, not her advice, not her love. No, they wanted her to work the Art to free them from whatever curse they had brought down upon themselves. Yeah, this was about the time when Kirke ought to tell them to get the fuck off Aiaíā, and maybe go fuck themselves with a stingray in the process.

She had no idea if Erinyes were real or not. Men believed in spirits who avenged kinslaying by driving the perpetrators mad. Maybe such existed, or maybe pangs of conscience did that work well enough. Either way, none of this was Kirke's problem.

Nor did Medea *deserve* her help.

She had murdered her kin, long held to be the foulest of crimes. If Aeëtes had sent a spirit against them, Kirke could, perhaps, break his hold upon it and thus free Medea and Jason. She could also practice a purification ritual and hope that cleansed them of the stain they had inflicted upon their souls.

But why should she do it? Why abrade her soul further with sorcery for an ungrateful wretch who cared only about herself? Why, why, *why* could Medea not have simply come here because she missed Kirke? Had that happened, Kirke would have sought to move Gaia herself for the girl's benefit.

She ought to send them away.

But there was something of Kirke in Medea, she knew, too. A bundle of lonely desperation, of rage at how her kin oppressed her on account of her gender. A moil of intellect and anxiety similar enough to what Kirke beheld in her own looking glass that to condemn it was to hurl judgment upon *herself*.

"I will free you from whatever haunts you if I can," Kirke said. "And when it is done you will leave here and not return. I will not aid you a second time."

"Aunt ..."

Kirke raised her hand to silence the girl. "Only you can judge whether your actions were warranted with Absyrtus. But with me ... You should have done better. You should have *been* better, Medea."

For once, someone should have come to save Kirke instead of the other way around.

32

HERAKLES

730 Bronze Age

In Eurystheus's inner sanctum, Herakles withdrew a golden apple from his satchel. He kept his face free of expression as he proffered the stolen prize. Light from the room's oil lamps glinted off the apple's skin, giving it the appearance of a sculpture. For this thing, the gods would have drowned Men in oceans of their own blood.

Whilst Herakles had, for caution's sake, sought to present the prize to the king alone, the man had insisted upon the presence of a guard. "Comus shan't leave my side," Eurystheus had said. And the stranger stood in the corner, watching them with a too-intent gaze. The king had not, at any point, made mention of the fact Herakles had been gone so very long on this labour.

His cousin reached for the apple, hesitated a moment, then snatched it from Herakles with greedy fingers. Though he said naught, the slight parting of Eurystheus's lips and his raspy breathing revealed his lusting desire for the apple. Still, his momentary pause indicated he had wit enough to fear the consequences of what he and Herakles had done. Should the Olympians—the other Olympians— ever learn of this, Herakles and Eurystheus would find themselves damned side by side.

From the way his cousin's gaze lingered upon the apple, Herakles began to wonder if he ever intended to taste of it or would rather have something to cuddle.

"Have you settled upon the final of my labours?" He was so close now. In the periphery, half revealed by the firelight, he saw the shades of his boys nodding along, almost able to reach out and touch the release from their torment. This last endeavour had nigh proved the death of him, which was, no doubt, what Eurystheus had expected and intended. But then, he supposed either way his cousin won— such labours would ensure he either received his treasure or got rid of his perceived rival.

Eurystheus's hungry eyes darted from the apple to Herakles's face for a moment. "Tale speaks of one counted among the greatest of monstrosities in the World. A beast so fell, even the damned fear to gaze upon its smouldering eyes. They say a three-headed hound guards the gates of the Underworld." The king curled his lip, impressed with his own cleverness. "I'd have his hide to adorn my wall."

"You speak of Kerberos?" Herakles could not help but scoff at the absurd demand. "Have your senses fled? How am I to reach a place not on Gaia at all?"

"That," Comus said, striding forward, "I can assist with."

Herakles whirled on his cousin's guard. Such positions tended to get filled by men with more brawn than wit, oft lacking the skills to do more in life than bully others. At first, he took the man's words as a threat to send him to Hades upon the point of a blade, but instead the guard produced a ceramic phial and held it toward Herakles.

"Poison?" Herakles folded his arms over his chest, refusing to accept the offered tonic. "You'd have me kill myself to reach Hades?"

Eurystheus snorted. "Tempting though that seems, you could not well return with the hound's hide, then. No, you see, my associate here assures me that with this draught, consumed in the right place, you can venture beyond our Realm and into the Underworld. So, Cousin, how badly do you wish to complete these labours of yours? Redemption is yours to claim, have you the mettle for it."

An image flashed through his mind of reaching over and throttling Eurystheus. The evil glint in his cousin's eyes told him the man knew well enough his proposal was absurd. Far and wide he had sent Herakles, to slay monsters and steal prizes that ought to have proved beyond all reach. But this? This defied reason.

He could walk away from this now. He ought to walk from it. Before he stood, his gaze scraped over the room, almost involuntarily. In the corner, Deikoon's shade mouthed a word. *Papa.* He had sworn an oath to his boys. They watched him now, plaintive, eyes begging him to complete his promised labours and release their tormented souls.

Perhaps sensing his deepening resolve, Comus drew closer, offering the phial once more. There was something off-putting about the guard, as if he occupied even more space than that of his admittedly large frame. A simmering malevolence exuded from that form, making his skin crawl. Had he seen the man under other circumstances, he would have taken him for a bandit and a sadist. Maybe that was still not far off the mark. What guard had tinctures that let Men walk betwixt worlds?

Herakles accepted the tonic this time, meeting the guard's unnerving gaze with his own determined stare. He would not back down. "If it can be done, it shall be done."

"It's not poison," Athene said, recapping the phial before returning it to Herakles. "Though I still mislike this whole endeavour. My mother once ventured to Hades's dark abode in the hopes of rescuing Persephone, and though she spoke little of it, I know things did not turn out well for her."

They sat upon a rock in a field beyond Mykenai, watching

twilight spread across the horizon. He had come here to think, and she had found him, perhaps having sensed his distress or foreseen it in the waters of her hydromancy.

"Will it allow me to cross into the Underworld?"

His adoptive mother folded her arms across her chest and clucked her tongue. "I believe so. My visions are rarely exact, though. I ... I have learnt something, Son. Another mortal whom I've tried to watch out for also attempted this sojourn not long back, and he did not return. I do not know whether or not he perished in the attempt, but I know he travelled to caves within Tainaros to make the crossing. And I know he had some sort of draught given to him by the witch Medea."

"Who tried this?"

Now she rubbed her arms. "Your friend Theseus. My, um ... descendant. I didn't realise his intent until it was far too late."

"What of this Comus? Is he, too, steeped in witchcraft to come by such a tonic?"

"I don't know that, but believe me, I intend to look into him." A pause. "Should we split the potion? Try to make the journey together?"

It would be a comfort to have her by his side. After a moment, he sighed and shook his head. "No, these tasks are mine alone. Besides, we do not know the draught would work if divided. I will go to Tainaros. If Ananke proves kind, I shall both slay Kerberos and find Theseus."

His mother nodded, but in her grey eyes he saw the obvious question: when had ever Ananke proved kind?

IN A SEASIDE CAVE of Mount Tainaros, to the sound of breaking waves, Herakles knelt beside Theseus's naked corpse. The young man had cast his clothes aside, presumably to dry them. Beyond that, Herakles could not say what had happened. The body was cold as ice but bore no signs of violence or decay. Had the witch poisoned him? If so,

Herakles would see Medea brought to justice, Jason's wife or no. Poison was a vile way to kill a Man.

He leant close to Theseus's ear. "I'm sorry, my friend. You deserved a better end than this." He supposed he would never know what had possessed Theseus to attempt so mad a quest. "Was it vanity?" Had Theseus chased glory even to the last, and lost his life so doing?

Or was his aim somewhat other? Athene had claimed that her mother had tried—and failed—to retrieve Persephone from the Underworld. What if Theseus too had sought to reclaim the soul of someone precious to him? Such a tempting thought. What if he could, instead of facing down the guard dog of Hades, retrieve the souls of his boys and restore them to life?

Oh, but that sounded more akin to idle fancy. Their bodies were ash, their bones long buried. The dead did not return from the Underworld, and to give in to such thinking would be its own vanity. Pursuing that course might well cost him the success of this endeavour to put their agonised souls to rest, and he could not risk that.

He patted Theseus's brow. "When I return, I'll see you have a hero's funeral."

The boy had died far too young. And now Herakles would walk the same path that had led to that death, and yet hope for a different outcome. Doubt crept in, and he cast about the cavern thinking to see his sons once more, and through them to steel his resolve. But for once, they remained elusive.

Herakles must do this alone, even as he had told Mama.

With a groan, he rose and withdrew the phial from its place at his belt. Athene had checked it and declared it safe enough. Which was not to say Herakles would find the tincture beneficial to his health. Still ... he had come here with a single intent.

One. Last. Labour.

So let it be done. Pulling the wooden stopper out, he tossed it aside, and downed the potion in a single gulp. It tasted of sour wine and bitter herbs, thick upon his tongue and cloying in his throat.

"Ugh." The discarded phial, at least, made a satisfying crash as the ceramic shattered upon the stones.

He took a step toward the back of the cavern, swayed, and found his balance giving out. A wave of vertigo sent him to one knee, and even then, he had to slap his palms against the stone to keep from pitching over sideways. The cavern rocked like a storm-tossed ship. He looked up, but the back of the cave receded before his eyes, disappearing into dark spaces deeper than had been there a moment earlier. The World contracted and contorted, wrung thin like a rag.

Herakles's stomach lurched. He clamped a hand over his mouth, struggling not to retch up the potion. The motion left a trail of afterimages of his fingers streaking through the air. For several moments he remained there, on one knee, willing the spinning and twisting to cease. When at last his vision stabilised, Herakles struggled to his feet.

A glance over his shoulder revealed Theseus's corpse, now farther away than where he'd left it. Farther, as though he had walked several dozen feet into the cavern, though it was not deep enough for that, afore now. Or rather, had he passed into some sort of Realm betwixt Gaia and the Underworld?

Who was Comus, to give him such a strange tonic? No mere soldier seeking employment for his skills, that much was certain.

But whatever the man's intent, Herakles was here now, and the only choice lay in pressing forward. He withdrew a torch from his bag. Seawater had left it sodden, so it took time to get the oil-soaked rag to catch but catch it did at last. The flames that spilt from the torch seemed muted here, as if they retreated from the gloom rather than the other way around. Too, the light had taken on a grey-blue tint, casting squirming shadows the colour of the Axeinos Sea in the dead of night.

Like venturing back into Tartarus. The thought further soured his stomach.

Before nerves could get the better of him, Herakles advanced. The tunnel ahead sloped downward, bending back upon itself many a time, like wild ivy spiralling down a massive tower, but sometimes cutting through the middle. The irregular passage seemed unnatural, yet certainly not Man-made either.

Did some other sort of being carve out these tunnels?

Maybe best not to ask such questions. Herakles was not certain he truly wished for the answers.

Down and down he went, his ears popping as he descended those sepulchral depths. The space reeked of stale air, tinged with a whiff of sulphur. The torchlight lost its bluish aspect yet remained suppressed, unable to push the darkness back by more than a couple of feet. Light was an intruder here, unwelcome and unprecedented.

Had Theseus come this way? Had his friend walked these steps before his death? Or did this strange Realm shift such that each of their experiences would prove distinct?

At last, the winding tunnel levelled off into a cavern, and Herakles was greeted by the sound of running water and distant, rumbling falls. Faint maroon light seeped from rents in the cavern walls, floor, and ceiling. From these gaps puffed out sporadic bursts of gas that stank like army latrines. Herakles gave them as wide a berth as possible.

Was this then the Underworld proper? The expanse stretched on much farther than he could see. He could wander at random, but it seemed wisest to head towards the sound of water and follow its course. Bards' tales spoke of the River Styx cutting through the Underworld, and mayhap it would prove true enough. He had no better route, either way.

AMID THE ROAR of cataracts spewing torrents of black waters, Herakles came to a field littered with desiccated trees. Smoke-like vapours wafted betwixt the trunks, whilst the fingers of branches clutched at any among the streams of shades who passed too close. A hapless man—pale and listless—got himself snared in those gnarled limbs, and Herakles watched, aghast, as the shade was drawn in through the trunk as though it was a permeable membrane. The shade moaned and flailed but could not manage a coherent word. And then it vanished. A moment later, the outline of a face protruded from the tree's trunk, mouth fixed in a permanent scream.

Now, as Herakles turned to look, he saw more faces etched into the bark of so many of the trees. A shudder wracked him. Were the dead sealed within still conscious, or were the faces but echoes of their passings?

He dare not press closer to inspect.

The waterfall pitched down from onyx cliffs, dark foam rising where it fell. The waters twisted a slithering path through the field before joining a much wider river in the far distance.

As he plodded through the wilted meadow, careful ever to steer clear of the trees, most of the shades paid him little or no heed. Many did not even look at him if he approached, as though so locked in whatever agonised pattern had settled upon their soul that now they could neither see nor hear outside the prison of their own memories. Some of them spoke, spewing nonsense or spiteful recriminations or half-formed laments. Others moaned or muttered or said naught at all.

A woman hissed at him, and Herakles spun, xiphos in his hand in a moment. The creature—half-woman and half-snake, her hair a writhing nest of spectral serpents coming in and out of existence— glared at him. Medusa? He knew the legend well enough, but though her gaze had met his own, it had no effect upon him. Herakles pointed his sword at her throat—a scar showed where the flesh was cleft in twain once already—and the Gorgon sneered, raising threatening claws at him.

"My ancestor smote you once already."

A veil of confusion washed over her face then. The nest of serpents upon her head vanished, replaced with wisps of pale red hair. Her tail had become lithe legs, half-concealed by her peplos. "Where am I?" The woman looked about as if seeing Herakles and this whole field for the first time. With a shake of her head, she wandered off. She'd gone perhaps a dozen steps when her form shuddered. The next instant, the snake-tail and writhing serpents had returned.

"We start to forget everything ..." A voice behind him said.

Herakles turned once more, this time to look into the face of the hunter Meleager. A weeping pit of raw flesh had replaced one of the Kalydonian prince's eyes, and like Medusa, flickers of confusion creased his features.

"I ... I ... know you ... Herakles."

Word had reached Herakles after the return of the Argo. A bitter tale of how Meleager's own mother had murdered him over a fatal dispute he'd had with her brother. Herakles thought it a poor parent who'd side with anyone, sibling or otherwise, over their own child. "I am sorry for the unhappy fate that befell you, friend."

Meleager squinted his single eye, peering hard at Herakles. "My ... fate ... Uh ... Who am I?"

The question left Herakles agape, falling back a step. Was this emptiness creeping over Meleager the same end that awaited all the dead? When he, at last, appeased the souls of his boys and saw them freed of their endless vigil over him, would they too fade into shells? He worked his mouth a moment before managing even a whisper. "Prince Meleager of Kalydon, son of King Oeneus."

"I ... Yes." The prince's shade nodded eagerly. "I knew you. And I knew him, too, the friend I came here to see. Oh, but it's harder outside the necropoleis. The walls blunt the Lethe somewhat. Venturing here ... it's ... ah ... venturing ... I know you!"

"Yes." Herakles nodded, heart clenched with pity for the prince. "Who did you come to see here?"

"Uh ... I came to see ... Oh. Theseus. He, um ... Hades had him ... Bound. Chained to an iron chair over an outcropping on ... an outcropping that juts over the River Styx. Yes."

Theseus! Did that mean he yet lived, or was merely his shade here? Unlike Herakles's sons, Theseus had a body, one as yet unspoilt. If Herakles could retrieve his soul, could he restore the young man to life? He grabbed Meleager's shoulders. "Where?"

"Where ... what?"

"Meleager! Where is Theseus? Upstream or down?"

"Up ... Oh! But Herakles ... I need ... I think I have a sister. I can't recall ... I ... I think ... I never took care of her as a brother ought to ..."

Herakles nodded. Whilst he empathised with Meleager's woes, the prince was years dead, and Theseus still had a chance. "Fine, fine. Listen, though. I must—"

"Marry her," Meleager blurted. "You're the only one who's come here ... only I ... I cannot ask any of the other hunters. They don't come to me ... Swear to see her cared for ... keep her happy ... I ... I think I have a sister. Why can I not recall her face or name? How could ... anyone have a sister they don't know?"

The pain creasing the shade's face and straining his voice was more than Herakles could bear. His former companion had lost his life and now, even in death, begged Herakles for one final request. Who was he to refuse?

Even if, when Herakles closed his eyes, it was Iole's face he saw in his dreams. But she was not for him, and maybe he could—should he somehow escape the Underworld—give a good life to the princess of Kalydon. Either way, he could not deny Meleager's earnest plea. "I swear."

"That's good ... I ... I think I must return to the city of Hades. The ferry is coming ... I must go ... before I lose ..." Whatever thought Meleager had struggled with slipped from his grasp, and he wandered off.

Herakles could not help but grimace. So, to survive here long, the dead had little choice save to march themselves to the city of Hades and beg succour from the God of Death. Those who could not or would not make the journey must fade.

And Herakles would not leave Theseus to such a fate.

❧

RACING UPSTREAM, following those black waters, Herakles came to an obsidian shelf as Meleager had described. It rose up, perhaps a score of feet above the water level, jutting forth like some giant's overgrown toenail. And there, upon the edge rested a chair of wrought iron, mounted to the stone with great spikes. Upon that ironic throne sat Theseus, bound in iron fetters that looped around his limbs and torso before threading through gaps in the throne's ironwork.

"Sweet fuck." Herakles could scarce believe what he was seeing. He hesitated a single heartbeat, then broke into a dead sprint to reach his friend. "Theseus!" he called.

The boy looked at him without recognition, his mouth ajar and head lolling slightly to one side. "Who ...?" Theseus asked when Herakles grasped those chains.

No, no, no. He could not have already lost himself so completely. "You are Theseus, son of Aegeus, Prince of Athenai. And you *shan't* succumb to this."

A single jerk rent the chains in twain, sending a piece of the iron link clattering over the obsidian ground. Whilst reminding Theseus of every adventure they had shared, Herakles unspooled the fetter from the throne and unwrapt his friend's limbs. The bindings had left his skin raw and abraded, and his flesh had a sallow, deathly colour that made plain his state. A state Herakles was determined to reverse, no matter what it took.

A feral growl sounded over the noise of both the river and the clanking iron. Another followed, and another. Herakles turned to see a hound plodding closer, first noting massive paws, then the black shaggy mass of the beast. Three heads, each almost as large as his torso. Flames simmered within those six eyes, all of which latched onto Herakles with Otherworldly malevolence. The tail rose above the hound's back, a hissing viper. The beast stank of sulphur, and yellowish fumes poured from those slavering jaws.

Beyond the creature, another monster approached, this one a Titan's desiccated and shrouded husk, but one standing nigh to twenty feet tall. The figure wore an iron crown and carried a massive bident whose points scraped along the ground as the dead giant dragged it behind himself.

"Hades?" Herakles asked, releasing his grip upon Theseus's bindings and turning his attention upon the monstrous hound and its master.

"The son of my brother, and his descendant, both here in my domain." Hades's voice somehow both rasped and boomed. "Perhaps I ought to arrange a banquet in honour of such esteemed guests ..."

This had not gone the way Herakles might have wished. For a moment, he clenched and unclenched his fist at his side. Still, he would not stand here and quiver, even in the face of his own destruction. "Hello, Uncle. I am afraid I'm going to need to take your dog." He jerked a thumb behind him at Theseus. "And the boy's coming with me, too."

Hades chuckled, a hateful, grating sound. "Your bravado apes that of your father, boy. And yet, in you I wonder if it is more affected than in Zeus, whose arrogance is vast enough to swallow sea and sky within its embrace. You have not the least grasp of what unfolds, here or above. Soon, I and *my* son shall bring both the living and the dead under our control. The cosmos will bow before us, and Zeus's hateful line shall at last be ground beneath my heel. You, and that boy, shall spend eternity having your memories devoured by the Lethe."

"Son?" Herakles asked. "That ... still works when you're dead?" Maybe Hades had the right of it. Maybe his bravado was but affectation. But if so, he'd wear it with pride and let no one, Man or Titan, alive or ghost, see him tremble with fear. He unshouldered his bow and dared a wry smirk. "As for squashing the Kroniads, that may not prove so easy."

"Tear his legs off," Hades commanded Kerberos.

Herakles had enough time to nock an arrow and loose before the hound closed. His missile took Hades in the shoulder; the god stumbled, crying out. Any further reaction Herakles could not see, given the hurtling mass of fur and jaws surging at him.

A snarling mound bowled him over and it was all he could do to brace and keep those snapping jaws from closing upon his face and throat. With his forearm, Herakles held back one head, twisting another with his free hand. Still, the third sank its teeth into his left bicep, piercing even his Pneuma-hardened skin. Waves of pain he could not quite suppress shot up his arm and into his neck as Kerberos strove to rip his limb straight from its socket. Scalding drool seared his flesh.

Though screaming in agony, Herakles managed to lock his legs around the creature and twist, sending the hound tumbling beneath him. With snarls to match those of his canine foe, Herakles heaved and wrestled, slamming heads one way or the next, until he managed a hold upon one neck, preventing that maw from reaching him.

That serpent tail hissed, darting in to bite his arse, venomous fangs latching on and refusing to withdraw. All he could do was grit his teeth against that.

With Potency flooded to its limit, he choked Kerberos. Held on until vertebrae crunched beneath his grip. Until eyes bulged and a bulbous tongue lolled to one side.

The chorus in his mind rose to a cacophony of voices urging him on. To slay. To slaughter. To end whole worlds and thus keep spinning the wheels of life and death.

Herakles grabbed the serpent stuck on his arse, planted a foot against Kerberos's flank, and yanked. Flesh rent in twain, and the hissing snake was torn out by the root. Kerberos yelped, rolling to its feet and watching him with its two remaining heads. Were this thing not an abomination feasting upon the souls of the dead, Herakles might have almost pitied it.

But Kerberos was no animal.

Wielding the snake tail like a whip, he lashed the hound across the face. It yelped, scrambling away, but Herakles closed in, slapping again and again with his improvised weapon. Venom blurred his vision and had his limbs shaking. He'd not have so much longer to accomplish this.

But if he failed, Theseus would languish here. His sons would wander, locked in eternal despair, losing themselves in forlorn shadows. So Herakles closed with the hound as it retreated. Tossing the serpent aside, he swept Kerberos up, hefted back first into the air.

He brought the monster down upon his knee, shattering its spine. Eurystheus would want proof. When it lay helpless, he stomped upon a head, then grabbed the top of its jaw and tore it free as macabre trophy to hurl at the feet of the corrupt king.

Then he remembered Hades.

Herakles's strength gave out, and he dropped to one knee and looked up to see the King of the Dead. But Hades retreated before a small army of ghosts closing in upon him. Men and women surrounded a cloaked figure who seemed keen to take the opportunity provided by Kerberos's death to revolt against the tyrant god.

It offered some small comfort to know even the dark god would suffer this day. Herakles's death would cost Hades more than his prized hound, he hoped. With a grim smile, he pitched face-first onto the blood-drenched obsidian.

33

THESEUS

730 Bronze Age

*S*oft hands massaged his abraded wrists. A woman's face hovered before his own, her ebony hair spilling about her face as she unthreaded the chains that bound him upon an iron chair. Tantalising wisps of memory danced before his eyes but flitted away from his grasp each time he struggled to understand them.

Somewhere nearby but unseen, a rising song soothed his weary soul. The woman laid a hand upon his cheek. Focusing upon her face was like trying to climb out of the most insistent of dreams when sleep strove ever to creep back over him. "Do you know who you are?" she asked.

He blinked. She had a vicious scar about her neck, worn raw. He had looked upon that very wound afore now, had he not? "I ..."

"Theseus."

"I ..."

The song was not for him, at least not entirely, and yet it felt as though it had begun to stitch together the tattered ends of his life.

Memories frayed and snapped apart were woven into wholes once more. And Theseus could have wept for the unspeakable muddle of relief and despair. There were times when emotions knotted together into unbreakable masses, when grief and hope and longing became one, and movements of the soul surged too large for temporal constraints like words or bodies. "Ariadne."

His great failure looked upon him. Took his hand. Eased him to his feet.

Beyond, Herakles lay bleeding, tossing and turning. A dark toxin worked its way *out* of a wound upon his arse. The shredded ruin of his arm seemed to knit itself together. All in time with the echoing, mournful, soul-stirring song.

And over Herakles, singing and strumming his lyre, stood Orpheus. Theseus could not have identified the language in which the bard sang, but its effect upon his friend seemed plain enough. For that awful thrashing abated, and Herakles opened his eyes before pushing himself up on one forearm. His right arm, for despite whatever glory lay within the words of Orpheus, Herakles's left arm remained mangled, and Theseus wondered if the demigod would ever again be able to use it.

Hand in hand with Ariadne, Theseus made his way to Herakles, then helped his friend to his feet. At last, Orpheus's stirring lament trailed off, and the bard nodded at him.

"Take care of my sister," Ariadne said, drawing his attention once more.

"Come back with us. Return to Gaia."

A sad smile creased her face, and she shook her head. "Even if I could, he would only come for me again."

Clarifying memories slammed into him, and he knew of whom she spoke. He wanted to beg her, but her expression brooked no argument.

"There is a war impending in the Underworld, Theseus," Orpheus said. "We are compelled to choose a side if we would not be slaves to Hades and Dionysus." The bard stole a glance down the slope, where Hades seemed to have retreated onto a ferry, driven back by a gathered army of the dead.

Herakles clapt him on the shoulder. "There may yet be time to return you to the world of the living."

Theseus looked to Ariadne again. A war here, and her entangled in it. If he left now, did he once more abandon her? But she had told him to look after ... Phaidra. And Theseus loved Phaidra more deeply than ever he had Ariadne. "I ..."

"Go," Ariadne bid. "Only passing fate ever joined us, and only for a moment. Live your life, Theseus."

Herakles's grip tightened upon Theseus's shoulder.

Yes.

They had to go.

EVEN HALF EXPECTING IT, still, a shock had settled upon Theseus when he looked upon his corpse. As Herakles had entered the cave, Theseus's friend had become no more than shadow, pushed back into the Mortal Realm, whilst Theseus's soul remained here, Ethereal. Across the haze that blurred the space between worlds, he saw Herakles kneel at his body, shaking it with fervent desperation. The demigod set beside Theseus's body a head of Kerberos—most of a head—as proof of his labour achieved. Seeing it there, beside his body, had Theseus feeling chilled.

Still, Theseus too knelt beside his friend and took the hand of his own corpse. And then he was opening his eyes, shivering and famished, and in such desperate need of a piss he could spare no words before finding a corner to relieve himself.

Wiser or more reckless than himself, Herakles had managed to bring a rowboat inside the cave, and in this, the two returned outside Mount Tainaros. Neither spoke much, both perhaps weighted by the momentous experiences they had undergone.

Perhaps in some lingering effects of the Lethe, Theseus felt himself forlorn and sullen, his thoughts ever a roil of half-formed regrets. At his side, Herakles carried his obscene trophy all the way to Mykenai, where the two of them parted with heavy looks. He was not sure they would ever speak of what they had endured in the netherworld. He was not certain he could ever give voice of it to anyone, even to precious Phaidra.

Theseus needed to return to Athenai, of course. But the thought of re-entering his life stirred further melancholies. He had failed Pirithous. Had left Hades's domain without so much as gazing upon his beloved friend's visage one last time, much less dragging him back to the world of the living as Theseus had so imagined. How vain he had been, to think he could defy every law of nature and restore life where it had fled.

And he was left here, lingering in the sunlight, whilst two people he had loved had taken their own lives. The bitter thought choked all others, and, in the middle of the beaten path running from Mykenai to Korinth, Theseus tumbled into the dirt and wept.

Both losses mingled into a drowning sea of grief, each deepening the other. He sat there, sobbing, beating an impotent fist into the obstinate ground. It defied him, refusing to crack beneath the force of his anguish.

It defied him, as Ananke too had mocked his arrogance for thinking to spite its design. But there was no going back. There was no reclaiming those lost. All he could do, in the end, was cherish those who remained.

Sooner or later, Theseus would need to go home.

THOUGH HE KNEW he ought to return to Athenai—to cling to Phaidra as he had resolved—Theseus had walked long roads, lost in his melancholies. It proved so hard to take that final step and return to the life he had left behind. As if, in stepping into those sandals once more, he would then have truly left behind Pirithous and Ariadne forever.

The new year had almost passed, winter giving way to spring, before Theseus's ship reached the port of Athenai. His long absence only deepened his guilt until that very guilt became its own reason for further delay. It had taken so long to muster himself to face the court. He hoped Phaidra would forgive him. He hoped she would understand once she had heard his tale.

Word came to him, though, that, in his absence, his father had taken a bride, who now sat as queen of Athenai. Whilst Theseus wished his father all happiness, given the choice, he would have seen his parents together. Still, this Queen Eriopis might do well, he supposed. He had not thought, however, to present himself to a new stepmother upon his return.

It made his passage across the throne room heavier. Though he would have preferred to look first upon his wife and son, propriety demanded he call upon the king, and he ... He looked up as he drew nigh to the thrones. The woman sitting beside his father, this Queen Eriopis, was the witch *Medea*. Theseus could not keep the glower from his face.

In his wanderings, tale had come to him of how she had murdered the children she had given Jason and fled into the night. Now she dared to sit there, beside Theseus's own father and pretend to be some other woman?

"Who are you, warrior?" His father demanded before Theseus could reveal Medea.

Theseus's mind reeled, even as the chorus of whispers filled the hall. Some of these people knew him, and yet, somehow, his father seemed oblivious to the truth.

The woman had bewitched his father. It seemed the only answer possible, and the thought had him narrowing his eyes, glaring at Medea. When she had conceded to aid him with her potion, Theseus had dared to image letting lie all the hateful deeds of her past. But this treachery stretched beyond all limits, and he would not abide it.

"You are bold, boy, to stare at a king's wife thus," his father threatened.

Medea's drugs had fearful power, that Theseus had seen first-hand, and his wrath would little avail him against such. So, forcing his face to calmness, he looked back to his father. "Forgive me, my king. I mean no disrespect. I am Theseus, recently come here through … some hardships."

The king settled back onto his throne, not quite appeased, but willing to listen. "What hardships are those?"

"Ah." Theseus shook his head at the question. He could not bear the thought of voicing all his travails to his father. He was not certain he could tell all, even to Phaidra, and now he longed to see her more than ever. "Those would be rather long in the telling, my king."

"Well," his father said, "then you must join us for a meal and regale us with your adventures."

"Despina," Medea called. "Bring the wine for our guest."

Was she now, having spoilt her marriage with Jason, content to play hostess and queen here? Was the desire for a more powerful husband the *reason* she had broken so violently with her first spouse?

Theseus joined Medea and his father at a table. The servants brought wine and bread and fish, and his father soon offered him a room for the night. Theseus accepted the offer, hardly knowing what else to say. *I would rather stay with Phaidra,* came to mind, but he had no idea what the king, having forgotten his son, now thought of his daughter-in-law. Nor dare he inquire about her.

Rather than feast, Theseus watched his father's face, desperate for even the least sign of recognition. Surely, no matter what Medea had done to him, he must know his son in the depths of his soul.

The king threw back his goblet of wine and wiped his mouth. "Have we met before?"

Theseus sighed. He looked first to his goblet, then glanced at the damn witch who had wrought this. Gods, but he wanted to scream in her face. To hurl bitter castigations for bringing this further suffering upon him, given what he had endured in the Underworld. For a time, he had forgotten his life. Now, he returned, and *it* had forgotten *him*. "Memory is a strange, slippery eel," he said, at length. "We think it lurks well contained within known hollows, only to find it has freed itself through unseen passages." He raised his goblet still staring at his father. "Sometimes, we recognise the eel only when it has crept around to bite us upon the arse." And so it had. He drained the goblet in one long swig and let it clatter noisily upon the table. "Such is the peril of memory."

His father cleared his throat, then rubbed a hand against his chest. "Ah. Well. I'm not sure I follow that." The king coughed. After a moment, he waved to a servant to refill his goblet. "In any event, I believe I was promised a tale."

Theseus nodded, watching the maid as she refilled the king's goblet. From the corner of his eye, he saw Medea's suddenly horror-stricken face as she watched his father about to take another drink. What? Why would she ...?

Poison!

Theseus lunged forward and slapped the cup from his father's hand, sending wine spilling over the royal robes.

"What the—" his father exclaimed. The king stood, unsteady, then pitched forward, catching himself with both hands on the table-top. *Father?* With a gasp, the king collapsed onto the floor before Theseus could reach him. The hall erupted into the chaos of rushing servants and calls for help.

Medea had poisoned his father. The thought hit him dead between his shoulder blades and drove all other thoughts out before it, raging like a maddened boar through his mind. The witch tried to slink away, but Theseus grabbed her by the back of the neck and slammed her up against a column.

Already, his sword had leapt into his hand, and he pressed the point against her collarbone. "Even along the lonely road I walked to reach Athenai, tale reached me of what you did to Jason and his children. Give me one reason not to run you through here and now, *witch*."

Medea's golden eyes widened and her mouth worked like a fish cast out of the sea. He saw himself finishing it, driving his xiphos through her deceitful heart and letting her blood stain the marble floors. "I carry your father's heir in my womb," she blurted. "Your brother would die too should you make good on that threat."

His sword hand shook with sudden doubt. No. A lie? She seemed in earnest. She deserved to die for all she had done here. All she'd done to Jason. Shit, she deserved death for what she'd done with her own brother, the kinslaying bitch that she was. He looked to where his beloved father lay dying upon the floor. The man had precious few breaths left, and Theseus would not waste more of them upon Medea. He lowered his sword. "Pray to whatever dark gods you worship, that once you have birthed the child and can no longer use it as an aspis to hide behind, I do not again lay eyes upon you."

Medea ran from the hall, and Theseus paid her no more mind. For he fell to his knees and clutched his father's hand. And he held him as he died.

❧

THESEUS HAD LOST HIM. It was *loss*, the word so commonly uttered one might forget the depths of its awful import. What is lost is gone from you, stolen by time and Fate. Cleft from those whose lives, whose very identities lay hopelessly enmeshed with the essence of them.

Loss left behind a hollow that might never be filled again.

The word sounded a pebble when beneath it lay a mountain.

Phaidra came to him, stared hard at him, face a mix of barely suppressed ire and sympathy for that damn loss. Forcing himself to meet her gaze, he could almost see her struggle with her desire to slap him. In the end, her better nature won out, and she took his hand in hers. "I am with you. I walk beside you in all these things."

Such promises meant more than mere words could ever express. It meant, as he scaled the mountain of his loss, he need not do so alone.

"And there is something else, husband." Bitterness creased her voice, despite the reassurance she had offered.

"What? What happened?"

Phaidra levelled a heavy gaze upon him. "It seems you have another son."

34

ATHENE

742 Bronze Age

Whilst Athene trembled, silently cursing the Moirai, little Hyllus approached the pyre they had built for his father, torch in hand. Athene wanted to scream at the heavens. To curse every last god and spirit. Could she have her son back, she would have invoked Nyx herself.

Instead, Herakles's ten-year-old son had to toss a flaming brand upon his father's corpse.

Hand to her mouth, Athene choked upon sobs she could not stifle. Already, the pyre had become an inferno, a blazing beacon against the black curtain of night. Smoke billowed up from it to vanish against the darkness. She could not make out the body beyond the flames. She couldn't see him. She would never see him again.

Somehow, impossibly, she still expected him to stir. To leap from the pyre and deny even this could be the end of one so great.

She knew Hyllus needed her. He needed her to be strong, to keep himself from collapsing in the crushing press on unfathomable grief. She knew it, but she had no strength left her now.

It was his mortal grandmother, Alkmena, who drew the boy into her arms and held him as he wept over his father's death.

As Athene watched them, a buried, brutal instinct sought to wriggle its way to the surface in her. For a moment, she looked into vengeance's seductive eyes and allowed herself to picture her blade plunged into Eurystheus's breast. Mayhap the king had arranged this, perhaps in concert with Dionysus. Athene would strike them all down. She would burn their World to ash, even as hers now popped and sizzled before her eyes.

No.

He would not have wanted her to become that person again. Athene had spent centuries striving to become a better person than the one who had so wronged the Kreiad genos. Still trembling, she forced her fists to unclench.

She had been too late to save her son. And she would need to find and deal with Dionysus—or Comus, or whatever name he wanted to carry in this incarnation—but not out of revenge. The chaos he unleashed would unmake the World unless someone stopped him. For the past decade she had failed to corner him. He had become a phantom, lurking in the wilds, appearing in one place to undermine Olympian authority, only to vanish before any of them could arrive and mete out justice. And it would be justice. Far too many innocent lives had fallen to the god's insane Bacchic revels and endless stream of monsters.

No, no. She would kill him, yes, but only to prevent further death. She needed to remain clear in her motives.

A log burst in the pyre, throwing a shower of sparks into the night air. Athene jerked at the sudden shock and pounded a fist—when had she clenched it again?—against her thigh.

Or maybe vengeance was warranted. Maybe it was too much to ask a parent to take any other course. Morality blurred beneath the obscuring ocean of grief. She had wanted to be a better person; but the person she had wanted to be was a *mother*.

And thus, whoever had driven Deianeira to murder Herakles, that person had ended two lives.

Iolaos walked beside Athene, bowed by grief, though he cast sporadic glances back toward the carts where Alkmena and Megara sat, the children among them. Hyllus and Mekaria were the son and daughter of precious Herakles, and Leipephile the daughter of Iolaos and Megara. None of them were safe in Mykenai any longer, Eurystheus had made certain of that. With Herakles gone, the king had set about securing his line's claim to the throne by persecuting Herakles's kin.

Athene had come within a hairsbreadth of striking the aging mortal king. In her anguish, she almost drew her blade and protected her grandchildren with bloody vengeance. But she would not become an assassin of kings, exerting her will through brute force like so many of her fellow Titans. She had to be better than that.

So, with their train of mule-drawn carts and the meagre belongings with which they had escaped their home of so many years, her charges fled toward Athenai and the shelter she felt certain her descendant Theseus would offer them. The road to Korinth would take days, then they'd need to make sail for the island.

For the third time that day, Iolaos opened his mouth but choked on whatever words he might have spoken. Herakles's nephew had lost his father some few years back, and that loss had cleft pieces of his soul like the fall of an axe. Somehow, he seemed to have taken the loss of his uncle harder still. An emptiness now filled his eyes, though he had sworn to raise Herakles's children as his own. The man had not inquired how Megara felt about that promise, and thus Athene had found herself with little choice but to insist the woman give her oath to treat them well and see no harm came to them. So long as Alkmena lived, Athene trusted her to keep Megara to that promise.

But the passing of nigh on to thirty years would not have washed away the unbreakable foundations of Megara's grief for her first children. Some wounds not even time could seal. Athene knew it. She bore such a wound now in the very pith of her soul.

Perhaps even Iolaos did not know what he needed to say. Athene laid a hand upon his arm in the hopes it might offer some shallow comfort. She had little more to give anyone at present. Loss had carved out her insides and left an aching hollow that would never again be filled.

Herakles's nephew swallowed and looked to her with those empty eyes. A mirror, no doubt, of her own vacant, shattered gaze.

So absorbed was she in these sorrows, she did not at first notice the figure awaiting them alongside the beaten path. When he caught her eye, Athene watched, too numb to manage a feeling upon seeing her brother. Ares seemed taller than last she had seen him, well over seven feet now, and clad in full panoply save for his helm.

His eyes, always tinged with malice, had now taken on a feral, lupine quality, and when he grinned, he revealed teeth too pointed. Realisation, razor sharp, pierced the shroud of her grief and Athene held up a hand to forestall the caravan. She could send the others around whilst she confronted her brother, but what if he had brought allies to harry her charges ahead? A risk she might have to take. She had no idea if he intended to accost her here, nor even if she could beat him if he did so.

"Get everyone as far down the road as you can, as quickly as possible," she said to Iolaos without taking her eyes from Ares. "Do not wait for me. Sail for Athenai the moment you reach Korinth and beseech aid from King Theseus and Queen Phaidra."

Iolaos hesitated but a moment before scampering off to see his family safe. Under his direction, the carts banked around the road, giving the God of War a wide berth.

Ares, blessedly, paid them no mind. Her brother's weighty gaze had locked upon Athene, beckoning, and she found herself with little recourse save to stride over to meet him. "The day of reckoning draws nigh."

Athene met his brazen declaration with a blank stare. "You've become a Gígas." She ought to have known. Herakles had told her of his encounter with Ares's son, Kyknus. Her brother had made up for his lack of Ambrosia by feasting upon the flesh of Man.

Ares shrugged. "'Tis not so bad as we were led to believe. The hunger grows and can only be sated in one way, but ... the *power*, Sister. Such power. Instead of a sip of tonic twice a decade, I may feast upon the Pneuma of my foes whenever it suits me. Perhaps you ought to try it."

"I think not."

Another shrug. "I offer you one final chance to join me. I shall fulfil the prophecy and cast down the tyrant king."

"He's our father."

Now her brother sneered. "That mattered little to him when he threw me off a mountain. Less still when he cast his own father into Tartarus. At least I've the decency to kill the old fuck rather than damn him to eternal torment." The sneer became a toothy grin. "Can you imagine the puissance imbued in his flesh?"

"He's our father," she repeated, having no good retort for Ares's accusations against Zeus. He had indeed done what Ares said, but Athene could not bring herself to allow harm to come to her father. Much less to allow her brother to *eat* him.

"Oh, Nyx's black arsehole, Sister. Do you yet believe that you will earn his favour by this? The man will dole out or withhold his facsimiles of affections, yes, but it is all manipulation. He shan't love you, no matter how loyally you serve him. He won't because he cannot. He has no love in him to grant."

Athene winced, her hand going to the hilt of her sword. "You devour."

"Your beloved Mankind?" Ares spat into the grass. "That's all I have for them. Gods do not trouble themselves over the woes of mortals."

"We are not gods." She eased her xiphos free. "Do not make me do this, Brother."

"No one makes you do aught, Athene." And yet, his grin betrayed his sadistic glee at the thought of crossing blades with her. He drew his own xiphos, whirling it once in the fading sunlight. "It's all choices."

"Then I have chosen."

That smirk widened. Ares lunged. His blows came with impossible speed and strength, forcing Athene back onto the defensive. Iron rang upon iron. Ares's fury became a whirlwind, and all Athene could do was fall back, driven from the road back into the high grasses.

Analytically, she judged his skill a hair beneath hers, but such mattered little given his Pneuma-fuelled fury. In desperation, she caught his blade on her own, winding and binding until she could sneak in a thrust. Her sword's tip scraped over his breastplate and clipped his arm but failed to draw blood. He had reinforced his skin to rock-hardness.

She'd need to land a clean, Potency-infused blow to have a chance of piercing his Steadfastness.

Another exchange, and another, and still, Athene fell back. Ares's assault continued as though her brother had tapped into a limitless font of stamina. Athene's arms ached from the strain of holding him off. Every parried blow came as a fresh shock to her muscles.

She managed to reverse one of his blows, her blade sweeping to cleave his chin. She threw enough Pneuma into the attack that, though her sword chipped, she drew forth a spray of golden ichor. The pain didn't even seem to register with Ares. His sandalled foot caught her in the chest and sent her hurtling twenty feet backward.

All the air was blasted from her lungs. The World became a blurred series of impacts. Next she knew, he had a foot upon the small of her back and a hand wrapt in her hair, yanked her head back and exposing her neck. The pull of it felt apt to tear her head clean from her shoulders.

Athene shoved against him. Before she could fight free, he drove the point of his sword between the bones in her forearm, pinning it to the ground. Athene wailed in agony. Pain blinded her.

Ares knelt upon her back. "Did you know, when Father first claimed Olympus, within its depths he found several chains of orichalcum. We never knew who first wrought these links, but they had remarkable uses." Some dim part of her mind registered the cold touch of metal upon her wrists. "Even if you shan't fight beside me, your Oracular insights might prove a boon."

The clamp of fetters shut off the flow of her Pneuma, and without that flow, all her pain crashed in upon her at once. Blissful darkness rose up to claim her.

35

HEKATE

1550 Silver Age

Cloying bands of shadow engulfed Hekate's body. They wrapt around her wrists, holding her arms immobile. They sucked at her shins, dragging her slowly down into hidden depths. They encircled her throat, worming their way into her nostrils, her mouth, her ears. Sickly sweet, promising eternal slumber. Peace.

If only she surrendered the sum of all her life, let go her myriad tribulations, and cast aside that perennial dread of the future that awaited her. Ephemera that had once been days and months of her memory flitted off, devoured by the consuming darkness of the Lethe as it pulled her under.

Even as consciousness teased at her senses, she heard that hypnotic call, that elusive offer that she could, *should*, stop fighting.

"Pyrrha?" A muffled voice emanating from a silhouette of light, blurred as though seen through the ripples of murky waters. "Pyrrha ..."

Almost imperceptible. It could have been a dream. It could have been wretched, merciless hope.

That quivering, faintly luminous figure paused above her, hand taking on substance even as it reached toward her. Until its fingers twined with her own.

No, let her fade. Let her embrace the delusion that blissful oblivion awaited rather than the eternal desecration of her soul.

Umbral fetters tugged at her as the hand yanked her upward. The shadowy tendrils snapped, popping like torn ligaments, hissing as if in pain at their prize being stolen from their very grasp.

Maybe the Penumbra had so bled into the Mortal Realm here that someone had reached through and found her. Maybe she—victim of her own stubborn refusal to submit to Fate—had called up enough of Mormo's power to help her shift back through the Veil. Either way, bewildered and reeling as though she'd drank the whole contents of that wine cellar, she lurched back into the real world, collapsing into her father's arms.

FLEETING IMAGES BLURRED into a miasma of sensation. Choking smoke clogging corridors, billowing through palace halls. Screaming men and women, all dashing about like an army of ants after someone kicked over their nest, desperate to salvage their precious home. Lamentations had replaced lyres. The scents of charred flesh and burning lives masked earlier aromas of the feast.

When at last her vision focused into a singular, painful *now*, she lay propped against a rock down by the Leontes River. Her bleary eyes took in numerous biremes and triremes, their crews having made way even at night. Little surprise, given the nightmare that had unfolded in the king's palace.

"Papa?" Was that memory real?

The crackle of flame came to her, the realisation it lay here and now, not in the muddle of her memory.

Turning sent jolts of pain shooting down her arm, making her painfully aware of burns that covered the whole left side of her body. Even now, ichor oozed from cracks within the charred ruination of her flesh.

"Shh," Papa said, scooting toward her. His fingers were ice upon her burning brow, but she let him ease her down, head into his lap. With one hand he massaged her right temple, wise enough not to even touch the other.

Despite the lachrymose tide rising in her, no matter how hard she tried to weep, her remaining eye felt arid as the parched Empty Desert of Kumari Kandam. As if the well of her sorrow had dried up, denying her even this momentary release from pain.

"I fear I have only a little Ambrosia," Papa said, breaking off a stopper on a phial with his free hand. He poured the golden liquid down her throat, a few drops really, but enough of that honey-sweet brew to allow her to slip into dreamless, healing slumber.

"You have little Ambrosia because you don't need it," Hekate said when at last she could no longer deny that sleep had left her. Dawn's harsh light pierced her eyelid, a reminder that even this moment with her father, the shelter she found in his arms one last time, would prove fleeting.

Everything was transitory ... everything, save the eternal Dark, ever writhing, always waiting for its chance to swallow her. Not only her, though. All the cosmos would become a feast hall set before the ravenous hunger of the Elder Gods. The souls of Man and Titan were the main course of a meal planned since the dawn of time.

Beneath her head, Papa's leg tensed at her words.

It didn't matter. She hadn't destroyed the moment because the moment was already gone. Or it was carved into stone, eternal as every other moment. Either way, it remained impervious to any alteration she might have made.

With a grunt of fresh pains—blessedly muted by the regenerative properties of the Ambrosia, though her left side remained a necrotic ruin—she rose to sit, gazing into Papa's sapphire eyes.

"Kronos—Ouranos—you and he were immortals from long, long before this Era, were you not?" His expression remained unreadable. "How many names have you carried, Papa? How many endings of the World have you borne witness to? And what happens after the eighth Eschaton?"

The anguish as he clenched his eyes at that, turning his head to the side, offered her the only confirmation she needed. They both knew how this ended.

"You're not part of the Gnostic Cabal, I think. So I have to wonder, are you their opponent? Are you the reason their every attempt to thwart Ananke ends in failure?"

"You cannot change Fate." He still had not opened his eyes.

"Really? You bid me find a way! When you saw my fate, when you saw my death, you implored me defy it! You have seen the future that, even *now*, I feel closing in around me. How could you let me believe an alternative lay before me, when you so clearly knew, even then, that time is *immutable*?"

"Because I could not bear the pain!" he blurted, eyes opening as he lunged forward, catching her arms in too tight a grip. Fresh agonies shot through her charred left arm, but Hekate forced down her shriek. What matter some physical suffering compared to what lay ahead? "Because ..." Papa's voice shook, falling into a whisper. "Because, even knowing what I knew, still I had to hope ... It's all we have ever had, this pale, fleeting hope."

Oh, but now even that hope had wilted on the vine, leaving a rotting husk where once it had bloomed. The stench of it sat between them, between the whole of their family. What if he had said, from the first moment, that none of them had free will? That all their striving would end in despair, the ashes of life flitting through their fingers? Enodia had given her the truth, so bald, so ruinous that Hekate could—though she knew why she had not allowed herself to see it before—no longer deny the reality: she could not counter her future self.

She squeezed her good hand into a fist. "Everything, even this conversation, even the thoughts giving rise to it—it was all written, plain as if carved into the Tablet of Destiny."

"He showed it to you."

"What is the Destroyer, Papa? This catalyst for Eschatons? I cannot shake the suspicion you still know more. That your hand lies behind this play. You let the World end, over and over, do you not? How many versions of the Earth have perished thus?"

"I could not stop it if I tried."

"But you won't try, because ..." Incipient fears coalesced with damning certainty. "Because it is the reaping of the harvest. A seasonal sacrifice that keeps the ravenous lords from kicking down the doors and devouring everything in sight. But even this solution can only last but so long ..."

The slack look on his face was answer enough.

"It is not mere Fate the Cabal fears but what lies at its *end*. That hunger out there, waiting in the Dark, clamouring for its last, unreserved gorging that will leave naught save an empty void in its wake."

"More than one brilliant mind has collapsed under the weight of such Ontos. Those already unhinged suffer all the more. Within the pages of his father's journals, Zeus has flitted away the last vestiges of his sanity, his mind unable to reconcile with the reality that there could be some power so far beyond himself as to defy comprehension. The Cabal, too, loses themselves in their blind struggle, thinking they understand. Yes, the Earth, or the life upon it, has faltered again and again." She had never known him to ramble. Had her impending demise so beleaguered him he could no longer play the part of the imperturbable font of wisdom?

"And you," he said, almost choking on the words. "Did you think to stop the kidnapping of Europa and Pandora? Did you consider doing so would unmake yourself, your daughters, and any children they would have? Your actions led to the kidnapping of Io, too, meaning if you removed yourself from the timeline, nigh the whole Tethid line would be erased from history along with you. Countless generations compounded over millennia affected by your actions or the lack thereof. It would not be only you condemned to oblivion but more lives than could ever be measured."

His words rained like blows, reminding her, too, that Athene had also given birth to a line of kings. How many hundreds, thousands of people would have ceased to exist if she had succeeded?

Fate, or at least the past, was inevitable. It had to proceed, because, as Kronos had told her, the cost of deviance was too great, even for the tattered remnants of Hekate's conscience. But if she could not risk changing what she had already lived, still, she would not give in. She would not allow her soul to serve as sustenance for demons or Elder Gods, nor would she consent to the eventual annihilation of the World.

"You created the Destroyer, did you not?"

Papa sighed. "Given the choice whether to allow the cosmos to be swallowed by the Dark, or to forestall the end with cyclical sacrifice, to find a moment's reprieve for Man, what was I to do?"

There it was—the desperation of his ploy, the whole cycle of Eschatons, a play for time.

And she would do better. Be more. And perhaps, unwittingly, Hades of all people had shown her the way. "But maybe you did create a solution, Father. You sired *me*. If I am to die, then I shall reign as Queen of the Underworld. And with the passing of eons, I will gather to me the power needed to challenge even the parasitic gods who make mockery of life. And I will do what neither you nor Kronos ever could. I will end both the gods and this wretched cycle you have begun."

She turned from him, for the last time, lest the tears spilling from his eyes sap the will she would need for this final step.

As IT MUST, the Box returned Hekate to the Golden Age, to the riverbank outside Thebes, where the winding road of her destiny had always led. Here, it would be ended and too begun again. Here, she must walk knowingly into her own death and embrace the torments of beyond.

The sorceries and necromancies she wove should help tether her soul to her corpse and prevent Aeshma from rising to claim her too soon. It would work, she knew, because Enodia already provided proof of her success. It had all already unfolded.

The sense of watching life play out in twisted panoply left her wandering as though somnambulistic. Was this how the Moirai perceived the bounds of time? Was this dreamlike dance of shadows the truth of their wretched Tapestry? Crouched amid reeds, silt sucking at her heels, Hekate watched the merciless procession of history.

You have given in to the madness … Mormo accused, its hollow voice further strained by an emotion the wraith must have found unfamiliar. Absolute terror.

Flush with Pneuma, her younger self raced along the river, seeking a crossing she would not find, desperate to reach the unreachable teenage Pyrrha before Enodia. Pity welled into her chest, but she squashed it.

"I want to help," Hekate heard the young girl saying, "but don't know how. If you help me, though, I'll try. I want to find out what happened to my mother that day. Can you tell me if you saw—"

Do not follow this course … Mormo ordered, its will rising in a vain attempt to seize control from Hekate.

It was time. Hekate shrieked, letting all the pain of tortured millennia pour forth. All the bitter self-loathing her abraded soul deserved, all the unspeakable vexation the Fates had inflicted upon her, they mingled into a scream so inhuman she could scarce believe it had ushered from her. A moment of defiance, and then, enhanced by Potency, she shoulder-slammed into the younger Hekate. The impact hurtled the other woman away, sending her tumbling several times before coming to rest amid a maze of roots.

All choices, all her life had been illusory. Her self-deception of free will had cast her unerringly down this path. Or maybe this, now, was her first true choice. She walked willingly into the Dark.

She stalked closer, coming to pause before the other Hekate, hovering over the fallen woman.

How those words rang in her ears, unforgettable. "Hope is the delusion with which we poison our souls. Like the apparition that is free will, we chase it because we cannot abide that our very thoughts arise not from our desires but from the chains of fate."

Her younger self pushed herself on her arms, turning to look at her. Hekate watched as gaping, mind-numbing shock washed over the woman whilst she strove to regain the breath blown out of her lungs. With gritted teeth, the other woman stood, making her vain attempt to stare down the Hekate of now.

The one who, at last, must become Enodia.

And Enodia could not allow pity to stay her hand. The World admitted no room for such indulgences as mercy. "So you would defy Ananke by killing your past self?" A pause. "As close as you draw, still apprehension escapes you." Summoning Khione's power, she coalesced ice crystals around her fingers. "If only we could have seen more, seen farther, maybe this could have been avoided. Now, it is the last choice—or illusion thereof—yet left to us."

Enodia swung, launching icicles like a rain of arrows, but Hekate twisted out of the way and swung for her ribs. Instinct—or unconscious memory—had Enodia moving faster, catching Hekate's wrist. Lest she give herself time to reconsider, to remember the agony, she immediately formed a lance of ice around her other hand. And she punched upward. Her conjured weapon ripped through Hekate's cheek, her nose, and left eye.

Despite Enodia's efforts to block out such memories, a haze of pain shot through her. She had to do this.

I will not allow this! Mormo wailed.

Yet seeing the fallen victim, the wraith's hunger rose, a gaping void in Enodia's soul. A desperate, bestial need for souls.

Consume her now, and you may yet live, Enodia promised.

On some level, Mormo knew it for a lie, she had no doubt. It still couldn't help itself, rising in her, forming claws thirsting to tear out Hekate's soul.

"Maybe, if I allow Mormo to feast upon your soul, this can be ended," Enodia said. For she had to provoke both incarnations of the wraith. She saw it when Mormo seized control of her past self.

A moment of indecision crippled her. And in that moment, Hekate-Mormo lunged, its skeletal claws ripping through Enodia's guts. A tidal wave of agony blinded her, stole vision and thought, filling her sight with red haze and screaming without apparent source.

Next she knew, Mormo had yanked out her intestines, sending Enodia pitching backward. She sat on her arse, looking up at the half-possessed Hekate.

"None of this matters," Enodia gurgled, ichor spilling over her lips and down her chin. She felt Mormo rising in her now, taking control, seized by some animal moil of dread and fury and hunger. Mormo had her now, but it didn't matter, because this had all happened before. She already knew how this ended, and thus, her mind grasped for somewhere else, some other thought, some distant memory that might serve to block the ravaging pain.

Her attempt to dislocate herself failed as the younger Mormo bit into her, teeth gnawing and gnashing, unleashing cyclones of agony. Until Hekate begged for death. Until thought slipped from her, a void rising up to claim her.

THE COLOURLESS EXPANSE of the Spectral Realm took shape around Enodia, its chill wind bearing the lamentations of the damned. Bearing Enodia's too, for she must count herself among them. The crushing torments of her death did not so much fade as lock into place. No longer a shifting, burning agony, it had become a constant pain intuition told her she would bear until the end of time.

Khione and Okypete flew free of her corpse, drained by her murder and yet hissing in fury at their own eternal enslavement. Perhaps they considered an assault against her now.

Caliginous tendrils wormed their way through the shadow

ground of this Realm, intent to arrogate her soul. Yet the sorcerous and necromantic bindings she had wrought kept her fettered to the corpse lying on the ground below her feet. The pull of conflicting forces yanked at all parts of her at once, threatening to rend her soul in twain.

Even the circling spirits broke away at the sight, no doubt realising powers greater than themselves laid claim upon her.

Enodia cried out in despair. She felt it as her mind was pulled apart like ligaments stretched too far until, at last, it snapped in a flash of brilliant agony.

Dimly, at first, she became aware of another pain, almost buried beneath the eddies of her wounds and the wrenching apart of her soul. A hollowness opened in her core, a seething void feeding upon itself and sucking bits and pieces of her down into a Darkness that lay not in the unfathomable expanses of this shadow Realm but *within*. A sense of putrid corruption seeped through her, spreading like oil upon water, until it had engulfed the whole of her. Even her good hand began to flay itself, skeletal claws piercing through her fingertips. Nails popped off as though squeezed out from beneath. Joints bent in arthritic twisting.

And below, the gaping wound of her gut began to spread, her flesh tearing apart at the seams, to reveal a miasma of seething darkness. Her own aura turned murky and solid, fraying into tattered wisps of a death shroud that might hide the shame of her wretched state.

As she became a wraith.

Pyrrha ... The voice, like a hundred razors slicing through her eardrums, it rose from the spectral landscape. Aeshma promising that not even her transmigration into such an accursed ghost would spare her from the demon's retribution. Not that ...

Wracked by uncounted torments, Enodia seized the tether holding her to her corpse. Like a lifeline, she tugged her Etheric form along that tenuous link. She was not finished yet. Not yet.

The World thrummed with indignant rage that she should dare deny an Old One its due. Tremors rippled the Etheric air, manifesting demonic ire. Yet Enodia kept pulling herself forward, down, into her corpse.

Into her only, however temporary, means of egress.

❧

EXIGENT PAINS only intensified as Enodia's soul possessed her former body. All the ruination of her flesh compounded with the abraded state of her soul.

"Atropos!" Her father roared. "Moirai! I will *destroy* you for this! I will burn down the whole of your abominable Tapestry for such an affront! If it takes me a thousand lifetimes, I swear—"

His words broke off as Enodia lurched upward. A stream of putrescence—all the ichor and contents of her ruined innards—flew from her mouth. Even as the retching abated, the remnants of her flesh corroded. Around her torn-out eye, her flesh sloughed off. Wracked with agony, she clutched her ribs whilst the whole of her left side melted, joining her face in a pile of gore mounding by her knees.

Her father gasped, falling backward, then scrambled away, shocked at what she had become. "Pyrrha ... what have you *done*?" He looked, then, to the younger Hekate, still there, on the ground herself.

The whirl of torment defied reason, and yet Enodia knew she would bear it. She rose, drifting over to her past self, to stare down at the helpless woman who must be made to fulfil the designs of Ananke. Hekate must follow her path to ensure Enodia's existence, and Enodia would attend to their future.

She knelt, snatching the clasp of the cloak Hekate wore, and yanked it free before draping it over her own shoulders. Though she did not need breath any longer, she drew in one in a vain attempt to calm her nerves. After raising her hood, she passed her hand before her face, calling up a glamour to disguise the state of herself as alive once more. It was not perfect, of course. She would need to conceal her face lest anyone see through the illusion and recognise her something dead and damned.

"I told you," she said, looking down on Hekate. "Hope is an illusion. And we would not want little Pyrrha to guess at the truth beneath Enodia's hood, would we?"

Her past self collapsed, seized by horror Enodia remembered all too well. Even Papa remained on his arse, trembling in unvoiced anguish, aghast at the price he must finally pay for his gambit against the Dark.

Oh, yes. Horror was all any of them would ever have now.

There was naught left, save to savour the glorious taste of despair.

36

PANDORA

399 Dark Age

After calling for his Immortals to tend to Artemis, Marduk himself half-escorted, half-dragged Pandora by the bicep down through the numerous tiers of the Hanging Gardens of Babilim. In moments, he would hand her over to his father, and her mind whirred for any line of reasoning she might use on Mithra, after having tried to murder him. She could see naught she could say that might save herself now. Mithra had bidden her to choose sides, and Pandora had, in moving against him, made her irrevocable choice.

"I am trying to save us," she pleaded, though she knew Marduk's simmering fury at her would prevent him from hearing aught she had to say. His vision was tinged with a red haze of paroxysm at the thought of someone trying to kill his father, and she could scarce blame him for that. Should anyone have struck against those Pandora loved, she would have done the same as him.

His only answer was to tighten his grip on her arm until she had to grit her teeth to keep from yelping at the pain. He guided her onward, through an open doorway, into the shadowed halls leading into the depths of Mithra's palace. It seemed unbelievable that it should all end thus. In every empty corner, she found herself scanning, searching, half expecting Prometheus to be here to save her one more time.

But there was no one here.

Pandora was on her own, and, bound with orichalcum, she could never fight free. If Marduk would not listen to her, it left only the chance to make a final appeal to Mithra himself. Though she knew it doomed to failure, she resolved to try. If there was one thing she knew about herself, she knew she would keep trying, to her last breath.

They rounded a bend, and Marduk drew to an abrupt halt, staring at a figure blocking the way. The wan light of sporadic torches set in the wall glinted off the aureate plates of her armour. It was dirty and dented, the breastplate of her panoply warped inward as though something had struck her a mighty blow. As ever, her eyes glinted like burning sapphires beneath her helm, almost luminous. When she strode forward, her steps were slower, measured. As if she was in pain?

"Nemesis," Marduk said, his voice thick with guarded emotions. He had little love for the Unseen assassin, Pandora realised. But how could she use that to her advantage?

"I must speak with the woman," Nemesis said. "Alone."

"She is *my* prisoner, held on charges of attempted deicide. I shall bring her before my father."

Nemesis's shoulder plate grated against her helm as she cocked her head to the side. "Would you defy an order from the Moirai themselves?"

Marduk's grip upon Pandora's bicep tightened once more until it felt like her bone would crunch and she could not hold back the hiss of pain. Then the prince eased off his hold and shoved her toward Nemesis. Pandora stumbled, but the other woman caught her and kept her on her feet.

"I want her back the moment you finish with her."

Nemesis offered no answer, craning her head to follow Marduk as he stalked past her and disappeared down another hall. The armoured woman looked around, then, before dragging Pandora alongside her. She picked a door, seemingly at random, and flung it open to reveal a dark room redolent with the scents of too much stored oil.

Releasing Pandora, Nemesis moved to a table, lit a lamp, then stalked back to close the door.

"Are you here to kill me, at last?" Pandora demanded.

"No," the golden woman said, her back to Pandora.

It might prove Pandora's one chance. Bound in orichalcum, she doubted she could overcome the assassin. But maybe, if she could wrap the chains around Nemesis's throat, she could choke her, assuming she could wedge the links under that helm. The thought of such a brutal assault left her queasy, but to fail to act might mean her own death.

Nemesis turned to face Pandora, stealing the choice from her, and a part of Pandora was almost grateful for that.

"Why do you serve the Fates?" she asked. "Why this wretched determination to hold fast to a timeline in which so many are condemned to futures they would never have chosen?"

"You hold choice up as the inviolate standard to which all must bow. Were the will truly free, surely then the self-interested masses would have sent the world spiralling toward oblivion long before now. You are quick to rail against a timeline whilst forgetting that, so long as it exists, so too does life."

Pandora shook her head. "Life is beautiful *because* of our wills. Choice is the fulcrum upon which the meaning of our lives swings. Even if all is written, at least grant it is written by choices already made rather than deny the very existence of free will."

Nemesis clenched a gauntleted fist. In the flickering lamplight, Pandora judged her armour might have seen its last days. Could such abuses be beaten out, the plates once more burnished to gleam in the light?

"If you did not bring me here to execute me, then why delay my reckoning with Mithra?"

Nemesis raised her head now, casting a heavy look at Pandora. "Execute you? Such were never my orders nor intent. I am bound to tread the river of time and follow its course." The woman reached up to grasp her helm. "But I would not slay my own blood." She pulled free that golden covering and let it drop, clattering upon the floor, and revealing her face.

Pandora gasped. Though her eyes had changed, had taken on an inexplicable blue gleam instead of their normal pale grey colour, she knew at once Athene when she looked upon her. Beaten and bruised, but stern and unbroken, jaw set in grim determination.

And all Pandora could do, upon seeing her granddaughter—her blood, as Athene had said—was sputter in aphonic stupor, wondering how she had never suspected the truth before. Had Athene been Nemesis all along? Or, instead, was this her future, something that had happened now? But Pandora had encountered Nemesis even during the Titanomachy, when Athene had been but a child. So what ... how ...?

The assassin cracked a faint smile, perhaps reading Pandora's growing mystification. Athene reached around to a bag at her hip. Even before she removed the Box, Pandora knew what she would show her. Of course, she had seen Mithra give Nemesis that Box last night. But for Nemesis, it could have been *years* for all Pandora knew.

Then, while Pandora yet reeled over that revelation, Athene pressed the Box back into Pandora's hands. Part of her wanted to question, but she could see only one reason for Nemesis to return the device back to Pandora: to further control her. The Unseen Order, perhaps the Moirai themselves, they wanted her to continue her trekking through time. The timeline already accounted for her vain, facile attempts to save the future, and her enemies counted on her to make those moves.

And *almost* she considered refusing the Box, spiting destiny, and striding into the unknown, head held high. But to remain here was to face Mithra's wrath, and surely he must slay her for what she'd done.

She had desperately sought for her lover to appear as if from nowhere and offer her a reprieve. Who was she to complain it had, in fact, been her granddaughter who had come to her rescue?

Besides, even if the Moirai thought her efforts to save the future futile, it did not mean Pandora was the type to surrender. As she had told Athene, will defined life.

Athene produced a key and unlocked the chains binding Pandora's hands. The moment they clattered to the floor, Pandora felt the flow of her Pneuma again.

Athene stepped away, moving outside the radius of the Box's bubble.

"I will never give up," Pandora said. "I will never stop fighting this."

"I know."

Pandora set the Box.

EPILOGUE

Asura Era, Golden Age

An ocean of bubbling naphtha surrounded Matarśivan, bursting into flaming geysers that scorched an ashen sky. His dreams were a maelstrom of chaos. Visions of destruction on a scale beyond imagination. He saw the World scorched by the burning sea, and with it came a tide of charred giants, incandescence gleaming beneath the prison of their skin, so like his master Agni's. The blazing giants set about mass slaughter even whilst volcanic eruptions buried the land in magma.

The whole of the cosmos caught in the conflagration.

And beyond it, insatiable maws gorging upon the souls of all those who fell, while grasping tendrils stretched out, enclosing the world, ever tightening, like constrictor snakes.

❧

Sweat-soaking and gasping, he tumbled from his cot, landing hard upon the stone floor of his tower. For a moment, he lay, panting.

The dreams were not always the same. Sometimes he saw a great flood swallowing whole continents and inundating the World. Once, he had seen a prurient darkness lurching out of the land and sky alike.

Why his mind played such tricks upon him, he could not fathom.

Mopping his brow and not bothering to dress, he pushed himself up and strode onto the balcony. In the Roil, much of the land seemed a sea of slow-moving obsidian shards as reality made and unmade itself. But beyond his tower, that incipient ground broke away to reveal empty, iridescent cosmos coruscating with nether lightning amid clouds of shadow. Every so oft, great fissures of flame would erupt out in the void.

Sometimes, he fancied he could see something in those fervid streams. It was why he had chosen this spot. Like a drunk feeding his addiction, he tempted his own madness by embracing it. By searching for meaning in delusion.

Like every member of the Dodecadic Circle, he'd built a Watchtower in the Roil. A refuge, as the Archons had suggested. As Watchers, they could pass freely between the Mortal Realm and the Otherworlds, and these bastions were meant to give them time away from Men, to gather their thoughts. Or perhaps—and he could see the need for it—to separate themselves. Men, always, withered and died, and their souls were drawn back to the Wheel of Life. Those he met passed their lives in the blink of an eye, and, if he got too close, he found himself torn asunder by the unending loss.

Forever lighting their pyres and burning away pieces of himself in the process.

Still, out here, the nightmares grew worse. The visions ... and a haunting intimation of something perverse stalking the shadows of creation. How could he not fear, knowing this amorphous unreality unpinned the fragile world of Men? How could he not dread, gazing upon the tenebrous sea that encompassed the cosmos?

They knew Mankind could not handle these truths, and thus, they shared little of what they knew lay beyond the Mortal Realm. Men who saw too much oft lost themselves in the dread apprehension of greater Truth. Perhaps the mortal mind could not grasp the limitless cosmos.

Or ... perhaps his could not either, and therein lay the root of his nightmares and growing disquiet.

Another conflagration ignited out in the void beyond his Watchtower, like a tumbling cloud of flame. Within its depths flitted images, and the deeper he stared the more the vision rarefied.

His beloved Aditi, her bronzed wings carrying her on nether winds as she drew nigh to the piercing obelisk that was his abode. Matarśivan blinked the vision away, rubbed his brow. If any Man under his care claimed to behold the future or some distant event in his mind's eye, Matarśivan would have called the speaker a liar or a madman and, either way, remanded him for care.

Yet he now spent more time gazing into flame, tormenting himself with the delusion that his hallucinations held some import other than the collapse of his mind. One could not see the future, of course. The implications of doing so would unravel causality. For a vision of the future must surely affect the viewer, thus affecting the future so beheld. Besides which, what would it mean for the most precious of all gifts, Man's free will? If a set future existed, how could the choices made in the present still hold any weight?

But there, a shadow in the sky drew closer. A winged woman, closing in on his balcony. Matarśivan's hand went to his gaping mouth, stifling a denial. This was not the first time he had witnessed something he had thought he'd seen in the flames come to pass. But this ... It was so direct, so immediate.

So irrefutable. Even if his mind had conjured the image of Aditi out of desire ... How had he imagined her garb? She wore a vermilion sari trimmed with gold filigree. The same as she had worn in his vision, and he had never laid eyes upon the outfit before today. Unaware of his distress—of the tremors that wracked the core of him —she alighted upon the balcony with a warm grin, though the set of her features revealed a weight upon her as well.

He went to her, grasping her upper arms in reassurance. His troubles could wait when she clearly came bearing her own. "What has happened?"

Aditi laid her head upon his chest a moment before pushing away. "Bloodshed, on a scale heretofore unknown." She swallowed. "War between my heirs and Danu's."

Matarśivan fell back a step, steadied himself against the balustrade. Oh, he'd seen something of that, as well. Both Aditi and Danu had left their carnal encounter with the Archons impregnated, and it had—at times—worn upon him that her first children were not his. Based upon their aspect, he'd guess them fathered by the golden-eyed Sun Archon, though given that all had lain with all that day, perhaps it could have been anyone. Perhaps, even, those first children had more than one father, for Aditi had borne triplets. In his visions he'd seen Adityas tinged with Fire as well, and perhaps even other elemental influences.

Either way, that moment had given rise to two great bloodlines in the World, and they had forever striven with one another for control of Mankind.

"You should not have given them the Amrita." Maybe there ought to have been no more immortals, beyond the Dodecadic Circle. And though Amrita bestowed only temporary immortality, it came too close, brought their kind too nigh in nature to that of the Watchers.

Aditi glowered. "I tire of this argument. I was not going to let my children wither and die like mortals."

"They are mortals. They are meant to die. Such is the Wheel of Life, as the Archons declared it."

In his mind, he beheld those vast, gorging maws so eager to devour souls. An eternity of screaming torment. No! Such was but figments of his tortured mind, and he needed to spend far less time here, in this non-reality.

Now Aditi had the grace to look somewhat abashed. "Yes, well, either way, they didn't want to share it with the Danavas, and now Danu's children slaughter far and wide for control of the Amrita."

Matarśivan might have once more castigated her for creating the golden brew in the first place, but it would have done no good, so he left it with a lingering look. What would this war mean? How many would die because of them?

Had they, had the whole Dodecadic Circle failed in their duty to guide and protect Mankind?

"Do you believe we can stop this war before it rages out of control?"

His beloved leant against the balustrade beside him, her lack of answer making plain what she thought of that. No, it was too late. And the greater question remained for him, regardless.

What was this madness that haunted him, intimating such dark truths about the cosmos? Try as he might to dismiss his nightmares ... if his vision of Aditi coming here in this sari had proved prescient, how could he assume no truth lay in his other imaginings?

"I have seen things," he ventured. Revealing his affliction would make him seem mad, but if he could not trust her, of all people, then he could trust no one. "I have seen some few things ... before they happened."

Aditi cocked her head to the side, watching him, perhaps searching his face for some sign of jest. Finding none—his heart hammered waiting for her response—she tapped a finger against her lip. "Some new manifestation of power from the Prana coursing through us?"

Prana. The power of life, bolstered in them by consuming the fruit of the Tree of Life. It had given them so many great gifts already. Could his visions and nightmares be born of the same? An explanation both blessedly simple and horrible, for it would imply he saw vestiges of real Truth.

"Perhaps," he admitted, though it did little to suppress his growing dread. Forming words felt like trying to retch up stones lodged in his throat. "I saw something ... appalling."

Aditi frowned. "Worse than the mass slaughter of my descendants and Danu's? *Worse* than Man drowning in blood from this war?" Her tone made it clear naught could ever seem worse than such things.

Matarśivan, however, could not help but disagree with that assessment.

AUTHOR'S NOTE:

While Medea was thus tormenting herself, the heroes were on their way to the ship, and Argus said to Jason: "Perhaps you will spurn my advice, but still I must give it. I know a girl who understands the brewing of magic potions, an art which Hecate, the goddess of the underworld, has taught her. If we could win her over to our side, I am certain you would be victorious in this task. If you agree, I shall go and try to enlist her favor in our behalf."

"Go if you like," said Jason. "I shall not prevent you. But we are in a sad way if our homeward voyage depends on women!"

—Schwab, Gustav. *Gods and Heroes of Ancient Greece*

MOST WRITERS EXIST on a spectrum between those who plan in detail and those who "garden" their stories, seeing what comes to them as they go along (of course, in reality, both kinds make it up as we go long, but planners do it at a different stage). I fall heavily into the planning camp, but this series required me to go even farther in that direction, knowing precise details about everything that would happen to every character. It necessitated writing parts of all nine books before the first was ever published.

Which is my way of saying, what unfolds in this book, especially for Hekate, I've been sitting on for a long time. Her chapters were, by and large, written for the whole series before I finished writing book 1 for other characters. So I've been waiting a long time to unleash the reveals and finally give some answers about Enodia and her motivations and why Hekate's life takes the course it does.

Those who've read *Gods of the Ragnarok Era* will have always known Hekate would head toward a dark, tragic future. In this book, we really see that coming to a head. I hope you've enjoyed the ride so far!

Special thanks to my family and my team that helps bring these projects to life: Sarah, Regina, Felix, Shawn, Tawny, and Francesca.

If you've enjoyed this book, I encourage you to join the Skalds' Tribe newsletter and get access to exclusive insider information and your FREE copy of Starter Library. **I generally send every week or every other; I promise not to mail more often than that.** No spam, no selling your email address to marauding warlords, none of that.

Join me here to grab a free novella and stay connected with me: https://www.mattlarkinbooks.com/skalds/

Thank you for reading,
Matt

PS Pandora's journey continues in *The Wrath of Artemis* ...
https://books2read.com/wrathofartemis

Join the Skalds' Tribe newsletter and get access to exclusive insider information and a selection of free books to kickstart your Matt Larkin library.

https://www.mattlarkinbooks.com/skalds/

ALSO BY MATTHEW LARKIN

Tapestry of Fate

The Gifts of Pandora

The Valor of Perseus

The Inferno of Prometheus

The Madness of Herakles

The Threads of Theseus

The Face of Hekate

Heirs of Mana

Tides of Mana

Flames of Mana

Queens of Mana

Gods of the Ragnarok Era

The Apples of Idunn

The Mists of Niflheim

The Shores of Vanaheim

The High Seat of Asgard

The Well of Mimir

The Radiance of Alfheim

The Shadows of Svartalfheim

The Gates of Hel

The Fires of Muspelheim

For my Juhi and Kiran.

Special thanks to my family and my team that helps bring these projects to life: Sarah, Regina, Felix, Shawn, Tawny, and Francesca.